Bloodsworth Island

Jeff Slate and David Rearden

First printing

Cover painting by Retta Jay

ISBN: 1-58851-351-3
PUBLISHED BY AMERICA HOUSE BOOK PUBLISHERS
www.publishamerica.com
Baltimore

Printed in the United States of America

For Barclay Brown (1941 - 1995) for providing us both with priceless guidance.

We miss you very much.

Acknowledgements

We want to thank the many people who helped us and provided support during work on this project. In particular we want to thank Nancy S. Feldman for reading so many pages.

Heartfelt thanks goes to Scott, Jeff's son, who gets the very highest marks for empathy, unfailing support and enthusiasm.

The Internet

To learn more about Bloodsworth Island and the authors, please visit the following sites on the Internet:

Book Web Site: www.BloodsworthIsland.com

Author Web Site: www.SlateRearden.com

Chapter 1

Bone & Banana Stew

Gene never expected to be engaged in the clandestine practice of medicine. But there he was in the jungle rainforest of Ecuador secretly dispensing medication. He had been ordered not to treat the natives, an order he had simply ignored for a time, until he got caught.

He wasn't sure why he had been so brazen. Was it because the order was stupid? That couldn't be it. There were lots of stupid orders with which he complied, but this one was stupid and destructive. Now he was ordered and warned. It would have been worse if he had been in Maryland, much worse.

He was going to treat Hiaroma again. And what would be the consequence of discovery? Well, he just didn't know, but it would be a lot more unpleasant than a warning. He would be careful this time. First he would have to get more Tetracycline. After the incident Alfred took all of the antibiotics away from him. They were now hidden in Alfred's tent, the medical supply tent.

Gene leaned hard on the crooked wooden pole. Losing his grip, he paused for a moment and then pressed again pulverizing the resistant skull fragment. A clattering sound of metal against stone erupted from a few yards away where a dying boy knocked a metal pot off a hammock and onto one of the many hearths in the village. It was the only sound that drowned out the constant noise of the rainforest that surrounded them, the rasping call of the lichen-mimicking katydid and the buzzing and chirping of the other insects. Gene crushed another bone discharging a burst of powder onto his T-shirt and dark blue shorts.

Gene had finished medical school six years earlier, but he had never finished his residency. Instead his residency had finished him. And although it had been difficult for him to accept, something in the series of events that ended his residency had derailed his career in medicine. Applications for other residency positions were rejected or drew no response. Interviews for jobs were hard to come by. Neither of the two interviews that took place resulted in a job offer.

Dr. Gallagher had turned Gene's life around by offering him a research position at Davenport Center on Bloodsworth Island in the Chesapeake Bay. As part of that job Gene and two other doctors from Davenport Center had traveled to Ecuador.

Life in the jungle had been hard on Gene. Fungus had found its way into every cleft on his body: toes, fingers, crotch, armpits. Streaks of brownish-red earth emphasized lines on his face, detracting from his boyish good looks and making him appear older than his thirty-two years.

Everything except some of the medical equipment had become dirty. A bath in the dingy brown water of the Cononaco River served to reduce the concentration of dirt. But Gene's light brown hair that used to glisten in the Maryland sunlight had become darker and duller in Ecuador. It flopped over his forehead and looked something like dying leaves about to fall from a tree.

On this trip to Ecuador things had become worse, worse than the omnipresent dirt and mosquito bites. Gene was surrounded by death and dying. He looked up past the bone fragments, past the makeshift lab and towards the river. Watching the slow, steady current, he imagined what it would be like to get into a canoe and ride down this muddy tributary into the Amazon. By riding the Amazon across the continent and into the Atlantic Ocean he could free himself from the carnage. The rasping calls and chirping sounds of the forest drew him back. They beckoned him to return and finish what he had begun.

It was hot, and he was sweating. Earlier he had been shivering from the cold as water had poured from the sky in torrents. The weather fluctuations were, he felt, the hardest thing to get used to in the western Amazon basin. Well, that was up until this. Until a few days before, these trips to Ecuador were the most fulfilling thing that Gene had experienced. The world of the xenophobic Orani Indians was so foreign, so fascinating, so full.

"Your time in Ecuador will be different, more difficult this time," Dr. Gallagher had said. Remembering his last moments on Bloodsworth Island, the salt air smell of the Chesapeake Bay mixed with antiseptic cleansers of the medical laboratories rushed back into Gene's consciousness. Dr. Gallagher knew what would happen in Ecuador, like he knew so much else, and Gene looked to him for guidance. Gene could still hear the soft, confident resonance of his voice.

"You will be tested there by a burden that would break a weaker man. But you are strong. You know what must be done." Those mesmerizing green eyes hung before him as though Dr. Gallagher were standing right there in Ecuador, next to the hearth where the bone and banana stew would be prepared. "This work is essential. We can't go on without it."

The round end of the wooden pole caught another fragment of bone against the side of the trough in the peach palm wood. Pressure and a twist of the pole turned the bone to granules of gray. Gene lifted the pole and pressed the rounded end into the moist earth. It came to rest against his shoulder.

Hiaroma, the village shaman, tried and failed to break a fragment of charred pelvis. Gene dropped his pole onto the ground. Walking around to the other side of the hollowed log, Gene placed his hands on top of Hiaroma's and together they crushed the fragment.

"I'm going to get more medicine for you," Gene whispered.

"Yes, Doctor Gene," said Hiaroma.

"Alfred took the medicine away from me." Gene remained with his arms around Hiaroma, so they could talk without being overheard.

"I know," said Hiaroma.

"I think it's helping you. You are better than most of the others."

"We need medicine for everybody. Do you have enough?"

"No. We don't. I told you that. We brought very little. We didn't expect everybody to get sick." Gene said "we," and he was certain that he hadn't known. He wasn't so sure about Alfred.

Gene let go of Hiaroma's arms. Although Hiaroma was tall for a member of the Orani tribe, Gene surpassed him by a head.

The shaman wore a swath of red cloth to cover his genitals and a black feather band on each arm. If the missionaries had not come through some years before, the standard attire for this ceremony and all other activities would have required less clothing. Despite the efforts to control and direct the behavior of the Orani, the primary, lasting impact of the missionaries had been the addition of small pieces of cloth and sometimes shorts to the wardrobe of members of the tribe.

Hiaroma was muscular, and up until the last few days, more agile than most. A week earlier he had claimed a wooley monkey after pursuing it for over three miles through the jungle. The first poison dart struck the monkey in the left leg. It happened less than 100 yards from the village. The animal was perched in a tree 120 feet above the ground. With a stiff leg the monkey traveled miles through the forest canopy with Hiaroma running along the ground in close pursuit. Thirty or so darts later, Hiaroma had pierced the animal's skin four times. The last dart hit the sluggish twenty pound primate dead in the heart. When it lost its grip, it fell only a few feet and became wedged in a sling shot shaped tree branch 100 feet above the ground.

Hiaroma yanked a long vine out of the forest and wrapped it around the trunk of a tree which would take him within four or five feet of the source of meat for the evening's meal. The vine was formed into a loose wreath that was large enough to accommodate Hiaroma's feet, one on each side of the trunk. With the vine to press his feet into the tree, Hiaroma climbed straight up. Using his right hand he reached out and grabbed a branch from a third tree that crossed above the branch with the monkey. With a hard yank, he forced the sling shot branch down, and when he let go the dead animal sailed up and away from Hiaroma. Several five inch straw-thin darts protruded from soft, brown fur as the woolly monkey tumbled to the ground.

The pursuit had been a long one for only twenty pounds of meat. It was food that Hiaroma would be proud to provide to the other villagers, but he would eat none of it. The hunter was never permitted to eat the flesh of an animal he had brought down. He could choose whether to hunt, but according to the customs of the tribe, he could not choose to eat part of the animal he had hunted.

Despite his physical prowess, a toothless mouth, deep grooves in his cheeks and time worn skin gave Hiaroma the appearance of a man in his sixties or seventies. Based on things Hiaroma remembered from his childhood, Gene estimated that he was fifty.

The ritual Gene performed with Hiaroma, crushing the charred bone fragments, had become all too common. "The spirits of our dead are happy when they come to a resting place inside the bodies of relatives," Hiaroma had told Gene weeks before when a teenage girl had died after falling from a tree. For the most part, Hiaroma and Gene communicated in Spanish. They were both fluent, though it was not the primary language for either of them. Hiaroma was good with languages. In addition to Spanish he knew some English. Gene had studied Spanish for years and had polished his skills on previous trips to Ecuador. Sometimes Gene would use a word or two of the Orani language which always pleased Hiaroma.

The bones they were processing were the remains of Hiaroma's brother. Earlier in the day, crackling, popping flames had consumed the body. There had been crying, some forced, some heartfelt. "You must cry louder," said Hiaroma. "Otherwise my brother's spirit will think you do not miss him enough. His spirit will not be able to rest." Hiaroma knew the emotional suffering as a result of the loss would be evaluated by the spirit of the deceased. Punishments or rewards for the living inhabitants of the village were linked to the quality of their mourning. "You must cry louder," Hiaroma instructed the villagers, and they complied. Whether they complied because of Hiaroma's authority or because he reminded them of a fundamental truth which they recognized, Gene didn't know.

"I know they are sick," said Hiaroma of the residents of the village, "but they seem to forget that my brother will return and give us pain or cause us to die if we do not care for his spirit." After the fire had burned out, the remaining pieces of bone were pulled from the ashes. Those were the pieces which Hiaroma and Gene had set about to crumble.

"My brother and all of us in this village have been cursed by the moon spirit," Hiaroma told Gene. "This happened long ago. The curse has not been lifted. I have tried, but the moon spirit is strong. It has power over us. Now the curse is passed from mother to child." He sat on a felled tree as he was weakened by the same sickness which had taken his brother and other villagers. "We are powerless. This curse makes our lives difficult. The moon spirit takes our food. Sometimes it brings animals we have killed back to life, and they run away before we can eat them."

Hiaroma beckoned Gene to join him on the log. As Gene sat, Hiaroma attempted to free a cord that was tied to the right side of his loincloth. After watching Hiaroma's frustration for a moment, Gene leaned over to help.

The small dark beak of a Black Throated Antbird twisted on the end of the string, as Gene lifted it away from Hiaroma. He held it a few inches from his face.

"Aaskouandy," said Hiaroma, pointing at the beak. "You need this."

"I do?"

"Yes. I watch you. I see things. I know how you are. The thin man gives orders. You follow. This will give you independence. It will give you freedom. You can have freedom from disease. You can have freedom from control by other people. It can give freedom to others as well." Switching to English, he said, "I will gift it to you if you gift me something."

Gene had grown accustomed to the trading methods of the Orani. They were better at it than he would ever be. On his first trip to Ecuador, he had been lucky to leave the village with his underwear. He had come prepared this time with many things that would be of interest to the Orani. It wasn't so much a value for value trade as a bonding tool, a way to build trust. Gene enjoyed the interaction.

Gene looked around for Alfred before he spoke. "I give you medicine."

"That's true," said Hiaroma. Disappointment and sadness tugged at his face, as he extended his hand, palm up, toward Gene. "Here. You take the aaskouandy."

"No," said Gene, realizing he had made a tactical error. He didn't want to ruin the trade for Hiaroma. After glancing around again, he spoke. "That wouldn't be fair. I don't have any medicine with me." Gene reached for his pack. It leaned against the trunk of the tree that had become their bench. "I'll find something, but I don't know if it will be good enough to trade for an aaskouandy."

Hiaroma's sadness vanished. With the little energy that he had, he managed a gleeful, toothless smile in anticipation of what Gene might offer.

Digging into the bottom of his pack, making a production of it, Gene pulled out a disposable butane lighter. "This is my last one," Gene said. "Do you think that it is a fair trade?"

"The aaskouandy is very powerful," Hiaroma bargained. Gene could tell that Hiaroma yearned for the lighter. "It may change form.

It would not be surprising if you wake one morning to find that it has become a talon or an arrow point. In a time of need it can become a jaguar or an eagle."

Gene examined the beak, feather remnants still attached to it, and the string dyed the color of burgundy. He knew that such a transaction was a serious matter. After what he deemed an appropriate period of time, Gene nodded and handed the lighter to Hiaroma who gratefully accepted the exchange.

"You must be vigilant," said Hiaroma. "You must protect it and care for it. Talk to it sometimes. Feed it. Listen to it."

"Are you hungry?" asked Gene of the aaskouandy, holding it at eye level. There was no response from the lifeless beak.

"If you fail to care for it, the aaskouandy will turn its power against you. You will lose the independence and freedom which it has granted you."

Gene wanted to put the charm to work. The beak twisted before Gene's eyes as Hiaroma rose and continued to pulverize the bone fragments. Gene wished the aaskouandy had power. He knew that Dr. Gallagher had power and wisdom.

Gene thought again about the last conversation with Dr. Gallagher before leaving Bloodsworth Island. He could still feel the sense of expectation that he experienced during their last meeting. Gene knew that he had been in the presence of a great man. It was when Gene left Dr. Gallagher's office the last time, when he turned, that he saw the light like a halo over Dr. Gallagher's head. A feeling of exhilaration had swept through his body that last time. It was not so different from the way he felt the first time he had been with Dr. Gallagher on Bloodsworth Island.

Dr. Gallagher had saved Gene from a life of pain and failure and impending self-destruction. Dr. Gallagher stepped in and changed Gene's life forever. As he and Dr. Gallagher walked toward the door of Dr. Gallagher's office that day he left, Dr. Gallagher said, "You know you are my favorite. You have a good mind and the will to do what's right. If something should happen to me, you will be the one to carry on in my place. I have already left instructions."

"But Dr....," began Gene, but he stopped himself. The words were wrong. "I couldn't possibly do what you do."

"You can with belief in our mission, with knowledge of what is right, with determination and most of all with faith. You will be tested in Ecuador, pushed to the very limit of your endurance, but this test you will pass."

Gene felt a pride and an inner power he had never felt before. "I will do my best to serve."

"You will succeed. Always remember that I love you, Gene."

"I love you too, Father."

Now he was in Ecuador, and this was the test Dr. Gallagher had spoken about.

"Moti sent the moon spirit to kill my brother," said Hiaroma. This was another peculiarity that Gene had gotten used to when in Orani territory. Their sense of time was different than the fast paced world that Gene was used to. A conversation from hours or days earlier would continue as though there had been no interruption. When Gene and his fellow researches arrived in the village after an absence of months, they were greeted as if they had only been gone for the afternoon.

"Who is Moti?" asked Gene. He had heard Moti's name before, when the conversation started two days before, but he couldn't remember who he was.

"Moti is a shaman in the village just up river."

"Why did he do this?" asked Gene, as Hiaroma spread the powdered bone with his hand.

"Because the moon spirit has cursed everyone in this village. This curse is passed to our children. Sometimes our children leave our village. They join a different village. In time the curse will spread. It will destroy the entire tribe. Moti knows that this will happen. One day the whole tribe will be cursed. Moti says our village hurts the tribe. Instead of helping me to lift the curse, he sends the moon spirit to kill us. He has great power with the moon spirit. You can see. He has made everyone in the village sick. I must work today. I must use all of my power to lift this curse. And I will harm Moti. I will bring together all of the spirits I can command. I want Moti to die. I will feel better when he dies. I will call the rainbow spirit and the sun spirit. The sun spirit is stronger than the moon spirit."

"Why would the moon spirit curse you?"

"It was our fault. It always is. We did wrong. But this curse is more than we deserve." Hiaroma let go of the wooden pole he had been using. Disease had depleted the energy from his body. With some effort he tipped the hollowed log that contained the bone powder and the last of the gray granules fell onto a mound of pulverized bone which had been collected on a palm leaf.

"You did wrong?" Gene grasped the log and brushed the last of the bone dust onto the leaf. With one hand on each of Hiaroma's arms, Gene guided him back to the bench log.

"It started with the young people. They were telling lies about who was sleeping with who in Moti's village. They said a child had been born with the beak of a parrot and the body of a worm. That can happen, but it was not true this time. To tell these lies was wrong. They knew it was wrong, but they went their own way. Now you see what has happened. We all have to pay the price for what they did." Hiaroma picked at the crusted blood on his cheek.

Gene knew that without the medicine Hiaroma would soon die like his brother before him. Hiaroma blamed the moon spirit. Gene thought that he and Alfred and Bruce, all from Bloodsworth Island, all of whom worked for Dr. Gallagher, had caused the death and suffering. How, he wasn't sure. Maybe it was the vaccinations. Maybe it was the invasive test for cystic fibrosis Gene had developed. Maybe it was the test Bruce had developed. Any of these things would explain why the villagers were all dying while Gene and Alfred and Bruce had not been affected. Gene felt sickened and disgusted, knowing that the help he had tried to provide had destroyed what he was trying to save.

Hiaroma reached for the wire mesh. The village had been little impacted by the outside world. Iron axes, metal pots, some cloth, the wire mesh, those were things members of the village had traded for. Gene steadied Hiaroma's arms and hands, so he could hold the wire mesh over a clean palm leaf. If other members of the village had been healthier, Gene would not have been allowed to help with this sacred ceremony. With Hiaroma's frail hold on the mesh, Gene began to filter the ground bone. Only a fine powder passed though the mesh. Larger pieces were discarded. Hiaroma formed a funnel out of a leaf and placed it on top of a dried and hollowed gourd. Gene poured the fine, gray powder into the gourd. Hiaroma was wise, and there was an enticing spirituality about him. That wisdom and spiritual nature reminded Gene of Dr. Gallagher and forced his consciousness back to his mentor.

Dr. Gallagher knew so much. He knew Gene would struggle in Ecuador. Had he foreseen the death and suffering? Why would he send Gene and the others here if he could foresee this disaster?

"Life has a purpose," said Dr. Gallagher to Gene years before, when Dr. Gallagher had rescued him. "Everything happens for a reason. You are suffering now. These difficult times will pass, and as you struggle you learn. You will get through these and other difficult times when they come." Dr. Gallagher's dark gray sweater matched his hair. His eyes were bright and alive. Gene looked at him, not certain that the misery he was suffering through when he met Dr. Gallagher would end. As time passed, Gene realized that Dr. Gallagher had been right.

Before he met Dr. Gallagher there were times when he thought that death might be better than the pain. Those thoughts ended with his first visit to Bloodsworth Island. With the move to Bloodsworth Island he had become busy, his life filled with directed work and the excitement of discovery. At times he imagined that chaos would not reign again. He had never really believed it, and the events of the last week had been the proof.

"No matter what happens," continued Dr. Gallagher that first time on Bloodsworth Island, "God will not abandon you. And I will not abandon you. You must not give in to fear." Gene didn't believe Dr. Gallagher, not at first. He had expected to be abandoned by Dr. Gallagher as he had been by his father when he was six and by his mother when he was 16. But during his four years on Bloodsworth Island Gene had come to know that Dr. Gallagher would not abandon him no matter what.

Hiaroma had started a ceremonial fire earlier. Above the flames a small, metal pot hung from a pyramid shaped frame made of sticks. Mashed bananas, water and some of the bone powder were added to the pot, as Hiaroma chanted in his native Orani language. Gene could pick out a few words, Hiaroma's brother's name, the names of spirits, the sun, the rainbow and the moon.

A top for the bone powder gourd had been tied to the spout using string woven from fibers from the inside of tree bark. Gene placed the top on the gourd and set it near the fire. Hiaroma and his family would be permitted to remember and speak of his dead brother only so long as powder remained in the gourd.

When the soupy banana and bone stew was ready, Hiaroma poured it into a ceremonial bowl. He was the first to drink. With half of the stew finished, he carried the bowl over to his brother's wife. She was barely able to sit up, but she took some of the thick liquid. The remainder of the stew was distributed among the surviving relatives.

"My brother's spirit will come to rest in our bodies," said Hiaroma to Gene. "In this way he will be at peace."

Now Gene had to worry about how to get some antibiotics out of Alfred's tent in the hope of saving Hiaroma's life.

Chapter 2

Missing Pills

Gene was supposed to be gathering blood and tissue samples from the villagers who had died. Alfred hadn't seen him helping Hiaroma. If he had there would have been a problem.

The stainless steel case for carrying samples was covered with tiny droplets of water from the earlier rain. Gene picked it up and started off toward the river where he could get a better view of the tents. Alfred stayed in the larger tent with all of the medical equipment and supplies. Gene and Bruce shared the other tent.

Gene had to find out where Alfred and Bruce were. If they were away from Alfred's tent maybe Gene would have an opportunity to get his hands on some of the Tetracycline Alfred had taken from him. It was the only hope for saving Hiaroma and maybe one or two others. It would work only if some kind of deadly bacteria had contaminated the vaccine or some of the testing material. That must have been what happened, because the antibiotic seemed to be working. Gene had given some to Hiaroma, and he was still alive, maybe not as healthy as could be, but alive. So many others had died.

If Alfred saw him poking around the tents instead of collecting samples, there would be hell to pay. The discipline wouldn't take place in Ecuador. Alfred would wait until they were back in Maryland, where Alfred and others had complete control of the environment. The discipline for multiple violations would be stiff and unpleasant, but Gene couldn't be concerned with that now. He would save Hiaroma if he could.

The small village was spread along the northern shore of the Cononaco River. The river flowed from the west, and the eastern half of the river formed the border between the Napo Province where the village was located and the Pastaza Province to the south. Sixty miles down river the Cononaco flowed into the Curaray River at the border between Ecuador and Peru. From there the water flowed 125 miles before reaching the Napo River, and another 125 miles from there the Napo flowed into the Amazon.

The tents were situated just to the west of the village. Alfred had said that the water in the river was less likely to be contaminated at that point. The top of the larger tent was visible behind the palm leaf covered roof of one of the huts. Gene headed east, away from the tents.

"Alfred!" shouted Gene. "Bruce."

No response.

The lifeless body of one woman had fallen from the string hammock in which she had waited to die. Her torso lay on the moist earth, and her left foot and right hand were held aloft, as they had become entangled in the twisted beige string of the hammock.

Toward the east end of the village Gene saw Alfred working at a medical table they had set up. It was the place where the villagers had been examined, tested and injected. Alfred wanted it as far from the tents as possible so the villagers wouldn't bother him when he was in his tent. He didn't like to talk to anybody, least of all Orani villagers. Bruce was some distance off, walking toward the river.

Gene approached Alfred.

"Alfred," said Gene.

Alfred looked up from the paper on which he had been writing. He was only a little taller than Hiaroma. His straight blond-turning-white hair hung down over his round glasses and was a different shade of blond than the darker hair in his mustache.

"Yes." Alfred was serious as always.

"I've got some samples in this case," said Gene. "I thought I might take them up to your tent. They need to be refrigerated." Gene held the case up in the air. He thought if he could get permission to enter the medical tent, he could search for the Tetracycline with little chance of being caught.

Alfred shrugged. "You know I don't want you in that tent."

Gene nodded.

"Leave the case here. I'll have Bruce deal with it. Take that one over there." His extended finger pointed toward a similar case with a duller finish. It rested on the ground behind the table.

"Ok." Gene placed the case he was carrying on the ground under the end of the table away from Alfred. He hoped Alfred would forget about it there, and hidden under the table, Bruce might not notice it when he came back from the river. He picked up the case Alfred had indicated and headed back toward the center of the village.

He was aggravated by Alfred's response. Not only did he fail to give him permission to enter the medical tent, he told him to leave the case with samples. Bruce might pick up that case and head up toward Alfred's tent at any moment. Gene was going into the medical tent. He was going to get the medicine for Hiaroma. Now he had to worry about both Bruce as well as Alfred showing up while he was in the tent.

Despite his concerns, Gene headed straight for the medical tent on the opposite end of the village. The new sample case fell onto the seat of a canvas chair next to the tent. The zipper on the screen mesh covering the door became stuck. Gene yanked it free and entered the tent.

Alfred's bed was on the left. A table visible from the outside through the screen mesh and a small refrigerator were on the right. Gene didn't want to be discovered. If Alfred found him, Hiaroma would die. Gene went straight for a cabinet not far from the small refrigerator. Inside was the Tetracycline bottle. He grabbed it and twisted off the cap. Empty. Alfred must have destroyed the stuff to keep him from using it. They had brought it for themselves, and they would be going back to Maryland in a few days. Alfred knew he wouldn't need it.

Gene recapped the bottle and put it back in the cabinet. He checked the other cabinets. No Tetracycline. No antibiotics. Gene knew he must keep his time in the tent short, but he dropped into one of the chairs next to table. From there he could see through the mesh out into the village. He would have a few seconds to escape if Alfred or Bruce came toward the tent. Of course they would be able to see him if they were paying attention, and Alfred would be paying attention.

The clicking sound of the village harpy eagle penetrated Gene's consciousness. Someone or something was moving in the village. The eagle functioned as an early warning system. Maybe Alfred was coming.

Gene opened the door of the small refrigerator. It was used to store the vaccine. Inside, on the door, was a large, transparent yellow glass bottle with about 30 penicillin capsules remaining. It was the only thing in the refrigerator other than vaccine they had brought for the villagers. Gene spun the top off. It came to rest on the wooden floor under his chair. The bottle had been marked with a printed white label "Ecuador E7341 - Penicillin." The designation E7341 was for this trip to Ecuador. Gene stood and dumped all of the capsules from the bottle into the front pocket of his shorts.

When he found the top, he twisted it on and slid the bottle back into place in the refrigerator door. He was aggravated by the transparent glass. If Alfred looked, he could see that the bottle had been emptied. In his haste Gene pushed his way across the tent, and knocked the other chair by the table sideways. He kept going, hoping Alfred wouldn't notice the chair or the missing penicillin. Outside he zipped the mesh, grabbed the sample case and headed back toward the village.

Chapter 3

No Accidents. It's all God's Will.

Standing against one of the giant pilings that supported Davenport Center, Gene looked out onto the salt marsh and the canal that ran into the Chesapeake Bay. Tar seeped from the columns, and the acrid odor of hot asphalt filled the air. An impenetrable fog concealed the bay and caused the marsh to appear as though it stretched forever.

There was noise around the building to Gene's right. Flapping. Ruffling. Scraping. Gene looked toward the east wing. He lived in the doughnut shaped, central portion of Davenport Center, and he worked in the east wing. Muffled squawks floated in the air through the breeze. The noise lured him toward the east wing of the building.

He stumbled on the footpath that traced the outer edge of the building, getting one foot caught in the wet cordgrass and muck that made up most of the land on the island. The mud surprised him with its tight suction grip on his boot. He stooped down to pull his leg free. A bright white, almost glowing human skull lay between the pilings, hidden beneath the massive structure of Davenport Center. The suction grip of the mud seemed unimportant. The entire ground beneath the mammoth structure was littered with luminescent human bone fragments.

A loud, mechanical, whirring sound startled Gene. It was something like a battery of automatic garage door openers operating all at once, maybe ten of them. The ground began to vibrate. An explosion shook the mud and muck, freeing Gene's foot and filling the dense, wet air with sparks and flashes and orange-black embers.

Gene was pulled toward the noise, floating in the air between the muck and the first floor of Davenport Center. After he passed under Davenport Center and came out on the other side, his body became vertical and he floated a foot or so above the ground. Thousands of birds spewed from the building. Seagulls, egrets, herons flapped their wings and squawked and cried in a desperate attempt to escape from

25

the shaking building. The explosions and the showers of sparks had their source somewhere behind Gene.

Feathers ripped and torn from the struggling birds filled the air. Several birds impaled themselves on sharp wires that protruded from the edges of the garage-like doors which had flipped open. A young dove broke its neck and still struggling came to rest in the space beneath Gene's feet.

Gene turned. There he saw Dr. Gallagher wearing a white robe and carrying a soft, white feather stick that somehow resembled the barrel of a shotgun. Bright flashes and sparks flowed from the end of the feather-barrel, and when Dr. Gallagher pointed the barrel into the air or at the ground an explosion and more sparks and embers issued forth. Dr. Gallagher floated forward. The white light surrounding Dr. Gallagher almost blinded Gene.

The cries of terrified birds rang in his ears. That sound blended with the moaning wind that seemed to emanate from the scattered bones that littered the ground beneath Davenport Center. Gene wanted to stop the noise, stop the explosion. The birds were frightened and in pain. Gene lifted his hands to comfort the birds.

"No," said Dr. Gallagher. "No comfort for the birds. Help me scatter them."

Gene knew Dr. Gallagher was right. Father had asked for help, and Gene would provide it. He reached for the feather barrel offered by Dr. Gallagher, but something pulled at his foot. Was it still stuck in the mud? He thought he had freed it. He remembered pulling it free.

"Gene," said Alfred, waking Gene by tugging at his foot. "I need your help." Alfred was the thin man Hiaroma had referred to when he gave Gene the aaskouandy.

Gene was still disoriented from the dream. Realizing that he was still in Ecuador was a disappointment. The fanciful image of Bloodsworth Island disturbed him, but the reality of the rainforest was worse. Alfred was a smallish man and always polite. But Gene could see an anger that welled up inside of him, ready to explode at any moment. That morning, as Gene awoke from his dream, Alfred looked to be in control. He always did. But Gene sensed that he had come with bad news.

Gene rolled over in his cot, and his eyes fell on four penicillin capsules on the canvas floor next to Alfred's sandal. Last night Gene had thrown his shorts onto the floor near the foot of the bed, and that's when the capsules must have fallen out. It was dark then, but there the capsules lay, visible in the light of morning to anyone who might choose to look. Gene had to get Alfred out of the tent before he noticed the evidence.

"Hiaroma's dead."

Gene was awake now. "When?" The antibiotics didn't save him. Gene had taken the penicillin to him after he left Alfred's tent.

"Sometime last night," Alfred said. "I found him in one of the shelters."

"He was a good man," said Gene. "I'm going to miss him."

"All right. We have another problem too. Bruce."

"What's wrong with him?"

"He's lost sight of our purpose here. There are a lot of sick people around here, but we still have our jobs to do." Gene admired Alfred's ability to keep focused on the goal, Dr. Gallagher's goal. "Bruce has been talking about walking over to the Via Auca to summon help. We can't have him disrupting the mission." The Via Auca was a road which cut a straight line north-south through the rainforest.

The road had been built alongside an oil pipeline by a partnership between the Ecuadorian Government and the oil companies. The Ecuadorian government wanted the pipeline, but the Orani did not. This road near the pipeline had been named for the Orani, in a sense. In Spanish, auca meant savage, which is how the Orani were viewed by nearby Ecuadorian inhabitants. The only people who ever used the road were Orani that were returning to the rainforest and pipeline workers who arrived periodically to patch the line if they noticed a dip in oil coming out of the region.

The members of the Orani tribe had become more restless as the oil companies cut further into their traditional land. As the drilling and exploration moved closer, different tribes fought for the remaining land. The natives watched as oil companies consumed what the Orani saw as an essential resource, the land that supplied their food.

27

Gene said nothing in response to Alfred's comment. He knew that Alfred was right and that Dr. Gallagher wanted to limit the number of people who had knowledge of their presence in Orani territory. Besides Bruce could never reach the Via Auca by himself. The road was sixty miles upriver, and there was no way to fight the river's current without a powerboat. Neither Bruce nor Alfred nor Gene could hack his way through 60 miles of jungle, so an overland route was also out of the question. Everybody in the village would be dead before Bruce could get to the road anyway. Even if Bruce got to the road, it wouldn't do much good. It was almost never used.

"I need your help," said Alfred. "We must examine the body, before we dispose of it." Alfred left the tent without noticing the capsules. Gene scooped them up and stuffed them back into the pocket of his shorts. He hoped that Alfred wouldn't notice the empty bottle in the door of the refrigerator.

Gene walked over to Hiaroma's home, a structure of wooden poles and palm leaves. He removed the aaskoundy charm from around his neck. It had not changed form overnight. He held it in the palm of his hand, hoping that somehow it could help. The hut was open along one side and Gene could see Hiaroma's body laying in a white string hammock, arms stretched down to the ground. That deep brown, wrinkled skin was covered with puss and clotted blood.

The dead gaze from Hiaroma's open eyes made Gene feel uncomfortable.

"Get some blood out of him before it clots up," Alfred said.

Alfred's presence made Gene uncomfortable. One of the pills might fall out of his pocket as several did the night before. He would get rid of the useless evidence at the first safe opportunity. He looped the burgundy string around his neck, tucked the bird beak back inside his shirt and walked down to the medical table to get some vacuum tubes and needles. In the days since the disease began in the village, there was little discussion among the three doctors about what was happening there. Alfred gave instruction and Gene and Bruce followed them without asking questions. Aside from the fact that those were the rules as laid down by Dr. Gallagher, it seemed only natural, since Alfred was older and more experienced.

Alfred was always so analytical and reserved, almost removed, and Gene usually avoided talking to him. They weren't friends. Gene didn't even consider them to be colleagues since they seldom even saw each other except during these trips to South America. Gene respected Alfred's work and focus, but didn't know very much about him.

Given the nature of their relationship, Gene was hesitant to strike up a conversation but at the same time couldn't stand the idea of remaining quiet. Their work was too gruesome for silence. Besides, Gene was concerned about what had happened over the past several days. One of the things that Dr. Gallagher stressed was that he wanted them to come forward to him or one of the paladins with any concerns. There were to be no secrets. Since Alfred was Gene's paladin, it was only right for Gene to tell him about his concerns.

"What do you think caused this to happen?" Gene asked. "I'm worried that we've done something awful here."

"Gene, you know better than that." Alfred grabbed the body of a teenage girl by the shoulders and dragged her a few feet to a point near the open side of the shelter where the light was better. "As Dr. Gallagher tells us, disease and death are the natural results of our actions. Those who do wrong suffer the consequences, and there is nothing that we can do about that."

"I understand that, but…"

"Do you?" Circling the girl's body, Alfred dropped down on one knee and looked into the dead girl's eyes. "If you understood that good people are allowed to live and the bad ones die, then you wouldn't think that we had done anything wrong. Don't you see, if we had done something wrong, we would be the ones to die."

"I see, but what did they do wrong?"

Alfred looked at Gene. "Look at where these people live. Have you noticed the indiscriminate sex, the food that they eat, the way they murder their enemies with those crude wooden spears. This is not what God wants."

"But what's to say that they're not just carrying out a different plan God has also laid?"

"Gene, what was your life like before you met Dr. Gallagher?"

"Bad."

"How is your life now?"

29

"Good. Well, until the last week or so."

"What would you attribute the improvement in the quality of your life to, barring the last few days?"

"Dr. Gallagher." Gene knew that Dr. Gallagher made him feel like he had a place on Bloodsworth Island and a purpose. Dr. Gallagher taught him how to look at the world in a new way. He provided answers to questions Gene had been struggling with for years. Dr. Gallagher had provided structure and guidelines and a way to look at the world that made sense to Gene.

"Weren't disease and sickness some of the things that he talked to you about?"

"Yes."

"What did he tell you?"

"Well..." began Gene, but his voice trailed off.

"I'll tell you what he told you," said Alfred. "Disease is a manifestation of the evil that people do. A person performs an act of evil, and that action opens up the person and his whole family to disease and eventually death."

"No. That's wrong. That's not what Dr. Gallagher believes. Sometimes there are accidents. Sometimes an innocent person can be killed by someone who is evil or by disease or by..."

"No! No accidents. It's all God's will." Alfred took one of the vials and a needle from Gene's rack and drew some blood from Hiaroma's lifeless body. His spirit would not come to rest inside the bodies of his relatives the way his brother's spirit had.

Gene didn't accept Alfred's explanation, but he could see the futility of further discussion.

Chapter 4

Spiritual Satisfaction

The light had begun to disappear into the jungle. Few sun rays reached the floor of the rainforest, except some distance away where the trees had been cleared following planting of manioc stalks. The women planted the crop. The men chopped the trees to expose the garden to direct sunlight. Manioc, a tuber, looked like mashed potatoes after preparation and was part of most Orani meals. As evening approached something seemed to pull the light away from the village, through the trees and into the distant darkness.

Gene was at a point where the generator behind Alfred's tent was as loud as the sounds of the insects. He had tired of collecting bodies by himself and wanted to know what Alfred and Bruce were doing.

Inside the medical tent a bare bulb glowed above a round, canvas-topped table. Alfred and Bruce sat across from each other in lightweight chairs made of aluminum tubing and camouflage pattern canvas. The raised wooden floor creaked as Bruce stood and leaned into the table, pushing it toward Alfred.

Bruce wore only khaki shorts and dark blue running shoes. His tanned skin was washed out by the incandescent glow, and Gene could see the sweat that had collected on his brow. Bruce's behavior was odd. Gene decided to watch and listen from a distance.

"We did this," shouted Bruce. "We murdered these people. It's the same as if we had shot a bullet into the head of each person in this village. It is no different." His voice was loud. It rang in Gene's ears and made him forget the generator and insects. Gene could see the profiles of the two men through the fine mosquito net that served as a door, Alfred straight and fixed, Bruce bent and broken. With evening approaching, they wouldn't be able to see him even if they looked in his direction. Bruce started to point at Alfred, but his hand swung around and grasped his own throat. He seemed surprised by the sound that had emanated from it.

Gene felt anxious. He knew Bruce had violated the nineteenth principle. The nineteenth principle provided that "[a]ll residents of

31

Bloodsworth Island will speak to each other in a straightforward conversational voice without any untoward or inappropriate intonation. Shouting, raising of the voice, cursing and derisive comments are prohibited as they inhibit clear, honest and loving communication and exchanges of views." Gene and Bruce both knew each word of all of the principles.

The pressure of Bruce's body against the table diminished as Bruce stood and turned away from Alfred. Alfred adjusted the table, his eyes still fixed on the point where Bruce's eyes would be if he had remained seated. Cat-like. That's how Bruce had once described Alfred. Bruce said that Alfred would watch and calculate and then spring into action. Gene now had an image of Alfred stalking and then pouncing on Bruce and devouring him.

"Please sit," said Alfred. His voice was cold, without emotion, the same as always. Gene wondered if Alfred would overlook Bruce's behavior. Whether such a transgression could be excused by anyone other than Dr. Gallagher, Gene had no idea. On Bloodsworth Island such conduct would not go without consequence. This was the jungle in Ecuador. There were only three of them. How Alfred would respond, Gene didn't know.

Bruce grabbed the brown and green leaf canvas back of the light chair. Holding it in place, he fell back into the seat. His expression was blank.

"We did," said Bruce in a soft monotone. "We have destroyed this village and the people in it."

"It is our job to study what has happened here, not judge it."

"Study?" said Bruce who seemed distant, distracted. "You have been irresponsible or worse. This was your project, and you were either paying attention or not. In any case, what is there to study?"

"We must understand the results of whatever tests we conduct. We can and will learn from this," said Alfred. "The second principle is..."

"I know what the second principle is, but it doesn't change the fact that we murdered these people. We murdered everyone in this village."

"That is not for you to say." Alfred's voice was soft, devoid of intonation. "You are here to perform the medical procedures expected of a doctor, to observe, to help, to record information. You are not here to jump to conclusions."

"I know," said Bruce. His movements were mechanical. "The second principle. But the second principle doesn't change what is true. The second principle doesn't change what we have done here, what we have done to these people." He strained to grasp the words, as if he were trying to remember a dream.

"You are inconsistent." Gene knew that inconsistent meant that Bruce's behavior was inconsistent with the rules of Bloodsworth Island. It was. Anybody could see that.

Bruce looked surprised when Alfred spoke. His eyes opened wider.

"Are you even able to recite the second principle?" asked Alfred.

"Oh, yes. I can recite it. 'Independent thought is prohibited. It is destructive to our group, to us as individuals and to...'" Bruce's voice trailed off. He looked as though his mind had disengaged from his body, as though he had experienced some kind of a short circuit.

"Something is quite wrong with you," said Alfred.

"Yes," said Bruce. "Even more is wrong with the people of this village. You know Dr. Gallagher is a good man, a sensitive man, a smart man, a man who is in touch with the meaning of life." His voice was wistful. "Dr. Gallagher would not tolerate this death and destruction. What has happened here has crossed the line for me, and I know it would cross the line for Dr. Gallagher as well."

"You have become the spokesperson for Father?" asked Alfred.

"I know him. I know what he thinks. I know what he wants. I know where he is leading us. And you are leading him and us astray. Maybe you and Gene are in this together. I don't know."

"Yes. Yes. Yes. I see now. You are under a great deal of stress. I'll give you a sedative. You'll feel better after that."

Bruce sat with his hands clasped on the table. Alfred opened a cabinet from which he pulled a syringe. He lifted a small vial of clear fluid from the refrigerator near the table. Gene knew that the only thing in that refrigerator was the vaccine given to the villagers and an empty penicillin bottle. If they brought any sedative with them, Gene was unaware of it.

Alfred filled the syringe. Bruce stood. Alfred put a hand on his chest and guided him back into the chair. As Alfred turned toward him, Bruce looked like he wanted to resist, to bolt from the tent. He started to rise from the chair again.

"Sit," said Alfred in a loud voice, as he moved close to Bruce and placed his hand on his shoulder. With a forceful shove, he pushed him back into the chair. "Don't move. Sit in the chair."

Bruce turned to the side and tried to get out of the chair again. Alfred's hand held him in place. That Bruce remained in the chair seemed more a result of persuasion and power of personality than physical strength. Bruce was too tired or disoriented to resist.

"Your arm," said Alfred, holding his hand out as though he expected Bruce to turn his right arm toward him. Bruce turned away, twisting in the chair. "Your arm."

Alfred moved around the chair and injected the fluid into Bruce's right arm. In the end, there was no resistance, only acceptance of the inevitable.

"Go back to your tent," said Alfred. "This will help you get the rest you need." Alfred returned the small vial to an empty butter dish that rested on the top shelf of the small refrigerator.

Gene decided to return to the task of collecting bodies. As he walked away from the tent a huge gray, black and white harpy eagle flapped its wings to maintain its balance on a nearby branch. Gene was just over six feet tall, but when spread, the animal's wings were wider than his height. A piercing long whistle and a series of short clicks emanated from the bird. When Gene first arrived, the sound of the beautiful animal with distinctive feathers protruding from the back of its head had startled him.

Quemperi, a small boy in the village, kept the eagle as a pet. A six-foot length of rope secured one of its large, muscular legs to the branch where it was perched. With sensitive hearing, the bird issued a loud squawk when anyone or anything approached the village. The ten year old Quemperi had been dead about 24 hours, but before that, when Gene had free time, the boy had on a few occasions taken Gene out on a hunt. Gene didn't have much free time in Ecuador or back on Bloodsworth Island for that matter. But Gene found time to watch Quemperi hunt with his primitive slingshot-like weapon. Adult Orani

34

used blow-guns with poison-tipped arrows, but they were very heavy and Quemperi was still quite small.

The boy always carried the slingshot. He kept it in a small red cloth pouch tied around his waist. After Gene found his body, he pulled the twine from around the dead child's waist and tied it around his own waist. The slingshot-laden pouch remained secured above Gene's right, rear shorts pocket. Quemperi's skill had amazed Gene on those occasions when he had followed the boy into the jungle. Gene struggled to keep up as the boy whipped through the heavy undergrowth. Quemperi usually hit his target, often a small monkey hidden in the foliage a hundred feet above him.

On one occasion Quemperi ran into a sharp stick which sliced into his calf. Gene carried him back to the village and bandaged the leg. As Gene worked, the boy taught Gene how to play bilboquet, an Orani game played with a stick and a small wooden ring tied to it with a string. The object was to hold the stick and swing the ring into the air, catching it on the stick. Gene hoped to find Quemperi's bilboquet stick and ring. He knew it was the boy's favorite toy, and Gene wanted to put it next to Quemperi's body.

The harpy eagle hadn't eaten since the day before Quemperi died. In the past Gene had watched as the boy flung a small monkey he had killed up toward the eagle. Using its massive feet to hold the monkey against the branch, the bird had ripped loose the flesh bite by bite. Quemperi had been lucky to catch this rare eagle. Two or three years pass between one chick and the next, and Quemperi could never have caught an adult. He and his father had captured it when it was an awkward young bird. With everyone in the village dying or dead, Gene knew he must be the one to set the hungry animal free.

With an open pocket knife in one hand, Gene maneuvered around behind the forest eagle which started squawking and flapping its wings. The bird might have trouble flying and nesting with a long piece of string hanging from its leg. It was important to make the cut close to the animal, even better to cut the string where it looped around the leg. The bird fell forward with wings open but maintained its grasp on the branch. Just then Gene grabbed the string and holding it taught cut the string from the bird's leg. The bird dropped from the branch and landed on the ground, free for the first time in its adult life. After a first awkward attempt to fly, the majestic bird rose up into the darkness and away from the village.

After freeing the harpy eagle, Gene checked on the few village residents who were still alive. For those who were conscious, Gene offered to bring water or anything else they wanted. One of them, a woman who looked to be in her twenties, had died since the last time he checked, and her young daughter clung to her. He moved the woman's body to the point where the path to the manioc garden left the village. Since the garden was the only clear area, that is where the helicopters which brought Gene, Alfred and Bruce had landed.

When he went back to check on the young girl, he found her clinging to a support at the edge of the hut. He lifted her and placed her in a hammock which he had watched her mother make out of about a mile of white, vine fiber string. With the crying girl in the hammock, Gene hugged her.

She looked up at him and said, "Moon bad," in Orani.

"Yes," said Gene using one of a few Orani words he knew. The girl knew that the moon was using its power to control her destiny.

"Moon bad. Moon bad. Moon bad."

Gene took her hand and sat down on the dirt floor with his back against a pole that supported the thatch roof and one end of the hammock. With his free hand, he pushed the slingshot in the red pouch out of the way. He remained with the girl, knowing there was nothing he could do to save her, holding her hand, waiting for her to fall into the peaceful unconsciousness of sleep.

When Gene finished medical school he had no intention of participating in genocide in a remote Ecuadorian village. Something had gone wrong, and he did not yet know what it was. He, Alfred and Bruce all worked for Dr. Gallagher in Davenport Center on Bloodsworth Island in the Chesapeake Bay about 90 miles southeast of Washington, DC. At Davenport Center, above the grand, glass framed entranceway was a sign "Knowledge Makes Us Free." And like the Principles of Davenport Center, Gene knew the goal, "We at Davenport Center seek a civilization free of inherited disease where those who are honest and hard working can prosper and live happy, healthy, fulfilling lives."

Gene and Bruce had both developed separate tests for cystic fibrosis, and Alfred and his team had developed a new DNA vaccine cocktail designed to immunize against certain diarrhea causing viruses, tuberculosis and malaria. The technology was new, and Alfred and Dr. Gallagher thought it was so promising that immediate human testing would be appropriate. They knew they would be unable to conduct such tests in the United States at the current stage of development, so they selected this remote village in Ecuador. Gene agreed that it would be all right also. He knew that human testing at this point would be extraordinary. On the other hand, he understood the technology, and he believed it was safe. He did not expect even a minor adverse reaction. Maybe it wasn't the vaccine. Maybe it was one of the cystic fibrosis tests. Both of the tests introduced foreign substances into the body.

In time the girl was silent. Gene stood. He laid the small hand he had been holding next to her side and leaned over to kiss her on the cheek. That's when he realized she was dead. With resignation and numbness, he carried her small body and laid it next to her mother's corpse.

It was late when Gene got back to the tent he shared with Bruce. Gene's period of spiritual satisfaction was scheduled to begin in minutes, at 10:48 pm. During this time of peace Gene was required to get in touch with his spiritual needs and to satisfy those needs through thought and contemplation. Absolute quiet was required. At the end of spiritual satisfaction, at 11:18 pm, Gene was required to go to bed. On this night, Bruce's period of spiritual satisfaction coincided with Gene's. On other nights the times might overlap for a smaller number of minutes or not at all, sometimes resulting in as much as an hour of total silence.

"Hi Bruce," said Gene.

Bruce knelt at the side of his cot, organizing things in his suitcase. "Hi," he said without looking up.

"How was your day?" asked Gene.

"Uh," grunted Bruce. "I mean, good."

Gene knew that Bruce was unhappy, but neither of them could discuss it. Each of them was permitted to discuss any concerns only with Dr. Gallagher or Alfred. Gene was agitated but did not discuss the causes of his agitation with Bruce.

During spiritual satisfaction Gene sat in one of the lightweight, camouflage fabric chairs. His body was calm. His mind wasn't. He couldn't stop the death and dying.

Concerned about whether he might have to violate some of the principles, Gene remembered the first time he heard them. They were stupid. That's what he thought. But he wasn't so sure anymore. No independent thought. It was an impossible prohibition. He couldn't shut off his brain. He had once discussed the difficulty of complying with this requirement with another component.

"I can't do it," said Gene. "Thoughts pop into my head. I get ideas. I dream. There is no way I can comply with the principle that prohibits independent thought."

"You must try," said the other component. "If you are sincere, if you are devout in your belief in Dr. Gallagher, you will succeed."

It was the next day when one of the Paladins approached him.

"I understand you are having trouble with the second principle," said the paladin.

Gene was surprised and hesitant and concerned, but he said, "yes."

"I understand," said the paladin. "We can offer you help. Would you like that?"

"Yes," said Gene. He was bothered by the offer, but he felt as though he had been caught. He believed he had no alternative but to accept whatever the paladin might offer.

"Come with me," said the Paladin.

Gene followed without comment.

The Paladin led him to a small room on the first floor of the west wing. The room was normal height but not much larger than a closet, maybe four feet by eight feet. The tile floor, the plain sheet rock walls and the ceiling had all been painted black, and there were large panels on the walls. The panels were soft, about two inches thick and covered with a black burlap material.

"This is the toilet," said the Paladin. He pointed to a six-inch circular hole in the floor in one corner of the room. "Food will be delivered once a day. The Paladins of Davenport Center want you to have some time to think, to meditate and to strengthen your belief. Independent thought is prohibited, and we want you to have time to think about how you will comply with that principle."

When the door was closed the room fell into a blackness darker than anything Gene had ever experienced. There was no light, nothing for his eyes to adjust to. And the silence pounded in his head. It was an odd, disorienting, uneasy silence. The panels absorbed all noise and produced absolute quiet. He could hear only a light roaring sound caused by the blood pumping through his ears and a soft, high pitched buzz that increased in intensity when he put his fingers in his ears. Whatever the noises were, they were coming from inside him.

The ventilation in the room was inadequate, something Gene had found in no other room at Davenport Center. In time the air became muggy and hot and as dead as the sound. There was nothing. No time. No light. No noise. Nothing to cushion the hardness of the floor. Nothing to cover the smell of his excrement that became pervasive over time.

Gene knew he couldn't stop his mind from working, but as the days passed in that room of silent horrors, he wished and prayed for it to stop. It wouldn't. He knew that, but he had learned something else. There were no private conversations at Davenport Center. However clear it might be to him that he wouldn't be able to give up independent thought, he knew that he would never again say to anyone that he was having difficulty following the principles of Davenport Center. Reality had become irrelevant. At Davenport Center he was living in a restricted, controlled environment where even discussing the violation of a principle resulted in immediate and harsh discipline.

At the end of a week he was set free, as free as anyone could be at Davenport Center. That freedom was tempered by a new found caution and wariness. He left the room wanting to follow the principles. His life would be easier if he did. Sometimes he convinced himself that he could.

Back in Ecuador during spiritual satisfaction, Gene's thoughts drifted to Kelly. He knew that was wrong. He thought of her long brown hair, her long, muscular legs, her big, dark eyes, her slim waist. He knew it was wrong to think about her in this way. The "body," the people who worked at Davenport Center with Gene, were to be Gene's life. He was to have no need that couldn't be fulfilled through them. But he did have a need. He needed Kelly. He yearned for her. It was wrong. It was a violation of the third principle. If only his desire could have been suppressed, that would have been the right thing. Gene sometimes wished he was strong enough to do that, but he wasn't. He couldn't.

She had a touch of Asian in the way she looked. And something about her reminded him of Alfred. The thought was distasteful to Gene, because Alfred frustrated him so. Gene knew he wasn't supposed to hate anybody, least of all a component of the body, but he did hate Alfred. The fact that Alfred reminded him of Kelly left a sour taste in his mouth. Overall though, they were quite different. Alfred was cold, analytical and irritating. Kelly was bubbly, outgoing, empathetic and supportive.

She worked at Davenport Center, in one of the labs. That's where Gene met her about six months earlier. To Gene, she felt like a natural extension of himself. Something just clicked with them, like they were meant to be together. It was the way he was supposed to feel about the body. She was so often on his mind. It was essential that he do everything within his power to keep the relationship with Kelly a secret. He knew the relationship violated the third principle, and he wished he had the strength to resist. He didn't.

On a few occasions they had found empty patient rooms where they could share a few moments together in private. Gene felt a force drawing him closer and closer to Kelly. At the same time, both sex and sexual desires were prohibited by the fourth principle. He knew he didn't have the strength to resist, not where Kelly was concerned. But it was wrong. He knew it was wrong, and he often wished he had what it took to combat this distraction.

She wasn't a component of the body at Davenport Center. She worked there, but she lived off the island. She would never be a component. As far as Gene knew, only physicians capable of performing genetic research had ever become components of the body.

Bruce knew about Gene's weakness. It had happened only a few weeks before they had left for Ecuador. It was the last time that Gene and Kelly had been together. As they were lying in a patient room,

Bruce walked into the room surprising them and himself. Kelly and Gene whipped on their clothes, and Kelly ran off down the hallway.

Bruce escorted Gene back to his quarters but said nothing. Gene was terrified. He knew that a violation of the principles would not occur without consequence. During a restless night, he pondered what his punishment would be. There had been ramblings about various torture devices that existed on the island to redirect people who had become misguided. By the next morning he was almost praying that someone would come for him and cure him of his weakness.

No one ever came. Several days passed, and by the time they had packed to travel to South America, there was still no mention of the incident. There could only be one explanation, Bruce had not reported him. That was a violation of the seventeenth principle.

After spiritual satisfaction, Gene pulled from his pocket the aaskouandy that Hiaroma had given him. "What can I get for you?" Gene asked the beak.

Bruce looked over from his cot. The silent Antbird beak twisted on the string.

"Yes," said Gene. "If I can help you in anyway, you let me know. Ok?"

Gene wondered if he saw movement in the beak, but there was no sound.

· "And if you can do something for mè," continued Gene, "please help us to stop the death in this village." Gene laid the aaskouandy on one of his sandals.

Gene had trouble sleeping. He worried about Kelly. He thought of the deaths of Hiaroma and Quemperi. And there was the penicillin bottle. Sooner or later Alfred would notice that it was empty.

41

Chapter 5

Too Much Thinking Gives You Ideas

Two days later, when Gene awoke, he could see that yellow splotches had developed on Bruce's arms and chest. Blood had seeped through his skin just beside his nose on his left cheek, and there were crusted remnants of blood under his nostrils. These were the same symptoms experienced by the villagers. Bruce would not have long to live.

"How do you feel?" asked Gene. "Is there anything I can do for you?" Gene wanted to make him comfortable. He knew there was nothing he could do to save his life. Only two of the villagers were still alive.

"No. I'll be all right."

Gene nodded.

Hearing a shuffling about outside, Gene left the tent and followed Alfred to the river. The water was brown. It always was. The daily rain cleansed the land and dirtied the water.

"Bruce doesn't look good," said Gene.

"Don't you have to get ready to work?" asked Alfred.

"Yes. I wanted to talk to you about Bruce."

"He has to get ready to work also."

"I don't think he'll be able to."

"He'll have to do the best he can." Alfred leaned his head back into the water. "We need him today. We've got to finish up around here and get ready to go. The helicopter is coming on Thursday."

"It looks like he's got the same symptoms as the villagers."

"What are you trying to say?"

"Something went wrong here. This isn't the result we wanted."

Alfred rinsed the soap off his face. "This was a medical test. We have data. We have blood and tissue samples. We will learn from this test like we would learn from any test. Look Gene, you're doing a really good job. You've worked hard. You haven't been disruptive. I need your strength to help get us through these last few days. Can you do that for Dr. Gallagher? We will learn from this. You can be confident that this testing will move us closer to accomplishing our goal. Please get ready for work, and try to see what you can do to get Bruce ready."

Gene was unsettled, but he didn't know what the value of an argument with Alfred would be. He went back to see Bruce who was still on his cot. Large scabs covered Bruce's face and hands, and his skin was close to the color of egg yolk. There was an open sore that started in the flesh below his lower lip, crossed the lip and continued on into his mouth. Fresh blood was splattered on the top of his right ear, the one with a black chain tattoo starting at the lobe and continuing halfway up the back edge of the ear. The hole was still visible, where the earlobe had been pierced. He had told Gene that he used to wear an earring that looked like a tiny padlock.

"Orange juice..." said Bruce. His voice was raspy and soft and hard to understand. "That cup... down there..." he said, lifting his arm an inch or so to point.

Gene held the cup, and Bruce sucked a little of the bright orange fluid through a straw. Gene didn't want to see Bruce die. The young man's head fell back against the tan canvas pillow, and his eyes closed. Fresh blood was splashed across his bare chest and had stained the canvas cot. Both fresh and dried blood spotted the white sheet that had been pushed onto the canvas floor.

"What can I do for you?" asked Gene.

"I'll be dead soon." A few drops of rain hit the tent. Bruce's head turned toward Gene. With his eyes partly open, he seemed startled. "I don't want to die in Ecuador," continued Bruce, struggling to open his eyes. "I don't know what happened... where everything went wrong." Bruce coughed a long, choking cough. "I thought we were safe. I thought we were going to eliminate disease." Gray and rust colored mucus dripped from one side of his mouth.

"We will," said Gene. "That's what Dr. Gallagher wants."

"Dr. Gallagher loves us. He would always want what is best for us." Bruce tried to adjust himself on the cot. "Something's wrong here Gene."

"Please Bruce, you know I can't talk to you about these things." Gene felt frightened. "I will go get Alfred. You can tell him about any concerns that you may have."

44

"Don't you get it? Alfred is the one who did this to me." Gene got it, but he didn't want it. He knew that what Bruce said was true, and he was concerned about what Alfred might do to him.

Gene loved Bruce the same way he loved all of his co-workers at Bloodsworth Island. Maybe he loved Bruce more. But he could not listen to him now. Were these the delusions of a dying man? Had something gotten inside of him and contaminated his body and mind? Dr. Gallagher had warned that this could happen.

Gene and Bruce met when Gene had decided to stay on at Bloodsworth Island as a full-time staff member. They were initiated into the body together and had memorized the principles together. They had eaten together many times over the past three years. They had become like brothers.

"Have you noticed that no one leaves the body alive?" asked Bruce.

"Please, Bruce. Don't!"

"Do you remember Alan Kurtzmann?" Bruce sat up suddenly and began coughing. The fit went on for almost a minute, climaxing with a clot of blood exploding from his throat and onto the sloping side of the tent.

"Lay back down. Let me help you," Gene said.

"No! Don't! Do you remember Alan?"

"Yes. Alan couldn't live by the principles. He was a failure at Davenport Center."

Bruce fell back on his pillow. "So what happened to him?"

"He left Davenport Center. I don't know where he went."

"Yes," said Bruce, turning over on his side now. "Right. I saw him take the ferry. He tried to sneak away, and I guess he got away with it for a time. But they found him and brought him back. At least they brought his body back. I helped Alfred perform an autopsy on him about two months after he left the island. Of course, Alfred tried to hide it from me. Alan's face had been mutilated. It was unrecognizable. Alfred told me a vagrant had been found dead on the ferry. I knew it was Alan though. The dead man had a birthmark on his left arm below the elbow, just like the one on Kurtzmann's arm. Alfred had no more luck hiding his identity from me than Kurtzmann had in hiding from Alfred. Alfred lied to me then, and he's lying to us now."

"What are you saying?"

"They tracked him down and killed him. Alfred performed the autopsy. Kurtzmann was murdered, killed by a blow to the back of the head. It wasn't very elegant, but that's what they did to him. That's what the autopsy showed. Alfred ordered me never to mention it to anyone. I wanted to get away from Bloodsworth Island ever since that time, but I couldn't figure out how to do it. I should never have trusted that man to inject me with anything." Bruce coughed and closed his eyes again. "More juice."

Gene pressed the straw into Bruce's mouth, and Bruce sucked in a little of the liquid. When Bruce didn't take anymore, Gene put the cup down. Bruce was unconscious, and Gene watched him. A foam of orange and red bubbles flowed from his mouth, and soon Bruce stopped breathing.

Gene hugged his friend of three years and covered him with the sheet that had fallen to the floor. The cool wind and rain blew against the mosquito netting and into the tent. Gene sat in the darkness of the tent. Bruce had protected him. He had been a good friend. Gene needed to stop thinking about this. Just like Dr. Gallagher said: "Too much thinking gives you ideas." Besides, Alfred would be waiting for him.

As he stepped out into the jungle, he pulled one of the canvas and aluminum chairs from inside the tent. The rain was heavier. With one hand on each side of the back of the chair, he lifted it over his head and with all the force he could manage, he slammed it into the base of a foot thick tree. Again he lifted it over his head and brought it down. Anger and hurt flowed from his body through the chair and into the tree. But the pain didn't stop. He smashed the chair against the tree and the wet ground until it was as mangled and tortured as his soul. It was then that he cried.

The loss of Bruce hurt more than he thought it would. Gene had not realized what an important part of his life Bruce had become.

Gene knew he could escape, at least for a time. He would be by himself during much of the trip back to Bloodsworth Island. There were plenty of places he could go, although there might not be anyplace other than Bloodsworth Island where he could practice medicine. If he failed to report to Bloodsworth Island, he would spend the rest of his life looking over his shoulder, until Alfred caught up with him. Then he would be dead. Maybe there would come a time when life on the run would seem the better choice. He wasn't ready yet.

Later that morning, the things that Bruce had said still nagged at him. No matter how hard he tried to focus on his work ahead, Bruce's words kept pounding through: "I should never have trusted that man to inject me with anything."

What was it Alfred gave to Bruce the evening when they had had the argument? Gene knew it had to be the vaccine. He hadn't seen anything else in that refrigerator, although he had focused only on the bottle of penicillin.

Gene looked for Alfred. Some of his blondish-white hair was visible fluttering in the moist breeze on the far side of one of the huts. It didn't matter what he was doing. The visit to the medical tent would be short this time. Gene entered Alfred's tent, and opened the small refrigerator. There were several clear bottles on the top shelf. One was in the butter dish. All of the bottles looked identical. Maybe the one in the butter dish had less fluid in it than the rest. All of the bottles were labeled. The labels indicated that they contained the DNA vaccine that Alfred and his group had developed.

Protocol for this study, like all of their experiments in the field, called for the destruction of all materials upon completion of the mission. This included tents, left over food and all medical supplies. Only the samples that they had collected from the villagers would be taken with them to Bloodsworth Island. Gene wanted to follow the rules, but he grabbed the bottle from the butter dish and dropped it into Quemperi's red cloth pouch next the slingshot.

When the helicopter came, they doused the village, the tents and the bodies with gasoline. From the manioc garden the helicopter lifted them into the air.

"I was packing up," shouted Alfred over the noise of the engine, "getting ready to go back."

"Yes," said Gene when he noticed that Alfred had stopped in the middle of a thought.

"And you know what I found?" He continued after a pause, "or rather didn't find?"

"No," said Gene. "How would I know?"

"I thought you might. I found a penicillin bottle. I didn't find the pills."

Gene was bothered by the implication that he had taken the pills, but he thought he would be better off talking about something else.

"All of these people died," said Gene. "I wonder why that happened."

"It seems to me that this is treading dangerously close to a violation of the seventh principle." The seventh principle prohibited questions. Components of the body would be told whatever they needed to know. "But you know what I've been wondering?"

Gene looked at him but didn't answer.

"I've been wondering what was in that stuff you gave those villagers." Gene had developed a test for the presence of the cystic fibrosis gene, and he had introduced test solution into each of the villagers. "Those people died, but what part did you play in it?"

The helicopter jerked to the right and Gene might have fallen out through the open side door if he hadn't been strapped in. That jolt focused Gene on the precariousness of his situation. Alfred was suggesting that Gene had something to do with the deaths of the villagers. It wasn't so, but Alfred was a paladin. Bloodsworth Island operated with a rigid hierarchical structure. In any dispute, right and wrong and facts and rationality would all be irrelevant. The paladin would prevail. No other result was possible at Bloodsworth Island.

Anger welled up inside Gene, but he didn't feel like he could argue with Alfred or even discuss the issue with him. He didn't want to follow Bruce. Gene fell into silence, realizing that he was riding toward Quito with a murderer. Despite the implications of Alfred's statement, Gene knew he was not responsible for the deaths. Alfred was. Bruce had a single argument with Alfred. One disagreement. And it resulted in the termination of years of service dedicated to Dr. Gallagher.

Even more astonishing, Alfred had made the decision on the spot and without consultation with Dr. Gallagher. He couldn't have communicated with Dr. Gallagher. They hadn't brought any communication equipment.

Gene felt that he was in the presence of a malevolent, capricious man. And yet he couldn't leave. No one ever left alive.

"We'll see what happens when we get back to Bloodsworth Island," said Alfred.

As the helicopter headed west, roaring orange and black flames consumed the village.

Chapter 6

Government Property — No Trespassing

The first time he had made the trip to Ecuador, Gene had thought that to fly from the East Coast of the United States to a country on the West Coast of South America would put him in a different time zone. But it didn't. Despite their locations on opposite coasts of different continents, Maryland and Ecuador were in the same time zone.

Alfred and Gene parted company when they arrived in Miami. Gene was to return to the Baltimore-Washington International Airport just south of Baltimore where a Davenport Center fleet vehicle was parked. It was Gene's job to pick up the car and return to Bloodsworth Island. Alfred had been able to get an earlier flight. He had spent less than two hours in the Miami airport, whereas Gene would be stuck there for more than 24.

As difficult as the trip to Ecuador had been, Gene thought back on the stroke of good luck that had brought him to Davenport Center after his residency was terminated. With no income and no family and plenty of debt, life became a frightening vision of impending doom. While he applied for other residency positions and sent resumes and visited hospitals, he began to sell everything he owned in order to live. After making no car payment for a few months, the car was repossessed. Public transportation made life more difficult still.

The medical books and medical equipment were the first things to go. Baltimore was a good place to sell such things. Next to go were the kitchen utensils, pots and pans. He sold the desk, bed, dresser, table and other furniture as best he could. When the television and stereo went, he thought it wouldn't make much difference. The electricity would be cut off in a few days anyway. His collection of novels he didn't want to sell, but he had no way to move a bunch of books around anyway. The last to go was an autographed copy of *The Late George Apley* which he had found years before at a flea market in Annapolis.

How the entire medical community was able to function as a single entity in denying him work and training, he didn't know. He only knew that he couldn't continue his residency and he couldn't find a job. Luckily he did get the job offered by Dr. Gallagher who called him the morning of the day the phone was to be cut off. Gene hadn't been able to pay the phone bill. If Dr. Gallagher had called four hours later it would have been too late.

That period of his life, after the termination of his residency, with no job, no money and no prospects, had been hard on Gene, but at the time he had not realized how close he was to the edge. All of his credit cards were maxed out. Everything he had owned was gone. Unable to pay the rent, he had agreed to surrender his apartment at the end of the week. As he sat in the Miami airport, he realized that if Dr. Gallagher hadn't called, he would soon have been giving his address as the southwest corner of Light and Redwood Streets.

Thoughts of Alfred and the death in the jungle occupied Gene's consciousness during much of the layover in Miami. Anger and frustration made him tense and alert and tired. Over time images of Kelly with her dark hair and eyes and slender figure interrupted his thoughts. He was drawn to her. And he knew it was wrong.

He couldn't resist the thought of her. That violated the fourth principle.

He wanted her. That violated the third principle.

He wanted to talk to her about what had happened, about his part in it, about Alfred and about what Alfred might do next. That would violate the seventh and tenth principles and maybe the eleventh.

These thoughts couldn't be expunged from his mind. That violated the twelfth principle.

Gene was not living by the principles he had accepted and by which he had agreed to live. The Principles were designed to focus attention on the important work at hand, eliminating inherited disease. To seek the goal set by Dr. Gallagher was the most honorable of objectives. There were places in Davenport Center accessible only to components. In one of those places a poster on the wall said, "Those who serve Dr. Gallagher serve Health. Those who serve Health serve God."

Gene thought back about the time when he and Kelly met. Social interaction and friendships between components and others were prohibited. Still there was contact sometimes. During the summer, about six months before Gene left for Ecuador, Kelly had been assigned to assist him with some laboratory work. The assignment was for two weeks, and that was the last time they had been scheduled to work together.

Except two weeks had been long enough. They liked each other. There was some kind of deep connection between them. The second day they worked together it seemed to Gene that all Kelly did was giggle at everything he said.

"Please hand me that autoradiogram," said Gene.

Kelly giggled and laughed.

"Are you all right?" asked Gene.

"Oh yes," said Kelly, as she continued to laugh. She handed him the autoradiogram.

As Gene sat in the airport in Miami, he thought the giggling seemed so out of character for Kelly. He knew that she was intelligent and poised and thoughtful. The girlish laughter and bantering of those first few days together was only one side of her personality.

"How did you get a job here?" Gene had asked on their third day in the lab together.

"Through my stepfather," said Kelly. "He knew about this place. Not many people do. He has a lot of respect for Dr. Gallagher."

Early in the second week of their time together, Gene began to tell Kelly something about Davenport Center. He knew the conversation would violate the eighteenth principle, but as he spent time with Kelly he felt driven to tell her as much as he could about himself.

"Why do you work here?" asked Kelly. "For me this place is a job. For you there are all kinds of restrictions."

"It is restrictive, and that's a pain in the butt sometimes. But in some ways, it's a great place to work. These are the best research doctors anywhere in the world, here at Davenport Center. All of us have been trained by Dr. Gallagher. There's no better physical research environment anywhere."

"Yeah," said Kelly, "but you can't go to a movie with me."

"Yes," said Gene, as he reached over and took Kelly's hand. It was the first time they had touched. "That makes me sad. But I can't get a job anywhere else. None of the doctors here can."

"You can't get another job," said Kelly. "That doesn't even begin to make sense. You're a doctor. You can get a job anywhere you want. You can get a great job."

"You're wrong. I can't. I've tried. I know it doesn't make sense, but I really can't get another job. I've been blackballed or blacklisted or both by the medical community. I can't go to any of the great research facilities. I guess I could get a job in some small town out in the country somewhere, but it wouldn't be the same. There's nothing wrong with that, but I'm doing cutting edge research here. This is the best medical research facility on Earth. My work here can impact the lives of millions of people. I can help to save lives and reduce suffering everywhere on the planet. I know there are restrictions here. Some of them are stupid, but this is an exceptional place to work. I can't do this anywhere else."

The two weeks together had been good and exciting, but even so, if the assignment had been cut short by one day nothing would have developed between them. It was on the last day of work together when they devised a clandestine method of communication. Gene knew about a loose doorframe on a public hallway where they could hide notes between the doorframe and the wall. They agreed on another doorframe some distance from the first. A mark there would indicate that one of them had hidden a note for the other to pick up.

While he waited for the plane and drank a cup of cold, putrid coffee, worse even than the stuff he'd had in Ecuador, he decided that the relationship with Kelly was too distracting. He had to end it. How could fantasies about this woman be more important than his work, more important than the mistakes that had been made? And Alfred was a loose cannon. He might accuse Gene of wrongdoing at any moment, and Gene didn't want to provide him with ammunition in the form of verifiable violations of the principles. Dr. Gallagher was wise to establish the principles as guidelines for the components. When he got back, Gene decided, he would change the relationship with Kelly. He would change it into the kind of formal, business relationship that would be appropriate under the circumstances. He would have no more wandering thoughts, no more sex, no more love for this woman he didn't really know.

It was late at night when Gene arrived in Maryland. It seemed as though he had been on airplanes or in airports for a week. By the time he got to the car, it was past midnight.

Near Annapolis he passed exit 22 which would have taken him to Old Bay Ridge Road where he and his mother had moved when he was seven. It was the place where she had drunk herself into an alcoholic stupor night after night. It was the place where he endured his childhood until he left for college at Stanford.

At Sandy Point, not far from Annapolis, Gene approached the William Preston Lane Memorial Bridge. It crossed the Chesapeake Bay at its narrowest part, only four miles wide. No other cars were at the row of tollbooths. Darkness and fog consumed the bridge. From the center, 200 feet above the water, Gene could see only the lights on a container ship anchored just to the south. The lights on Kent Island at the eastern end of the bridge did nothing more than brighten the fog. On this cold, early December night, the bay was not littered with hundreds of sails from the boats of Sunday sailors, as it would be on a clear fall weekend.

The constant misty rain was the December weather that Gene was accustomed to, different from the daily rains in Ecuador. Crossing onto Kent Island, Gene noticed a sign saying that it was the location of the first English settlement in Maryland. Gene passed the Pizza Hut, the Burger King, the Taco Bell and the various gas stations and shops which served the summer traffic on its way to the Atlantic Ocean beaches in Maryland and Delaware.

At Cambridge he turned off of route 50, the only highway in that part of the state, and headed south on small, shoulderless roads that would take him to what he knew would be a deserted dock at the southernmost point of land south of tiny Crocheron, Maryland. In the morning he would take a ferry to Bloodsworth Island.

At the end of the road Gene drove through an automatic gate and pulled into a gravel parking lot that contained other Davenport Center fleet vehicles. A large sign hung above the entrance that said "Government Property - No Trespassing" in bright red letters. The car stopped only a few feet from the water of the Chesapeake Bay.

Alfred had always been stable and predictable and boring. But as Gene leaned the driver seat back he remembered Alfred's comments on the helicopter. Would he carry out one of the implied threats? The prospect bothered Gene. Defending himself against an accusation by Alfred would be difficult or impossible and ultimately futile.

Chapter 7

Land Outside-In

It was cold inside the car when Gene woke. Standing on the gravel, he pulled on the dark blue jacket he had been using as a blanket. The fog had lifted overnight and the sky was bright blue with wisps of clouds to the west. The luggage shook and rattled as it bumped across the gravel and over a rough looking grassy area separated from the gravel by a lengthy, rusted iron pipe. Gene walked up onto a concrete dock at the edge of the bay. The trees on the northern shore of Bloodsworth Island were visible, but Davenport Center was another mile to the south, on the north edge of Great Cove Creek. From the concrete dock Bloodsworth Island looked large, flat and deserted. He could see Tigs Cove at the northern tip of the island, a wide mouthed, narrow cove that barely amounted to a cove at all. Fin Creek ran along beside Fin Creek Ridge and emptied into Tigs Cove, but the mouth of the creek and the ridge looked just like everything else, bluish-green and flat. The island bore no more evidence of human intrusion than the Ecuadorian rainforest 100 yards from what used to be a thriving Orani village.

For twenty minutes on Saturday morning Gene stood near the dock and waited for the ferry to arrive. He pulled the zipper of his goose down jacket up an extra inch or two so that it almost touched his Adams apple. To lessen the impact of the cold, wet wind he walked back and forth, making an oval pattern on the concrete. He was at the edge of a massive estuary, 30 miles wide at one point and 190 miles long, where the fresh water of 150 tributary rivers and streams mixed with the salty water of the Atlantic.

Facing south Gene saw the ferry coming up Tangier Sound, past Piny Island Cove on the east side of Bloodsworth Island. It was early December, and the cold weather had reduced the levels of phytoplankton and zooplankton, leaving the water of the Bay bright and clear.

Dark brown denim pants and worn running shoes had replaced the shorts and sandals Gene often wore in Ecuador. Gene shivered. He was having trouble making the transition from the comfortable warmth of Ecuador to the biting cold of Maryland.

The ferry shook as it pulled up to the pier, its rumbling diesel engine belching noxious smoke. Foster Kennedy had once been painted in black letters on the gray hull. The F in Foster and the K in Kennedy were so badly weathered that only a fine black outline remained where the edges of the letters had been. The other letters had fared better, but only the last letter in Foster had survived with more than half of its black paint intact.

Gene waved to the only crewmember on board other than the captain. Gene had seen the guy before but didn't know his name. They had never talked except to exchange greetings. The captain and crew of the ferry were not components of the body of Davenport Center, and they didn't live on Bloodsworth Island. Gene assumed they lived at one of the stops on the ferry's route, in Wenona or Crisfield or on Smith Island.

The Foster Kennedy bumped against the pier, and the crewmember jumped onto the dock, taking the bow breast line with him. After securing that line, he walked toward the rear of the boat where he grabbed the stern breast line.

The large boat had red painted metal benches that would accommodate over one hundred passengers on the main deck. The seating area was enclosed with loose-fitting plastic windows that blocked gusts of wind and created an even flow of frigid air throughout the cabin. More passengers could ride on top, above the red and white striped metal awning, but there was no protection from the weather on the upper deck.

When the boat left for Bloodsworth Island, Gene was the only passenger. The crewmember steered the boat. Mick Ingel, the captain, a burly old man with a white and yellow beard approached Gene and sat on the bench next to him. Maybe the old man's beard had once been white, but it looked dirty. He looked dirty. His hands were black with grease.

"Hi," said Mick.

"Hi, Mick," said Gene. The captain had always been friendly to Gene, but they had never had a conversation. More passengers had been on board the ferry when Gene rode it in the past.

"Did you know that the Monitor and Merrimac battled only 80 miles south of here?" asked Mick.

"What?" Gene smiled. He felt like he had to shout to be heard over the loud engine noise. He had not slept well in the cold, cramped quarters of the Davenport Center truck and he felt as if he were half-asleep. Gene's stomach was a bit upset and he felt nauseous as the boat began its journey.

"You know, the Civil War ships. They were the first ironclad vessels to engage each other. It happened in the Bay near Hampton Roads, Virginia."

"Interesting," Gene said.

"Dr. Gallagher."

"Dr. Gallagher?" asked Gene.

"I saw him this morning."

"Really," said Gene. "He's usually not up and about this early." Gene had seen him before noon on only a few occasions.

"So what do you think of your Dr. Gallagher?" asked Mick.

"I like him." Gene could smell Mick's sour, tobacco laden breath mixed with his pungent body order.

"Yeah," said Mick. "I read a story."

"A story?"

"Yeah. About him."

"Oh. Where?"

"I don't know. *People* or *Time* or someplace. It's been a couple of years. It said that he's not married?"

"Yes. I know that."

"He was born in a strange place."

Gene nodded. He wanted to be polite, but Mick's body odor was unpleasant.

"The Virginia Colony for Epileptics and Feebleminded. In Lynchburg. He was born there. His mother was a patient."

"Is that so?"

"Yeah. She wasn't epileptic. Wasn't feebleminded either. He was born on April 20, 1939."

"You have a good memory for details," said Gene.

Mick twisted his head to the right and glanced up at the metal canopy. The constant noise of the engine and vibration of the boat filled the break in the conversation. Mick looked as though he might be considering Gene's comment, but he continued without acknowledging it. "He had a younger half sister."

"I never met her," said Gene, although he knew Dr. Gallagher had a sister.

"Nope. Suppose not. She's dead. Had a curved spine or something. She lived her whole life on a couch. Couch potato. She must have been a couch potato. A real one." Mick stopped talking. His eyes were fixed on the eastern shore of Bloodsworth Island that was now off the starboard side of the boat. His expression was serious, concerned.

"What's wrong?" asked Gene.

"Couch potato."

"Couch potato is wrong?"

"Yeah. She wasn't a couch potato. A couch potato decides to sit on a couch. It's voluntary. A couch potato doesn't have to be a couch potato. She had no choice. She was like a vegetable. She never got off the couch. But it was different than being a couch potato. Some other kind of vegetable. Let's give her a whole group of vegetables. Legume. She was a couch legume. I don't mean to be cruel. I just think we need a different name."

"Uh-huh," Gene replied.

"This couch legume died when she was four. Dr. Gallagher was very moved by her death. 'One of the greatest losses of my life.' That's what he said. Something like that."

Gene looked at Mick's pock-marked face. Deep creases marked his pink-yellow skin. "I've heard him mention his sister."

"You meet his girlfriend?" asked Mick.

"Girlfriend? No. I don't think so. I didn't know he had one."

"That's what I don't know. The story writer guy thought so. The doctor wouldn't answer questions. Not about her. Wouldn't admit he had a girlfriend."

"Does he have a girlfriend?"

"Don't know. The writer guy thought so. He didn't say it though. He didn't come right out and say it. But that's what he thought. Those story guys can give you an idea sometimes without saying the idea. That's what they can do. That's what this guy did. Is he a nice guy, this doctor?"

"Yes," said Gene. "Yes he is."

"And he's smart too," said Mick.

Gene nodded.

"He's got to have a girlfriend then, I think."

It was still early in the morning when Gene left the boat and started walking toward Davenport Center, a massive, sprawling structure with beige concrete walls. The building, two stories in some places and three in others, had room for offices, living quarters and research laboratories.

Bloodsworth Island was on the east side of the Chesapeake Bay across from the mouth of the Potomac River and sixty miles south of Annapolis. When he was in high school and lived in Annapolis, Gene had passed it a few times when he had been out boating with friends. The island had been used by the Navy as an impact area for target practice. There was always danger from unexploded shells. And since Dr. Gallagher had taken it over, the entire shoreline had been made even more treacherous for boaters. Jagged boulders had been placed just beneath the surface of the water all around the island to discourage visitors, and the area had been marked with warning buoys.

Gene pulled a suitcase on wheels and carried a shoulder bag as he entered Davenport Center's grand hall, an immense room that cut deep into the building. The lighter clouds to the east were visible through the rain spotted glass pyramids that formed the roof of the atrium. On the left side of the room, where the trees, stream, waterfall and indoor lake were located, a full size model of Santa's entire North Pole operation was under construction.

Gene wanted to see Kelly. Their relationship, although odd in many ways, was also a significant one for him. He knew it had to end, but at the same time, he was driven to see her. Sometimes she was all he could think about, especially when he was in Ecuador. It was hard to listen to the Orani villagers making love twenty feet away and not feel envious of them. Sex seemed to come so easily to them.

Gene walked under the dangling sleigh and reindeer and passed the encased Gallagher Fitter Family Trophy which rested on a pedestal between the elevators. Behind the trophy hung a gleaming Clapper

Medal with a shining silver image of parents draped in fine silk cloth, arms outstretched toward their newborn child. Gene climbed up the stairs to the second floor.

The small window in the metal door on the second floor gave him a view of the vacant, curving hallway. As he looked through it, he saw Kelly come into view. She wore the distinctive bright yellow lab coat designed for people who worked on Bloodsworth Island but were neither components nor component candidates.

Gene was surprised to see Kelly so soon. It was Saturday, and usually she didn't work on Saturdays. She must have worked all night, which she did sometimes. Otherwise she would have been on the same ferry Gene took that morning. This was a good time too. After having been gone for so long, no one would be expecting him. They could spend some time together. Maybe they could find a vacant patient room where they could have some privacy. There was a lot on Gene's mind.

He pushed the door open. "Kelly," he said in a voice too loud for the morning. "It's so good to see you." The door slammed against the suitcase on wheels, and at the same time Gene realized he didn't want to attract attention by shouting in the hallway.

Kelly looked up and stared at him for a moment and then looked down without speaking.

A small, blue and yellow box of Frosted Flakes fell from Kelly's hand and hit the floor when Gene grabbed her wrist. He pulled on her arm in an effort to drag her in the direction from which she had come. She yanked herself free and stood still. Gene felt like he was going to burst. He wanted to be with Kelly, but there would be serious trouble if a component of the body found him in the hallway talking to her.

"What are you doing?" asked Kelly who was ten years younger than Gene and four inches shorter. "You can't just show up here after being gone for months and act like you just got back from lunch."

"Come on," said Gene who had continued down the hall dragging his suitcase. "I need to talk to you. This is important." He pushed open the door to the kitchen and motioned for Kelly to follow him. When he saw one of the cooks chopping onions for breakfast omelets and another preparing a vat of oatmeal, he grabbed the door to the pantry and held it open for Kelly.

Kelly sauntered in with a frown on her face, her long dark hair bouncing off her back. The bright light in the pantry from a bare incandescent bulb reflected off the shiny white buttons on her lab coat.

"You're acting like a madman," said Kelly as she dusted off the top of a large carton of puffed rice cereal so she could sit. "I don't know what you could be thinking about. You've been gone for who knows how long. You didn't call. You didn't send me a letter. Nothing. What am I supposed to do, just sit around and wait until you decide to waltz back into my life?"

Gene had become agitated. The problems with Alfred were on his mind, and he wanted to see Kelly. He had even considered talking to her about Alfred and the things that had happened in Ecuador, but the encounter wasn't going well. His eyes darted from place to place around the room, from sacks of flour to cans of chocolate sauce to tiny boxes of cereal.

"Kelly, I missed you," said Gene.

"Give me a break," snapped Kelly. "You go away whenever you feel like it. You don't tell me where you're going. You don't tell me when you're coming back. You don't tell me anything, and you don't know what's going on in my life. Then you show up one day. No warning. No nothing. And the first thing you do is yank me into a food closet."

"I thought about you all the time I was gone."

"Very persuasive. I suppose you don't know the customs. If you care about somebody, if you think about them, you give some indication of it. You might call or write a letter. I'm sure there are different customs in different places. Maybe you're more comfortable with the customs of Antarctica or Neptune."

"Kelly, I do care for you." He reached out to touch her hand.

She pulled away. "In this country when there hasn't been any contact for so long, that sends a message."

"I thought about you. I missed you. I wanted to be with you."

"Your hands have healed very nicely then."

"What?"

"Your hands have recovered. Surely they must have been broken so you couldn't dial a phone or write a letter."

"I wanted to talk to you. I just couldn't do it."

"I know. That's the problem. That's what I'm talking about. It's not like you were on top of some mountain somewhere or out in the middle of the desert. And all of this sneaking and hiding around here. You've got no freedom to do anything. It's insane. I've never seen anything like it. I just can't stand it."

"There was just no way I could contact you," said Gene. He wanted to tell her about Ecuador. Things would be different if she could only understand what had happened and share the horror he had experienced. He wanted to break it off with her, but not like this. She had to know that he cared for her.

Kelly looked at Gene without speaking. A deep sadness had taken over her body and pushed out the playfulness and the upbeat attitude that Gene remembered. Something was different.

"What's wrong? " he asked.

"Nothing." She got up off the box of puffed wheat and turned away. Her nose was an inch or so from a gray metal shelf with bottles of sweet hot mustard and jars of olives stuffed with white almonds.

"No," said Gene, "something is wrong. I've never seen you this sad."

She turned toward him. "You don't know me. You don't know anything about my life."

"Yes I do. You were born twenty-one years ago on September fourth here in Maryland. I don't know what hospital. Then when you were five you visited Bodega Bay, California just before you moved to Illinois. Five years later you moved back to Maryland."

"Ok. Ok." Kelly smiled for the first time.

Gene touched her arm, and this time she didn't push him away.

"Come on," said Gene as he grabbed one of the giant cereal boxes and pushed it up against the shelves on one wall. Gene pushed the box Kelly had been sitting on over next to the other box.

"What are you doing?" asked Kelly.

"Making a place for us to sit."

"Right here on these cold tiles?"

"Well ... yes."

Gene sat with his back against one of the boxes and, taking Kelly's hand, guided her into a sitting position against the other box with her legs stretched out in front of her and flat against the floor.

"I'm still mad at you," said Kelly.

"I know. Who wouldn't be?" He didn't want to love her. There was no time or space in his life for this kind of love. But he did love her and want her. Could he walk away? It wasn't an option. He was anxious and irritable and tired and yet she had such an effect on him that he just wanted to be with her.

"Don't make light of this," she said, yanking her hand from him.

"I'm not," said Gene, taking her hand back. "I wish I could have contacted you. I ached to spend time with you. Sometimes all I could think about was planting a kiss right here on this smooth, pretty cheek." He leaned over and kissed her on the left cheek, just below the eye. As he pulled away his lips brushed against her ear, and he gave her another light kiss on the tip of her ear lobe.

"You worked last night," observed Gene.

"Yes."

"Will anybody miss you now?"

"No. I was just getting ready to go home."

"Let's just sit here then."

Gene took Kelly's hand again and used the index finger of his right hand to draw spokes on the back of her hand from her wrist to the tip of each finger and her thumb. Flipping her hand over he did the same thing on the palm side and then started tracing the lines on her palm. In time they both dozed off.

"Maybe this week we can have another pantry date," said Gene when they woke up. He touched her forehead and the corner of her mouth.

"It's unique," said Kelly. There was playfulness in her voice. Some of the anger had dissipated during the nap.

"So what's been going on with you?"

"I'm still mad at you."

"I know. You should be. I know how you feel. I spend plenty of time mad at myself."

Kelly smiled.

"So what's going on?" asked Gene a second time.

"I'm having trouble with my family. My stepfather wants to see me."

"You mentioned him before. Isn't he the one that helped you get this job?"

"Yeah. I hate him. He's a cruel, angry, malicious man." She was frightened and shaking.

"Oh," said Gene who was bothered by Kelly's physical response when she talked about this man. "What does he want?"

"I don't know. It's got to be trouble. No good can come of it. He's mean."

"Yeah?"

"He treats me like a slave, and he gawks at me, and he buys stuff for me, and puts his hands on me, and he calls me tramp like it's my name. There's so much. Richard, that's his name. My father died when I was ten, and Mom married Richard too soon for me. Thrift you know. The funeral baked meats did coldly furnish forth the marriage tables, except this guy didn't murder my Dad. Mom didn't even know Richard until after my Dad died."

Kelly had never mentioned Richard's name to Gene before. Although she and Gene had spent a good number of hours together over a period of months, she had said close to nothing about her family. This discussion was quite different from anything Gene had heard before.

"This guy sounds bad," said Gene. "When did your mother marry him?"

"I don't know. Ten years ago. I moved out as soon as I could, but that was only a couple of years ago."

"Is he mean to you every time you see him?"

"Man is not truly one, but truly two. Sometimes he's the doctor and sometimes he's the mister. It's the mister that hurts. He tries to be nice sometimes, but he's not good at it. I feel sorry for Mom. She has to live with him. He calls her fatty. She's not overweight, but that doesn't stop him."

Kelly stood up and sat back on top of the box of cereal. She adjusted her lab coat to cover her legs. "He's a big man, not fat but tall and strong. You'd notice him in a crowd. With his deep voice, loud even when he whispers, he can out-talk anybody."

"Could you do anything?"

"Not much. One time I fought back. It happened a few years ago. I was a sophomore. From time to time I would see a bruise or a scratch on Mom. She always had some kind of excuse, but I wondered if Richard was doing something to her. They would have these loud, loud arguments. One time I came home, and they were arguing. I could hear it while I was still on the steps. Of course you could hear his voice a block away.

"When I opened the door, I saw them in the living room. Mom was pushed way back over this old couch we have, and Richard had one of his massive hands around her throat. I knew she wouldn't be able to talk, the way he was squeezing her. His voice was booming. I heard something like, 'Don't do that again you fat fucking bitch.' I don't think he saw me come in. I don't know if it would have made any difference. His face was red. I could see this big blood vein bulge right in front of his ear. I remember the blood vein. It was blue against his red skin. I found a plate. It shattered and pieces went everywhere when I slammed it into the back of his head. That knocked him over, and he didn't react for a time. I told him that I would kill him if he ever touched Mom again. He got up and left the house. When he came back he was peaches and cream, but I knew he hadn't changed. He was crying and apologetic. There were flowers and a box of candy. Mom let him stay. I told her not to. It didn't make any difference. I guess it's ok to strangle her if you give her a Hershey bar later.

"Things got better. Maybe he thought I really would kill him. The man is Beelzebub in pressed khaki pants and a starched shirt. No permanent press shirts for him. He makes Mom work all the time keeping his wardrobe and the house in order. It's not her strong suit either, but he's turned her into a slave that responds to his every whim.

"I never saw him touch her again, but the bruises came back. Mom won't leave him. I had to get out. I haven't had much contact with him since I moved. I only visit my mother when I know he's at work. Then he called yesterday. I've been ordered to appear at the house."

"Are you going to see him?" asked Gene.

"I have to. If I don't go there, he'll just come and get me, and I don't know what he might do to Mom."

Gene wanted to protect her. "Can I help?" he asked.

"You can't help. You're unreliable, and you're never here anyway. You don't have the freedom to go from one room to the next. I can't imagine what use you could be."

Gene groaned.

"Am I wrong?" asked Kelly

"I want to help. I want to do what I can. I guess your parents were divorced?"

"Dead. I told you. My father's dead. He died when I was ten in a place called Bad Ems in Germany. They have these hot springs there. It's a spa town. You know, those Europeans have spas where they go to rejuvenate themselves."

"I guess I've heard of that. I'm not sure."

"It's a beautiful place. The River Lahn flows through the middle of town. In the winter, when I was there, you can see steam coming up off the river where some of the hot springs boil up underneath the water. I guess it's famous as spa towns go over there. Kaiser Wilhelm and some Russian Czar used to go there. There's a Russian Orthodox Church on the south bank of the river, a yellow-white structure with a gray top and bright blue onion domes."

"What happened?"

"Dad was in a spa near this little room where hot water shoots up into the air like a continuous geyser. He drowned."

"He drowned?"

"Yeah. Mom and I went to China for a few weeks, and when we came back we found out that he was dead. He died while we were gone. He went to Germany. We didn't even know he was going to Germany."

"I'm sorry," said Gene.

"Yes. So am I. Before we even knew he was dead, they cremated his body and spread his ashes over the River. We never found any of his things. Maybe somebody sold his suitcase to pay bills or something. Maybe he didn't have a suitcase. But his spirit is still with me, still supporting me, still guiding me. He comes to me when I need help. Sometimes his presence is very strong, almost overwhelming."

"I know it's hard to lose your father," said Gene. "My father just went away too, only I don't know what happened to him."

"Gene, I really care for you. You're the sweetest, most thoughtful, most sensitive guy I've ever met. But you've got this crazy thing going on here, and I end up getting neglected. I need to take care of myself. I can't rely on you."

Kelly stood up, straightened out her lab coat and opened the door. "Kelly ... ."

"Look. I want you. I need you. But I can't have you. What am I supposed to do with that?"

"Kelly, please."

"I've got to go now. We'll talk again later. I missed you."

"I missed you, too," said Gene.

"I've got to get some rest before this pound party I'm going to tonight."

"Pound party?"

"Yeah. Everybody brings a pound of something, whatever they want, popcorn, chips, cookies, shrimp, anything."

Gene smiled a sad smile. He wished he could go to the pound party with her.

Kelly turned away and walked through the pantry door. Gene grabbed his bag and threw it over his shoulder and tried to orient his suitcase on wheels. By the time he was able to get out of the pantry, Kelly had walked halfway around the doughnut shaped corridor and went down the short hallway that led into the east wing and toward the laboratory where she worked. Just then Gene saw Dr. Raines walking toward him.

"Dr. Nolan, welcome back," said Dr. Raines.

"Hi," said Gene as he passed the hallway Kelly had used and then walked past Raines.

Raines was the newest doctor on the staff. He had arrived about a month before Gene left for South America. Gene always felt uncomfortable around Raines. He seemed insincere. Raines appeared to be a nice guy, always smiling and full of energy, but Gene wasn't able to read him like he could most people. There was a coldness about Raines that made it hard to get to know him. The other thing that bothered Gene was that Raines was always putting his hands on Gene.

"Dr. Nolan?" Raines said as he made a U-turn in order to follow Gene. Raines put his arm around Gene's shoulder. "It's good to see you again. I was wondering if you could explain something to me?"

Gene stopped and turned. To shake Raines' arm off, he leaned over to fiddle with his suitcase. "How can I help you?"

"It's the lab coats. There are all of these different colors. The assistants have yellow ones. I could tell that. The last time I saw you in one, it was violet. Mine's brown. Then I saw a doctor the other day in a yellow one. I just don't know what the rules are."

"First of all, Dr. Raines, you should be reading the Davenport Center manual. Anything you need to know is in there. If you're still confused about something, anything, you should talk to your paladin, not me. There is some structure here, you know."

"I'm sorry Dr. Nolan. Please forgive me."

Gene turned to walk away and then stopped. "Wait. No. I'm sorry. I didn't mean to be so abrupt. I'm tired. Let me try and explain it to you. Your coat is easy. All new staff members use brown coats until they have performed a task which Dr. Gallagher deems worthy of additional responsibilities."

"What kind of task?" asked Raines.

"It's different for everyone. You'll know when the time comes. When it does, you'll be given a violet lab coat like mine, and you'll become a component of the body. There are a lot of different types of violet lab coats. Your paladin wears a violet lab coat with silver metallic piping around the collar, down the front and around the bottom edge. Dr. Gallagher usually wears a violet coat with gold metallic piping, but sometimes he wears a white coat with gold piping. People wearing violet with red piping are on special assignments."

"What about the yellow ones?"

Gene pulled Dr. Raines over to the side of the corridor, so that it would be difficult to overhear the conversation, not that it mattered in an empty hallway. "Yellow coats are worn by outside-ins"

"Outside-ins?"

"The outside-ins are people who are not and never will be components of the body, and who work in Davenport Center. There are two different kinds of them. Take your assistant Kelly. She's what we call a land outside-in, because she lives off Bloodsworth Island. An outside-in who lives on Bloodsworth Island is known as an island outside-in."

"How about an outside-in who lives on Smith Island?" asked Raines. "Would that person be a Smith Island outside-in or a land and island outside-in?"

"I guess either of those would do, but we call them land outside-ins. An outside-in who lives off of Bloodsworth Island is a land outside-in even if he or she lives on a houseboat, not that anybody does. I guess we could add a new category called water outside-ins for people who live in house boats. Hasn't been much of a problem I don't think. Have you learned about combos in your training yet?"

"No, I don't think so. I know about those little pretzel snacks with cheese in them."

Gene smiled. He knew that he and Dr. Raines were both supposed to take all of the various Davenport Center labels seriously, but Gene didn't feel like it was a serious matter. At the same time the words often provided simple shortcuts to express complex ideas or relationships. "A combo is a family, although it really includes any grouping, of individuals recognized by the members of the combo. Traditionally, combo is used to refer to a wife, husband and any children. However, a husband and wife with no children is a combo as is an unmarried parent with one child."

"These combos, are they just for outside-ins?"

Gene thought about Raines' question. In becoming a component each person took an oath to dissolve all family relationships retroactively and to perpetuity. This commitment had not been difficult for Gene, since he had no family at the time that he came to Davenport Center. Denial of these family relationships and refusal to speak of them was not so different, Gene thought, from one of the practices of the Orani. Once all of the powdered bone from a deceased family member was consumed, that person was never again given life through the words of the family members. Once the oath of Davenport Center was taken, no previous combo life was ever again to be recognized through word or thought.

"Well combo is for everybody, I suppose." Gene was not yet sure what Raines knew about the body, so he thought it best not to talk about details. "There's more, just so you know. The word single is used to refer to an individual combo member. The words high and low are used to distinguish between adults and children. So, for example, a high f-single is an adult female member of a combo. A low m-single is a male child."

As he left Dr. Raines Gene's thoughts turned to his concerns about what Alfred might do. Could Gene engage in some kind of preemptive strike against Alfred? He decided to begin preparation for a meeting with Dr. Gallagher.

Chapter 8

Systus R

"I know he was a good doctor," said Alfred. "But the mission was in jeopardy. He was out of control, and I didn't want to risk losing Bruce and Gene both."

The two men were in Dr. Gallagher's second floor office, near the Mission and Conscience Department. It was the office Dr. Gallagher used to receive visitors from the outside.

"That couldn't have happened," said Dr. Gallagher, as he leaned forward onto his desk. "Gene is absolutely loyal. I've already selected him for ceremonial migration to the next level. He will never turn against us. You need to know that."

Alfred looked flustered, and he appeared not to want to argue with Dr. Gallagher. With a yellow highlight marker, he fiddled with the eleven pens which lay on the plastic portfolio from which he had extracted the pens and a yellow pad he had brought for notes. On the left were four expensive looking, big barrel, capped fountain pens with gold bands. Each pen was a different color, blue, green, black and red, all marbled. Next to those pens were five dark gray pens with subdued color bands and matching but much brighter pocket clips of shiny black, blue, green, fluorescent orange and fluorescent red. The collection was capped off by blue and green felt tip pens which matched the blue and red pens in the pocket of his lab coat.

"I'm sorry Father," said Alfred. "I thought I was doing what you would have wanted."

"Just let me make decisions concerning termination of staff members from now on." Dr. Gallagher swiveled back and forth in his armed desk chair. "Tell me more about the mission."

"Other than the incident with Bruce and some issues with Gene which we can talk about in a minute, everything went as planned. After we performed physicals and tested everyone in the village we injected them with the vaccine... well, the virus... and we got just the results we were expecting."

"So, that virus is 100% lethal then?" asked Dr. Gallagher.

"Yes, just as we expected. It worked just as well on Bruce, and he was genetically quite different from the villagers."

"Overall what's your judgment on the efficacy of Systus R? Are we ready?"

"I think so." Alfred had previously conducted experiments with a modified version of the Systus R virus called Systus Ra. Systus Ra was an attenuated version of the Systus R virus modified so that it wouldn't cause disease. Systus Ra turned out to be more effective than anticipated in infecting cells carrying at least one copy of the cystic fibrosis gene. Since it infected the mucus membrane cells lining the throat and nasal passages, it demonstrated that Systus R would be an effective airborne pathogen. The test virus also infected birds and copies of the virus were expelled in waste products. "This test of Systus Rb was the last piece." Systus Rb was a version of the Systus R virus modified to prevent airborne infection. Alfred and Dr. Gallagher had hoped it would cause disease, but transmission of the virus from one person to another or to birds would be impossible. "I believe that Systus R will behave exactly as we expect. It's ready for release now... well, except for the need for replication. That's simply a matter of time. There are no further technical issues to be resolved."

"Good. Good work. As you know, release of this virus will be our first effort at actual implementation of our plans. Other viruses, perhaps other techniques, will follow, but your virus will be the first to be released into the environment. You have every right to be proud. You have accomplished with cystic fibrosis what others here at Davenport Center have yet to accomplish with other diseases."

"I have done the best I could," said Alfred. "The result is good. It is just what we wanted, but I am only part of a great organization. Without your guidance and without the support of the other components here at Davenport Center, this couldn't have been done."

"Yes. It is a proud moment for you and for all of us. This will give some of the other doctors around here a richly deserved kick in the butt. If it can be done with cystic fibrosis, it can be done with other diseases. They will realize that they have failed where you have succeeded. The experience can't help but focus their energies."

Dr. Gallagher got up and walked around to where Alfred was sitting. "Alfred, I want you to know that if anything were to happen to me, you will carry on in my place. I have already left instructions."

"I don't think anything is going to happen to you, Father."

"Life is fragile. You are the one I trust, Alfred. You work hard. For years, many years, you've been by my side."

"Thank you, Father. I am humbled by your confidence."

"Now," said Dr. Gallagher, "let's talk about Gene. You mentioned issues. What issues?"

Chapter 9

40,000 Volts

Davenport Center consisted of a massive, round core building of three stories with a rectangular, two-story building attached on each side. From above, the whole thing looked something like a giant doughnut with square wings.

In his apartment, Gene turned the bottle of vaccine over in his hand. It was the bottle he had taken from the small refrigerator in Ecuador. It contained proof of what Alfred had done, perhaps the only evidence that remained. On the other hand, Alfred had produced the vaccine once. He could do it again. If Dr. Gallagher wanted to know what had been injected into the Oràni villagers, he could get the information from Alfred.

He and Alfred and Bruce had traveled a long way to find human subjects for medical testing. Gene thought it was strange that they had traveled 2700 miles to perform human tests when such tests were often performed right in Davenport Center.

Dr. Gallagher had developed an effective approach to attracting volunteers for his various drug and medical tests. Davenport Center was large and isolated, and Dr. Gallagher provided an enticing resort atmosphere. The demands on the volunteers were light, and all had the opportunity to relax or to participate in sports and social functions. The staff had access to as many test subjects as they needed. The doctors had the opportunity to conduct both short and long term testing in a convenient, controlled environment.

A person who came to Bloodsworth Island for the purpose of participating in a medical test was known as a VTS or volunteer test subject. The components would sometimes joke that somebody might become an ITS or involuntary test subject. It looked to Gene as though that happened in Ecuador with the villagers and Bruce.

With all of the outside-ins and the VTSs living and working on Bloodsworth Island, Dr. Gallagher said it was essential that the living and working areas for the components be isolated from other areas. Access to the third floor component living areas was controlled by

Sarah Vorschrift. To get past Ms. Vorschrift without proper authorization would be like trying to drive a bulldozer up to the front door of the White House. It just couldn't be done without being observed.

Gene was able to move between his living quarters on the third floor and his work area on the second floor without any fear of coming into contact with an outside-in or a VTS. In fact, because of the rigid schedules developed by Dr. Gallagher, two components might go for a year or more without having contact. This could happen even if they lived or worked within a few feet of each other.

Gene decided to take the bottle of vaccine with him to the meeting with Dr. Gallagher. Something had gone wrong in Ecuador, and only Dr. Gallagher would be able to straighten it out. Gene loved and respected Dr. Gallagher and didn't believe he would condone the carnage in Ecuador. On the other hand Gene realized that Dr. Gallagher was, without question, responsible for the operation of Davenport Center. There was a chance that he directed, approved or acquiesced in the operation. The bottle was tucked inside Gene's right, front pants pocket as he left his apartment.

Dr. Gallagher had two offices, one on the third floor and one on the second floor. The third floor office was part of his living quarters. In that office he received only visitors who were components of the body. The second floor office where Alfred and Dr. Gallagher met was used to receive visitors from outside of Davenport Center. Gene had an appointment to see Dr. Gallagher in his third floor office.

The third floor corridor ran all the way around the inside portion of the floor, next to the doughnut hole. The rooms were all located along the outer wall of the building. Gene's apartment was less than 90 degrees around the doughnut from Dr. Gallagher's quarters and private office.

Looking through the windows toward the doughnut hole, Gene could see Santa hanging below on wires which stretched down from the glass pyramids above. Dr. Gallagher always saw to it that grand seasonal displays like the North Pole in the main entrance hall were prepared. He arranged parties and guest appearances by such holiday personalities as the Easter Bunny and the Halloween witch. Santa Claus would begin his visit soon, and caroling was scheduled for

Friday evening. Each year the minister from Smith Island would come up to lead the singing.

Gene entered Dr. Gallagher's office, located on the north side of the building. The north wall of the office was glass from floor to ceiling. The window faced in the direction of the ferry dock just south of Crocheron where Gene had caught the ferry that morning. It provided a panoramic view of the vast expanse of Bloodsworth Island to the north and west. To the east was Tangier Sound and the eastern shore of Maryland.

Dr. Gallagher was on the phone. Wearing a weathered yellow rubber coat appropriate for a fisherman, he looked out of place in an office with expensive furnishings. A worn, dark blue, knit watch cap lay on the desk next to a pair of old knit gloves.

Gene moved to one of the burgundy colored leather wing chairs near the edge of the red, gold, green and tan geometric pattern carpet. In front of Gene was a large mahogany desk that had been polished to a reflective dark brown. Dr. Gallagher leaned back in his large leather chair and gazed out the window as he listened. The phone rotated back and forth with the mouth piece moving from his throat to his forehead as Dr. Gallagher yawned.

The room was large and had high ceilings like all of the rooms on the third floor. Past the edges of the carpet was a tongue and groove honey-colored oak floor that gave way to chair rail height solid oak paneling. Opposite Dr. Gallagher's desk was a forest green loveseat, a cherry coffee table with a see through glass top and two more of the burgundy wing chairs.

Behind Dr. Gallagher was a small, framed poster with the words, "It is not enough to know, one must also apply. It is not enough to want, one must also do." Above the loveseat were two large posters. One, at first glance, seemed to have only words, "Heritable Disease is the Scourge of Mankind!" It looked sort of patriotic with letters arranged on three lines, the first in blue, then white then red, all on a shiny gold background. Upon inspection, it would become clear that the letters were made of people. The people in the blue letters were smiling and playing games. The white letters were made of people lying in hospital beds surrounded by doctors and nurses. The red word

"Mankind!" was made of twisted and misshapen bodies piled on top of each other.

The other large poster had a healthy man carrying on his back and shoulders a drab olive green boy with deformed arms and hands and a gray girl with a grotesque face. Below were the words, "You are carrying the load!" The man was struggling. His face was red and dirt streaked. The weight had pushed him down from the blue sky and green trees at the top of the poster toward a desolate area at the bottom where all that remained were black tree stumps, gray smoke and glowing orange-red embers, all remnants of a burned forest.

After listening for a good while, Dr. Gallagher spoke into the phone. "To resolve that, you will need to talk to Dr. Edwin Roybal. He's the only one who can help you. His extension is 2417."

Gene knew that Dr. Gallagher was trying to get rid of whoever was on the other end of the phone. Dr. Edwin Roybal didn't exist, at least not in the flesh. He was listed in the Davenport Center phone book, and he had a telephone extension and a voice mail box. Whenever Dr. Gallagher didn't want to deal with someone, he would tell the person that only Edwin Roybal could handle the matter. Leaving messages for Dr. Roybal was like dredging the Chesapeake Bay for the Loch Ness Monster. Nothing would come of it.

"Yes," said Dr. Gallagher. "I believe he's in his office now. I can transfer you. In the future you can dial him directly using his extension."

Dr. Gallagher dropped the phone into the cradle and jumped out of his chair. Gene stood. Dr. Gallagher pulled the yellow rubber coat off and hung it on the back of his chair, before he walked around the desk and gave Gene a bear hug. At 5 feet 10 inches Dr. Gallagher was two inches shorter than Gene, but something made him look tall, even imposing. Under the coat Dr. Gallagher wore a blue, green and tan plaid flannel shirt, khaki pants with navy blue suspenders and large black rubber boots. His eyes were bright and alive and seemed to provide a window to a great store of knowledge. The red in a bandanna stuffed in his shirt pocket emphasized the healthy looking rosy highlights on his cheeks.

"Gene, it's so good to see you," said Dr. Gallagher as he held Gene close to him, patting him on the back.

Gene pulled Dr. Gallagher close to him. The hug felt good, secure and familiar. Gene was glad to be back where Dr. Gallagher could help and protect him. Gene sometimes saw an image in his mind of Dr. Gallagher leading him through a field of potholes. Gene was able to navigate around these potholes of life with his help and direction.

"It's good to see you, Father," said Gene. "It's good to be here with you."

"I just got back from Smith Island," said Dr. Gallagher. Smith Island was south of Bloodsworth Island. It had a couple of hundred residents and a declining economy based on fishing. "It's part of our community health program."

The doctors of Bloodsworth Island provided free medical care to anyone in need. Dr. Gallagher and other doctors spent several days each month diagnosing and treating various medical problems, focusing on the most serious. Most of the effort was expended in less affluent communities to the east of Bloodsworth Island.

"We met with a young mother this morning. She's about 30, and she's been in continuous pain since she was in a car accident in Ocean City a couple of years ago. Her right arm is deformed and immobile, and it's affecting her shoulder and back. She can't raise a family like that. We're going to take care of this for her. I'm worried about the nerve damage, so I don't know if we'll be able to regain complete mobility for her. But we're going to straighten that arm, so it will look normal. And we'll take care of that pain. After that we'll see what we can do about the mobility. I'm hoping we can do something. We're the first ones to give her hope. She gave me a one-armed hug, and she was crying when she left. We'll get a good result for her."

Dr. Gallagher motioned for Gene to sit on the green loveseat. Dr. Gallagher sat in one of the wing chairs.

"There was this big pompous guy there. He must have been related to her some way or another. Maybe he was her husband or brother or father or son. I don't know. He was sticking his giant, pock-marked nose in everywhere and asking all kinds of irritating questions. We'll probably do the surgery at the hospital in Crisfield, but I don't know. It could happen someplace else. This guy was asking all sorts of questions about where and when and how. So I told

81

him, 'We're going to do this thing right here and right now.' I started rustling around in one of the bags of stuff we had there. I said, 'I think we've got the razor blades we need to make the incision. And there's some bailing wire around here somewhere. We can suture with that. We might not have everything we need, but we'll do the best we can.'"

Gene was both entertained and aggravated by the story.

"That guy strutted around the room like he was trying to walk and stand at attention at the same time, and then he just left. That was the best thing, I guess. He wasn't being any help. This guy reminded me of a professor I used to have in college. He was one of those guys who has a lot of rules about how everything ought to be. I guess you could call him a rule oriented type of guy. I used to take such pleasure in irritating him. I knew the stuff he was teaching, but I did everything I could to make him think I didn't."

Dr. Gallagher leaned forward in his chair. "This professor," he continued, "walked around like he had a pole up his butt. His movements were all sort of mechanical and precise and jerky, like he was walking in a parade. One day he gave a lecture and talked about some issue in biochemistry for half an hour. I forget the issue, but he had broken it down into such simple straightforward terms that it was clear that everyone in the class would have understood it. So he decided to ask me some simple question. I gave him an answer that made no sense whatsoever. He looked crestfallen that someone could have so misunderstood his lecture. I knew the stuff, but I wasn't about to let him know that. We danced around each other for some several minutes there, and everything I said would make less sense than whatever I said before.

"At the end of the class he took me aside and said something like, 'I think that this biochemistry just isn't for you.' I said 'ok,' but then I went and studied. I really studied that stuff. When the test came I got an A on it. I think it might have been the highest grade in the class. He said, 'I don't believe you could have gotten this grade. You must have cheated.' I said, 'Well I did get that grade. You can test me again.' He did, and I got a 99 on that test. He finally gave me the grade, but he never did understand it."

Gene laughed.

Dr. Gallagher was full of energy, and now that the various stories were finished, all of that energy was focused on Gene.

"Before we get into this Ecuador thing," said Dr. Gallagher, "I've got something really exciting to talk to you about."

"Yes?" said Gene.

"You know that you're genetically perfect."

Gene didn't respond. He just looked at Dr. Gallagher.

"Every doctor here is. It's one of the requirements. Through our work here we've come across some young women who are also genetically perfect. We've already constructed a ranch style, multi-unit living complex over near Annapolis. We have room for twelve families, all of which will have genetically perfect children."

Gene squinted, as he contemplated Dr. Gallagher's introduction.

"In January," continued Dr. Gallagher, "you and eleven other doctors will be married to the twelve women we have found. This will really have very little impact on your life. You will live and work here as you do now. You'll spend one afternoon each year with your wife. The objective is to produce genetically perfect children not to distract you from your work. You will be scheduled for visits as needed."

"I don't know what to say," said Gene. He did know what to say, "no" and "that's ridiculous," but he believed he couldn't say those things.

"You think about this. You'll have a wife and a family of genetically perfect children. I know that in time you'll be as excited by this as I am."

Gene wasn't going to be excited by this. He wasn't going to do it if he could avoid it, but he had no idea just how much room he might have to maneuver. Kelly wouldn't understand this.

"Just give this some time," said Dr. Gallagher when Gene didn't respond. "We'll talk about this again before the marriage ceremony. I'll try to get a photograph of your fiancé so you can see what she looks like before the wedding."

"Yes," said Gene. "Let's talk about this again."

"I know there were some difficulties in Ecuador," said Dr. Gallagher.

"Yes. There were. What happened was horrible."

"I knew it was going to be hard for you. But you're a strong, disciplined man. You know what's right, and you're able to do what must be done."

"So many people died."

"I know. Sometimes death is a cleansing process."

Gene was confused by Dr. Gallagher's responses. "Have you had an opportunity to talk to Alfred?" asked Gene.

"He got back yesterday. His flight connections turned out to be better than yours. We talked about what happened. He wanted to get right back to work. He was able to spend yesterday afternoon and evening in the lab."

"It was a disaster," said Gene. "We must find out what went wrong."

"Wrong?" Dr. Gallagher repeated the word as he leaned back in the chair. His eyes fell on the "You are carrying the load!" poster which hung just above Gene's head. He appeared to be struggling to understand Gene's view. "Sometimes things happen that we don't expect. That doesn't always mean that what happened was wrong. On the other hand, the loss of Bruce was a significant one. He was a talented doctor. I don't know what made him so uncooperative, so opposed to everything we're doing here. I didn't know you were going to test him for cystic fibrosis. As you know, we've done detailed genetic testing on all of you. He didn't carry the gene."

"I didn't test him," said Gene. What was Dr. Gallagher saying? Would it be appropriate to mention the bottle of vaccine in his pocket?

Dr. Gallagher nodded and cocked his head.

"I think I know what went awry down there." Gene substituted the word "awry" for the word "wrong," although "wrong" was what he meant.

"I see. We can talk about your thoughts in just a moment. As it turns out, we've done some testing here. Some of it was underway before you got back. Alfred finished it up and analyzed the results. That's what he did yesterday afternoon and evening. Alfred is a dedicated and responsible component. We're lucky to have him. We now know what happened in Ecuador."

"What did Alfred find?" asked Gene. He knew this was trouble. Alfred was hostile to him, and it was about to come out. Now that

Alfred had poisoned Dr. Gallagher's mind, it would be impossible to determine what Dr. Gallagher thought before Alfred got to him.

"You developed a test for cystic fibrosis. It's a very clever approach. Your test for the presence of cell surface receptors was inspired."

Victims of cystic fibrosis develop abnormal mucous in their lungs, and that mucous traps bacteria and encourages infections. Channels on the surface of mucous membrane cells will not pass chlorine ions from inside the cell through the membrane to the outside of the cell. The result is that water is retained inside the cells. This keeps the cells from drying out, but the mucous outside the cells becomes thicker than normal.

The disease only develops in those individuals who have two genes that code for the defective chloride channels. The parents of these individuals each have one gene that creates a working chloride channel and one gene that creates a defective one. The parents' mucous membrane cells are able to pump the chloride ions out through the working channel, but where both parents are carriers of the defective gene, one child in four will have two defective channels which together cause the disease.

Gene had been able to develop a virus in the laboratory that would attach itself to the defective chloride channels and nothing else. The virus then injects its genetic material into the cell. Once inside the virus would take over the invaded cell and turn it into a slave laborer following the instructions of the test virus.

From a tropical Hatchetfish, Gene had taken genetic code responsible for the production of a luminescent green pigment. That gene had been inserted into the test virus, and that forced the invaded cells to use all of its resources in the production of glowing green dye. The virus was not given any genetic material to reproduce itself, so in time each invaded cell would die and be replaced with a healthy mucus membrane cell.

Gene was certain the test would cause no harm to test subjects. At the same time evaluation of test results was simple and straightforward. People with at least one cystic fibrosis gene would appear to have throats lined with green neon lights. The glow was visible across a dark room. The test virus had no impact on people without the gene.

"Thank you," said Gene in response to Dr. Gallagher's compliment.

"The approach is very clever and one that we have already adopted for other types of testing. The ease of evaluating test results is appealing. On the other hand, this is an invasive test."

"Yes," said Gene.

"We maintained samples of the viral test fluid here. These samples were preserved from the batch you used in Ecuador."

Gene glanced out the window in the direction of Tangier Sound. He didn't know that samples had been maintained, but he wasn't surprised. All of this discussion of his test had made him uncomfortable.

"Alfred has just completed evaluating the results of tests on that batch. Something was wrong with the batch you prepared for use in Ecuador. It was still an effective test for the presence of the cystic fibrosis gene, but at the same time it destroyed the lab mice. That batch was contaminated."

"Contaminated?" Gene knew that he alone would have been responsible for any contamination. He had developed the virus, replicated it and prepared the test solution. "Contaminated with what?"

"I don't know. Maybe it was another virus. Maybe it was some kind of toxin."

"I'll look at it. I want to try to find the problem."

"That won't be possible. We were so surprised by the results that we performed many tests. None of the Ecuador batch is left. We have tested other batches, and we found no similar contamination."

"What could it be?"

"I don't know, but I do know who was responsible for it."

Gene felt empty. Dr. Gallagher was saying that he had been responsible for all of the carnage in Ecuador. The coarse dark blue fabric of Gene's pants held the bottle of vaccine on top of his leg. Without taking his eyes off of Dr. Gallagher, Gene used his right hand to nudge the bottle over to the side of his leg and out of Dr. Gallagher's view.

JEFF SLATE AND DAVID REARDEN

"How about Alfred's vaccine and Bruce's test?" said Gene. "Did you test those?"

"Yes. Of course. We're not sloppy here, Gene. We tested both of those at the same time."

"I don't know what happened," said Gene. "I don't know what to say."

Silence filled the room. It was an uncomfortable silence for Gene. Dr. Gallagher touched his chin and leaned his head back. Gene knew his eyes had come to rest on the age worn photographs of Ellis Island which covered the portion of the wall to the left of the two large posters. At the top the photographs were labeled "Congressional Hearings, November, 1922," and at the bottom they were labeled "Carriers of the Germ Plasm of the Future American Population."

Gene was lost. It was as if his body had been abandoned and was tumbling without direction through some cold, dark vacuum. He had been careless about the preparation of the test serum. That's what Dr. Gallagher was saying. It might be a lie, a story concocted by Alfred to protect himself or to hurt Gene. It didn't matter. The damage had been done. Dr. Gallagher now believed that Gene had done something wrong. Gene would be punished for wrongdoing whether or not he had been careless. It jolted him when he realized that he was viewing the deaths of everyone in an entire village in terms of the amount of embarrassment and trouble it might cause him.

Gene knew that Dr. Gallagher could not have incompetent staff. The project was critical. There was only one alternative then. Dr. Gallagher would have to take action.

Dr. Gallagher pulled his eyes from the old photographs and met Gene's. Gene looked away. His eyes came to rest on the comfortable, soft fabric of the moss green pillow on the other end of the love seat. The silence was punctuated by the constant, soft sound of blowing air heard everywhere in Davenport Center. Gene knew that his future hung in the balance, but it was hard for him to think about that in the abstract.

Then a small refrigerator that was built into a mahogany credenza behind the desk kicked on. Dr. Gallagher's eyes were still fixed on him.

"I know this is difficult," said Dr. Gallagher.

"With all of the test solution gone," said Gene, "it will be hard to determine the source of the contamination."

"Yes, but not impossible. We have tissue and blood samples from everybody who died in that village."

Gene leaned back and glanced out the huge window to his left. Analyzing the samples to find out what had been in his test virus solution made him uncomfortable.

"I know you are concerned about the contamination and the deaths in Ecuador," said Dr. Gallagher. "It's important that you understand that I am here for you. I am always here for you, no matter what happens. We will put this thing behind us, and we will continue on with our work. You are a component of the body. You have my support. You are responsible for those deaths, but you don't need to worry. I will protect you. You will get past this. We will get past this. Your dedication to me and to the principles of Davenport Center is the most important thing. As long as you are here at Davenport Center, I will see to it that no authority from outside Davenport Center will be able to touch you."

The phone rang before Gene was able to formulate a response, but Gene recognized the negative implication of what Dr. Gallagher was saying. If somehow Gene were to leave Davenport Center and survive, Dr. Gallagher would see to it that he was prosecuted for murder or manslaughter or some kind of gross negligence.

Dr. Gallagher stood and touched Gene's leg. "That will be Marion. I've got to take this call." From the front of his desk he picked up the phone. "Dr. Gallagher." There was a brief pause. "Yes, Marion. I tell you what, I've got one of our best young doctors here in the office. I'd like to put you on the speaker phone."

Dr. Gallagher put the call on hold and motioned for Gene to move to one of the wing chairs near the desk. "I wanted to talk to you about this before she called," said Dr. Gallagher. "We'll talk after the call."

Gene sat in the same wing chair he had used earlier, and Dr. Gallagher pushed the speakerphone button. He remained standing behind the desk.

"Marion, are you there?" asked Dr. Gallagher.

"Yes."

Gene detected irritation in her voice. He knew she was agitated about something.

"Dr. Eugene Nolan is here with me," said Dr. Gallagher. "He is one of our best young doctors. He has been working on this project for the last three or four years."

"Hello," said Gene.

"Look Marcus," said Marion without acknowledging Gene, "there are problems with this contract, and I'm going to get them straightened out."

"Problems?" said Dr. Gallagher.

"Don't act innocent with me," snapped Marion. "You know what I'm talking about."

The lines in Dr. Gallagher's forehead had become creased and the tops of his cheeks had turned bright red. His eyes were focused on the black phone on his desk. "A number of issues have been raised," said Dr. Gallagher. "Would it be possible for you to refresh my memory on your specific concerns?"

"I don't know why we have to go over this again," said Marion. Her words were short, clipped. Her voice was strong and firm with a raspiness that suggested that she smoked cigarettes. "Here it is again. You are over budget and behind schedule. As far as I can tell you haven't made a delivery on time or within budget since the beginning of time, not under this contract, not under the previous one, not under the one before that."

Dr. Gallagher dropped into his chair. There was anger and defiance on his face.

"I'm sure there have been some problems," said Dr. Gallagher.

Gene was surprised by the contrast between Dr. Gallagher's appearance the moment before he spoke and the soothing, reassuring tone he used with Marion.

"We are looking into the problems," said Dr. Gallagher. "We are making every effort to resolve problems as we find them. We are just as concerned as you are."

"I don't think so." There was no anger in her voice. It was a simple, matter-of-fact statement. "I want a list which contains the name of every person employed to work on this contract. For each employee I want a resume and the total hours spent on contract work broken down by year, month, week and day. I want a list of every task assigned to each employee, the date of assignment, who made the assignment and the date of completion. I want a list of all uncompleted tasks. I want the work history on each of these tasks, and I want to know why each of them hasn't been completed. For uncompleted tasks I want detailed plans for the future including employee assignment and anticipated level of effort required to complete the task."

"It would require a great deal of effort to compile this information," said Dr. Gallagher.

Marion didn't respond.

"Have you talked to Peter about this?" asked Dr. Gallagher.

"I'm the contracting officer. I told you what I want. Peter's got nothing to do with it."

"I'd like to send Gene out to talk to you next week."

"You can send Santa, Mrs. Claus, and a dozen elves if you want. I don't care. I just want the information."

"Let's schedule a time."

"I'll schedule a time, but if he doesn't have the information I want when he gets here, it's going to be a short meeting. You can make this difficult or you can make it easy. Either way, it's going to happen."

After the phone call ended, Dr. Gallagher paced back and forth in front of the window. "I don't know what's she's trying to do to me. If she keeps this up she's going to destroy this place and all we've worked for." Dr. Gallagher looked only at the credenza as he walked east. The west wall of the office to the right of the large posters was covered with photographs of ramps to buildings, lifts on buses and other facilities designed to aid the disabled. At the top was a banner, the left side in red with white letters and the right side in blue with white letters. On the left it said, "Hey You!" On the right were the words, "Get Out of The Gene Pool." His gaze was fixed on an eye level photograph of a parking meter with a blue and white handicapped only designation on it when he walked to the west.

In some ways, Gene felt like Dr. Gallagher was oblivious to his presence. "She's out of control. She's got power for the first time in her worthless life and she's going to use it. I caused Davenport Center

90

to rise out of this swamp. It's the best genetic research facility anywhere in the world, and all she wants to do is destroy it."

Dr. Gallagher looked at Gene. "It's what I've warned you about," he said. "We're builders. She's a destroyer. You'll see her next week. She's got this insane sort of wild look in her eyes. You'd have to chain her down to keep her still. You can imagine a wire with the capacity for 110 volts. She's that wire with intermittent busts of 40,000 volts running through it. She shakes, recovers from the shock, spits venom and sets about to destroy anything in her path. She's after us now. It's Peter's fault. Peter has been very supportive of our efforts. He and I have been friends for years. Still, he's nothing but a gregarious, ineffective boob. He can be pleasant as long as you don't mind being bored, but he can't control the direction of his piss stream. Now he's got Marion working for him. He can't control her. He can't control anything."

Dr. Gallagher sat back in the wing chair by the loveseat. Gene moved back to the loveseat.

"This is a new kind of assignment for you," said Dr. Gallagher. "I've talked to Marion and others have talked to her, all with no luck. I'm hoping you can work with her. You're the best we've got, and although this is going to be difficult, you can handle it."

"What is all of this about? If Peter's in charge, why doesn't he just move her to a different job?"

"We tried that. He can't. These people in Washington are after me again. This isn't the first time, and it won't be the last. Peter can't control it. It's somebody above him, maybe his boss, maybe somebody in the White House, maybe somebody else. I can't find out who it is. The orders are coming from Peter's boss. Peter can't control his subordinates. He surely can't control his superiors."

Gene nodded.

"You can see all of this," said Dr. Gallagher extending both arms and pointing in every direction at once. "It's expensive."

Gene knew that everything on Bloodsworth Island and the operation of Davenport Center would have been expensive, but he had never been as focused on money or financial matters as some.

"The money has to come from somewhere."

Gene nodded.

91

"For the most part it comes from the federal government. This island belongs to the Navy, but they let us use it. Some of the money comes from the Navy. The financial arrangements that support our work are complex, but one of the most important sources of funds is through contracts with NIH." NIH is the National Institutes of Health in Bethesda, Maryland. "Marion has now got the job of contracting officer for our biggest contract with NIH. I don't know what she's trying to do, make a name for herself I suppose. All she can do is destroy. She can't build as we have. It's now your job to keep her off our backs."

Gene was surprised when he realized he had been transformed by all of this. Dr. Gallagher had pledged to continue to support him and to protect him from anyone who might want to harm him, whether inside or outside of the body. Now Dr. Gallagher was entrusting him to handle negotiations concerning Davenport Center's most important contract. Gene felt pleased and excited and proud. Davenport Center was his home, and he knew that he would always be able to count on Dr. Gallagher. This is where he wanted to stay, and he could see now that, although he might be insecure about it again at some point in the future, Dr. Gallagher was not going to abandon him. And then there was Alfred. He would have to deal with Alfred.

"How am I going to do that?" asked Gene.

"You've got to go over to Bethesda and deflect her, get her confused, talk to her, something. I don't know."

"She doesn't sound like she's going to be easy to deflect."

"Well you'll have to do it. What she's asking for will be a significant drain on our resources. We can't provide it. We've got important work to do here, and she wants to turn the whole place into an army of bookkeepers. We can't function that way. She wants to dismantle Davenport Center tile by tile. When she's got the building down she'll pull the pilings up, one by one. She and people like her will drive us back to the Stone Age. This place will be a swamp again."

"Maybe I can take her out to lunch and see if we can accommodate her needs in some other way. If I talk to her, she'll see that what we're doing here is good and then I can work with her to define what else she needs."

"Good. I think you can pull it off. It's going to take everything you've got. At the same time it's taking you away from the work you're doing here. But this is important. If we don't stop Marion, none of us will be doing anything. Try to find out what she wants. What is the minimum that will satisfy her? Tell her that compiling the information she has requested will cause a significant hardship. Tell her that it will delay important research and waste the government's money."

Dr. Gallagher wore a strained expression. In the time Gene had been associated with Dr. Gallagher, Gene had seen Dr. Gallagher angry, agitated and melancholy at different times. But something was different. Penetrating the successful man's aura of confidence and wisdom were fear and concern about the damage this woman might do. Gene could feel that Dr. Gallagher lacked confidence. It was the first time he'd ever seen it.

"You might as well know," said Dr. Gallagher.

"What?" asked Gene.

"Marion and I used to have a personal relationship. You know that saying about scorned women and fury and what hell hasn't got."

Chapter 10

Living In Fear

"You are very tense," said Madame Charlotte. "Just relax for a moment. Your attitude will interfere with the reading."

Madame Charlotte sat in a large, ornate chair of carved wood. The back and seat of the chair had been upholstered with red velvet into which a pattern of flowers and vines had been woven. The chair was tall, and Madame Charlotte's head was a foot below the top of it. The top of the chair back was wood carved into an intricate design of mingled trees, leaves and vines. Pointed wooden mushrooms adorned the back of the chair on the left and right, one directly above each of the rear chair legs. Below the carved wood was a strip of green fabric edging which separated the carved wood from the red velvet. Below that was the top of Madame Charlotte's head accented by a string of coins she used to pull her long black hair off her face.

Richard, Kelly's stepfather, sat across the round, dark wood table from Madame Charlotte. The table was made of carved wood in the same style as the chair with ball-and-claw feet and legs consisting of twisted serpents. A modest sized crystal ball, the center clouded by imperfections, rested on a brass stand in the center of the table. Incense of cinnamon, anise seed and bayberry herb burned on the stand behind Madame Charlotte.

Richard, a stocky man dressed in farmhand overalls and a black leather jacket, seemed out of place in the elegant though cluttered Victorian parlor. A bushy, blond moustache, extending four inches on each side of his nose, provided a softness to the otherwise sharp features of his face. On the right it swept out to the side and then down past the corner of his mouth. On the left it went down first, covering his mouth, and then over to the side.

He had been in a go-go bar the night before, where he had talked to a woman. She had told him that she thought the bar was cold.

"My life is crap, nothing but crap," he had said to the woman who continued to wear her calf length black coat with a collar made of long, wispy black feathers. "One problem comes. Then another problem comes. Then another one. Shit follows shit."

"Same as me," said the woman. Standing beside Richard at the bar, she placed one of her shiny black platform shoes with the thick metallic silver soles on the brass bar. The bottom of the coat fell off of her leg to expose the leopard design pants. The coat opened all the way up to the bottom of her yellow blouse.

"There's got to be more to life," said Richard.

"I don't know," said the woman. Her deep red hair looked as though it had been piled on top of her head. Most of it had drooped off to form a haystack shape. A few strands fell into her eyes.

"I think it must be hidden from us. Not everybody can see it."

"Yeah. I see this spiritualist. She talks about the same shit that you're saying. Maybe you should talk to her." She told Richard where to find Madame Charlotte. "She's helped me a lot."

Now, there he was in Madame Charlotte's reading room. He had already paid this bejeweled woman with the yellow and sky blue billowing skirt ten dollars to have his palm read. The skirt was decorated with two parallel red stripes near the bottom edge and bluish-purple bunches of grapes with green vines and leaves. She wore a bulky sweater with narrow horizontal stripes of yellow, blue, orange and purple. Richard leaned forward against the table. His jacket rubbed against itself and squeaked as he moved. He laid his left palm in front of the woman with the tannish-yellow skin.

"That's better. Don't worry, I won't bite it."

She grasped his hand with both of hers, twisting it from side to side to get the best view in the dim light. With two fingers she traced the long line down the center of Richard's palm. Her touch was light, sensual, seductive. She looked up at Richard, almost as though she had been startled by something in his palm. Then she squinted and studied his face, as if she were trying to look deep into the soul of a man who carried such shocking information on his hand. She looked back at his palm.

"Oh yes. I see why you've come here." She rubbed his palm with a soft touch as if to verify that the lines she saw were creases in Richard's skin and not dirt or discoloration. "This is a crucial moment in your life. You are very fortunate to have found me. I can help you with this. I only hope it is not too late."

"What is it? What do you see?"

"Many things. I see many things. The question is where to start when there is so much."

"I've got to know. What is it you see?"

"First I see family. I see trouble with your family."

"It's my wife isn't it?"

"Yes. Yes. It's your wife. She has caused you much trouble."

"She's been real difficult lately. Nothing I do seems to keep her under control. I work hard all day, you know. All Catherine does is sit around the house on her fat butt. When I get home, I expect the place to be clean and to get a little supper. Is that too much to ask for?"

"No. That's not too much to ask. But there is more here. I see more. Catherine has caused you trouble, but it is not her fault."

"Not her fault? Whose fault is it then?"

"There are enemies. You have enemies. And there is still more. Something is inside you, something important." Madame Charlotte shifted in her chair and leaned back.

"Kelly left. Hasn't been the same since."

"This woman Kelly does not feel like your enemy. Although maybe your enemy is close to her, related to her somehow."

"No woman. Kelly isn't a woman. She's a girl. Catherine's daughter."

. "Yes. She is near to the spirit I feel. The spirit is very strong here. Could it be Kelly's father? There is an imbalance there. I can feel that imbalance. There is turbulence here. The spirits are in turmoil. This is a very difficult time for you."

"The tramp's father, Catherine's first husband, is dead. She picked a real loser. Stupid. He was stupid. Died years ago."

"The spirits of the dead can be very powerful, perhaps the most powerful of all. And Kelly is a woman, like it or not. That explains some of what I see here." She pointed to a place on his palm where some small heavy lines intersected with a much longer line that ran from the base of his index finger to his wrist. "Women always cause men confusion. Two women together can make a man crazy."

"Kelly is not a woman. She is just a girl. She's only twenty or something."

"Your mind is telling you that she is a girl, because that is how you remember her. Her mama has the same problem I think. But she's a woman now, ready to go out and make her own life."

"They don't seem like very sensible decisions to me. The girl's got no judgement. She just picks up one day and leaves her mother and me without giving us any notice. I could do a better job of directing her life than she has."

"I think that to have your wife more stable, you must think of some way to convince Kelly to spend more time with her. It is clear that she has left a void in her mama's life that has left her feeling empty."

"I had that same thought myself," Richard said. "I asked Kelly to come up to the house so I could talk to her."

"That sounds good. I hope you can work something out with her. We will see what else is in your palm." She looked back down at his outstretched hand once again.

Richard reached into his pants pocket with his free hand and pulled out his lighter and began flipping it around. As he pulled the cover back, a small flame appeared, which he extinguished with his thumb. He repeated this process several times, until Madame Charlotte dropped his other hand.

"Do you mind? This takes concentration."

"Sorry, it's an old habit of mine. I'll put it away."

"Let me see that!" The gypsy grabbed at the lighter, but Richard pulled away. "Let me see it."

He handed her the stainless steel lighter. Embossed on one side was a gold shovel, surrounded by an elaborate border.

"This symbol," said Madame Charlotte, tapping the golden shovel, "what is the significance of this symbol?"

"When I was a kid my older brother, Leo, used to beat up on me a lot. He was bigger than me. That louse made my life miserable. One day, after school, he was pushing me around and giving me a lot of crap to impress one of his friends. I was pissed. So I went around to the shed behind the house and pulled a shovel off the wall. It was heavy. I had trouble carrying it. When Leo saw me coming around the house he started charging at me. He said, 'I hope you brought that thing out here to dig your grave 'cause I'm gonna kill you.' So as he neared, I steadied myself, lifted the shovel and wham!" Richard clinched his fist, raised his right arm and then brought his elbow down hard against the top of the table. "I slammed that shovel right into his ugly face. Hasn't bothered me since."

"Yes," said Madame Charlotte. "You have an aura about you. I felt it when you first came in. It is an aura of forcefulness. You are a powerful man who will not be stopped."

"It was a turning point in my life. He never bothered me again. I wasn't living in fear of that little fart anymore. I had confidence. That shovel gave me confidence. I knew I had power. When I was in the army, I bought that lighter. It's been my trademark ever since."

She handed the lighter back to him and he put it in his pocket. "We must continue," she said. "There is a very potent force at work here. It is the spirit of the child's dead father. It is evil and very strong. I can feel the foreboding presence of that spirit."

"That man, even though he's dead, has made my life shit. Sometimes I think Catherine would rather be with him than me. And he left this burden on me, the burden of raising his kid. It was a dirty, thankless job."

"It is his spirit that fuels the curse. This curse must be removed. It is your only choice. You will never have happiness so long as that curse is in place. I can work with you. I want to work with you. I want to help you. This is very serious. We must act quickly, otherwise it will be too late. I want nothing for myself. I only want to help you. There will be costs of course. We will need a crystal, some special candles, a few other things. You will only need to cover my expenses. I will make nothing."

Chapter 11

So Says One. So Say We All.

"Dr. Nolan!" The insistent but conversational level voice was that of Sarah Vorschrift.

"Yes?" said Gene, as he turned toward her. They were in the hallway near Gene's lab. It was late afternoon.

"There's a problem."

"A problem?"

"Yes. Dr. Gallagher told me to inform you that we have received some unexpected results from the blood test. He said you'd know why. He seemed quite bothered. It wasn't the test results that upset him, I don't think."

"Well, what was it?"

"He kept muttering something about integrity. He was angry. You know how he can get. It was better that you couldn't see him then. You will meet with him soon enough. It will show up on your schedule. This way he will have an opportunity to cool down."

After Dr. Gallagher told Gene that he was to be married in January, Gene had been ordered to report to Medical Services for some blood work. He didn't know why blood was to be taken, but he thought it might have something to do with last minute testing prior to his impending marriage. Dr. Gallagher had talked about genetic perfection, and Gene had seen to it that the blood labeled with his ID number reflected anything but perfection. Before reporting to Medical Services, Gene drew some blood from a VTS with a number of debilitating genetic disorders.

Gene thought he had gotten away with substituting one tube for another, but things didn't look good. He didn't know what went wrong, but something had. This was trouble and it could be disastrous. The price Gene might pay for this kind of deception could be quite high.

"He said I'd know why?" said Gene.

"Yes," said Ms. Vorschrift.

"What did he mean by that?"

"I'm sure I don't know."

By substituting the blood, Gene had hoped to cause confusion that would take long enough to straighten out so that he could avoid the marriage in January. There were plenty of other doctors at Davenport Center. Someone else could get married in his place in January.

This upcoming meeting with Dr. Gallagher was one more problem and a serious one at that.

~ ~ ~

It was past midnight, past the time when Gene would normally have been scheduled for spiritual satisfaction, past the time he was often scheduled to be asleep. Gene was in a small, dark room, an antechamber, along with several other components. Many of these rooms occupied the perimeter of the huge, circular Ceremonial Chamber, the room where the most sacred ceremonies of Davenport Center took place. This was an area of the west wing of Davenport Center accessible only to components.

In the antechamber Gene had changed into his costume for the beginning of the ceremony. He wore all black, socks, shoes, gloves and a hooded cape--nothing else. Gene had worn the same costume many times before, and although it was almost new, everything looked old and worn. The shoes had painted scuffs and cut gashes. Holes had been cut into the socks and gloves, but the edges of the holes had been bound with black thread so the holes wouldn't unravel the cloth. The hooded cape was heavy and thick and, like the other clothing, had been created to give the appearance of years of abuse. A reflective stone crystal of milky white was secured by some black elastic bands on the back of the cape, behind Gene's right shoulder.

The door opened automatically, and Gene and the other components in that room went down several steps and along a narrow passageway which took them into the Ceremonial Chamber. The discordant sounds of pianos, strings, an occasional horn, wind, rain, rattling, crashing, and breaking shook Gene's body. The volume shifted between soft and deafening, and the noises were disconcerting.

An overwhelming smell of rotting garbage filled the room where the temperature was close to freezing.

A raised roof and sunken floor permitted a high ceiling in the chamber. The floor was black marble, and the ceiling and curved wall of the chamber had been painted black. When Gene entered the room, the only illumination was provided by small lights in the ceiling which projected tiny red numbers onto the floor. Gene found his place in the room where the number 48 appeared on the marble. The small columns of red light were dim, and the numbers were difficult to read against the black floor. Gene found his place, because he knew where the 48 would be relative to his antechamber. Adjusting one side of his cape to protect him from the cold floor, Gene fell into a position of uncomfortable death.

Many components were in place when Gene entered the room, and more came, antechamber by antechamber, until the components, all dressed in costumes like Gene's, were distributed throughout the room in positions of agony or death. Some new components would be experiencing the Ceremony of Unity of Action for the first time. With everyone in place, the small columns of light went off, plunging the room in blackness.

In time a column of bright, white light illuminated the center of the room. Dr. Gallagher rose from beneath the floor, standing atop a small, circular platform that pushed upward until it became level with the floor. The sound changed to a single note of a clarinet high above the room which blended with the sounds of a soft summer breeze until it was joined by strings and a piano. The sound was different now, no longer discordant. Instead it was pleasant and uplifting. The temperature changed and the rotting stench softened.

Dr. Gallagher was dressed in a white business suit, shirt and tie. The fabric shimmered and glistened in the light like a metallic white or mother of pearl. In the blackness behind Dr. Gallagher, to the northwest of him, was a massive, realistic looking mountain made of metal, rock and glass. The top of the mountain was made of sharp rocks and soft edged boulders, and the lower part was covered with trees. White glass served as snow caps for the dual peaks, one of which was higher than the other. The mountain rested on a giant, round metal plate which had six inch metal legs.

"The messenger has arrived," said Dr. Gallagher in an amplified voice that boomed throughout the room. High up above the floor in the direction Dr. Gallagher was facing, a photograph had been lit from behind. The image was of a dove taking flight from within a burst of light. To his sides, also high up, lights flashed behind stark images of men, women and children. A prisoner sat on a metal bed in his cell. One group of men worked as slaves. On a flat bed of parched, red earth, a child made bricks. A woman searched through garbage in front of a decaying industrial landscape of black and gray factories and train tracks.

In front of Dr. Gallagher was a metal pole on which a rectangular control panel had been mounted. The process of gathering the components began. Some of the components were gathered individually, others in groups of two, three or four at a time. The process was always the same.

When it was Gene's turn, Dr. Gallagher directed a light from above to illuminate the crystal on Gene's back. The crystal came alive, glowing and reflecting the light directed by Dr. Gallagher. Other components had similar crystals fastened in other places, on the bottom of a foot, behind the knee, next to the waist, on the back of the head. With the crystal sparkling in the light, Gene stood and removed all of the black clothing, placing it in a pile beside him. He took the crystal and clipped it to a loop of red cloth ribbon taken from a pocket inside the cape and hung the crystal around his neck. He stood in the cold air, naked except for the crystal, arms lifted skyward, his body bathed in white light.

"Blessed are your feet which brought you here," said Dr. Gallagher. His voice boomed from speakers near the ceiling. "Blessed are your hands and body which do the work of Davenport Center. Blessed is your soul and spirit which have been set free. Blessed is your mind which is now free to dream a grand dream. Blessed is that spark inside you that has now been ignited into a roaring fire by your work here at Davenport Center."

Gene fell to the floor, his body jolted by the cold, black marble. Pulling his knees up to his chest, his right hand touched the soles of his feet, and his left hand was on the top of his head.

"My soul," said Gene, "my spirit and everything between my two hands is dedicated to Dr. Gallagher and will work tirelessly for the principles of Davenport Center."

The black raggedy clothing had been replaced by new clothing. Gene pulled on pants and a shirt of light gray with thin red strips down the outside of the legs and accenting the collar and cuffs of the shirt. A red leather belt supported a small knife on the left side. The knife had a black handle adorned with a small diamond shape of red enamel. The knife was inserted into a golden sheath. He slipped on a gray hat like one an elf might wear.

"I have transformed you into a warrior for all that we hold dear," said Dr. Gallagher. "As part of the whole we can do more than individually we could ever dream of accomplishing. Now take your rightful place as a component of Davenport Center."

Gene headed for his position next to the metal and rock mountain. He formed part of an incomplete circle around the edge of the plate that supported the mountain. As he reached the structure that towered over his head, he leaned into it and pushed with all of his might. The structure remained immobile. Gene stood by the mountain, watching and waiting for the transformation of the remaining components. The process was the same for all, but the uniforms differed somewhat. Some had accents of different colors, blue, yellow or green. The paladins wore silver with accents of gold. When all were in place around the mountain, Dr. Gallagher spoke.

"I have delivered each and every one of you here, free of slavery, free of restraints that limited your accomplishments. You have become a component of Davenport Center and together we work without limits. We are free, resourceful and powerful. We will make a difference. We will leave a permanent mark. We will change the world forever. Millennia from now, when some may have forgotten our names, our influence will still be felt."

The temperature in the room had become comfortable. The foul odors had been removed and replaced by the pleasant odor of the Chesapeake Bay salt air. The images of pain and struggle had been replaced by various of images of light and clouds and angels and mountains and forests and pristine buildings and families and well dressed, hard working people.

In response to light signals by Dr. Gallagher, the group reached down and grasped the edge of the metal plate that supported the mountain. Together they lifted the towering structure and moved it across the room and out of the way.

The light directed the components to form a circle. Dr. Gallagher was just to the north of the circle and just outside of it. The mountain was in darkness at the side of the room.

"I am the fuel that fires the engine," said Dr. Gallagher.

"So says one. So say we all." The group responded in unison.

"I am the solid rock that anchors us in place with unchanging values and goals."

"So says one. So say we all."

"I am the light that guides us and without which we would do nothing but wander without aim or direction."

"So says one. So say we all."

"I am the source of power and vision and mystical sight."

"So says one. So say we all."

"I am the channel and conduit for communication for all higher power in the universe."

"So says one. So say we all."

"Individually we are powerless. Together and with focus and direction we have moved this mountain and we will move others."

"So says one. So say we all."

Chapter 12

God's Plan

Peter Snyder's silver Volvo pulled to a stop next to one of the giant logs on the gravel parking lot of Hank Dietle's Tavern on the Rockville Pike about two and a half miles north of NIH and on the other side of the Washington beltway. Peter popped out of the car. His movements were short and jerky, suggesting both a high level of energy for his fifty-three years and a low level of coordination. At the same time he was able to move his five foot six inch wiry frame across the gravel without any indication of the club foot caused by osteomyelitis when he was a child.

Hank Dietle's Tavern was an anomaly on the Rockville Pike. Surrounded by large, modern townhouses, ten story office buildings of gleaming, mirrored glass and a glitzy shopping mall, it stood out as one of the few remaining original structures on the Pike. The building would not have been out of place as a country store at a lonely rural intersection with an abandoned house across the street.

Marion got out of the car. Two inches taller than Peter, she looked the part of a powerful business woman. Although she had a significant amount of gray, it blended with her short, almost black hair. Her navy blue suit was striking against the silver of the Volvo and out of place in a gravel parking lot. Fine lines around her eyes gave her a mature, distinguished look. The corners of her mouth were pulled into a perpetual frown, and that frown dominated the oval face no matter what other expression might try to push its way through. This caused some people to be wary of her.

It was colder than usual for a Washington December when Peter used the cinder block steps to climb onto Hank Dietle's gray painted concrete porch. Although the sky to the west was gray, there was only clear bright blue to the east with a few diffuse clouds back in the direction of NIH and downtown Washington. With a nose that made him look something like a chicken, coarse yellow skin and a disheveled green suit, Peter blended in with the time worn, dirty tan brick facing. He stood next to the easel style billboard that was in front of the large window to the left of the door. In large black letters the billboard advertised "Homemade Soups and Sandwiches," and in red "Cold Beer To Go."

Marion stepped onto the porch and tried to look through the dirty window on the right side of the door. Past the window, which looked like it hadn't been cleaned in a couple of years and past the red and blue "Happy Hour, Monday - Friday, 4 - 7" sign, Hank Dietle's was a small, one room affair. A young woman with a ponytail and wearing a dark gray dress with pink flecks played pool by herself.

"You brought me to lunch here?" exclaimed Marion.

"Yes," said Peter. "It's a great place. Not many places like this left." Although Peter irritated most people after a period of time, his extreme extroversion mixed with his small town Indiana charm won over many during an initial encounter.

"I'm sure that's true," said Marion.

Inside on the right with the pool table were three small booths. On the left was a pinball machine, two video games and seven more small booths. An eight stool bar filled the back of the room. A lighted orange and green O'Douls sign hung on the left, and a neon blue Lite sign had been nailed to the wall on the right. A giant inflatable red video game character sitting on a yellow rocket hung in the front near the pool table. A big man with close cropped, dark hair, a bushy blond moustache and dark rimmed glasses played the Tank Command video game, and three guys were gathered in the back next to the bar. All of the booths were empty.

The woman playing pool waved and smiled. Peter led Marion to the booth nearest the door. Soon the woman with the pony tail laid the cue stick across the corner of the pool table and took Peter's and Marion's order.

It had been more than 25 years since Peter and Marion first met. They were next door neighbors in Montgomery Village in Gaithersburg, Maryland where they became good friends. Marion was godmother to Peter's oldest child. Even so they had lost contact over the years. It was Marion's interest in the job at NIH that reunited them. The lunch at Hank Dietle's was their first together in many years.

"How did you get this job?" asked Peter.

"You hired me," said Marion. "That's how." She had been working for Peter only since the week before Thanksgiving.

"I know I did," said Peter in a way that suggested he wished he hadn't. "But I had nothing to do with it. I only made the offer."

"I though you wanted to hire me."

"I did. Of course I did. But the decision was out of my hands. I was instructed to do it." When Peter first found out that Marion wanted the job, he was ecstatic. It was after she started working that the trouble started. Her interest in Dr. Gallagher became apparent to Peter within a day or two after she began work at NIH.

Marion nodded.

"Nothing like that ever happened to me before," said Peter. "How did you pull it off?"

"I've got a lot of related experience, and I know people. I have friends all over Washington, all over the world, but it's the ones in Washington that count right now. It's funny. When I selected this job it never occurred to me that you might be in a position to help me get it. I would have called you. I knew you used to work at NIH, but I didn't know that you were still there. I had no idea I would be reporting to you."

"You didn't?"

"I wanted this job. I was happy to find that we would be working together."

"How did you make it happen?"

. "I don't know myself for sure. Perhaps it's better not to know everything. I've always wondered about things that are invisible. So often it's the things that are invisible to us that control our lives. When something happens, there is always a reason. We've been brought together again. As we work in these jobs, we'll discover the reason for that. We'll come to understand why this has happened."

The waitress brought a ham and cheese sandwich on whole wheat toast for Peter and tuna salad on white bread for Marion.

"What is your interest in Dr. Gallagher?" asked Peter.

Since Marion started work, Dr. Gallagher had had many conversations with Peter. Dr. Gallagher had ordered Peter to move Marion to a different position where she would have no authority over the Davenport Center contracts. In the past Peter had always complied with Dr. Gallagher's requests. Over a period of many years he had developed a cooperative subservience so far as Dr. Gallagher was concerned. This time he just didn't have the power to do what needed to be done.

"I'm concerned about him," said Marion. "I'm concerned about what he is doing. He's been spending money like there's no end to it. I don't have a list, but he's over budget on this task, over budget on that task, over budget everywhere."

"Aren't you being too hard on him? You haven't even met him."

"I have. I know him... well, knew him... quite well in fact. It was years ago. I hadn't seen him in quite some time. Then something happened. He gave a speech downtown at a medical convention. I was there. It was a big affair with the Secretary of HHS, the Surgeon General, the Vice-President. I don't know who else. Lots of people. Everybody was there. You were probably there too. I shook hands with him afterwards. As soon as I touched his hand, I felt this energy flow up my arm and into my body. I had forgotten his power, and it was worse than before. He's become more powerful, and he's more focused than he used to be. It was like he wanted to take over my body, my consciousness, my whole being. I wouldn't let him. Not again. Not this time. I jerked my hand away. He seemed surprised. I think he has grown accustomed to his power. Maybe most people let him in. I don't think he even recognized me. It's not surprising after so many years. Still I felt it was somewhat embarrassing considering the kind of relationship we once had." Marion pushed a pickle wedge to side of her plate.

"You never mentioned Dr. Gallagher to me," said Peter. After Marion got the job at NIH, Dr. Gallagher had told Peter that he had known Marion when they were in college together. Dr. Gallagher didn't elaborate, and Peter didn't indicate to Marion that he had this piece of information.

"Peter," said Marion, "come on now. You don't know everything about me."

Peter made a half-hearted attempt to smile. "Are you after him because of the way he shook your hand or because of a personal relationship that went bad?"

110

"The way you phrase the question makes the whole thing seem ridiculous. Aren't you belittling the importance of human relationships?"

Peter didn't respond.

"It's so hard," continued Marion, "what you're talking about. You're taking this intellectual sort of approach. Let's put this in that box and we can put this other thing here in that box over there. You want to slice and dice everything this way, and if that doesn't work, we'll slice and dice it that way. You know that's wrong. You know it's misleading. Important things have so little to do with the mind."

"But why are you after him?"

"I'm not *after* him, but let me tell you this. That night a couple of months ago, he was talking about eliminating inherited disease. I just have to tell you that it bothered me. I was thinking, there's all of this talk about evolution and that we came from rodents or something. Let's just say that that was God's plan, that He created people through this evolution process. We can start with a mouse. Then for some reason the mouse gives birth to something that isn't quite a mouse. Maybe it looks a little funny, especially to the other mice. Maybe its nose is a little different or its front paw looks like a hand. What if the other mice came along and said this mouse that looks different has a disease. We're not having any funny looking mouse around here they all say. Then boom. There goes this animal that's maybe a little bit more than a mouse. It turns out that this rodent was an essential link in the chain from lower life to humans, and it ends up that we're not here. Who is to say what is an inherited disease and what changes are part of God's plan? Are we going to let Dr. Gallagher do that?"

"I don't know," said Peter who looked confused.

"I was thinking about this evolution thing. You know how some people have pictures of the family on the mantel. Wouldn't it be funny to have a picture of great grandmother 5000 generations back and there on the mantel between the photos of Uncle Henry and Aunt Bertha is a picture of a mouse."

Peter's smirk fell into a smile of patient suffering.

"Well, back to Marcus Gallagher," said Marion. "First things first. I want to know what he's doing. The whole thing is shrouded in mystery. I want to get some facts. That doctor from the swamp already sent two people to try to confuse me. They tried to talk me out of getting what I want. Another one's coming this afternoon. His name is Gene Nolan. He's a doctor. The other ones weren't. I've done research. I found out about him. I made a couple of phone calls. I know a lot, and I'm going to test him when he gets here. I'm going to find out if he's truthful, if he's honest, if I can rely on him. The other two were slimy snakes. If Marcus Gallagher sent them, doesn't that make you wonder about him? Still, if Gene Nolan shows up without the report I'm just going to turn him around and send him back with a fire under him. I'm not putting up with Marcus Gallagher's crap ever again."

"But what has he done wrong?"

"You tell me. You know the answer to that question."

"Well, nothing. He's done nothing wrong. What he built on that soggy island is truly remarkable." In an excited state, Peter had raised his voice. The man playing the video game only a few feet from the booth where Peter and Marion sat turned toward them. "He has established the foremost genetic research facility in the world."

From his position, the video game man could only see the balding back of Peter's head and the brown-gray hair combed over the top. The man with a crisp, starched shirt of subtle tan and green plaid looked past Peter and straight into Marion's eyes. Marion appeared startled, and a real frown reinforced the perpetual one.

"And the results?" said Marion as a statement more than a question. She leaned forward and tried to direct her voice toward Peter and away from the video game man with the sharp creases in his forest green pants. "What about results? He was supposed to deliver the report for task order number seventeen whatever the rest of the number is a year and a half ago. We got bupkis."

"There are reasons he hasn't delivered it yet."

"Reasons. There are always reasons." Marion looked away from Peter. "Peter, this guy is looking right at me." She nodded in the direction of the video game man.

Peter turned. "Richard. I didn't know you were here." Peter jumped out of the booth. "Come on over."

While still next to the video game, Richard pulled a silver lighter from his pocket.

"There's somebody I want you to meet," said Peter.

As Richard walked the short distance around the brown plywood booth, he flipped the lighter over in his hand.

"Richard Halpin," said Peter, "this is Marion Latterner. I've known Marion for years, but she just started working for me at NIH a couple of weeks ago."

Marion looked at the lighter as Richard shifted it to his left hand so he could shake hands with Marion. On one side the lighter was decorated with a golden shovel and the golden letters "R.H." The color of the bushy blond moustache looked out of place next to Richard's darker hair. Marion's hand disappeared into the palm of his massive fist.

Marion nodded without speaking.

"Hey," said Richard. His deep voice reverberated throughout the room.

Richard didn't say anything else to Marion, but he was in the bathroom when Peter stopped in just before he and Marion left.

"You going to remember that lady?" asked Peter, as he stood at a urinal next to the one Richard was using.

"That old sow?" said Richard. "I hope not."

"Take a good look at her," said Peter. "Do what you can to get a fix on her face. You might need to recognize her one day."

Richard shrugged. "All right, but I ain't saying it won't hurt."

Peter smiled.

Richard went back to the video game. A few minutes later Peter and Marion left the restaurant.

"Who is that guy?" asked Marion in the car on the way back to NIH.

"He's one of my drinking buddies. I've known him for years. He's a great guy."

"He was giving me such a strange look. Is he normal?"

"Normal? Is that really the point? He's a great guy. I enjoy spending time with him. It's got nothing to do with normal."

"Well," said Marion, "he gives me the creeps. He's calm on the outside, but he's got this force surging through him. It's like a sword made out of lightening, but it's all mixed up and doesn't know which way to go. There is evil there I think. Maybe it's confused evil, but it's there. The potential is there." There was silence for a moment before Marion continued. "That guy was odd, but sometimes I wonder if my perceptions are right. The feelings are so strong and the images are clear and sharp, but what if my subconscious is toying with my conscious, sending false signals and sitting back to watch my confusion."

"Yes," said Peter. "I remember you told me that before. You said something about your grandmother."

"That's right." Marion didn't say anything else as they passed the Boy Scouts of America Building on the way back to NIH. She had talked to Peter about her concerns many times over the years. About her grandmother she had said, "She was crazy as a loon. She died in an institution. I don't know which one. I don't know when. My mother won't talk about it. She thinks the whole thing is a secret from me, but it's not." About her mother she had said, "My mother has been in and out of institutions. She's unstable, but she can get by." When she talked about herself, she often told Peter, "I'm terrified that I'm crazy just like my mother and grandmother."

Chapter 13

Independent Thoughts

Gene was in the lunchroom. He tried to put the issues concerning the blood test out of his mind. For the moment he would concentrate on a way to strengthen his position and weaken Alfred's.

The schedule was tight for the afternoon. As usual every minute of time was accounted for. Lunch was from 12:38 until 1:03. Cataloging samples from Ecuador would take place from 1:03 until 1:57. After that he had until 2:04 pm to pick up a list of employees from Sarah Vorschrift. By 2:16 he was to be changed and ready for the trip to NIH. At 2:22 he would be at the dock in front of Davenport Center, and at 2:25 the ferry would leave. The appointment with Marion was at 4:30.

Schedules for the components were not standardized. Lunch breaks started and ended at what seemed to be random times. It was toward the end of Gene's lunch break. The component lunch room was on the second floor of the east wing not far from Gene's lab. It was an elegant space. The ceiling was decorated with cherubs, braids and flowers all of carved plaster, and the white of the ceiling and walls blended with the carved white marble of the fire place. Flickering flames of the winter fire were captured by the crystals in the chandelier and reflected around the room by the massive mirror above the mantel. The white and crystal of the room matched the white tablecloths and crystal accents on the round dining tables. A deep red carpet covered much of the oak floor and provided the room with some contrast to the white. The carpet picked up the color of the red ornaments in the Christmas decorations on the mantel, on each table, on the walls above the oak chair rail and hanging from the chandelier.

More information. That's what Gene needed. The existence of the vial of vaccine he had brought back from Ecuador had caused him a great deal of anguish. He thought of the second principle, "Independent thought is prohibited. It is destructive to our group, to us as individuals and to our goals." There was more to the principle, but the rest didn't matter. Gene knew he had violated it. The seventh principle was trouble too. "Questions about Dr. Gallagher, about the body, about Davenport Center and about the work we do here are not permitted. I will be told everything I need to know, and unknown information can only serve to distract me from my work." By keeping the vial, Gene was seeking information that had not been provided to him.

Gene knew he was in violation of those principles and others. The eighth principle provided, "If I ever have any concerns about anything that happens at Davenport Center or anything that any component is involved in I will express these concerns to Dr. Gallagher or a paladin." Gene had not expressed his concerns to Dr. Gallagher even though he had had an opportunity to do so. And principle thirteen provided, "I will always be truthful and completely open with Dr. Gallagher and any paladin about everything I have seen, done or thought." He hadn't been, and he continued not to be.

For now he was both satisfied and tortured by the fact that he would have an opportunity to test the vaccine. It was 1:02 pm. He was scheduled to be back in his lab in one minute. Two other components were at the table with him. He stood and nodded but didn't speak.

This is the time, he thought as he started toward the solid oak door. A good place to start would be to inject the vaccine into a couple of mice. He could observe the impact on the mice. No matter what the results, the test wouldn't resolve all issues, but he would know more. Gene pushed open the door.

The mice. There were no test animals in Gene's lab. Anyone who came into the lab would know the mice weren't supposed to be there. Maybe he could hide the cages in one of the cabinets. That might not be good for the mice, but the vaccine might not be good for them either. Then there was the problem of getting the mice into the lab. There was never a free minute in Gene's schedule. Worse than that, the mice were kept in the west wing. That would require a long walk from the east wing, and the return journey would have to be with mice in a cage if he were lucky enough to get his hands on a free cage when he got there. Any component would know that he wasn't supposed to be in the west wing. On the other hand, none of the other components were supposed to be there today either.

Without much of a plan, Gene decided to see whether he could get some mice. He walked past his lab and toward a door from the east wing to the doughnut shaped central portion of the building. It was a path that should not be in use by any of the components. He pushed open the door to the circular corridor and there right in front of him stood Sarah Vorschrift.

"Oh?" said Ms. Vorschrift. She looked at Gene as though what she was seeing didn't quite make sense. Her long, curly hair slid across her shoulders, when she tilted her head. She wore a heavy knit sweater decorated with a tree, a fireplace with stockings and dozens of red, blue and silver packages. She stood silent, waiting for Gene to speak.

"Hi," said Gene.

Ms. Vorschrift twisted her head and squinted.

"I'm just going up to my quarters," said Gene. He knew this was trouble. This was not the shortest way to his quarters.

"That's not on your schedule," said Ms. Vorschrift. She knew. She made up the schedules a week in advance and then reviewed them each day before they were distributed and made any necessary last minute changes.

Her response was not threatening. Gene interpreted it as a question. He believed that Ms. Vorschrift would think that something quite cataclysmic must have happened to cause behavior that was inconsistent with the schedule. In Gene's mind, Ms. Vorschrift was simply asking to be informed about the cataclysmic event.

"I just wanted to get something," said Gene.

"I see," said Ms. Vorschrift, pushing the blonde hair off of her face, exposing smooth, youthful skin. "Well..."

"That's ok," said Gene, interrupting her. "I'll get it later."

"I think that would be best. Perhaps you can discuss this aberration in your behavior with Dr. Gallagher when you discuss the results of the blood test. I'll mention it to him."

Gene turned and went back to his lab angry about the encounter with Sarah Vorschrift.

Sometimes the restrictive environment of Davenport Center drove him crazy, but he knew there was no way out. None of the principles explicitly required a lifetime commitment. No one had ever told him he couldn't leave, but he had suspected it from the beginning.

117

Thinking back he couldn't remember what made him realize that he had made an irrevocable commitment when he took the oath. The week he spent in the dark, uncomfortable, muggy room thinking about how to banish independent thought had bothered him. He didn't leave Bloodsworth Island after that. It didn't even occur to him to try. Perhaps it was then that he realized on a conscious level that he couldn't leave. He didn't want to be locked in a small dark room for a week. That it happened still shocked him sometimes. He knew he would never tolerate such abuse. The fact that he didn't leave could only mean one thing... that he couldn't leave. He remained because it was not within his power to do otherwise.

The last conversation he had with Bruce, the one in Ecuador when Bruce was dying, had emphasized the point. Since he had returned from Ecuador, Gene had thought about leaving several times a day. He knew he could get off the island. Soon he would be driving a Davenport Center car in order to get to Marion's office. He could drive anyplace he wanted. No one would know. But if he did get away, he knew the paladins or somebody else would track him down and bring him back. Listening to the story Bruce told, Gene learned for the first time that one of the components had tried to escape and had been caught. Somebody had tracked Alan down and brought him back for examination on the autopsy table.

But past the technical issues of how to escape lay a more difficult question. Even if he could get away and be safe, could he just walk away from Davenport Center and let events take what course they may?

There was an evil force at Davenport Center. It was a pervasive force that had taken control of Gene's body and maybe his mouth, but it couldn't control his mind. He could think despite the prohibition in the principles. He would think independent thoughts. But could he act on any of those thoughts? The constraints at Davenport Center were real and effective. ·

Chapter 14

He Can Be Good

In 1798, the Marine Hospital Service had been established to care for merchant seamen. The MHS was later directed to check passengers on arriving ships for evidence of infectious disease. In 1887, as part of those new responsibilities, the MHS opened a one-room laboratory in the Marine Hospital in Stapleton on Staten Island in New York. That small laboratory, which soon identified the bacteria that caused cholera, was the origin of NIH. When Gene drove onto the NIH campus in Bethesda, Maryland, it had become a sprawling complex of 75 buildings on 300 acres of land with enough trees and grass to give visitors the impression of a park-like setting. Marion's office was in Building 10, a giant reflective cube of mirrored glass on the northern side of the campus near Cedar Lane. In the lobby Gene noticed that someone at NIH shared Dr. Gallagher's interest in posters. One poster had alternating splashes of red and pink on a black background. Upon examination it was possible to see that the splashes spelled the word chaos with the letters stretched wide and thin into almost unrecognizable form. At the bottom were the words, "The Head and Heart of Chaos, Nonlinear Dynamics in Biological Systems." Another had three giant molars in bright white that occupied the lower third of the poster. The space above and between the molars was black. Above the teeth were the words, "Effects & Side Effects of Dental Restorative Materials." The words, "Dental Restorative Materials" were in giant amber letters just above and partly obscured by the teeth. The other words were in the center of the poster in small red letters.

The last poster Gene noticed was a white one with two small, brown, windblown trees on the side of a gentle slope. Below the trees were the pink words "Imagine God." Gene resolved to try.

The tenth floor of the building had a typical government look. The walls were plain white rising above a floor of marbled navy blue and white tile to a dropped ceiling of white foam material. The metal door frames and doors had all been painted the same color as the walls.

119

Next to each door was a white room number pressed into black plastic and held in place on a brown plastic track.

Gene knew he needed somebody to talk to. Dr. Gallagher had told him that it was the components of Davenport Center against the natives of the parched land. That was how Dr. Gallagher referred to anyone who was not a component of the body, as a native of the parched land, whether or not they lived on Bloodsworth Island. No one from the parched land would understand, Dr. Gallagher would say. It wasn't that certain natives couldn't understand. Over time most would come to appreciate the mission and goals of Davenport Center. The problem was that, coming from a chaotic world where everyone was bombarded by streams of random information, no one could be expected to maintain the necessary clarity of thought. Natives would have no option but to become callous, unable to recognize foresight, unable to understand the visionaries of Davenport Center. They did not have the luxury of time to reflect and understand in the tranquil and ordered environment of Bloodsworth Island. That's what Dr. Gallagher said.

For Gene, talking to a component was useless and dangerous. The component would have no opinion in the first place, and in the second place Dr. Gallagher or a paladin would be informed of the discussion within a few minutes after it was concluded. Gene had already paid the price for such an indiscretion on one occasion.

Gene had thought about talking to Kelly, but she had her own problems right now. Gene knew she was in turmoil over the telephone call she had received from Richard.

How about Marion? She was a native of the parched land. At the same time she knew something about Bloodsworth Island, and maybe she had enough distance from it to be objective. "She's dangerous. She will interfere with our work." That's what Dr. Gallagher had said about her. Would she be unreasonable or irrational because of her past relationship with Dr. Gallagher? Gene decided that he would try to understand her during this meeting. He would begin to determine whether she was somebody he might confide in.

Marion's office was on the north side of the glass cube. From her window some of the houses of north Bethesda, a couple of high rise apartment buildings near the Washington beltway and trees on the northwest edge of Rock Creek Park were visible. Like the hallway, her office had the standard issue government look: white walls, gray tight weave nylon carpet and brown everything else. A surprising number of shades of dark brown filled the room. The large, sturdy but low cost desk was a deep, milk chocolate brown. The imitation leather seats and backs of the heavy side chairs were reddish brown. The laminated shelves on one side of the room were coffee brown. A small wooden dish on her desk was dark acorn brown.

Marion got up and walked around her desk to shake hands with Gene.

"I'm glad you were able to come by today," said Marion. Her manner and tone were friendly, different than Gene had expected, but the downward turn of the corners of her mouth into a perpetual frown bothered him.

"I brought some information from Dr. Gallagher," said Gene. Dr. Gallagher had described her as a viscous serpent, although she wasn't acting like a serpent. She looked older than he had expected. Both she and Dr. Gallagher would be in their 50s, Gene guessed, but Dr. Gallagher's brown hair showed little evidence of gray. He had a youthful, vigorous appearance. Marion looked older with more gray and pale, whitish skin.

"Good. We'll look at that in a minute." She motioned for Gene to sit in one of the side chairs. The wooden arms and legs had been stained to a dark, cooking chocolate brown to compliment the reddish brown seat and back. After pulling another side chair to face Gene, Marion sat. She took the large kraft paper envelope Gene had brought and laid it on her desk.

"So," said Marion, "tell me, how long have you worked for Marcus Gallagher?"

"Three years, or maybe it's been four now."

Marion nodded. "All of the time on Bloodsworth Island?"

Gene felt like he was walking in a minefield. He and Dr. Gallagher had spent forty-three minutes that morning discussing how to persuade Marion that the requests she was making were burdensome. They hadn't spent any of the time discussing how to handle questions about himself. He could think only about the eighteenth principle. It provided, "Except as explicitly authorized by

Dr. Gallagher, I will never disclose or discuss any information concerning Dr. Gallagher, any paladin, the body, any component or any work done by the body or by Davenport Center with anyone who is not a component of the body." Anything he said might get back to Dr. Gallagher. He had hoped to begin to develop Marion as a confidant, but that would take time.

"Yes," he said. To say anything else would violate the eighteenth principle. He knew he was leaving out the various trips to Ecuador, but the trips to what used to be an Orani village were not permanent assignments to work in Ecuador. He hated the half-truths.

"I see," said Marion. "You've worked only on Bloodsworth Island?"

She didn't believe him, he was sure of that, but he was committed now. "My permanent assignment is Davenport Center on Bloodsworth Island. It has always been that way."

"Our language is so imperfect. In some ways it is like trying to see what is around us by looking only at shadows. Have you had any trips away from Bloodsworth Island?"

"Yes. Well, I'm on a trip away from Bloodsworth Island right now. But still I work on Bloodsworth Island, not here."

Marion smiled. "You have this goodness inside you. I felt it when I touched you, but it's all mixed up in the spaces between your thoughts and feelings. And you are so intelligent, so clever. That makes things harder for you sometimes."

Gene sort of half smiled. He found Marion to be appealing. The connection she was trying to establish was attractive, but it made him uncomfortable at the same time. "I brought information for you. It's in that envelope," he said, pointing to the envelope on her desk. "I came to talk about how much effort would be required to gather all of the information you've requested."

"Oh, yes. We'll get to that. Have you made any other trips off of Bloodsworth Island?"

"Yes."

"Where did you go on those occasions?"

"I'm not prepared to talk about such things. Dr. Gallagher has not authorized me to discuss my work."

"Such a jumble there is inside you, but the truth is there, hiding in the darkness and light. And you always do what he says?"

"Yes. Of course. He's my supervisor."

"How about trips to Ecuador?"

She knew he had been to Ecuador, he realized. He had no idea how much information she had. There was no use trying to obfuscate any further. At the same time, he didn't want to risk the consequences of violating the eighteenth principle.

"I am not authorized to discuss my work at Davenport Center. You wouldn't want someone in your office going out and telling everything that goes on here."

"All right," said Marion. She sat back in her chair. She seemed calm, easygoing. There was a curiosity, an interest in Gene. Her friendliness seemed to be genuine. "Let's talk about your life before Marcus Gallagher."

"Is this discussion to be about me or about Davenport Center?"

"We didn't get very far talking about Davenport Center."

"I brought you some information. Why don't we go over that material?"

"We will, in time. Let's talk about your life before you worked for Marcus. You can talk about that can't you?"

"Yes."

Marion smiled. "Good. The truth must be discovered between the edges of our consciousness and the limits of our knowledge."

Gene looked at Marion but didn't respond, and he realized now that this was the very opportunity for which he had hoped. He could tell her about himself and his past. It was a violation of the eighteenth principle but a minor one which would not harm Dr. Gallagher or Davenport Center. Still it was enough of a violation that if Marion mentioned the conversation to Dr. Gallagher, Gene would find out about it soon enough.

"I'm interested in you. I want to know who you are. Can you just tell me about yourself? We might as well start early. Where were you born?"

"San Diego."

"Siblings?"

"No. None that survived. I had a sister who died when she was about a year old."

"Died of?"

"I don't know. Maybe I knew once, but if I did, I forgot."

"And your parents, what were they doing in San Diego?"

"My father was in the Navy. He was stationed there."

"I see. What is he doing now?"

"I don't know. My parents divorced when I was four. I lived with him for a time, but when I was six I went back to live with my mother. He dropped me off one day, and I haven't seen him since. I think he must be dead. I hope he is sometimes. If he's alive that means he has ignored me for 25 years after he abandoned me. It's hard for me to think about that, to think about what that means."

Marion nodded. Gene saw an empathetic sadness in her face. "And your mother?" asked Marion. "What's she doing?"

Gene glanced out the window. Near the shortest day of the year, only remnants of sunlight remained. Red and white car lights flickered through the branches of the leafless trees. Traffic was heavy on both Cedar Lane and Rockville Pike. Christmas lights were visible on a couple of the houses. A small tree in one yard had been decorated with flashing lights of red and green and yellow and white, and Santa made of all white lights stood nearby.

Gene liked Marion. She had a disarming quality about her. Unlike the serpent Dr. Gallagher had described, she seemed quite human. She was interested in him, and he felt she could see inside of him. She had an aggressive side. Gene had heard it on the speakerphone, but she had another side as well.

"She's dead," said Gene in answer to Marion's question about his mother.

"I'm sorry."

"Yes. So am I."

"Do you want to talk about it?"

Gene did want to talk about it. He found Marion to be appealing and thoughtful and incisive. Looking past that frown, Gene could see that she was an attractive woman, and she had a seductiveness that touched Gene's soul. It was an emotional rather than sexual connection. He felt as though he received something from her that was different than the support he got at Davenport Center. She was interested in him and his life. At Davenport Center Dr. Gallagher loved him and supported him, but he was interested in the doctor he had become. Marion was interested in Gene as a whole person with a history and a life before Davenport Center. In some ways she was like Kelly but with a maturity that Kelly didn't have.

"She used to drink. Too much sometimes." Gene leaned back in the chair and glanced at the ceiling. "Often. She drank too much often. We used to have fights about it. When I was little I poured the stuff down the sink. I filled the bottles with water and food coloring. I got pretty good with the colors. I could make water look like whiskey or rum. Vodka was easy." Marion seemed interested in every word.

"We had a real thing going. I poured the stuff out, and she bought more. She was a waitress. She didn't make much money. It wasn't long before she didn't have enough money to pay the rent. She was screaming at me and blaming me for everything that went wrong. She was overweight too. I can still remember her pudgy fingers wrapped around an empty bottle. 'You're killing me,' she said. 'I need this.' Even so I poured out a bottle of Scotch she bought with her last dime. With no rent money, we got evicted. That's when we moved from California to Maryland. We lived with somebody she knew here, Helen. Mom said it was temporary, but it wasn't. Anyway, she started going to meetings and stopped drinking for a time."

Marion looked at him, and Gene saw that empathetic sadness he had seen earlier.

"She started again," said Gene. "We fought about the drinking, and I tried never to do anything to support it. I was sixteen when she called from some bar. She was drunk, and she wanted me to pick her up. Sometimes she had a car, and I would go get her to keep her from driving. This time she had gone to work with Helen, our housemate. I knew she had no way to get home, and I thought if I made it hard for her she might think about that the next time she wanted to get drunk."

Gene paused. There was anger and sadness in his expression. "There wasn't a next time. Helen went home with some guy, and she gave Mom the keys to her car. It was the Wednesday night before Thanksgiving, and the roads were wet. She killed herself on the way home. The car skidded off the pavement and into a telephone pole."

"I'm sorry," said Marion in a way that suggested she really was.

"Life was harder after that. I had no place to go, but Helen let me stay with her. I can't imagine what would have happened to me if she hadn't."

"You must have fond memories of her," said Marion.

Gene glanced out the window again, this time into the darkness of night. No sunlight remained to soften the harsh glare of headlights and streetlights.

"I always liked peanut butter sandwiches," he said. "I still do. Mom made them for me on English muffins, until I started doing the same thing myself. And she would make this jam. She used small, wild blackberries with no seeds or maybe they had real tiny seeds. It's not like the stuff you buy in the grocery store with hard seeds big enough to crack your teeth. She made the jam whenever she could get the right kind of blackberries, so it seemed like I got it about once every five years. We had some of it this time, maybe about a year before she died. It was my favorite. The best I've ever had."

Marion was focused on him, focused on every word.

"I got a busboy job at the restaurant where she worked. I was young, but the owner let me work there anyway. Sometimes these guys would show up. Maybe they were businessmen. Some of them would be dressed in suits, and others wouldn't be. This place had kind of a country-western theme with wagon wheels for decoration on the walls and water glasses that looked like wooden barrels. It was odd in an area where fish and crab restaurants are pretty common. A lot of guys would go there and get drunk.

"Mom wasn't the sexiest thing alive, but some of the guys didn't care. They would tap her behind when she walked by. I got in a shouting match with one of them one night. I told the guy to keep his hands off the waitresses. That night things were worse. Some good sized, middle-aged bald guy was grabbing at Mom. He was drunk, and he would grab at her or smack her on the rear whenever she was within reach. I took that for as long as I could. Then I just walked over and clamped a headlock around that guy's neck. I yanked him sideways out of that booth. He got stuck between the table and the bench. I pulled, and he popped out of there like a cork coming out of a bottle. I dragged him across the floor. He was stumbling and walking as best he could with his torso parallel to the floor. We bumped into some tables and knocked over a couple of chairs. It's a good thing he was drunk. He was a big man, and I was scrawny, not so different from now."

Marion smiled. Gene took it as an indication that he had gained enough weight over the years to move out of the scrawny category.

"When I got to the door with him, I turned him around and backed him out. There was a step outside at the edge of the parking lot. He stumbled, and I let go. His butt came to rest right there on the yellow parking space line, and that's when I told him I would break his neck if I ever saw him grab another waitress. I told him he'd better learn some manners if he wanted come around anymore. I went back to the table. I got his coat and threw it out the door on top of him.

"When I came back in after throwing the coat, Mom hugged me. Two other waitresses started clapping. The guy who owned the place wasn't so happy though. He told me if I ever touched one of his customers again that my mother and I both would be fired. I knew that wasn't fair. 'You can't control your customers,' I shouted at him. 'You don't have the backbone to do what needs to be done.' As it turns out, he didn't fire either one of us.

"That night Mom and I went home together. It was unusual. She didn't go out with any of her boyfriends, and she didn't go out drinking with Helen. It was late when we got home, and neither of us had eaten dinner. She sat down and turned the television on, and I told her I would put something together. I got out some English muffins and some of that blackberry jam with the little berries. It was the first time I ever made dinner for her, not that it was much of a dinner.

"We sat there on this little couch we had and ate our sandwiches and fell asleep in front of the TV watching some re-run. She was proud of me that night for protecting her, and I was proud of her for not drinking. I wish we had had more nights like that. I don't think I'll ever have that blackberry jam again. I don't know how to make it, and I don't know where she got the berries."

Marion listened, and Gene told her more. He talked about his return to California with an academic scholarship at Stanford and his return to Maryland to attend medical school at Johns Hopkins in

Baltimore. He talked about his residency at a different hospital in the same city.

"I never finished my residency," said Gene.

"What happened?" asked Marion.

"Things were going pretty well there up until a couple of patients died unexpectedly. There was a malpractice suit, and the whole thing started winding its way through the court system. The suit was against the hospital and Dr. Tanner and others. I was named as a defendant at the beginning, but my name got dropped before it was over. While the suit was going on, the hospital established its own independent board of inquiry. At least they called it independent.

"I ended up testifying against Dr. Tanner before the board of inquiry and in court. While the trial was going on, after all of the testimony and arguments were over but before the jury came back with a decision, the case got settled. Some people say settled out of court, but it was more like settled in the middle of court. I don't know the amount of the settlement, but I know it was a lot. Information about the settlement was never made public. Dr. Tanner had murdered the patient, I'm sure of that. He was clever about it, but I don't care. That's what happened. Somehow that seemed to be forgotten when the case got settled.

"The board of inquiry was going on at the same time. I talked to some of the doctors who were on the board. I was certain that they were going to remove Dr. Tanner from the staff of the hospital. I thought they might discipline him in some other way as well. I don't know what kind of power they had. Anyway, the day after the settlement, the board met and voted that there was no evidence of malpractice or wrongdoing of any kind. The board apologized to Dr. Tanner for all he had suffered as a result of the case and dismissed all charges against him.

"I felt like I had been punched in the stomach. The only way the board could have reached that conclusion was by ignoring my testimony. Still, that board of inquiry was sort of a bittersweet thing. That's where I met Dr. Gallagher. He wasn't on the staff of the hospital, but he had been asked to participate as a member of the board. After the last meeting he stopped by to see me. He gave me his card. He said something like, 'You're an exceptionally intelligent man. I think that you can still have a bright future in medicine. If you decide to pursue it, please give me a call.'

"I thought what Dr. Gallagher had said was very odd. I *was* pursuing my future in medicine right there, right then. But Dr. Gallagher knew what I soon discovered; that I had violated some unwritten policy of all hospitals or of staff doctors everywhere. That policy is never to testify in a malpractice suit or at a board of inquiry against another doctor. Retribution for my malfeasance was swift and certain. Doctors who had been my friends wouldn't talk to me, and worst of all, I was assigned to work under the direct supervision of Dr. Tanner. I didn't realize it at the time, but the moment the board exonerated Dr. Tanner they implicitly terminated my residency. There were flourishes and discussions and pain and shouting yet to come, but the die was cast. My residency was over. With my newfound troubles, I soon forgot about Dr. Gallagher's odd comment.

"I tried to work with Dr. Tanner, but it just wasn't to be. I was no longer in training to be a physician. I was doing the work normally assigned to orderlies. I cleaned bedpans, and I mopped blood, vomit, and whatever else might get onto the floor. I became an errand boy, picking up and delivering blood and urine and tissue samples. The hours were horrendous. I was groggy all the time.

"I realized I couldn't work under Dr. Tanner. I talked to everybody who would talk to me which turned out to be a pretty short list, and I asked for a reassignment. That just wasn't to be.

"I tried to do the best I could under the circumstances. I assigned some of my tasks to orderlies and looked for ways to continue learning the things I would need to learn to practice medicine. It wasn't long before Dr. Tanner found out that I wasn't delivering the samples as he had requested. He tracked me down."

Thinking about the incident, Gene remembered what it was like to be there in the room with Dr. Tanner. Gene sat in a metal chair in front of a gray metal desk with Dr. Tanner behind it. They were in some kind of small patient conference room in the hospital. Right in the middle of the otherwise empty desk was a two-thirds full urine sample bottle with the top off.

"I thought I told you to deliver this to the lab," said Dr. Tanner.

"You have asked me to deliver urine samples," said Gene. "I don't know about that one."

"Yes. I asked you to deliver this one."

Gene shrugged. He felt defiant, backed into a corner. He had nothing left to lose.

Dr. Tanner jumped up out of the gray folding chair and knocked it over. "This one," he said, raising his voice, pointing at the urine sample. "I asked you to deliver this one to the lab."

"Right," said Gene.

"And did you do it?"

"Did the urine sample make it to the lab?" asked Gene.

"Yes."

"Then I guess I did it."

. "You didn't," shouted Dr. Tanner. He leaned over the desk toward Gene who had remained seated. "You didn't. Someone else brought this into the lab."

"All right, but it got there."

"That's the trouble with you. You refuse to follow orders. You see no need for a structured, ordered environment. If things were left to you, there would be disorder, anarchy and chaos."

"Dr. Tanner," said Gene, "I want to learn how to be the best physician I can be."

· "You've got a long way to go. And before you learn that, you've got to learn discipline. You've got to learn your place. I'm going to teach you. Before I'm done with you, you will be disciplined. You will understand your place in this hospital." Dr. Tanner went to sit, but he hadn't noticed that he had knocked the chair away from the desk. He landed on the floor next to the overturned chair.

Gene jumped up and went around the desk. He helped Dr. Tanner up and pulled the chair upright for him. With Dr. Tanner settled, Gene went back to his chair.

"Do you see this urine sample?" asked Dr. Tanner. His voice was calm, but there was a stern, angry look on his face.

Gene stared at Dr. Tanner. There was defiance in his eyes. He didn't look down. He didn't answer Dr. Tanner.

"Do you see this urine sample?" shouted Dr. Tanner.

"I see it," said Gene, still without looking down.

"You will learn discipline," said Dr. Tanner. His voice was soft. Again Gene said nothing.

"Drink it," said Dr. Tanner, pointing at the urine sample, his voice still conversational.

Gene didn't move.

"Drink it!" There was a sternness in his voice.

Anger consumed Gene, but he remained seated.

"Now, Dr. Nolan!" shouted Dr. Tanner through clenched teeth.

Gene stood and grasped the urine jar. As he raised it from the desk, he tilted it and threw the yellow substance toward the still seated Dr. Tanner. The fluid splashed onto his chin, soaked his shirt collar and wet the top of his tie and the front of his white lab coat. Gene returned the urine jar to the desk and turned to leave the room.

"Your insubordination is out of control," yelled Dr. Tanner, wiping the dripping liquid from his face. "This will be the last thing you destroy in this hospital."

Gene was silent for a moment, sitting in the chair near Marion.

"That's what drove me out of that hospital. I left right then. I haven't been back since."

"Did you call Marcus?" asked Marion.

"No. I guess I had forgotten about him. I don't know what happened to that card he gave me. It had been months since I had seen him. Although he was on the board of inquiry, I only talked to him that one time at the end. He was the last thing on my mind. I never did call him. I tried to get another job, but no one would talk to me. I guess I should have called him, but I never thought to do it. I was depressed, and I had no income and no money. For the second time in my life, I was living somewhere with no way to pay the rent. The day before I would have taken up residence on some street corner, Dr. Gallagher called. If it hadn't been for him, I don't think I would ever have practiced medicine again."

Marion nodded. It looked to Gene as though she wanted to reach out and touch him, hold him, but she didn't.

Gene looked out the window again. A few fine snowflakes bounced against the glass. He hadn't been paying attention to the sky earlier, but there must have been clouds.

"Would you like to take a break for a minute?" asked Marion. "I can get a soda for you or some coffee."

"Ok," said Gene.

They walked down the hall together, and when they returned to Marion's office, they were laughing. A can of Super G Mandarin Orange soda was in Gene's right hand. Marion touched Gene's arm and guided him back to the chair he had used before. After moving some papers, Gene scooted the soda can onto the edge of the desk.

"Look, Gene," said Marion. "Let me tell you something. I know Marcus. I've known him for years. He can be so charming and endearing that people lose themselves in him. It's hard to describe what happens when he works his magic, but in the end it wouldn't be inaccurate to say that people lose their minds when they're around him.

"Once we were traveling together, driving down Interstate 95 from New York. We stopped at one of those rest areas where there was a restaurant and a couple of gas stations. Inside the snack place, there must have been twenty people in line in front of us. It wasn't more than a minute and a half until one of the women came out from behind the service counter and walked straight up to Marcus and asked what he wanted. He told her, and we got our stuff and checked out ahead of all the people who had gotten there before us. I know this sounds strange, but he stands out in a crowd. He gets treated differently, like a celebrity might be treated. The effect is the same on strangers and on people he's known for years.

"He lived in an apartment with two of his fraternity brothers. They didn't pay the rent for a couple of months, and the landlord was livid. A week or two before Christmas, about this time of year, Marcus decided to visit the landlord. He went to the office and talked to the guy and his wife and some of the employees. The man had a construction business, and when Marcus showed up there was a carpenter there, maybe a plumber and a secretary. Before it was all over, the landlord forgave the two months rent, and Marcus promised that they would do their best to make the rent payment due on January first.

"His spell doesn't work on everybody, but I've seen him do this kind of thing over and over again. The most amazing thing about it is that he doesn't ask for special favors, but people do things for him anyway. He just walked into the rest stop and got in line, and he went to see the landlord to work out a payment plan.

"I could give you a ton of examples. I used to enjoy being with him, because I would be the beneficiary of some of the special treatment. It was sort of exciting and new for me, even though he was used to it. In some ways it made him kind of endearing. It wasn't like he expected special treatment or demanded it. Often he didn't recognize that the treatment he received was different than the treatment others received.

"On the other hand, he's got a cruel side. I've seen that side too. He's the king of broken promises and dashed expectations.

"One of the last times I saw him in college, he asked me to go to some Broadway bound play at the National Theatre downtown. It was before the Kennedy Center was built. Now that I think of it, John Kennedy was probably president at the time. Marcus had the tickets, and I was to meet him in front of the theatre. A bunch of his fraternity brothers had gotten together and decided to take dates. I stood out front waiting for Marcus, as one by one his fraternity brothers showed up with their dates. As they went in, maybe 15 or 20 of them, I said hello and told them I was waiting for Marcus. I stood out in the entrance lobby until intermission, waiting for Marcus and worrying about him. At intermission he came out with some other date. I was angry and hurt and embarrassed in front of all of his fraternity brothers and my friends. I realized that as each brother and his date got inside and saw Marcus they understood that I was outside waiting for something that was never going to happen. Maybe I should have made a scene, but I didn't. I just walked away.

"I had thought that we were going to get married. We had planned our life together and talked about our wedding. But I guess he had his own plan. That incident at the theatre broke up the relationship. It wasn't the only cruel thing he did, but it was the last and the most egregious.

"It's so surprising when you see his cruelty for the first time, because he comes across as kind and gentle. But there's something else there. He takes pleasure in tormenting people and seeing them writhe in pain.

133

"I never saw him much after that, and the relationship ended without any kind of a discussion or fight. It took me years to recover from the experience. I never forgot about him though. I went to see him speak a few months ago. I think his cruel, immoral side has become dominant, and on that night, the night of the speech, I decided to do something about it.

"I know he can be good. I know many people see that. I know he can be self-centered and destructive, and he can't hide that from me anymore. It's all in there together, the charm, the self-centeredness, the clever humor, the arrogant disregard for others and the depravity.

"He tricked and abused me before, just like he's using you right now. I know it's hard for you to see... maybe impossible... but when it suits his purpose, he'll throw you out like one of yesterday's doughnuts."

"I don't know what to say," said Gene.

"Say nothing. Listen, absorb and know." She was silent for a moment. "All right," she said, as she reached for the envelope Gene had brought. "Let's talk about these papers. It's what I expected," said Marion when she saw that the only thing in the envelope was a list of the current employees at Davenport Center. "That man has done nothing but confuse and delay. It has got to stop."

Gene felt loyalty to Dr. Gallagher and interest in this appealing woman he had just met and didn't really know. "This is just the first step," said Gene. "That's what he told me to say."

"Yes," she said, raising her voice. "You tell him that it's not good enough." There was fire in her eyes. She hurled the papers and envelope over her desk toward a worn, dark tan colored, metal trash can that was against the wall. The envelope and papers hit the edge of the can and scattered over the worn nylon carpet. The chair she was using twisted to the side with a sharp movement as she stood and looked out the window. "I'm going to get him. I'm going to stop that bastard." It was an involuntary, guttural murmur not directed at anyone.

Marion turned toward Gene. "That man has been spending our money as if there's no end to it." Her voice had become louder again, as though she were speaking to an auditorium full of people. There was anger in her eyes, but Gene could see past it. It wasn't directed at him. There was something beneath it and behind it that was for him. For him there was interest and caring and concern. "He's a year late and ten million dollars over budget on every task order. Accountability. He doesn't know the meaning of the word." Marion turned toward the back of her office, and her voice changed. It was soft, close to a whisper. "He will learn. I'm going to teach him."

She went back to her chair. "That crap isn't what I want," she said, pointing toward the trash can, "and Dr. Pompous knows it. I'm going to get that man under control, and he'd better get used to the idea."

"He wanted me to tell you that this is the first step," said Gene. "He said that he will gather more information. He said the things you've asked for are not as important as ... . "

"Not important!" screeched Marion. "That's just like him to confuse the issue. He needs to understand who decides what is important. I do. Not Marcus. I decide."

"I feel uncomfortable as an intermediary," said Gene. "He told me some things to say to you. Do you want me to tell you what he said?"

"I'm not mad at you Gene. I feel like you're a kindred spirit, that you have been caught up in his web just like I was. I know it can happen. But you'll get through it, like I did. I'm not angry at you. I'm angry at him. Tell me what he said, and if I start shouting, just remember that my words are directed at him not you."

.   "He said it will take tremendous resources to prepare that report. He said it will detract from the research at Davenport Center. He said it will cost the government money."

"Cost the government money?" repeated Marion. "He costs the government money. Not that I would ever kick you out of my office, but you can tell Dr. Pretentious that I did. You can tell him that I want that report now. Tell him... oh... tell him..." She leaned back in her chair and glanced up at the ceiling. "Tell him that he's got one week to get it over here. Tell him that if I don't have it in my hot little hand by a week from Friday, I'm going over to that damned island with so many government accountants and inspectors that our combined weight will push that soggy marsh another foot or so into the water. Before that island sinks, we'll go through every record out there, and we'll get the information ourselves."

Marion walked back over to the window and looked out into the darkness again. "Oh I don't know how best to handle this," said Marion. "I'm going to call him. I know you'll have to provide a report. You can tell him whatever you like, whatever you think best."

She turned toward Gene. "I've really enjoyed meeting you," she said. "I hope to see you again. I want to see you get through this."

Chapter 15

Get It Right

That same evening, while Gene was driving back from NIH, Kelly left Bloodsworth Island. She took the ferry to the dock just south of Crocheron where Gene had waited on the morning after he returned from Ecuador. Kelly lived about twenty miles north of Crocheron between the towns of Church Creek and Gum Swamp. The house she had rented was on a deserted, gravel road off of route 335. Although she was isolated, the area was peaceful and quiet and safe.

It was dark when she passed through the Blackwater Refuge, but even in bright sunlight the marsh water at the sides of the road looked as black as pools of oil. In December the area was dense with waterfowl and other birds migrating from the north. At this time of year Kelly often saw tundra swans from Canada, geese and bald eagles. Within the last week she had seen the rarer golden eagle.

As she drove a light snow began to fall. The turnoff to her house was on the right. She continued north toward Cambridge where Richard and her mother lived.

Catherine, Kelly's mother, had been born in Virginia of Chinese immigrant parents who ran a successful Asian artifact importing business in Washington, DC. Neither parent had much time for Catherine, and she was raised by an oppressive grandmother who lived with them. Catherine was bright and sociable. Coming from the repressive environment at home, she was overwhelmed by the freedom she had had as a student at the University of Maryland. As an attractive, slim woman with waist-length, black hair, she had plenty of opportunities for parties and dates. She accepted every invitation not in conflict with some more promising opportunity, and that took a toll on her academic success. During her senior year Catherine ended up in need of a tutor.

Catherine was not attracted to her tutor, but he was serious and dedicated to her mastery of the work. At the end of finals, when she believed she had passed some exams she had been worried about, she decided to take her tutor out for drinks. The next morning, the two of them woke up naked in her bed. Catherine turned out to be pregnant, and her father forced her to marry the tutor. Nine months later Kelly was born.

The marriage to Kelly's father was an uncomfortable one, a good experience in a tutoring relationship having failed to provide a solid basis for the marriage. The family was living in Michigan when Kelly was ten, and Catherine decided that it was time to expose her to the Chinese half of her heritage. Catherine and Kelly spent almost six weeks traveling and visiting in China. During the time, Kelly's father was to have moved the family back to Maryland. When they returned, Kelly's father wasn't in Michigan or at his new job in Maryland. He had no siblings, and both of his parents had died before Catherine met him.

It took almost a year before Catherine got a copy of the death certificate showing that he had died in Bad Ems, Germany. As far as she knew, he had no reason to be in Germany, not that the free flow of information between them had been a hallmark of their relationship. By the time of the trip to China, he had little to say to Catherine and often failed to inform her of any plans he might have. They had argued the night before Catherine and Kelly left for China, and all Catherine knew of her husband's plans was where he would be working in Maryland. After she received the death certificate, Catherine took Kelly to visit Bad Ems, a small, pleasant resort town on the River Lahn.

The week following her return from Germany, about a year and a half after the trip to China, Catherine married Richard. Within a year after that Richard adopted Kelly. Catherine's marriage to Richard had been tumultuous, punctuated with episodes of violence directed for the most part at Catherine and not Kelly.

Richard and Catherine took their daughter out to dinner for her eighteenth birthday. That night, after they got back from the restaurant, Catherine went to bed and left Richard and Kelly alone in the small living room dominated by a massive, black entertainment system with a huge television and stereo speakers four feet high.

"Thank you for dinner," said Kelly, as she started toward her bedroom.

"Just a minute," said Richard. "I wanted to save the best gift until we could be alone." He leaned over and pulled from under the couch a small box wrapped in silver paper with red ribbon. "Now that you're eighteen, you should be able to dress like a woman, not a little girl."

Kelly didn't look enthusiastic, but she opened the box to reveal a miniscule red silk teddy.

"Put it on," said Richard. "I'd like to see you model it." His face turned to a smirk in an effort to conceal a smile.

"All the subtlety of Paul Lazzaro," she said under her breath. Raising her voice, she said, "You're a pig." She threw the box and its contents at Richard's feet and turned toward her room.

"You'll wear it eventually, Cupcake. I'll save it for you. You're eighteen now, not off limits anymore."

The following week, Kelly rented the house north of Gum Swamp.

When she pulled up in front of the small brick house where Richard and Catherine lived, the snow was still light. The protruding metal fixture next to the front door threw yellow light onto the living room picture window, where the closed curtains had been pushed up against the glass. The cream-colored backing of the curtains was discolored with brown streaks and water stains.

The yellow painted wooden front door opened as Kelly stepped onto the small landing. The aluminum storm door had a brown H in some scroll work below the glass. It swung open. The room was darker than usual. With an outstretched left arm and anger in his manner, Richard held the door. He grabbed Kelly's shoulder, pulled her into the room and flung her onto the couch, next to her cowering mother.

"Let's get right to the point," said Richard. "You're moving your greasy, independent ass back in here. You shouldn't have left us in the first place, and your mother has paid the price while you've been out frolicking and doing just whatever you please whenever the spirit moves you. I hope that gives you the satisfaction you were looking for. I just want you to know that your period of misspent youth and idleness is over. You're going to learn to tow the line. Capish?"

An old style floor lamp with a glass bowl shaped top and no shade had been knocked to the floor. Shattered pieces of frosted glass were strewn over the floor along one wall and around the foot of one of the speakers. A wooden chair had been knocked against the front curtains, leaning against the green vines and pink flowers on the fabric and pushing them against the glass. A red, green and gold Chinese vase, the only concession to Catherine's Chinese heritage and her parents Asian antique business had been knocked off an end table. It was cradled unbroken by newspapers and magazines in a rattan basket. Of the two black metal table lamps, one had been knocked to the floor, the bulb broken, and the other one, still lit, teetered at the edge of the end table where the vase had been. The only other light in the room was reflected around the corner from a ceiling fixture in a short hallway off of the living room.

Catherine covered a bruised eye and cheek with her right hand. Her shoulder length hair was in disarray, obscuring part of her face. Kelly pulled her mother toward her. After pushing her hair to the side, she tried to examine the injured face and eye in the poor light.

"Mom, what has he done to you?"

"He doesn't mean any harm," said Catherine.

Kelly turned toward Richard who stood in the center of the small room. The light from the lone lamp hit him full in the face. "I'm calling the police!" snapped Kelly.

"Hey babe," said Richard. "No problem. That's a really fine idea. As long as you're going to be on the phone with them, you might as well tell them to bring an ambulance. We'll be needing that, too." He yanked the wooden chair upright and away from the front curtains. "Or maybe a hearse." He appeared to be distracted, perhaps thinking about the question. He looked back at Kelly. "You don't need to worry your pretty little head about that. Just tell them that we have a body here, because we will. The police, let them handle the logistics. Is that copacetic?"

Kelly glared at Richard, but she didn't move from the couch. Richard stared back. After a period of silence, Richard spoke.

"Good. I thought so." Richard stood and went over to the side of the couch next to Catherine. "Your mother and I have decided that you are going to move back home with us. Your mother seems to have difficulty handling the cooking and cleaning on her own." He grabbed Catherine's hair and yanked her head away from Kelly and down onto the arm of the couch. "Isn't that right, honey?" he asked through clenched teeth.

"YESSS!" Catherine shrieked out of pain.

Kelly slapped at Richard's arm and leaned over to hold her mother.

"Now," said Richard, "put your sweet ass back in that piece of crap car and go get your things. You've got two hours. Capish?" He maintained the grip on Catherine's hair, his fist clenched tight, the tendons, veins and muscles defined and casting small shadows on the inside of his wrist where his arm extended past the cuff of his starched brown and yellow stripped shirt.

Kelly looked at her mother. "Come with me," said Kelly. "There's room in my house. You can get away from this craziness."

Catherine's face was rigid. There was fear in her eyes which seemed to plead with Kelly to follow Richard's instructions.

"She ain't going nowhere," said Richard. "And there's no craziness to get away from. She screws up cleaning or cooking, and she's got to pay the price. That's all. I don't want to hurt her, but there's got to be some discipline around here. You're going to get it right. That's why you're coming back. By cooking and cleaning you'll be helping around here and if you get it right, you'll be protecting your mother."

"If you hurt her," said Kelly, "I'll see you rot in jail."

"I'm not going to hurt her," said Richard as he released Catherine's hair, "as long as you do what you're told. Now go. And if a policeman shows up here, she'll be dead before he gets through the door."

Kelly kissed her mother. "Do you want me back, Mom?"

Catherine looked at Richard then at Kelly. "Yes. Maybe that will help." Her movements and voice were mechanical.

Chapter 16

Freedom of Movement

Gene had to strengthen his position before his next encounter with Dr. Gallagher. He wanted to test the vaccine he had brought back from Ecuador. That would put him in a better position. Considering the problems with the blood test and that Alfred must be spewing into Dr. Gallagher's ear, Gene needed all the help he could get.

That night when Gene got back from NIH he stopped by the place where Ms. Vorschrift worked, just outside the entrance to the component living quarters on the third floor. She wasn't at her desk which was built in behind a large, dark mahogany counter. A solid wood door behind the counter lead to the component living quarters. There was a camera above the door. It was aimed so that it would pick up anyone standing at the counter. Gene sat at her desk so that he wouldn't be picked up by the camera, not that he would be out of place at her desk and not that anyone would be looking at the image broadcast by the camera.

The counter, at the edge of a gold and red Chinese carpet, was at one corner of a large, well-appointed entrance foyer. The room had wallpaper with a flower and bamboo design above the chair rail and textured, jewel-colored emerald paper on the lower portion of the wall. There were large, dark leather wing chairs spread throughout the room and several cherry tables of various sizes. Gold garland was draped from the ceiling molding. A Christmas tree stood in one corner, and a menorah and a Star of David decorated one of the table tops.

Gene picked up his schedule for the next day and stuffed it into his pocket without looking at it. He began to shuffle through the other papers on Ms. Vorschrift's desk. Many of the components had not yet picked up their schedules. It was the daily VTS list which had patient room assignments next to each name that he was looking for. The current one was on the desk, but he couldn't find the one he wanted, the one for the next day. There wasn't much turnover in the VTS rooms, so he studied the current schedule for a moment in an effort to identify a vacant room.

The next morning Gene looked at his schedule. He found it to be devoid of flexibility as it always was. At the same time, he was determined to get his hands on some test mice. If there were no problems, it would take fifteen minutes to go over to the west wing and get back with some mice. There was no provision for fifteen minutes of free time in his schedule. There never was. His breakfast was nineteen minutes, from 7:48 to 8:07. After that he had six minutes to brush his teeth, and he had to be in his lab by 8:13. He couldn't skip breakfast. The paladins would know within minutes, and Dr. Gallagher would be informed when he got to his office.

7:48 was late for breakfast. It was possible, he thought, that he could report for breakfast on schedule and leave without eating. Although Gene didn't know, he guessed that some people were scheduled to start breakfast as early as 6:57. In the past his breakfast had been scheduled to begin at times ranging from 6:59 to 8:03. With people coming and going at different times, he could leave right after he arrived, and as long as Sarah Vorschrift wasn't there, perhaps no one would notice. He decided to try.

When he left breakfast, he walked down one of the corridors in the east wing. The hall was empty. After he passed the door to his lab he decided he would be better off wearing a lab coat. He grabbed a lab coat from his lab, went back into the hallway and was soon out of the Mission and Conscience Department. Now in a public hallway, he headed for the short corridor which connected the east wing to the doughnut shaped central part of the building. While he was in the public hallway, he felt like he had put himself at risk. He wasn't scheduled to be in any public area on that day, and his presence there would seem out of the ordinary to many. As he rounded the corner into the circular hallway he bumped into a woman of about thirty who was dressed in earth colors. She carried a giant stained glass, holiday crab decoration, and the collision caused it to slip from her hands. As she grabbed at it, one side of the green and red translucent crab hit the carpeted floor. The large claw on the right side broke off.

The top of the crab, made of one large and several small pieces of glass, was connected to the body by hinges at the front. The top popped open, and about twenty lab mice which had been hidden in the body of the crab took off in all directions. The woman leaned over, and her long brown hair reached the floor almost before her hands did. The bright light in the hallway reflected off the sequins in the horse on the back of her beige jacket.

Gene didn't recognize the woman, and she wasn't dressed like an outside-in. She must have been a member of some combo or a VTS, most likely a VTS, Gene thought.

"What are these mice?" asked Gene as he leaned over and scooped up two of the white animals at once.

"They were going to be pets," said the woman. "I was going to give them to my nephews."

Gene stuffed the two mice he had picked up into the pocket of his violet lab coat. "Where did you get them?"

"Over that way," said the woman, pointing toward the west wing, "room W2016."

Gene knew what kind of mice were kept in that room. These were lab mice he could use. One was scurrying along next to the wall, and he leaned over and grabbed it. "I'll get a cage." Gene dropped the third mouse into the pocket with the other two.

He ran toward the west wing where he pulled two cages out of one of the supply closets. He stuffed the three mice he had picked up into one of the cages and started back toward the scene of the broken crab. The crab was on the floor with the top closed, and Gene could see the woman with the sequin horse now joined by Sarah Vorschrift chasing along after a mouse which had made its way around to the front of the building. Gene placed the empty cage on the floor next to the crab and took the cage with three mice and hid it in one of the cabinets in his lab.

By the time Ms. Vorschrift captured the mouse near the front of the building, Gene had returned from his lab and was in the process of transferring the mice in the body of the crab, about ten of them, into the second cage.

"I'll take care of that," said Ms. Vorschrift as she took the cage from Gene and dropped the most recent capture in with the others. "Madam," she said looking at the sequin lady, "we need to have a talk. Please pick up the remnants of that crab and follow me." She looked at Gene. "And Dr. Nolan, isn't this the second time in as many days where you have been off-schedule? I will add this incident to the agenda for your next meeting with Dr. Gallagher." Then with the mouse cage held level, Ms. Vorschrift led the mouse thief into an elevator.

Gene stood and watched the elevator door close. He was aggravated that every time he tried to do something he ran into Sarah Vorschrift.

Gene thought about the woman in tan and brown, probably a VTS, who had been able to come into Davenport Center and pick up twenty mice without authorization. How she had gotten into W2016 without an ID card, he didn't know. She had freedom of movement. Gene didn't. She could walk around after breakfast and pick up mice or do anything else she wanted. Gene was a component of the body. His efforts were important in accomplishing the goals of Davenport Center. And yet he didn't have the same freedom as the woman with the mice.

Chapter 17

The Contamination

That afternoon Gene was scheduled to perform testing on some of the tissue and blood samples from Ecuador. The time was short, as it always was. To complete all of the work which had been scheduled would require continuous, diligent effort. Busy as he was and under pressure as he was, Gene still had difficulty focusing on the work. He was angry at Alfred who had murdered a village full of people and was lying to avoid responsibility. The lies implicated Gene, and Gene hated that the most.

Gene pulled a pen and some paper from his desk and started writing a note to Kelly. From looking at the list of VTS room assignments on Ms. Vorschrift's desk, he had identified a vacant room. He asked Kelly to meet him in that room at 5:07 pm. He was scheduled to be in his lab until 7:14 pm. Dinner had been scheduled late for him, so he thought he might be able to meet Kelly and spend some time with her without being noticed.

Taking time for the meeting with Kelly, Gene wouldn't be able to get all of his lab work done. But he had already decided to have an unscheduled meeting with Alfred. He wanted to confront Alfred, to have it out with him. The lies, Alfred must be forced to take responsibility for the lies. Gene didn't know how long the meeting would take, but he hoped to point to it when someone noticed his lack of accomplishment for the afternoon.

He took the finished note and folded it so that it was small and only an inch and a half wide. With the note and a blue marker in his pocket, he was ready to go. Alfred's lab was on a corridor parallel to the one on which Gene's lab was located. Gene left his lab and started walking down the hall in the direction away from Alfred's lab. It was unusual to leave his lab when it wasn't on his schedule, and he felt uncomfortable about it. Still there was the eighth principle, and he thought that would give him the authority he needed to walk down the hallway. On the other hand, the eighth principle would provide better support for his actions if he had been going in the other direction, toward the meeting with Alfred.

Gene left the Mission and Conscience Department, the area where his and Alfred's labs were located, an area to which Kelly did not have access. Down the hall, the note slid into position between the doorframe and the wall, where it would be difficult or impossible for a casual observer to see it. Back down the hallway, near the entrance to the Mission and Conscience Department, Gene pulled the blue marker from his pocket and made a short mark at eye level on the wall next to a doorjamb. He didn't know if Kelly would see the blue marking. There was only about three hours between the time he marked the door and when he hoped she would be able to meet him. Even if she saw the mark, she might ignore it. He knew she wasn't exactly mad at him, but she was disappointed or frustrated or something. That was perhaps the next best thing to being mad. Even if she got the note and wanted to see him, she might not be available at 5:07 pm.

Back in the Mission and Conscience Department, Gene headed for Alfred's lab. When he got there, he knocked.

"Yes," said Alfred as he pulled the door open. He was a slight man, thin and short, and the silver piping on the bottom edge of his violet lab coat almost touched the floor.

"I have come to talk to you," said Gene.

"Oh," said Alfred, his lips pursed, a lock of his blond hair crossing the furrows of concern on his forehead. "This meeting isn't on my schedule. Could Ms. Vorschrift have made some mistake?"

"No," said Gene, "it wouldn't be on your schedule. It's not on my schedule either."

"Not on your schedule," said Alfred, distracted, apparently unable to comprehend the meaning of Gene's unscheduled action. "Well then... what... what would you be doing here?" Alfred stood in the doorway and blocked Gene's entrance into the lab.

"I need to talk to you."

"Yes, that very well may be, but I know you are familiar with the Form 1386. What would be the purpose of that form but to request a meeting? Following that request I'm certain that Ms. Vorschrift would see to it that a time and location for the meeting would appear on both our schedules."

"I have concerns about what happened in Ecuador. According to the eighth principle I am to express those concerns to Dr. Gallagher or to you."

"That principle also says that you are not to discuss those concerns with anyone else."

"I know."

Alfred stood in the doorway sandwiched between the doorframe and the door. His left shoulder pressed against the metal frame, and his left arm crossed his body behind him so that he could grasp the silver doorknob with his left hand and hold the door against his right shoulder.

"Discussions required by the principles," continued Gene when Alfred didn't respond, "are not required to be scheduled using a Form 1386. The instructions on the form are explicit on that point."

"True enough," said Alfred.

"Although interestingly enough, this point is not covered in the principles."

"Well that is as it should be," said Alfred as he released the doorknob with his left hand. "That form is purely an administrative matter. The process of preparing and handling that form does not constitute any part of the guiding principles which provide the fundamental underpinning for Davenport Center."

The door swung open, and Alfred stood to the side so that Gene could enter the room. Alfred's lab was larger than Gene's, perhaps twice as large. Neither lab had a window. Gene had a small desk on one side of his lab, in the back. Alfred had a carpeted area in one of the rear corners which was separated from the rest of the lab by a burgundy cubical divider. On the office side of the divider was an imposing desk made of metal with a matte black finish. Against the coarse fabric of the cubical divider were two heavy chairs of black metal tubing with deep red fabric backs and seats. Gene sat in one of the chairs. The matching manager's chair behind the desk was adjustable, and it had been adjusted to a height that would prevent it from sliding under the desk. Alfred sat behind the desk and looked tall in the chair.

"I talked to Dr. Gallagher," said Gene.

"Yes," said Alfred.

"About Ecuador. About the deaths in Ecuador. He said you did some testing."

"I see."

"You did do some testing, didn't you?"

"Yes. Yes. Of course."

"And what did you find?"

"Perhaps we could go about this a different way," said Alfred. "I don't understand the point of this inquiry into the details of my work. You came here to express your concerns in accordance with the eighth principle. Why don't we start there. That would seem to be the appropriate place to start. Tell me what it is that you are concerned about."

"It's the deaths in Ecuador. I am concerned about them. I want to understand what happened."

"Aren't you in the process of analyzing the samples we brought back from Ecuador?"

"Yes."

"That should help. That should give you and us a great deal of information about what happened there."

"But what about the contamination? I want to know about the contamination."

"The contamination?"

"Yes. I want to know about the contamination."

"You think the samples from Ecuador are contaminated?"

"No. My serum."

"You think your serum was contaminated?"

"Yes. That's right. What was the nature of the contamination?"

Alfred didn't respond for a moment. The force of his right hand against the edge of the desk pushed his chair back and twisted it some. His eyes became fixed on a stainless steel centrifuge which rested on the black slate counter.

"I'll tell you what I think," said Alfred. "I think this discussion, short though it has been, has already become confused and unfocused on more than one occasion." He looked back at Gene. "I'm a little hard pressed to understand why. First you tell me that you want to express concerns as required by the eighth principle. That makes

150

sense. But when you started talking you said something like, 'I want to understand what happened.' Well, that's where the confusion begins. You are well aware of the fact the words, 'I want to understand what happened,' do not express a concern but rather request information. You come here quoting the eighth principle, but surely you remember the seventh as well. 'Questions about Dr. Gallagher, about the body, about Davenport Center and about the work we do here are not permitted. I will be told everything I need to know, and unknown information can only serve to distract me from my work.'

"Perhaps we can start again," continued Alfred. "Let me attempt to summarize, you are concerned about the deaths in Ecuador."

"Yes," said Gene. "When we arrived in Ecuador there was a thriving village full of living, breathing men, women and children. When we left no human life remained. Those smiling, crying, laughing, struggling people had become fuel for fire and food for bacteria and maggots."

"What you say is true, at least the facts devoid of embellishments are true. Those people died. Have you got other concerns?"

"I think that's an important concern."

"If you're concerned about it, which you obviously are, I think it is important that we understand your concern. Do you have any other concerns?"

"I didn't test Bruce for cystic fibrosis."

"You didn't test him?"

"That's right, and he died, same symptoms as the villagers."

"I see. You are concerned about Bruce's death. I believe that is subsumed in your more general concern about the deaths in Ecuador."

"You injected Bruce with the vaccine, didn't you?" Although the question was accusatory, Gene's tone of voice was quiet and soft and non-confrontational.

"That's ridiculous."

"Then how was my serum contaminated?"

"That is a question. It violates the seventh principle."

"You know about these deaths," said Gene. "You know I had nothing to do with them."

"I am beginning to wonder if your visit here today is nothing more than a veiled attempt to seek information. You know that requests for information are prohibited by the seventh principle. You know that you will be provided with all of the information you need to know. You know that random pieces of information such as you are seeking here today can only serve to distract you from your work." Alfred remained calm as a fourth grade teacher might.

"What was the nature of the contamination?"

"You are suggesting, it seems to me, that you be given the authority to decide how research will be conducted. If you do that, then other doctors will want to be given the same kind of information to make the same kind of decisions. This sounds to me like a recipe for anarchy. We are under real time pressure. Our work must be focused. We can't have every doctor at Davenport Center chasing one dream after another as random thoughts pop into their minds."

"I just want to know about my serum."

"You want to know so that it will influence your behavior and work in the future. Are you suggesting that you should begin to direct the research of Davenport Center?"

"No."

"Are you suggesting that you know better than Father how our research is to be conducted?"

"No."

"Are you suggesting that you decide what issues are to be resolved first by our research?"

"No, of course not. But I was not responsible for the deaths in Ecuador."

"You don't know that. You couldn't possibly know that. Are you in a position to determine what is and what is not a mistake?"

"Well, yes. I could be."

"This is exactly what I suspected. Surely you can see that the requests you are making suggest that you are moving dangerously close to independent thought. You know that independent thought is the only true obstacle to our success. You know that independent thought has the power to destroy us. Have you taken the time to reflect on the wisdom of the second principle?"

Gene knew the answer to that question. He didn't want to spend another week in that dark, muggy, smelly room. He also realized that he was not going to accomplish anything by further discussion with

Alfred. He resolved to end the encounter without further controversy. The concerns had been expressed, but when Gene left he felt even less satisfied and more angry than when he had arrived.

On the way back to his lab, Gene decided he couldn't let this rest. What Alfred was doing was wrong, and he wasn't going to tolerate it. Gene turned on his right heel and headed for Dr. Gallagher's office. Dr. Gallagher and Gene reached the door to his second floor office at the same moment.

"Father," said Gene.

"Yes," said Dr. Gallagher, as they stood together in a small Mission and Conscience Department antechamber to Dr. Gallagher's office. There was tension in Dr. Gallagher's manner. He seemed to be under pressure.

"I need to talk to you," said Gene.

"I'm late for an important appointment. Several people are waiting in my office."

"This will only take a second. I need your help."

Dr. Gallagher put his arm around Gene. The pressure on Dr. Gallagher seemed to dissipate as he pulled Gene close against him. "You're so important to me, Gene. Tell me what's on your mind."

They sat in the two chairs which were in the antechamber.

"It's Alfred. Something's wrong. I don't know how to say this, but..."

Dr. Gallagher looked at Gene with no sense of urgency in his eyes.

"Well," said Gene, starting again, "I don't think my serum was contaminated. I think Alfred's vaccine caused those deaths."

"What makes you think that?" asked Dr. Gallagher.

"I didn't test Bruce. Alfred injected him with the vaccine. He died with the same symptoms as the villagers. I think Alfred killed Bruce, and he's lying about it now to protect himself. I'm his scapegoat, I guess."

"This is a very serious matter."

"Yes. I have a concern. I wanted you to know about it."

Dr. Gallagher stood. "We don't have time to resolve this now. We will discuss it later. We have other things to talk about also. Sarah gives me a longer list each day."

"Yes, Father."

"We will talk more." With that Dr. Gallagher swiped a magnetic card through a card reader next to the door. The latch clicked open. Dr. Gallagher disappeared into his office.

Gene remained frustrated. He had felt driven to tell Dr. Gallagher about Alfred, but now he wondered if he'd done the right thing. Were the lies Alfred's or Dr. Gallagher's?

When Gene got back to his lab he pulled the mouse cage from the cabinet. The three rodents looked healthy. He got some water for them. Food was a problem that he would have to deal with soon. The test conditions were not the best, not what would be expected at Davenport Center. But Gene hadn't conducted any clandestine testing in the past.

Taking one mouse from the cage, Gene used the blue marker to color the base of the animal's tail. After the mouse was marked, he slid the marker onto the countertop and injected the mouse with some of the vaccine he had brought back from Ecuador. With work on the first mouse complete, he performed the same marking and injecting process on a second mouse. He left the third, unmarked mouse as a control.

Chapter 18

Leave This Island Now

It was 5:07 when Gene arrived outside of the VTS room where he had asked Kelly to meet him. Next to the door and against the beige colored wall was a dull gray aluminum sign holder with a glass cover. Behind the glass the name of the person staying in the room could be inserted. Only beige wall was visible through the glass, and that meant that no one had been assigned to the room. That was as Gene had hoped.

With one movement, he knocked on the door and pushed it open. There were two workmen in the room squatting on the floor near the bathroom and fiddling with some wires. They looked up at Gene, and Gene looked at them. These men were a problem. Without speaking Gene nodded at the men, neither of whom he recognized. They seemed disinterested and after a moment resumed work. Gene glanced at the furniture. The room looked like a comfortable hotel suite with an overstuffed chair in one corner. Across from the chair was a small dark wood desk and a round snack or lunch table. Gene thought he would try to convey the impression that he had been sent to check up on the workmen. They were installing a camera in one corner near the ceiling to make it possible to observe whoever was in the room.

Gene stepped back out of the room and let the door close. The hallway was empty, but it might not be for long. The room was at the southeast corner of Davenport Center. To the north was a long corridor with many doors on both sides, most of which led to other VTS rooms. Toward the west a corridor ran along the front of the building. On the south side of that corridor was a long bank of narrow floor to ceiling windows which faced the boat dock. In December the days were short, and at 5:07 pm it was already dark outside. The lights down at the dock threw small shadows which emphasized the spaces between the planks. There was just enough light to see, in the distance, on the south side of Great Cove Creek, the saltbushes and cordgrass.

Gene decided to stand at the edge of the corridor which ran along the front of the building. From there he would be able to see Kelly, and

155

he believed he would be inconspicuous. There were few doors on that corridor and little traffic. As he waited, hoping that Kelly had gotten the note, hoping that she wouldn't ignore his request, he noticed the stairwell to the first floor. They would be able to talk in there if Kelly showed up.

It was already 5:12. There was movement and talking up along the north running hallway. Maybe people were getting ready to go to dinner. Maybe a component was checking on a VTS. Maybe Ms. Vorschrift was making her rounds looking for anyone out of compliance with one rule or another.

At 5:16 Gene decided there was no reason to wait any longer. Kelly knew his schedule would be tight and that every minute counted. When he was ready to leave he glanced over toward the room with the two workman and saw Kelly walk up to the door.

"Hey," said Gene just loud enough for her to hear.

Kelly turned toward him, her hand held in the air, ready to knock.

"I almost didn't come," she said.

"I'm glad you did." He leaned over and kissed her on the cheek. "Come in here." He pulled open the door to the stairwell. "Some people are in that room. We should have some peace in here. This door leads to an alarmed door downstairs. Nowhere else. I don't think anybody will come through here."

They went into the stairwell. The door closed behind them.

"This place has a sort of other worldly feel to it," said Kelly.

"I don't have much freedom around here."

Kelly rolled her eyes.

"I can't just do whatever I want whenever I want to," said Gene. "Let's go down there," said Gene, pointing toward the first floor.

"Why?" Kelly was agitated and more combative than Gene had ever seen.

"If we go down there we'll be next to that metal door. Nobody will be able to see us or hear us, and nobody will come through unless there is a fire or something."

"This cops and robbers stuff drives me nuts." She stood still on the second floor landing.

"Come on." Gene motioned for her to move. He went down a few steps to a painted black metal landing located halfway between the first and second floors. When he turned and looked, he found that Kelly had followed him. He continued on down the last half flight of stairs to the first floor.

"I saw you put that mark next to the doorframe," said Kelly. "I went right back into my lab. I knew you didn't see me."

Gene smiled. "You were looking for the mark?"

"I feel so helpless around here... around you... in my life. I thought I could at least take charge of something. I could control whether I got that note, so I didn't go get it."

"I'm glad you changed your mind. I really wanted to see you."

"I didn't get it for hours. Then I broke down just a few minutes ago. That's why I'm late."

"I miss you, Kelly. I think about you all the time."

Kelly looked away. The exposed incandescent bulb in the ceiling above the second floor landing provided the only light in the stairwell. It was a harsh light that in places made Kelly's dark hair look white.

"What happened with your step-father?" asked Gene. "Didn't you have to go see him?"

Kelly looked back at him. The black metal stair railing cast a shadow across his chest. She looked at his eyes and up and down his body. "I did see him."

"What happened?"

"I see why I think I love you sometimes. You can be good."

Gene smiled a small smile. He put one foot on the light gray rubber tread on the bottom stair.

"He's pure evil. I moved back in with him and Mom last night. I've got no choice." She told Gene about the incident with Richard.

"What a bastard," said Gene. "And your mother won't leave him."

"She's terrified. This is a miserable, stinking world." She moved away from Gene as far as she could in the small area. "But I'm going to talk to her. I'll see if I can get her to move. I'm afraid of Richard. That man is crazy, just crazy. I don't know what he might do. I'm afraid for Mom. She won't leave him. She won't call the police."

"Can you call the police?"

"I don't think so. Mom won't cooperate. If the police were to show up and come into the living room, I wouldn't put it past Richard to pull out a gun and shoot her right on the spot. The police would all be standing around, but there would be nothing to do. It would be too late."

"I'm sorry your life is so difficult now. I know there's not much I can do to help, but I want to do anything I can."

"Ok." Kelly touched Gene's arm. "How are things with you?"

"Things are rough for me right now. It's not the same as the stuff you're going through, but it's pretty hard on me all the same."

"Can you talk about it?"

"I'm not supposed to. I can tell you that some things have happened, things that have me worried. When I was away some people died where I was. It's causing me a lot of trouble."

Kelly looked at him as though she were struggling to understand.

"It's all disjointed and out of context," said Gene. "It's just that I'm worried all the time. I have trouble sleeping. I don't know who to trust. I wish I could spend more time with you."

"We have a few minutes now," said Kelly, as she touched Gene's cheek.

They sat on the floor. Gene crawled over the speckled yellow, red and gray floor tiles to a place underneath the metal landing between the first and second floors and behind the half flight of stairs that came down to the first floor. Kelly crawled in beside him. They sat in silence, their backs against the wall, Gene's arm around Kelly's shoulders.

"I missed you, Kelly," said Gene, as he unbuttoned her yellow lab coat and slid it back off her shoulders. "I've wanted to spend more time with you." He kissed her and caressed her neck. "You're so important to me. Sometimes I think you're my only connection to reality."

Kelly was less resistant than he thought she might be. In time they had both removed their shirts and stretched out under the landing. They kissed, and for a time they just held each other in silence.

"I love you, Gene," said Kelly.

"I love you, too," said Gene. He knew he didn't say that to her often enough. It hurt him to say it, to realize that it was true. It hurt him to want her but not be able to have her.

"I want you, Gene. I want to be with you more."

"Yes. I want that too."

Soon Gene's pants were pushed down around his ankles, stuck where they wouldn't slide over his shoes. Gene was excited and looking forward to squeezing their bare flesh together. It was a sensation he had missed for months and wanted to feel again. He unfastened Kelly's skirt and started to pull it down.

"Can you leave this place?" asked Kelly.

"This stairwell?" Gene was frustrated by the question. All he could think about was Kelly and how much he wanted to be with her.

"No, not this stairwell. Davenport Center. This island. Can you leave this island?"

"Yes."

"I want you to be with me. Can you leave this island and be with me?"

"Yes, I suppose, in time."

"No," shouted Kelly, pulling at her skirt. "Not in time. Now! Can you leave this island now?"

"I want to be with you, Kelly, but it's complicated."

"No," she said, as she put her bra on. "Complicated? Complicated? That's what I'm supposed to listen to? I'm not going to do this again, not until we get this... this... this I don't know what it is straightened out. Is this a relationship? I don't know what the arrangement is. I've never seen anything like it before. I've never heard of anything that even resembles what we're doing. I don't understand it. It makes me crazy. There are times when I really need the support you could give me, and you're nowhere around. I can't get in touch with you. I can't call you. The best I can do is wait until the next day and write a note and make a mark on the wall. Even then it could be days before I hear from you. What is this? What kind of thing is this?" Kelly had pulled her clothes back on and was turning her lab coat right side out.

Gene yanked his pants back up and started to get dressed.

"I don't know what to say, Kelly. I want to be with you." The aaskouandy which Hiaroma had given Gene was on a string. He slipped it over his head.

"What's that?" asked Kelly.

"It's a charm. A friend gave it to me."

159

"Curiouser and curiouser," said Kelly, shaking her head, but she didn't seem able to focus on the aaskouandy. "You don't want to be with me enough. If this place is causing you so much trouble, why don't you just get up and leave? You're a doctor. You can find a job somewhere else. You can find a good job."

"It's not that simple. I told you that. I can't get another job."

"It can be that simple. You could just get up and leave. You could take the ferry one day and not come back. You can get a job as a truck driver. You could work at McDonald's. You can get some job."

"I want to be with you."

"Then you can just leave."

"I can't right now. Maybe soon. I'm trying to get things straightened out here. How about you? Even if I could leave here right now, can you just get up and leave? Can you walk away from Richard, from your mother? What would happen if you left the house one morning and just never went back?"

Chapter 19

Component of The Body

Late that night Gene stepped into a small, dark room in the west wing. The door closed behind him. The ceiling, floor and walls were black and smeared with dirt. The smell was foul, like rotting flesh, and the temperature was an uncomfortable cold. There were discordant sounds of scraping, banging and crumpling metal, screeching, moaning, crying and voices in agony. On the wall to the left were dimly lit photographs of people dying of starvation and malnutrition. On the right there were photographs of people suffering in hospital beds and dying of disease.

Gene removed his shoes and all of his clothing and pushed the things through a hole in the side of a vertical, metal conduit that funneled everything into an incinerator on the floor below. The grit on the floor pushed into the soles of Gene's feet, and the cold made him shiver. Soon the door on the wall in front of him slid open. Light from that room illuminated several black obstacles of irregular shape which were between Gene and the open door.

"Move to the right, around the obstacles which block your path." The voice was Dr. Gallagher's coming from the next room.

The next room was small, but Dr. Gallagher was standing on one side and not yet visible to Gene. Gene maneuvered around the obstacles and stepped into the room with Dr. Gallagher. This room, painted white, was warm and clean. The door slid shut behind Gene. The foul smell and loud sounds were gone.

"I have led you away from your life of pain and despair," said Dr. Gallagher. "Soon you will move into the next room. There your body will be cleansed to remove outside influences, to remove dirt and contamination and earthly symbols of smiting and to clear and open your mind for receiving new information about the tasks before us. Your mind will be free. Your soul will be pure."

Dr. Gallagher handed Gene something that looked like a cubed bit of fruit, perhaps a piece of the flesh of an apple.

"Taste this," said Dr. Gallagher.

Gene bit the piece of fruit. A powerful bitter taste filled his mouth followed by a stinging, hot, burning sensation.

"This taste will remind you of the pain and bitterness you have left behind."

Gene wanted to spit the fruit onto the floor, but he swallowed it. Swallowing was required by the ceremony.

Dr. Gallagher lifted fresh, clean clothing from a small table and handed the small pile to Gene. On the wall behind Dr. Gallagher was a cape and other clothing on a hanger. Dr. Gallagher lifted the hanger off the hook on the wall and handed it to Gene.

"I give these to you freely," said Dr. Gallagher. "Take this clothing as a symbol of your new life and the freedom you have here at Davenport Center."

A door on the opposite side of the room slid to the side, and Gene entered the ceremonial cleansing room with undergarments under one arm and the clothing on the hanger draped over his back. The door closed behind him, and Gene was again alone.

The room was the size of a large bathroom. The floor was polished granite, and the bits of white, gray and black sparkled in response to soft pulsating lights of various colors that bounced against it from all angles. The walls were made of panels of rose-colored marble that ran from floor to ceiling. The edges of the panels were joined with strips of reflective gold metal. The mild odor of sandalwood filled the air. The clothing fit inside a small closet with a marble door, and a latch held the door closed.

Gene slid into the cleansing pool. For preservation and protection, lavender and rosemary had been added to the rippling water. Gene felt pulsating jets emanating from the sides and beneath the surface. The sounds of the swirling water blended with the music of light bells, a flute and a harp.

Using soap Gene removed from his body all remnants of the dirt and grit from the first room. Clean and with washed hair, he leaned back against the side of the pool. Over time the sound changed to the beating of a heart and the groans of labor pains. The jets in the pool fired full force then stopped and then repeated the sequence.

Fast moving images of sunlight, of birth, of people working and of happy families at home flashed on a screen on one side of the pool.

Then a slow moving stream of words began to scroll across the screen. Gene read the words aloud.

"This water cleanses me. It has removed all of the contamination, all of the pain, all of the limitations and restrictions from my body, from my mind and from my spirit. The contamination of the world, the pain, the limitations, the restrictions have flowed from me and into this water."

With that the drain opened and the water began to flow out of the pool. Gene stood with his feet spread apart and his arms outstretched to his sides. Each hand grasped a bar on opposite sides of the pool. Jets of warm air blew hard against Gene and swirled around the room, drying his body. The scent of sandalwood had been replaced by the mild aroma of frankincense. Gene read more.

"This water with all of these negative and harmful influences now flows down into the ground, into Mother Earth where it too will be cleansed. With this I am born again."

The blowing air stopped. Gene opened the closet with the clothes and took a glass of white, milky fluid.

"With this I drink the mother's milk of rebirth."

Gene swallowed the white fluid which had a sweet taste of apples and cinnamon.

Taking the clothes Dr. Gallagher had given him, Gene got dressed. As he lifted a shimmering white robe with gold highlights, he saw on the shelf, hidden by the robe, a clear yellow penicillin bottle. The bottle glistened in the harsh light. He touched the bottle, and it rotated, as he swung the robe over his shoulders and fastened the clip around his neck. As the bottom of the bottle faced him, he read the label, "Ecuador E7341 - Penicillin." It was the penicillin bottle from Ecuador, the one that had been in the small refrigerator.

It was then that he noticed that the bottle wasn't empty. A yellowish plastic looking thing lay against the back of the bottle. Gene lifted the bottle and turned it in the light. But when he realized that it was a human ear with a chain tattooed from the ear lobe up the side, he dropped it. The glass shattered against the granite floor, and the ear bounced behind a cabinet.

Alfred had brought Bruce's ear back from Ecuador, and now it was lost behind a cabinet. Gene trembled, frightened by the incident,

163

but he didn't know what to do but continue with the ceremony as if nothing had happened. He slipped a blindfold into place. The door opened, and Dr. Gallagher took his arm and guided him into the next room.

"We will now learn to penetrate the darkness," said Dr. Gallagher. He led Gene to a chair in the next room. "I will be your vision. You will learn to work with and rely upon the help of others here at Davenport Center."

With the blindfold still in place, Gene followed instructions from Dr. Gallagher. There were small wood, metal and plastic objects on a table before him. There were cubes, pyramids and other regular and irregular shapes, some joined together, others not. Only Dr. Gallagher spoke.

"Originally," said Dr. Gallagher, "God did smite certain evil people and groups by placing disease in their genes."

With Dr. Gallagher's hands guiding his, Gene took a cube and an irregular shaped object and joined them together.

"As times have changed, the descendants of those people who God did smite have mingled with the worthy people, and now the descendants of the worthy and the descendants of the evil live in the same communities side by side. Now the burden of this disease, the disease of the evil, has fallen onto the worthy people. The worthy now care for and even perpetuate the evil. This was never God's intention."

Again with Dr. Gallagher's guidance, Gene moved various objects around the table, joining some, separating others, mixing them all.

"Knowledge has been imparted unto me. The worthy people have suffered long enough. God has made it our mission to remove all of this evil from Earth. We are to relieve the burden of the worthy people."

Dr. Gallagher's hand guided Gene. They continued to rearrange the objects, discarding some.

"The word of God is unyielding. His direction is clear. We have the technology to cleanse the Earth of this evil. That is what we have been directed to do."

Dr. Gallagher lifted Gene's arm, directing him to stand.

"These are to be discarded as the source of bad protoplasm," said Dr. Gallagher, as he aided Gene in placing damaged and unused pieces into a trash receptacle. On the table there remained three chains of connected pieces. Holding Gene's hands, Dr. Gallagher directed him to place the chains into three sets of indentations in the door into which the chains fit as a hand into a glove. The door popped open.

"These sequences, the source of health and wisdom, have now opened for us the door to all opportunity."

With Gene's blindfold still in place, Dr. Gallagher guided him out of the small room, down a few steps and out into the Ceremonial Chamber. Gene was taken to an open place in the circle of other components. Dr. Gallagher took his position in the center of the room and at the top of the circle of components. This was a special ceremony. Its purpose was to recognize Gene and the entire body of Davenport Center for the innovative screening test which Gene had developed, the test which caused a luminescent glow to emanate from the throats of those people who have at least one copy of the cystic fibrosis gene.

Pointing at Gene, Dr. Gallagher spoke. "By his work this component has benefitted us all, as we together have benefitted him." The other components were not blindfolded. "By his work we have moved closer to a better life for all.

"It would be possible to think of this effort in a vacuum, to think that one person has made this monumental innovation. But that is not so. This is great work. This is a great achievement. But it is not an accomplishment of one. This is an accomplishment of many. Together we have achieved this, and together we will achieve much, much more. Triumphs which will startle the world, which will garner the undying accolades and appreciation of future generations are now within our grasp. We are all part of this, the greatest moment in all of human history.

"Our destiny, the destiny of this planet and perhaps the destiny of the entire universe hang in the balance. What we do now will echo throughout all of history. Together we will be strong. Together we must be swift. Together we will be decisive.

"We here at Davenport Center have an opportunity to make a profound contribution to our world and to the universe. We have seized and we will exploit this opportunity. But what do we ask in return? We ask not for gold. We ask not for comfort. We ask not that the work be easy. We ask only that we make a difference.

"We look to the future with an unflinching view of the reality of a better, healthier, more prosperous world. We work only with the knowledge that we are right, that what we do here must be done. We will change the people of this planet to perpetuity. Our only reward is that we will bathe in the gratitude of all future generations."

Chapter 20

What Should I Expect From A Cripple?

Dr. Gallagher sat at the controls of his R44 Astro helicopter, as he approached the Naval Medical Center in Bethesda, Maryland from the north. He had come to pick up Peter Snyder, Marion's supervisor, who worked at NIH, which was located just on the other side of the Rockville Pike. It was a little after 1:00 pm, and Peter stood in front of the Naval Medical Hospital, waiting for Dr. Gallagher to bring the medium sized, white and dark blue helicopter in. Peter's cheeks were red from the wind and the December cold.

The helicopter touched the ground in the same place where the president's helicopter would land. With the sixteen-foot rotor slapping the air overhead, Peter ran up to the right side door and slid into the front seat next to Dr. Gallagher. The two back seats were empty. The helicopter allowed Dr. Gallagher to make this trip from Bloodsworth Island in less than an hour compared with the two or three hours it might take using water and then land surface transportation.

Back in the air, Dr. Gallagher headed northwest above Interstate 270 toward Frederick. Before reaching Frederick, he looped off to the south of 270, and brought the helicopter to rest just north of Sugarloaf Mountain, a low rise mountain with a summit of 1,282 feet. They were in a rural, sparsely populated area of Maryland and close to a striking, large home built on rolling land adjacent to the mountain. A cold gust rustled the leafless branches of the oak and tulip poplar trees not far from the helicopter. Dr. Gallagher motioned for Peter to follow him across the large yard to a glass enclosed patio on the back of the house.

Inside, a round metal table with a glass top had been prepared for them. Steam rose from the frothy hot chocolate in two Christmas mugs on the table, and there was a chopped salad of lettuce, cucumbers, fresh green beans, carrots and walnuts ready for each of them. Dr. Gallagher wore hiking boots, forest green pants and a yellow oxford cloth shirt. An attractive blonde woman of about 30 appeared from inside the house, and Dr. Gallagher handed her his pale green goose down winter coat.

"Thank you," said Dr. Gallagher.

The woman smiled a half smile and bowed her head an inch or so but didn't speak. Peter, dressed in a dark brown suit and less well prepared for the bitter cold outside, decided to keep his suit jacket on. The woman left the room.

"I thought you might like to come out here," said Dr. Gallagher to Peter. "I know you haven't been here in a long time."

"Yes. It's a delightful place. There's such a nice view. It's so clear today."

"Please sit," said Dr. Gallagher, waving his hand in the direction of the table. "So, have you finished your Christmas shopping?"

"No," said Peter as he sipped his hot chocolate. "It's always the same. I say I'll be ready, and then I'm not."

After a lunch of beef, barley and vegetable stew and small talk, Dr. Gallagher called for his coat.

"Would you like a coat to wear?" asked Dr. Gallagher.

"No, I don't think so," said Peter.

"Suit yourself," said Dr. Gallagher as he pulled open the outside door. He went outside, around the house, away from the helicopter and started walking along a rocky trail that led toward the mountain.

"But the helicopter..." said Peter.

Dr. Gallagher motioned for him to follow. "I need to talk to you."

"Yes, but it was warmer in there."

"I know, but there are fewer ears out here."

About a half mile later, after walking up the side of the mountain, they came to a rock outcrop known as White Rocks. Dr. Gallagher looked fresh and exhilarated and ready to hike miles further. Peter was having trouble breathing.

"This air is choking me," said Peter. "Every breath feels like a knife in my lungs. I'm afraid to inhale."

"Fear of breathing sounds like a self-curing disease if ever there was one."

Dr. Gallagher sat on one of the rocks that was about the height of a stool.

"You want to sit?"

"No," said Peter. "I'll just stand here and shiver."

"Ok."

"What's this about?"

"It's beautiful up here, isn't it?" Dr. Gallagher looked out over the rolling hills.

Peter rolled his eyes. "It is. It's also cold."

"Yes. Yes. That's so. I'll get to the point. Marion, that woman, is a thorn in my side. I think the wound is infected and beginning to fester. Something has got to be done."

"This is the government, you know. We have a lot of meetings. We talk. We discuss. We chat. We write memos to summarize the meetings, but we don't do anything fast." Peter folded his arms tight o his body and shook back and forth.

"She is on a rampage. Her mission is to destroy Davenport 'enter. You must get her under control."

"I'll do the best I can."

"Don't do the best you can. Stop her. Get the job done. You can ansfer her to another job. You can fire her. You can give her so 1uch work she can't keep her head above water. You can send her to an Francisco or Honolulu or Phoenix for a couple of years. You can omote her. Give her a better job somewhere else. This is not an :haustive list. Find a way."

"I've tried."

"No more 'I've tried.' Get that woman under control. Do it lay. I don't care what you do or how you do it. Just do it now."

Peter didn't respond, but he looked sad and lost, almost like he ;ht cry.

Dr. Gallagher started in again. "All right. If you decide that it's much for you, that you can't do it, that's ok. I understand that. ` jobs are big jobs. Some jobs require skill and finesse and veness. Maybe you don't have those skills. Maybe you're some ᶠ sorry ass wimp. What should I expect from a cripple? If you the job, if you don't have the skills required to do the job, you me. We'll find another way."

Chapter 21

Ignorance & Idiocy

In the early part of that afternoon Gene had been working in the west wing with another component. Some laboratory equipment needed to be tested and calibrated, and they worked on it together.

Gene had just returned to his lab in the east wing. He was still quite shaken up after finding Bruce's ear. Not only that, he was scheduled to spend time with Alfred starting in only a few minutes. There were parts of Davenport Center which Gene had never seen. That afternoon Alfred was to give him a tour of part of the first floor of the east wing.

"I will be told everything I need to know..." That was part of the seventh principle. There was not a free flow of information at Davenport Center. Gene would be told or shown something, and there was a reason. Nothing happened without a reason. Dr. Gallagher or one of the paladins had decided that Gene needed to know more about the operation of Davenport Center.

Gene knew that Alfred had been responsible for the ear, and that frightened him. The paladins and Dr. Gallagher had power over him, and to incur their ire, as he had obviously done, was the behavior of a hotheaded fool. Gene resolved to be careful with Alfred this afternoon.

The time was short, but Gene wanted to check on the mice he had injected with the vaccine from Ecuador. He hadn't had an opportunity to look at them in the last two days, and he was curious to see how they were doing. The door to his lab was open. It was always open unless the schedule provided otherwise, which it didn't on that day. If the door were closed when Alfred arrived, some explanation would be required.

Gene was ready for Alfred, and he had a minute or so to spare. He squatted and pulled on the cabinet door where the mouse cage was. The smell was putrid, mouse feces and urine and maybe the rotting flesh of the one of the rodents. Gene hadn't had the opportunity to spend much time taking care of the mice. He wanted to. But food was hard to come by, and he didn't have the supplies he needed to keep the cage clean. The smell was pungent. Gene worried about it, but he knew that air circulation system in Davenport Center was good.

The space was too small to get a good look at the animals without removing the cage from the cabinet. There wouldn't be time for that. He couldn't be standing in the room, holding an unauthorized rodent cage when Alfred arrived. The fingers of his right hand twisted the cage and pulled it toward him. The scraping sound frightened one of the mice. It ran to the far end of the cage. The other two remained still. They had splotches of clotted blood where white used to be. Gene took a pen from his pocket and poked at one of the mice. The small body moved as though it were a stuffed toy. Yellow and purple splotches reminded Gene of the deaths in Ecuador. The cabinet was dark, and he couldn't see which mice had the black marks at the bases of their tails, but Gene knew what had happened. He knew what had caused the yellow, the purple, the rust-colored scabs and the deaths.

There was noise in the hallway. Gene pushed the cabinet door shut, but the twisted cage had become wedged in the small space. He yanked the door open, adjusted the cage and slammed it shut just as Alfred arrived at the door.

"Hi," said Gene as he turned to greet Alfred. Gene thought he saw Alfred's nostrils flare. Would it be possible for him to miss the piercing, repulsive odor?

"This way," said Alfred. He motioned for Gene to follow him down the corridor.

Fresh air entered Gene's lab from the ceiling just inside the door and left through an exhaust vent in the rear near his desk. The stench would soon be pulled from the room. These dead mice were trouble and a relief at the same time. Now he knew what happened in Ecuador. Alfred was a murderer, not that he had ever had any doubt about that, but now it was clear. The dead mice provided an even better reason to handle Alfred with care.

Alfred turned, and Gene followed him into the hall. They went to an elevator which Gene had never used. It was at one end of the Mission and Conscience Department. Gene knew there was no easy way to get to the first floor of the east wing. He and Kelly had been at the bottom of a stairwell, but to leave the stairwell on the first floor would have set off an alarm.

On the first floor, Alfred led Gene to an electronic platform truck which was parked against the light green cinder block wall a short distance from the door to the elevator. The truck was loaded with large brown paper bags that looked like each of them might contain about fifty pounds of something. Alfred started rearranging the bags on the bed of the tiny platform truck.

"Want help?" asked Gene, breaking his silence. An offer of help couldn't set Alfred off, he thought.

"No," said Alfred. "I got it."

It was hard for Gene to stand and watch the small man struggle with the heavy bags, so he helped despite Alfred's response. Together they rearranged the bags in order to provide room for Gene. They had cleared a place all the way down to the bed where Gene could put his feet. There were a couple of bags just behind the clear area where Gene could sit, and they had formed a back rest out of other bags.

"There you go," said Alfred, slapping the bag on which Gene was to sit. Alfred didn't seem to be angry at Gene. If anything his omnipresent coldness seemed less pronounced than usual.

"Ok," said Gene, as he jumped up onto the platform. The bags contained birdfeed. There were birds in Davenport Center. They were used for testing Gene had assumed, but he didn't know anything about the nature of the testing. He had never done any work with birds. And this small platform truck carried hundreds of pounds of birdfeed. When he was in Ecuador, Gene had dreamed about a large number of birds at Davenport Center, but except for the wild birds outside, he had known of only a few birds in the building. He guessed it would take those few birds about a thousand years to eat to all of the food. As he sat on one of the sacks, he hoped that the bags would be stable. "Dr. Gallagher killed his sister."

"What did you say?" asked Alfred.

"'Dr. Gallagher killed his sister.' That's what it says right here," said Gene as he pointed at one of the bags. The words were written with the thick red lines of a large felt tipped marker.

Alfred looked embarrassed. He grabbed the offending bag. Gene helped him to flip it upside down. "I find it inappropriate when people say that. It's not true. People shouldn't deface property with graffiti. And it's inaccurate. It's not accurate. Dr. Gallagher never killed his sister." Alfred was in a state of mild agitation. It was the closest thing to anger Gene had ever seen from Alfred.

"Why would somebody write that?"

"Failure of core principles, I guess. This is the behavior of someone who has a depraved mind and was raised without any respect for authority." There was silence as Alfred walked around the vehicle examining the other bags. Alfred was on the other side of the truck when he spoke again. "Dr. Gallagher left his sister alone for a few minutes in one of those small rubber wading pools. Maybe it wasn't the best thing he ever did, but he told me that he was very sorry for it. If he could trade places with his sister, I'm sure he would. She was young, 4 years old. She suffered from curvature of the spine. She couldn't move much without help. You can hear the pain in his voice when he talks about her. Some people say he drowned her, but I don't believe it."

Alfred climbed into the driver's seat.

"Let's go," he said, as he set the vehicle in motion and made a sharp left turn, bringing the front of the truck right up against the left wall. He backed up against the right wall and then started off in the opposite direction. The whir of the small truck's electric motor made an echoing sound. The soft rubber tires of the vehicle turned against the yellow, red and gray speckled tiles and made a soft, almost inaudible, sound.

"Over here on the left," said Alfred, "is the east wing ventilation system." He stopped the truck and gestured with his head in the direction of a set of double doors. "It's not really what I wanted to show you, but I figured I'd point it out as long as we're down here. You'll never find a better, safer air filtration system. No virus, no infectious microorganism of any kind gets out of this building, I don't care how small it is."

"I knew we had a system to eliminate airborne contaminants."

"I'll show you," said Alfred as he jumped out of the driver's seat. Gene followed him into a massive room cluttered with silver air ducts, copper pipes, black motors and giant deep blue metal structures which looked like furnaces. "Every room in this entire building has a separate air intake from outside. All of the air comes from the west side of the building. And every room has a separate exhaust on the east side. No air from one room ever gets into any other room. Every room gets clean air all the time."

Gene was not surprised by what Alfred was saying, although up to this point he had not been aware of the details of the operation of the system.

"We control the air flow through every room on the east side of the building," continued Alfred. "This is the main system. There are smaller, backup systems located all over the building. None of the air from any room exhausts to the outside without being filtered through four separate 0.3 micron filters. We also control all of the airflow through all of the laboratory laminar airflow cabinets here as well. As you know, this place is filled with Class III Microbiological Safety Cabinets. "

"Yes," said Gene.

"The equipment necessary to keep all of the air clean all the time takes up most of the space in this room. There's a similar room in the west wing which controls the air in the rooms on the west side of the building. Both rooms have backup ventilation systems with electrical generators so that we never have to worry about contamination. I think you know that every room in this building could be used as a Class III microbiologically safe room with independent laminar airflow."

"No. I didn't know."

"Enough of this air. It's not the point of our time down here today. It's the birds I wanted to show you. Well, not really the birds. They're upstairs. But this is a part of the system I want you to understand. Not here. Let's go. I'll show you."

Back on the small truck Alfred took off down the hallway. There were many intersecting hallways, and Gene had lost his orientation. In time Alfred stopped. He grabbed the bag with the graffiti on it.

"You grab a bag," said Alfred.

They went through a door. Gene found himself in a space that was more like a hallway than a room. It was narrow and perhaps 100 feet long. A pair of conveyors ran the entire length of the wall with matching conveyors below running in the opposite direction. Alfred dropped his bag on the floor and ripped open the top.

"Help me with this," said Alfred.

Together they lifted the bag and poured its contents into one of the giant stainless steel supply bins at one end of the conveyor belt. When they were done with Alfred's bag, Alfred grabbed Gene's bag.

"Let's see what you've got here," said Alfred. He examined the bag. "This one's different. The one I had was for birds that eat seed. Your bag is for the birds that eat meat. This stuff goes into this bin." He pointed to a second bin beside the first one.

"We'll put more of the food in here in a minute," said Alfred. "First I want to show you a couple of things. The feed in here," he said pointing at the supply bins, "moves down one conveyor belt or the other, seed on the left, that dried meat stuff on the right. The conveyors fills up these little metal boxes. When the boxes are full of food they are pulled up by the chains. They dispense the food into the rooms upstairs where the birds are located. There are sixteen of these metal boxes, two for each of the rooms along this wall upstairs."

The vertical chain arrangements looked as though they were made of stainless steel bicycle chain. Aside from those chains, there were what looked like water pipes leading up into each room and a drain pipe leading down. The seventh principle prohibited Gene from asking about these.

"If one of the food boxes upstairs is full, any excess food tumbles back down one of these plastic shoots onto the lower conveyors. That food goes back to the bins and gets re-circulated on one of the outgoing conveyors. The water supply comes from here also," said Alfred. "Upstairs. We'll see it later, there are automatic sprayers which keep the floors of the rooms washed and clean. The waste water flows out here." Alfred pointed to one of the drain pipes.

"Birds," said Gene. "This arrangement would support hundreds of birds." Gene decided to attempt to ask questions by making statements.

"Yes. It does."

"I've never done any testing on birds."

"We do testing on birds."

"It seems to me that birds would be troublesome. Genetically they're not close to humans. They wouldn't provide a valuable or useful model for testing. In fact I'm not familiar with any value such animals would have in a testing environment."

"An interesting point," said Alfred. "It's just that difference that fascinates us. The genetic differences have presented and do present some difficulty. Although we have had spectacular success with what might be called bridging with one virus. We have developed a single virus that will infect humans and over half of the species of birds we've tested including most of the long distance migratory birds. This has been very gratifying work."

"I understand. The objective is to develop a virus that will infect both people and birds."

"Yes." Alfred led Gene back to the truck to get more birdfeed.

Gene was frustrated by Alfred's response. He had made the statement to obtain additional information. He wanted to know why Alfred wanted this virus. Understanding such a virus that existed in the environment would be one thing. Developing a virus with this objective would be dangerous. He wanted more information, but he knew he couldn't ask for it in a direct way.

After they had filled both of the supply bins, they returned to the small truck. There remained two bags, and Gene sat on those.

"We've got a new project for you," said Alfred as they started down the hall. "It is one particularly well suited to your talents and experience."

"Good," said Gene.

"This issue of cross infection between birds and humans needs more work. What we have done so far is perfect for its intended purpose. That success came early and was gratifying. But we have not been able to expand that early success. The virus we've developed has some aggravating limitations. We can attenuate the virus so that it maintains its ability to infect both birds and humans without causing disease in either. This is obviously valuable for testing. But we have had no success whatsoever in one important area. We have not been able to modify the virus so that it attaches to a different receptor in humans. The receptor to which the existing virus attaches is an important one. We needed that, but we need to target other receptors as well. This is critical, and it is work for which your talents are particularly well suited. Of course receptors alone will not give us the comprehensive approach that we need, but one issue at a time. Solve this problem, and there will be others."

"I found Bruce's ear," said Gene. He had held his anger and frustration and hostility in as long as he could. Gene knew he didn't have the power to fight with Alfred, but his drive to confront him forced its way to the surface.

"Yes," said Alfred. "I know. You're a good man, a bright, hard working doctor, but you accused me of injecting Bruce with the vaccine. Next you went to Father and said that the vaccine was responsible for the death in Ecuador, a statement which is contrary to all of the information available to you. You followed that up with the same accusation about Bruce and the vaccine. The whole thing was just too much. It was more than we could tolerate. The ear was a warning, simply that. Nothing more. I wanted to remind you that consequences can flow from such behavior. If you continue your excellent work and live by the principles, you can forget about the ear." As always Alfred spoke in a mild mannered, conversational tone.

Chapter 22

Just Talk To Him

"That woman has been put on this Earth to make my life miserable," said Dr. Gallagher.

Alfred didn't respond.

It was past midnight, and the two men were in Dr. Gallagher's third floor office. The night was clear and crisp, and hundreds of stars were visible through the large window that looked out over the northern part of Bloodsworth Island.

"A civilization free of inherited disease where those who are honest and hard working can prosper and live happy, healthy, fulfilling lives. That's what I want. Is that a crime?"

"No," said Alfred.

Alfred sat in one of the wing chairs in front of the desk. Dr. Gallagher paced around the room.

"Should I be subjected to harassment and persecution and driven to the ends of the Earth for that?" He punched the wall on the left side of the window, next to the photograph of a parking meter with a handicapped only designation.

"No."

"That's all I want, to eliminate disease, a Herculean effort in and of itself. For what purpose should I be forced to fight battle after battle with the National Institutes of Health before I can fight disease? Partners. We should be partners. Right thinking people would know that the interest of all would be best served if we worked together. I don't understand this need to be at cross-purposes. That woman is the manifestation of cynicism and cruelty and hatred."

"What has she done?"

"It isn't what she's done, although she's done plenty. It's what she's about to do. It was supposed to be a surprise, like Pearl Harbor all over again. She still thinks it's a surprise. She's going to come swooping down on this island in the morning. She's missed December 7th by a few days, but she'll probably get the time right. She's arrogant. And she seems to have this omnipotence. She answers to no

179

one, not to her boss, not to his boss, not to the Secretary, not to the Congress."

"It seems to me that arrogance would flow naturally from omnipotence," said Alfred.

Dr. Gallagher stood for a moment with his hands on the back of his desk chair. As he started back toward the window, he twisted the chair and flung it against the wall.

"What does she want?" asked Alfred. He seemed to be unbothered by or at least accustomed to Dr. Gallagher's behavior.

"She wants to make my life miserable. She wants to destroy everything we've done here and everything we stand for. She wants to go through every piece of paper on this island. She will disrupt our work. She's developed this intense hatred for me many years ago, and now she has transferred it so that she hates all of us here at Davenport Center. I don't know why this is happening now. She's hated me for many years. I don't know what the catalyst was. All I know is that she and her cohorts have the destructive force of a nuclear weapon."

Dr. Gallagher sat on the loveseat across from his desk. Alfred twisted his body in the wing chair in order to look at him.

"What can we do to get ready for her?" asked Alfred.

"We'll be ready," said Dr. Gallagher as he jumped back up off the loveseat. "Sarah's been working on it. We'll be ready. We want to eliminate disease. Why is that so wrong? Jesus didn't want the sick and disabled around either. He knew they should not remain on Earth. He knew they were a problem. He cured them. That's how he dealt with it. But we can't cure them. Only He has that power. We don't. And up to this point He has not seen fit to grant us such power. Still, like Jesus, we must rid the world of lepers and all with disease or disability."

Dr. Gallagher pushed his desk chair back into place behind his desk and dropped into it. He became still, a sullen, angry look on his face. For several minutes there was silence in the room except for the soft sound of circulating air. Dr. Gallagher focused on one of the posters behind the loveseat. Alfred looked at a small white bowl with a copper rim which was on Dr. Gallagher's desk. The bowl had been made from a portion of the skull of a quadriplegic man. "At least he can be useful in death," Dr. Gallagher had said to Alfred years before when he requested that the bowl be fabricated for him.

"How did it go with Gene this afternoon?" asked Dr. Gallagher. His mood had changed, leaving no remnant anger or frustration.

"It went well. He knows that he will be developing a virus that can infect both humans and birds."

"I want you to keep an eye on him. He's moving into a position where he will be able to provide a very high level of service. He must be absolutely dedicated to the project. I don't think this will be a problem, but I want you to be aware of his moods, his spirit, how he responds to things. If there is some issue, let's catch it and deal with it early. We must be sure that we understand him completely."

"What do you want me to do?"

"I'm going to give you everything we've got on him," said Dr. Gallagher. He gestured toward a stack of notebooks, folders and papers about ten inches high on the corner of his desk. "Take a look at this stuff first. You can start with his autobiography."

The autobiography was a detailed document each person prepared before he or she could be accepted as a component. These autobiographies were to contain information concerning every major event, every major decision and every major turning point in the person's life. Information concerning drug or alcohol use, sexual experience and any illegal activity was to be included.

"You should also check out the Others Book," continued Dr. Gallagher. That notebook was yellow and contained copies of any information about Gene which had been submitted by any other component or by a paladin. "After you've gone through that or maybe at the same time, you'll need to go over the Today Books." Each component was required to submit on a daily basis a Today's Items Report. That report consisted of a detailed entry for each important thought, emotion, problem, action or success that occurred during the day. All of Gene's reports had been filed in several blue notebooks known as the Today Books.

"There are some other things in there also," said Dr. Gallagher. "You'll find his medical records, his psychiatric evaluation and any incident reports. I don't know, maybe there are some other papers also. After you've had an opportunity to review this material, then you can begin to focus on him. I want you to know everything there is to know about him. If there's any chance that he's going to cause a problem, now is the best time for us to understand that."

"I think he's a good man," said Alfred. "He can wear his heart on his sleeve. Sometimes he reminds me of you.

Dr. Gallagher gave a slight nod in acknowledgement of Alfred's comment. "Well he's your responsibility now."

"Any suggestions about how best to approach him?"

Dr. Gallagher turned in his chair and leaned forward onto the desk. "The objective is just to gather as much information as possible. Focus on him. Pay attention to what he does. Make him an important part of your life. Minor things, things that may seem mundane can still be important. Together many little pieces of information may give us insight into his reliability, insight that just isn't available without this kind of detailed study." Dr. Gallagher rubbed one side of his face.

"Don't do anything odd," continued Dr. Gallagher. "Just talk to him. Show an interest in him. I think one of the best things you can do is tell him something about yourself. After that, listen to what he has to say. Most people like to exchange information, not exactly piece for piece but exchange information in a general way. Share your life with him. Open yourself up to him, and he'll open himself up to you. Do what it takes to make him comfortable. Over time you'll develop a personal relationship with him, a relationship where he will trust you."

Chapter 23

Native Of The Parched Land

The next morning Gene was awakened at 6:03. As the grogginess of sleep faded, an understanding of the relationship between Dr. Gallagher and Alfred flashed into his consciousness, and it frightened him. Dr. Gallagher had told Alfred everything about their short conversation. That was not the behavior of someone suspicious of Alfred. Rather it was the behavior of someone who was not surprised by Gene's accusations, someone who was directing Alfred or at the very least working in concert with him.

The gray and tan curtains in his bedroom opened automatically, exposing nothing but blackness outside. The wrought iron ceiling fixture flashed on as did the light green ceramic lamp next to his bed. An alarm started buzzing. The only way Gene could quiet the alarm or regain control over the lights was by entering the bathroom. The intermittent blaring of the buzzer would return if he left the bathroom within four minutes.

Gene's bedroom was large and attractive. The light yellow wood of the trim and ceiling molding accented the gray walls. A large armoire of darker wood stood on one side of the bed, the side nearer the living room. Gene's comforter was gray, lighter than the walls, with a hint of the tan from the curtains. When Gene threw off the comforter, one side caught on the top of the iron and glass night table and almost knocked the lamp to the floor. The bed of heavy wrought iron provided solid support as Gene grabbed hold of a section of the curved iron at the foot and pushed himself up onto the floor.

He hit the floor and kicked a copy of *American Sphinx* across the room. It landed on one side with pages twisted back. After straightening out the pages and replacing the cover, he hid it in the bottom of the armoire under some maps and other papers. Kelly had read it, and she recommended it to him. But no one at Davenport Center had authorized him to read a book containing such controversial ideas. He knew he would be better off to hide it.

There was a photograph on the wall near the door to the bathroom. It was an old, black and white photograph depicting a boy of about eight or ten and a baby girl in a dress. The boy, a strained look on his face, held the girl. When Gene thought about the photograph, which he didn't on this occasion, it seemed to him that the boy didn't want to hold the girl. The faded caption read: "Marcus Gallagher caring for his younger sister Vivian."

Breakfast had been scheduled for 6:41 am, earlier than ever before. It was short, too, scheduled to end at 6:57. After breakfast Gene had time to brush his teeth, and then he was scheduled to report to Dr. Gallagher's second floor office at 7:03. His entire day had been blocked off. The next scheduled event was a late dinner. It was unusual to get such a schedule. The last time it happened, he had been scheduled to report to Alfred's lab. Bruce and Alfred were also there, and the three of them spent the day preparing for the trip to Ecuador.

On this occasion he didn't know who would be in Dr. Gallagher's office or how he would spend the rest of the day. Gene knew it wasn't likely that Dr. Gallagher would be there. He couldn't remember if he had ever seen Dr. Gallagher awake at 7:00 am before.

There were so many unresolved issues, from the blood tests Gene had manipulated to his impending marriage to Ms. Genetic Perfection to the incidents in the hallways with Sarah Vorschrift to the deaths in Ecuador. Discussions of these incidents would be trouble, and for the moment Gene wanted to avoid such discussions.

Putting thoughts of Dr. Gallagher to the side, Gene hoped to squeeze an extra couple of minutes out of his morning before he left for breakfast. Gene's shower was a fast one, using less time than had been allocated for it. Every movement was quick, directed. With his underwear, socks and shirt on, he knew he was a few minutes ahead of schedule. To get out of the bedroom he pushed an overstuffed chair covered in soft, rust-colored fabric to the side and jumped over a matching hassock.

The living room was as attractive as the bedroom. The ceiling was high. There were glass pyramid skylights along the outside wall like those which provided the roof for the grand entrance hall just inside the main entrance to the building. The sky above the glass pyramids was still black. Beneath the skylights were plants. A small tree of some kind reached almost to the ceiling, and beside that tree was a painting which depicted a scene from the 1924 Kansas Free Fair. A crowded wooden stage was festooned with red, white and blue banners. A man stood behind a huge podium, and a member of each of the four groups behind him carried a placard tacked to the top of a pole. The placards read, "Small Family," "Average Family," "Large Family" and "Grade A Individuals."

Cream-colored loveseats faced each other across a cast iron coffee table with a glass top which matched the furniture in the bedroom. There was a large, dark wood shelf unit on one wall with aged looking, yellow columns running from floor to ceiling on either side. On the coffee table was a copy of *The New Decalogue of Science*.

Gene went to the office area in the far corner of the living room. There he fell into the wooden chair behind his small oak desk. Using both hands, he wrapped several sheets of used paper over the top of a yellow pad and started doing some calculations. There were about 280 million people living in the United States, he guessed. Five percent of that number was 14 million people. If there were 6 billion people in the world, then 5 percent of the world population would be 300 million people. These numbers bothered Gene. There was a scowl on his face as though he had eaten something sour.

He wasn't sure that the numbers were right. He didn't really know the population of the United States or the world, and he wasn't sure about the five percent. He had always thought that about 5% of the population carried the cystic fibrosis gene, but he knew the number didn't tell the whole story. The rate of occurrence of the gene varied in different ethnic and racial groups around the world, but he couldn't remember what the differences were. All that remained in his mind was the general number of 5%. That bothered him. When a half of a percent error in the frequency of occurrence would mean that 30 million people might survive or die, the difference between 4.5% or 5% and 5.5% was important.

Gene resolved that he would talk to Dr. Gallagher at the first opportunity. It would be difficult. It amounted to asking questions about Davenport Center and the activities there. That violated the seventh principle. And it would be obvious to Dr. Gallagher that those questions could only be based upon suppositions and analysis that were the result of independent thought. That violated the second principle. Gene had often been instructed to recite, "Independent thought more than anything else has the power to destroy us and thereby prevent us from doing the good which we have set out to do."

There were other issues as well, even more serious than violations of principles 2 and 7. Gene had pledged to follow the direction of Dr. Gallagher. That was, as Gene had always been told it should be, contained in the first principle. "I pledge my being, my heart and my spirit to be faithful to the will and direction of Dr. Gallagher. I will obey without question all orders of Dr. Gallagher and of my paladin appointed by Dr. Gallagher. I recognize this as the only true path to happiness and success." And Gene had taken an oath. As he took the oath, he repeated the words, "I will follow without hesitation or question the principles and all orders and instructions from Dr. Gallagher."

What was happening at Davenport Center bothered Gene. At times he knew it was wrong. At times he thought it was wrong. At times he wasn't sure he knew what was right and what was wrong. Hadn't he taken an oath to follow the orders of Dr. Gallagher? Didn't he believe in the principles of Davenport Center? To discuss this matter with Dr. Gallagher, wouldn't he have to expose his weakness, his inability to follow the principles of Davenport Center? Wouldn't he have to turn everything he believed in on its ear? His body ached. The conflict made him feel as though his skull might explode.

What if Dr. Gallagher asked him to destroy the lives of 14 million people or 300 million people? The people would be gone, and their deaths would wreak havoc on the lives millions more who suffered the loss of combo members and friends and associates. It would be wrong. Nothing could be more obvious than that. And if he were to decide that what Dr. Gallagher was doing was wrong, would he have the will to resist? Would he have the capacity to do what was right? Would he have the capacity to know what was right?

Gene wondered whether he could simply decide not to follow Dr. Gallagher based on a whim and what might be the most irrational of assumptions. What Gene knew and didn't know seemed so ephemeral to him. Should he, based on random pieces of unverified information, simply decide to change paths? Should he ignore the leadership and direction of the man who, of everyone on Earth, had done the most for him? Should he ignore the fact that Dr. Gallagher had provided him with direction and a purpose in life? Should he ignore Dr. Gallagher's ultimate goal of the betterment of mankind? Should he turn against the man who more than anyone else had been kind, thoughtful and loving toward him? With the information he had, with his limited understanding, should he betray his oath and the man who had rescued him from the downward spiral which had consumed his life?

Just after 7:00 am, Gene headed for Dr. Gallagher's second floor office. The waiting area was accessible by the public via Dr. Gallagher's secretary's office which opened onto the circular corridor in the doughnut shaped center portion of the building. It was also accessible from the small vestibule in the Mission and Conscience Department, an area of the building open only to components, where he and Dr. Gallagher had met. Gene hesitated for a moment in the vestibule. The room was small, furnished like a living room with a carpet of royal blue and gold and furniture of dark hickory. The chair rail and ceiling molding were white wood with gold accents, and there was a large painting in a dark wood frame with gold highlights on one side of the room, between the two chairs. The painting depicted a burning mansion in the foreground and a towering castle behind it. The mansion doors were locked, and terrified guests clawed at the windows in a vain effort to escape. Engraved in a brass plate at the bottom of the painting were the words "Banquet Near Tîrgoviste Castle."

Gene pulled open the door to the waiting area. That area and Dr. Gallagher's second floor office were covered with the same blue and gold carpet used in the vestibule. The door to the Mission and Conscience Department pushed itself shut with some force. From the waiting room side, the door, once closed, no longer looked like a door. It looked just like the rest of the wall. Even if someone in the waiting room found the door, it would not be possible to open it without an ID card with the correct magnetic code.

"Gene," said Dr. Gallagher, "it's so good to see you." He grabbed Gene and gave him a bear hug. Gene hugged back. The embrace was a comfortable one.

"It's good to see you, Father."

"Come on in. We've got many things to discuss, and I doubt we have much time."

They went from the waiting room into the office, and Dr. Gallagher closed the door behind them. The arrangement of the furniture was the same as in the third floor office, but the color scheme and accents were different. Here the dominant colors were the royal blue and gold of the carpet with dark wood and accents of white. The burgundy leather of the wing chairs had been replaced with a heavy weave fabric of various shades of blue with specks of gold and white. Across from Dr. Gallagher's desk was an oil portrait of Karl Pearson with an icy, remote expression. Not so different from Alfred, Gene thought. The frame was the same as that used for the burning mansion, dark wood with gold highlights.

Behind Dr. Gallagher's desk in a blue enamel frame accented by a pair of fine gold lines was a framed copy of the United States Supreme Court opinion *Buck vs. Bell*. On a table by one wall were several copies of a book, *The Jukes in 1915*.

Gene sat in one of the wing chairs in front of the desk.

"We've got a serious problem," said Dr. Gallagher. "And I believe you're the best person to handle it. Marion is going to be here this morning, and I think she intends to bring along an auditor or two. The visit was supposed to be a surprise, but it isn't. The warning has given us an opportunity to take some steps so that we can be ready for her."

Gene was interested in the visit by Marion, but he was still agitated by his thoughts earlier that morning. The two men were alone. This would be an opportunity to talk to Dr. Gallagher, and Gene intended to take advantage of it.

"This woman continues to drive me crazy," said Dr. Gallagher. "She imagines we're doing something horrible out here."

"I know," said Gene.

"She is a native of the parched land. Her appearance is not abhorrent, but she is a serpent. An appealing appearance can't hide her intention to mislead, confuse and destroy." Dr. Gallagher dropped into the chair behind his desk. "I'm going to take care of her. I'm looking at various alternatives, but in the mean time, I want you to be responsible for dealing with her. Show her around. You know where she can go and where she can't."

"Yes."

"Her disposition can change in an instant. Her natural state is corrupt, vicious and cruel, and those characteristics she cannot hide from us. We've got boxes and boxes of documents for her auditors to scrutinize. You take her over when she gets here."

"Where?"

"All the material is in the west wing, as far away from here as I can get her. For today the room is known as our document storage facility, but of course you'll realize that it's one of our training rooms. We moved the stuff in yesterday. Here." Dr. Gallagher handed Gene a paper. "The room number is on here. As for Marion, we've been over this before. You know what to tell her. I know that you have the natural talent for handling people, even such a vicious, malevolent woman."

Dr. Gallagher pointed at the document he had just handed Gene. "I will talk to Sarah today. For the moment, the things you need to know are on that paper. Sarah will help you with anything else you need."

"Everything she's going to want isn't in that room, although there is plenty of paper there. That paper I gave you has a list of the things that she will eventually figure out that she wants. Whether she'll figure it out today or next year, I don't know. You'll have to use your judgement in dealing with the stuff. Obviously you won't show her the paper I gave you. We've pulled twenty or thirty things that I know her auditors are going to want. The stuff ranges from every document relating to a particular contract or task order to individual documents such as receipts and purchase authorizations. Everything's on that list, what the document or documents are, and where you can find them. Don't show her any of those things today. She probably won't realize these things are missing for weeks. Then, for every four or five additional things she wants, show her one. Tell her we're looking for the other stuff. Stretch it out as long as you can. Try to take a year or two. We can discuss strategy as things move along. The objective is to use this missing material to distract her. I don't know. Maybe she won't even figure out that this stuff is missing."

"Father," said Gene, "there are some things I need to talk to you about."

"What things?"

"I have concerns. I want to talk about some of the work we do here."

"What exactly?"

"As you know, I am bothered by the deaths in Ecuador. I want to talk about the implications of those deaths. And my new assignment..."

"Oh, yes," said Dr. Gallagher, interrupting Gene. "These are important things, and we have a number of other matters to resolve. I am ... ."

The phone on Dr. Gallagher's desk rang.

"I... uh... don't let her out of your sight while she's here," said Dr. Gallagher. He picked up the phone. "Yes."

The door to the office popped open.

"Hello?" said Dr. Gallagher into the phone.

Marion stormed into the room. Gene folded the paper Dr. Gallagher had given him and slid it into his pants pocket. Dr. Gallagher dropped the phone back into its cradle.

"Wait," shouted Sarah Vorschrift who followed her in. "You're not allowed to barge in here."

"Yes I am," said Marion. She glared at Dr. Gallagher. "I know you have misspent funds out here, and I'm not going to stop until I get you under control."

"Marion," said Dr. Gallagher, "what a surprise. I didn't know you were coming out here today. Even so, it's great to see you. I'm so glad you're here."

"You must be working on a winged swine project," said Marion.

"We would," said Dr. Gallagher, "but no money." He smiled and he came around the desk and started to put his arm around Marion.

"Don't do that," said Marion. "Your physical presence saps my energy."

Dr. Gallagher moved to where he could see several people in the waiting room. "I see you brought some friends with you," he said. "Come on in." Dr. Gallagher swung his arm high into the air and waved for the four serious looking men and one even more serious looking woman to come into the office. "Marion, please sit down."

Gene held out his hand to Marion.

"Dr. Nolan," said Marion. She nodded at Gene, and the anger in her face softened.

Dr. Gallagher went back behind his desk. "What a pleasure that you've all come," said Dr. Gallagher. "What can we do to make your visit a pleasant one?"

"We're here to conduct an audit," said Marion. "All we need is access to your accounting records."

"Dr. Nolan can take you over to our record storage room. I'm sure that you can find whatever it is that you're looking for."

"All we want are the records."

Everyone in the room was seated except for one of the auditors who stood next to the loveseat and Sarah Vorschrift who guarded the door with an agitated look on her face. Dr. Gallagher rose from behind his desk and went over next to Ms. Vorschrift.

"You will have access to the records."

"After we've spent some time with the records," said Marion. "I want to talk to you."

"I'm afraid that will be impossible," said Dr. Gallagher. "I'm leaving the island right now. Perhaps we can talk when I return."

"You'll be back this afternoon!" commanded Marion.

"No. I don't think so. I've left you in the best of hands. I'm sure you'll find everything you need." With that Dr. Gallagher slipped past Sarah, used his ID card to open the door from the waiting room to the Mission and Conscience Department and let it close behind him.

Marion jumped to her feet, but Ms. Vorschrift blocked her entrance to the waiting room. "Come back here," shouted Marion. "Come back here, you coward." She pushed her way past Ms. Vorschrift. Marion ran her hands over the wall looking for a door. "Where did he go?" she shouted at Ms. Vorschrift.

"He went out over there," said Ms. Vorschrift. She pointed to the door on the other side of the room, the one that led through the secretary's office and out into the circular corridor.

Marion dashed out into the hallway and after looking in both directions along the circular corridor, headed back toward the office muttering. "If the Prince of Darkness has a mystical castle with hidden entrances and compartments, this is what it would look like." She entered the office. "All right, Gene," said Marion in a louder, pleasant voice. "That man makes me so angry."

Gene took Marion and the auditors over to the room on the second floor of the west wing where the document boxes had been stacked.

"This is where the materials you are looking for are stored," said Gene. He opened the door with a swipe of the ID card which hung on a chain around his neck. The ID card hung outside his shirt. The aaskouandy hung on its burgundy string underneath his shirt.

The room was large and bright with fluorescent light. It was as gray as Marion's office was brown. Charcoal gray plastic chairs on shiny round, silver legs were lined up behind row after row of sturdy tables with medium gray plastic surfaces. The square table legs rested on commercial grade carpet of a shade of gray between the color of the tabletops and the color of the molded chairs. The back wall had been covered from floor to ceiling, from light gray wall to light gray wall with white record storage boxes. A pervasive musty smell filled the room.

The auditors began to examine the boxes which had been stacked along the back wall to a depth of four boxes from the floor up to about four feet and to a depth of three boxes from there up to the ceiling. Marion and Gene watched from a location near the door. Soon each auditor was working in silence, having claimed several boxes and a table.

"Let's go get something to drink," said Marion.

"All right," Gene said.

They went to the cafeteria in the central part of Davenport Center on the second floor, passing the pantry where Gene had talked to Kelly on the morning when he returned from Ecuador. Marion and Gene each got a cup of coffee and sat in a windowless section of the cafeteria which had the carpet, tables and chairs similar to the ones in the room where the auditors worked. The tables were wider. Not much else was different.

Gene felt like he had the unaccountability of a VTS. He was required to keep an eye on Marion, but that provided a sort of freedom of movement to which he was not accustomed. Without Marion, coffee would be unavailable except when it was on the schedule.

Marion's permanent frown dominated her face, but it was clear to Gene that she was making a distinct effort to smile. He felt from her the same kindness and interest in him that he had felt the first time they met.

"I think there are more documents," said Gene, referring to the documents on the list Dr. Gallagher had given him. "I'll search for them. I'll tell you what to ask for."

Chapter 24

Amniocentesis

The next morning Gene sat at the desk in the back of his lab. He wanted to see Kelly. She had said she wanted them to spend more time together. He wanted that too. But her demand that he just get on the ferry and not look back didn't make sense to him. There was trouble at Davenport Center, and if there was something he could do to straighten it out, he would do it. That would take a little time, but Kelly said there was no time. Now. She wanted him to leave now. The sound of her words pounded in his brain.

Could he just leave Davenport Center? It had played such an important part in the transformation of his life. It was the only place he had felt comfortable and loved and important since his mother died. Since before that really. Since his father left him. Maybe before that. Maybe since he was born.

He loved Kelly. He had admitted that the last time they were together. It was an admission both to her and to himself. But it wasn't like he knew her. Would it make any sense to leave the stability, the comfort, the excitement of Davenport Center for a woman he loved but didn't know?

The entrance that Gene used to enter the Mission and Conscience Department from the public area of the east wing was through a plain, unmarked door that looked just like any other door on a hallway that looked just like any other hallway. The place where Gene and Kelly left their notes and marked the doorframe was in the public area of the east wing not too far from the entrance to the Mission and Conscience Department.

There were not as many opportunities for Gene to get into the public areas as he would have liked. There was the omnipresent risk of running into Sarah Vorschrift who in an instant recognized any action or behavior which had not been scheduled. At every opportunity he had checked the doorframe, looking for a mark from Kelly. Each time he had made the dangerous journey to the public corridor, he had been disappointed.

The day after Marion's visit was to be a busy day for Gene. He was scheduled to prepare a report concerning the time he spent with Marion. After that, the documents which had been hidden from the auditors had to be reviewed and cataloged. During that process he could identify the most important ones to tell Marion about. And medical tests, chemical analysis of various specimens which he had been given, were scheduled for the afternoon. The work load was heavy and the time was short. However the hidden documents were spread throughout Davenport Center. That would give him more freedom of movement than on a typical day.

He decided to try to meet Kelly in one of the document rooms. After he composed the note, he headed for the public hallway. Although he passed several violet clad components and one paladin in violet with silver piping, he didn't run into Ms. Vorschrift. The locations of the hiding place for the note and of the doorframe to be marked had been selected because they were close to the lab where Kelly worked and not too far from the nondescript entrance to the Mission and Conscience Department. With the note in place, he went down the hall and pulled a marker from his pocket.

"It's you," said Kelly in a loud voice just after he turned toward the wall with raised marker in hand.

He spun from the doorframe before the felt tip of the marker had touched the cream colored paint. Kelly was sixty feet down the hall. The hall had been empty a second before. If it hadn't been, he never would have turned toward the wall to place his mark.

"I want to talk to you," she shouted, as she walked toward him.

He wanted to see her too, but the commotion she was making brought terror to his eyes. He pointed to the place where he had hidden the note and started walking back toward the Mission and Conscience Department at a fast pace.

"Don't you run away from me," shouted Kelly as she dashed down the corridor after him.

Gene stopped. When Kelly caught up with him, she put her hand on his chest, pushing him against the wall.

"Do you know what you've done to me?" asked Kelly.

Gene knew this noise would bring Ms. Vorschrift or worse, if worse could be imagined. His eyes bounced up and down the still empty corridor where he was pinned against the wall.

"I don't think I know the answer to that question," said Gene. He squirmed from beneath her finger, crossed to the other side of the hall and with his ID card opened one of the doors. "In here."

There was pain in Kelly's face, but she followed Gene into the small room which turned out to be a darkroom. Gene flipped a light switch, and a bare incandescent bulb on the ceiling struggled to illuminate the black walls. She pushed the door closed.

"What's wrong?" asked Gene. There was a serious problem. He knew it. He had never seen her like this.

"It's bad."

Gene was concerned. He went to hug her, but she pushed him away. He leaned against the black slate countertop as close to her as she would let him be. "Tell me what it is."

"I know I should have told you this before. I just didn't want to given the way things have been between us lately."

"What are you talking about? What should you have told me?"

"I'm pregnant." She held her hand up when he tried to approach her. "I'm four months pregnant."

"Four months?"

"I found out right before you disappeared for over a month, and when you got back, well…"

"It's not how I envisioned us starting a life together, but having a baby with you would really be something."

"You're not having the baby. I'm having the baby. You've already done your part. After that all you've done is abandon me."

"I haven't abandoned you. I'm not going to abandon you." Gene hated the idea that he would abandon anyone he loved. He was angry at Kelly for even suggesting that he would do such a thing. He knew what it was to be abandoned, and that was not what he had done. He tried to calm himself before he spoke to her again. "I want to go through this with you," said Gene. "We'll go through this together. I wanted to talk to you. I wrote you a note today. You know that."

"That's good. A note every week or so, that's what I'm looking for in life. Who would want to be bothered by all of those conversations we might have had? And what about meals together? We've never had a meal together, but what couple would want that? In fact we've never gone anywhere together or done anything together, and now I find you've written me a note. Who would want those other things when they could have a note every now and then?"

"I wanted to talk to you. I'm in love with you. I wanted to talk."

"I want more than notes and talk."

"So do I. There'll be more. Things are bad for me here right now. I've got to get some things straightened out."

"Go ahead. Take your time, two days, two weeks, twenty years. Take your time."

"I want to be with you," said Gene.

"Then let's get off this island right now."

"I can't."

"When?"

"Soon. After Christmas or after New Years Day. A couple of weeks."

"That's good. Why should we spend Christmas together?"

"I want to be with you." Gene tried to hug her again, but she pushed him away. "I want us to go through this together."

"There's more." Kelly looked tired. There was fear in her eyes.

"What?" asked Gene.

"I don't know what to think. I don't know what to do. I'm terrified. You don't know the whole story. I've just come from the doctor. It's deformed, and I'm afraid of it. This baby has muscular dystrophy."

"How could you know that?"

"My doctor did tests."

"What tests? Amniocentesis? DNA?"

"You tell me what tests. You're the doctor."

"These tests are not typical for a woman your age. Why would you have these tests?"

"Would you listen to me?" said Kelly. Water welled in her eyes, but she held back any tears. "You're the doctor. I don't know. The doctor I went to said the tests were normal. She said she does them on every pregnant woman to be certain the baby will be healthy."

"What doctor? How did you find this doctor?"

"She's my gynecologist. She came with this job. She doesn't cost anything. Everything is free, office visits, tests, medication... everything."

"Is she here at Davenport Center?"

"No. In Easton. But Davenport Center pays the bills."

"What kind of muscular dystrophy?" asked Gene.

"Kind? That's good. Let's compare diseases. I want to know which genes go where and how the chemicals mess up the cells. We can compare the cell damage for this disease with the cell damage from other diseases. Messed up cells, that will be the topic of our discussion. That way we won't have to deal with the problem or talk about this baby."

Gene tried to figure out what he could say without setting Kelly off. "What did the doctor say?" he asked.

"It's a boy. The baby's going to be a boy. She said the baby would develop initial symptoms between 2 and 5. He would have trouble getting off the floor or climbing stairs and he would fall easily. She was real graphic when she talked about what would happen. She said the muscles in his legs would be too short. Those muscles would pull his foot down, so he would have to walk on his toes. He wouldn't be able to straighten his foot after a time. She talked about severing the tendons. He would be in a wheelchair by the time he is 13, and then he would die around 20. I don't know what to do. I'm terrified of this."

"I'm here for you," said Gene. "I love you."

From Kelly's description Gene thought that the baby had Duchenne muscular dystrophy. Gene had studied muscular dystrophy, and some of the doctors at Davenport Center did work on the disease. It was an X-chromosome linked genetic disease which showed up almost exclusively in boys. Women had two X-chromosomes. Women who were carriers of the disease had one good X-chromosome and one that carried Duchenne muscular dystrophy. Carriers did not develop the disease, because they still had one good X-chromosome. Males on the other hand had one X and one Y-chromosome, and the X-chromosome always came from the mother. An X-chromosome from the father resulted in a female child, and a Y-chromosome from the father resulted in a male child. When a boy received the disease carrying X-chromosome from his mother, he would develop the disease. 50% of the male children born to a female carrier would receive the gene and develop the disease, and 50% of the male children would be born without the gene. 50% of the female children would be born without the gene, and 50% of the female children would be carriers of the gene. Although the female children with the gene would not develop the disease, they could pass the gene to their children. In a significant percentage of the cases of Duchenne muscular dystrophy, about one-third, the mother is not a carrier. In those cases the disease is the result of a new mutation. Gene would tell Kelly everything he knew about muscular dystrophy when she was ready to hear about it.

"My gynecologist is telling me I have to get an abortion," said Kelly. "She told me that I have no choice. She said I have to get an abortion."

Gene turned toward her and embraced her, and this time she let him.

Chapter 25

Agamemnon

"We're making real progress toward the elimination of genetic disease," said Dr. Gallagher as a tray-laden waitress approached.

Dr. Gallagher sat across the table from a man in a tan and gray plaid sports jacket. The man, apparently not a slave to fashion, wore a drab olive, narrow tie, and the collar on his synthetic looking blue shirt was twisted to the side. The heel of one of his cowboy boots rested on the wooden base of the table, and his black western style hat was on the seat of the chair next to him. They were in O'Donnell's, a traditional seafood restaurant on the north edge of Bethesda. The restaurant was convenient, only a block or so from the NIH campus, and viewed as a real treat by Dr. Gallagher's guest. From the window facing Rosedale Avenue, an asphalt parking lot was visible across the street. In the room where they were seated, one wall was decorated with a huge net of black string, some cork floats and a painting of a lighthouse on the Chesapeake Bay.

The waitress served baked salmon to Dr. Gallagher and a combination plate with some crab and some lobster salad to his guest.

"Best lobster salad in Washington," said the man in his Oklahoma accent.

"Yes. The food is good here." Dr. Gallagher continued, apparently unbothered by the fact that the man had ignored his earlier comment. "And our Board of Governors is composed of some of the most prestigious names in medical research. Two members have been recipients of the Nobel Prize. We have some of the most highly respected authorities in genetic..."

"Come on Marcus," said the man, interrupting Dr. Gallagher. "You're a good guy. I know that. I know you've got enough brains out there to sink that island. Why are you talking to me about this stuff?"

"You've got a woman working for you. Her name is Marion Latterner. She's causing me trouble."

"Well, I don't want that." Each word was clear, sprinkled with more than a hint of his western accent. "I was hoping to enjoy a great meal in peace. They bother me about this stuff across the street all day long."

"I know," said Dr. Gallagher. "I'm sorry to bring this up. All of these technical and administrative details are aggravating. The thing is, I felt like I had no alternative but to bring this to your attention."

"Well I don't want my people running around causing trouble."

"I know that."

"Who is this woman again?"

"Her name is Marion Latterner. She works for Peter Snyder."

"Well, I don't know. I don't know who she is. They don't tell me hardly anything about what goes on over there. Every time I want to know something, I have to go find out for myself. I'll look into this, and I'll do what I can. What do you want me to do with her?"

~ ~ ~

That afternoon Dr. Gallagher was in the Hart Senate Office Building in Washington. He walked along a corridor which was open on one side and overlooked the giant atrium. The atrium was higher and square but otherwise not so different from the one at Davenport Center. After reaching the office of the senior senator from the state of Maryland, it wasn't long before she came to meet him.

"Senator," said Dr. Gallagher, "it's so good to see you."

"Yes," she answered, "it's good to see you too, Marcus. It's always good to talk to the chief architect of a facility that makes Maryland famous. What brings you here today?"

"Have you got a few minutes?"

"Yes. Come on back."

They started back toward the Senator's office.

"I've been having this trouble," said Dr. Gallagher as they walked, "with NIH. I am hoping that you will be able to help me with it."

"I would certainly be interested in hearing about it."

After Dr. Gallagher finished the discussion, he headed toward the office of the other senator from Maryland. Finished there, he headed over to talk to some of the Members of the House of Representatives.

~ ~ ~

Gene hid the hypodermic needle and test tube in the pocket of his lab coat. There were other things too, a translucent rubber strip to restrict blood flow, cotton, a small bottle of disinfectant, some adhesive tape. Kelly and Gene were going to meet that afternoon in one of the document rooms, as Gene had suggested in his note.

After Gene and Kelly had talked that morning, Gene decided that he wanted to test Kelly to find if she was a carrier of genetic disease. Specifically, he wanted to know if she was a carrier of the cystic fibrosis gene. When they were having a clandestine relationship and occasional sex, it didn't seem important. Now there was a baby, and he and Kelly were talking about some kind of more permanent relationship. And Alfred was loose with the vaccine or whatever it was he had used in Ecuador. He believed that, despite Alfred's and Dr. Gallagher's reviews, the test he had developed and used in Ecuador was safe, but he couldn't have Kelly running around Davenport Center with a luminescent green glow emanating from her throat. He would take her blood back to the DNA typing lab and analyze it along with other samples.

Soon Gene was in the west wing, on the second floor, in a small, windowless storage room which was about the size of two combined walk-in closets. Shelves of gray metal were spaced to hold row after row of document storage boxes. There was a small, sturdy table with a folding metal chair at one end of the room. A box of documents rested on the table. Gene flipped through the papers in an effort to review them, but as he waited for Kelly, it was difficult to focus.

He thought about what life would be like with Kelly. Independent decision-making. That was normal wasn't it? His mother used to tell him that it was an advantage for him that she had not been around so much when he was small.

"This allows you to make independent decisions," his mother would say.

But he wondered whether he could prosper or even survive outside of the structured environment of Davenport Center. It was that structured environment which had saved his life. The direction and focus and love provided by Dr. Gallagher created a safe haven where Gene had been able to prosper and succeed.

The baby pushed its way into the conscious regions of his mind. What would it be like to care for a child with muscular dystrophy? What if Kelly was a carrier of the cystic fibrosis gene? He knew he wasn't a carrier, but what if the child was also?

Kelly pushed open the door.

"How do you feel?" asked Gene. He stood behind the table.

"It's too much. This is all too much for me."

He approached her, and she let him hug her.

"I've got nowhere to turn," said Kelly. "I can't talk to anybody. I don't know what to do."

"We have some time," said Gene. "You're only four months pregnant."

"She's pressuring me to have an abortion."

"I know."

"She wants me to abort this baby."

"Maybe we should give this baby a name. Not the real name. Not the name he would have, but just a temporary name, so we can refer to him without saying 'it' or 'the baby.'"

"All right," said Kelly. "How about Agamemnon?"

Gene twisted his head to the side and pressed his lips together. "Ok," he said. "Agamemnon it is."

"She wants me to abort Agamemnon."

"How do you feel about it?"

"I don't know. I want to have Agamemnon. I want our relationship, yours and mine, to be stable. But our relationship isn't stable. It isn't even a relationship. I don't want to have an abortion. I want to raise and love Agamemnon. I don't want him to suffer a life of pain. I don't want him to live in a wheelchair. I don't want him to deteriorate to a mass of unresponsive muscles. I don't want Agamemnon to die at 20." Her voice was even and steady.

"This is a horrible thing," said Gene.

"What about you?"

"I don't know. I love you, and I know that all of this has been difficult for you to deal with on your own. But I can't say that I'm happy about having a child that has muscular dystrophy. It's a frustrating concept to invest all of that energy and money in a child that I know is going to die."

"What does that mean? I don't understand. Are you saying that you want me to have an abortion too?"

"That's not what I'm saying. I don't know. We need to think about it. Maybe."

They stood in silence for a moment, leaning against shelved storage boxes. Gene moved the box off the table and pushed the papers to the side. He sat on the table and motioned for Kelly to sit beside him.

"I need to take some blood," said Gene.

"Blood?" asked Kelly. Her voice was loud. The evenness was gone. The sound was closer to a squawk. It reminded Gene of the harpy eagle he had set free in Ecuador. "You need to take blood?"

"Yes."

"Another test?" Her voice got louder still. "Another test? You want to do another test?"

"Yes." Gene's voice was soft, gentle.

"You know what happened the last time I got one of these tests! I found out that Agamemnon was going to die. You want me to go through that again?"

"No! No. Of course not. But I need to take blood." His manner was comforting. His voice had a reassuring quality about it. "I would like to do a test."

"What test?"

"I don't want to alarm you, I just want to find out more about what is going on with you and this pregnancy. I want to find out if you carry certain genes."

"If I do, does that mean Agamemnon will have another disease?"

"It's difficult to say, but it is extremely unlikely."

"Then why do you need to know?"

205

"I'm a scientist and a doctor. I will tell you everything that I discover. I'm not trying to keep any secrets from you."

"Oh, all right," said Kelly. She looked tired and worn. The skin on her face was drawn tight. Her mouth was pulled into a frown that resembled the permanent one on Marion's face. Whatever ability she might have had to resist on other occasions seemed lost. Only exhaustion remained. She would be compliant.

Gene guided her to the chair behind the metal table. Neither spoke. When the blood had been drawn, Gene slid the test tube with the rust red fluid into his lab coat pocket and taped a cotton ball in place over the tiny puncture wound.

Chapter 26

Over It Now

The next day Gene was scheduled to meet with Alfred for two hours and seven minutes starting at 9:39 am. Gene entered Alfred's lab right on time.

"I wanted to spend some time with you this morning," said Alfred. "We have been working together for a time, and I think we will work even more closely in the future."

"Yes," said Gene. "All right."

Alfred gestured for Gene to close the door behind him.

Gene hated Alfred. That was a violation of the sixth principle. "I will have no likes or dislikes." But he knew better than to show it. The man seemed cold, calculating, impersonal and dangerous. As far as Gene could tell he had murdered the people in Ecuador and told Dr. Gallagher that Gene was responsible. And he had murdered Bruce. That would have been a violation of the ninth principle. "I will not physically, verbally or by thought attack Dr. Gallagher, any paladin or any component." Did the paladins have a different set of principles? That was possible. And was Gene violating the ninth principle that very moment by thinking about Alfred in this way?

Gene wondered what he might do that would cause Alfred to murder him. Maybe Alfred would keep both of his ears.

Then there was Kelly and the life together that the two of them had talked about. Maybe that life and the thought of raising a family were only the most ephemeral of dreams, a fantasy that would remain forever unfulfilled.

"There is a research project you are to handle," said Alfred. "Our time together this morning will be divided into three parts. During the first part of the meeting I will outline the project for you. After that, for the second part of the meeting, we will spend a few minutes getting to know each other better. The last part of our time together will be spent discussing the project. You will need to understand what is required and the deadlines involved."

"Ok." Alfred seemed more distant and more mechanical than usual.

They moved to the back of the lab. Alfred sat in the chair behind the desk. Gene's hair pressed into the fabric of the burgundy cubical partition, as he sat in the heavy chair of red fabric and black metal tubing. The carpet on the floor in the office area of the lab felt soft and strange. There was no carpet in Gene's lab.

"This is an overview," said Alfred.

"Ok," said Gene.

"This is a two-part project with one objective. We want to know how to get at various genetic diseases. That's the objective. Part 1. You will do a thorough review of the literature and all reference sources. Based on that review you will summarize, catalog and present all currently available information concerning every known genetic disorder. Part 2. You will identify research needs. Where information is not available, you will a design a plan for the research that would be necessary if we are to have the information we need." Except for a single sheet of paper in the center, there was nothing that could be described as clutter on Alfred's desk. As he talked, his eyes were fixed on the paper.

"For the moment," continued Alfred, "let's look at dividing the results of your work into five different categories. Those categories would be: dominant genetic disorders; recessive disorders where the person had one gene but does not express the disease; recessive genetic disorders where the person has both genes and expresses the disease; x-linked genetic disorders where the female carrier has one copy of the gene; and x-linked genetic disorders where the disease is expressed. During the third part of this meeting we can discuss and analyze whether there is a better way to present the results of your research. Maybe you've got some ideas."

"Those categories make sense to me," said Gene. He had noticed before how Alfred had a way of going into too much detail. Gene knew what Alfred wanted before even Alfred seemed to know. Gene listened for a good while, as Alfred provided an overview that was closer to a detailed view of the information he wanted.

"There are other factors," concluded Alfred. "Obviously we have a lot of this information, but it's spread all over the place. When you're done, all of the information will be in one place. It will be a real help in providing direction for our future work. Let's take a break now. We can spend some time getting to know each other. After that we can go over this literature search in more detail, and we can talk about planning future research."

Gene didn't want to get to know Alfred better. Even if he did, how would the whole thing start? Gene thought that Alfred would need to go first. The two men sat in silence for a moment.

"Did you fornicate before you came to Davenport Center?" asked Alfred after a time.

Gene didn't answer right away. He didn't want to answer the question at all. He thought about what he might say.

"Well... I...," said Gene.

"Perhaps we can start this a different way," said Alfred. "I'll tell you something about my life first."

Gene had never experienced anything quite so odd as this, not even at Davenport Center. He knew that something was driving Alfred to have this conversation. It wasn't Alfred's choice to talk to him, and Alfred didn't know how to go about it. There must be some Davenport Center rule about such conversations, Gene thought.

"Yes," said Gene. "That would be nice."

"I was married once, you know."

"No. I didn't know." Gene knew nothing about Alfred except that he worked at Davenport Center.

. "Yes. I was married, and I had a daughter."

Gene was surprised by this discussion. In speaking the words of the oath which they both had taken, each of them had pledged that he would renounce previous relationships. The oath provided, in part: "I hereby renounce all previous relationships and dedicate myself to the principles of Davenport Center. I retroactively and to perpetuity dissolve all previous and existing combo and other relationships, and from this point forward it is as though those relationships never existed."

"I was married and living in Illinois," continued Alfred. "That's where I was for my residency. It was the last year of my residency, and I was getting ready to move to Maryland to work at NIH. My wife was Chinese. Our daughter was 10, and she, my wife, wanted to take her to China for three months to introduce her to the Chinese half of her heritage. We couldn't afford it, but I agreed anyway. Our marriage wasn't the best, and I thought a three-month break wouldn't be so bad."

As Alfred spoke Gene became conscious of the fact that he had a slight accent. Gene had noticed the accent before, but unlike Henry Higgins he was unable to place it. He didn't know whether it was from some part of the United States or evidence of his having spoken some other language before mastering English. He wanted to ask Alfred where he had been born, but the seventh principle caused him some discomfort. According to that principle all of the information a component needed to know would be provided to him. That same principle prohibited questions. Even in the middle of this strange conversation, where it seemed like the effects of some of the principles were being held in abeyance for the moment and that Alfred might be, in his clumsy way, soliciting questions, Gene was uncomfortable asking one of a paladin.

"I took them to the airport in Chicago one morning. They were going to Seattle and from there to Tokyo and finally to Bejing. We didn't have much, and we had sold everything that wouldn't fit into suitcases. That was the last time I drove that car. It was a Buick, a blue one, a nice car but in bad condition. I didn't want to take a chance on driving it halfway across country. The car had already been sold. I dropped it off and took a cab back to the airport. That afternoon I flew into Baltimore. The next morning I woke up in a hotel room in the Bethesda Marriott on Pooks Hill, and I found out that the plane from Seattle to Tokyo, the one they had been on, crashed in the Pacific."

"I'm sorry," said Gene.

Alfred looked sad. Gene doubted that Alfred ever felt much that might be called an emotion, but what he seemed to be experiencing must have been the next best thing.

"Well it happened long ago. I'm over it now. The first thing I did was call the airline to see if they were on the plane. They were. I expected that. I mean why wouldn't they be? Still I wanted to check. After that all I had to do was sit and think. The plane had crashed in the middle of the ocean. There was no plane, no bodies, no effects, no nothing. I wasn't all that enthusiastic about the job at NIH, and while

I was in that hotel room on the seventh floor, I remembered meeting Dr. Gallagher and what he had said to me. I met him at a seminar in Washington earlier that year when I was there interviewing for the NIH job. He gave me his card and said, 'If you ever need any help with anything, just give me a call.' I remembered him. He made a deep impression on me. I'm not much into that spiritual nonsense, but I felt some connection with Dr. Gallagher the first time I met him. It was like there was this glow around him. I liked him. I wanted to know him, but I figured nothing would ever come of it. I had thought of him several times since he gave me that card, but I didn't have any reason to call him. Then I realized that day in the hotel room that I did need help."

"Dr. Gallagher would be able to help," said Gene.

"He did. He asked me to come out here to Davenport Center for a visit. I did, and I never left. I didn't show up for that job at NIH. I never called. I know I should have, but I didn't. I guess people don't show up for jobs sometimes. It probably wasn't the first time it ever happened to them. They must be over it by now. Sometimes I worry that we'll be dealing with some contract at NIH, and somebody will realize that I didn't show up to start that job. What about you?"

Alfred's story impacted Gene. It softened his dislike. But he didn't trust Alfred anymore than he would a fuzzy and appealing polar bear. For Alfred and the polar bear, Gene figured, the attraction and the viciousness were about the same. He remained uncomfortable with Alfred and avoided telling him anything about his life.

Chapter 27

A Curse on The Woman

Dr. Gallagher pulled open the door. He was in a suite in the Bethesda Marriott, the same hotel Alfred had stayed in when he left Illinois.

"Why are we meeting here?" asked Peter.

Dr. Gallagher pushed the door closed and gestured for Peter to take a seat at the table in the combination living room-dining room.

"I've got something important to talk to you about," said Dr. Gallagher, "and I didn't want to risk being overheard."

Peter sat at one end of a cherry dining table. Dr. Gallagher had already ordered lunch from room service, grilled salmon with broccoli and rice for himself and medallions of beef with mashed potatoes and carrots for Peter.

"The food looks good," said Peter.

"Yes," said Dr. Gallagher. "It is good. I knew you would like it. You might want to start while it's still hot."

Standing beside the table, ignoring his salmon for the moment, Dr. Gallagher pulled a letter from his pocket and dropped it on the table next to Peter's bread plate.

"Look at this," said Dr. Gallagher.

"Looks like a letter from NIH," said Peter.

"It is. That woman is asking about trips to Ecuador. She says she didn't find any information about trips to Ecuador when she was out at Davenport Center."

Peter looked over at the letter, a piece of beef dangled from a single prong of his fork. Wine sauce dripped onto the corner of the table.

"It looks like she just wants the accounting records."

"She didn't find any information about Ecuador," said Dr. Gallagher, his voice loud, "because I didn't give her any information about Ecuador. It's none of her damn business."

"All right." Peter stuffed the beef into his mouth. He pushed the paper toward Dr. Gallagher's empty chair as he chewed and swallowed the meat. "You're right. This is delicious."

"Peter," said Dr. Gallagher as he pulled his chair out on the other side of the table, "something's got to be done." His voice was softer, more conversational. "She must be stopped right now, at this moment. She cannot be permitted to proceed further. This destructive snooping must stop. I don't know what she might find. It doesn't make any difference. She's rabid. Whatever she finds, she'll blow it out of proportion. She'll take something that is nothing and bludgeon us to death with it. She'll use whatever she finds to destroy us. It won't make any difference to her whether what she finds is significant."

"I know you've been unhappy with her. But how much damage can she do? Is this different from other audits you've been through?" When Dr. Gallagher didn't respond immediately, Peter looked out the window. "You get a great view of Rock Creek Park from up here, and the Beltway too, for whatever that's worth. I'll bet it's nothing but four long lines of tail lights at rush hour."

"I see," said Dr. Gallagher, shaking his head and pursing his lips as though he were trying to get a bad taste out of his mouth. "Well, you're right. We've been through plenty of audits. It seems like there is some kind of audit every year or two. But this is different. The people who have conducted audits in the past were fair and evenhanded. You know. You've been involved. In the past auditors weren't looking to put us out of business. They would review the records, and if there was a receipt missing, maybe they would disallow the one expense or another. The whole process was typical of what you'd expect. They were looking for the types of problems that normally turn up, and the responses were sensible and justified. Those people were just doing their jobs. No bias. No vendetta. This woman is different. She wants me crucified. She won't stop until she's tasted blood."

"Yes," said Peter. "She's different. But what can I do? I've talked to her. You know that. She won't listen. She won't stop. She acts like she's got no boss, and she certainly doesn't take direction from me."

"That's my point." Dr. Gallagher still hadn't taken a bite of his salmon. He scooted his chair around to the side of the table, nearer to Peter. "Look Peter, I know that what we're doing is good. It's right. It's for the betterment of all mankind. The trouble is, not everyone would understand all of the things we've done. If Marion were to pull something out of context, she could cast a shadow over the whole operation. When you're doing something that's this big and that has been in operation for this many years, of course somebody could find something wrong. The government regulations are complicated, and I've never read them all. I'm sure you haven't either. There are bound to be violations of this rule and that. The result is that Marion is going to make us look bad, and there are bound to be technical violations of who knows what law. Some prosecutor is going to get it up his butt that this is a high profile case and a good way to make a name for himself, and you and I will end up in jail. That's what could happen here. That's what will happen here if she's not stopped."

Peter, who was about to slide a chunk of glazed carrot into his mouth, seemed to lose interest in his food. He dropped the fork back onto the china plate with a floral design around the edge.

"What do you want me to do?" asked Peter.

"I want you to stop her. I don't want you to talk to her anymore. Now is the time for action. Distract her. Change her direction. Send her to do research in Madagascar. I don't care. The time for talking is gone. I want her stopped, and I mean now. I don't want to hear another peep out of her."

"I'm going to need some money," said Peter.

~ ~ ~

· Late that afternoon Peter went to meet Richard at the bar on Rockville Pike where he had had lunch with Marion.

"What's up?" said Richard.

"Yeah," said Peter. They sat at the booth closet to the front of the bar, the same one he and Marion had used. "Rolling Rock," said Peter to the waitress. "Two bottles."

The waitress smiled, nodded and left.

"I've got a job for you," said Peter.

"Good. I could use the money. Dr. Gallagher again?"

"Yes. The pay's good, too."

Richard smiled. "Dr. Gallagher is my benefactor. He's done an awful lot for me. What job?"

"That woman. You met her here. I was having lunch with her. Do you remember?"

"Yeah. I do. She had this frown. Gray hair. I wasn't looking to bang her."

"That's the one."

"What does Dr. Gallagher want?"

"She's causing problems at work. Dr. Gallagher and I want her to stop causing problems. You've got to do something that's going to distract her. It has to be enough so that she won't be able to focus on her job."

"Ok. What?"

"I don't care. Dr. Gallagher doesn't care. It's your choice. Be creative."

The waitress returned with the beers.

"Everything you need is in here," said Peter after the waitress left. He handed Richard an envelope with a thousand dollars, a photograph of Marion and information about her family, home, office, schedule and habits. "You'll get twice what's in here when you're done, and of course we'll pick up any expenses."

~ ~ ~

It was night when Richard entered the Victorian house in Easton.

Candles burned on the table against the wall. A spindly column of smoke from incense rose toward the ceiling. On the round table in the center of the room a brass stand for the spherical crystal rested on the heavy red and gold fabric of the tablecloth. The flames of the candles were caught by the crystal ball and diffused by the imperfections inside.

216

"I see a man," said Madame Charlotte. "A small man with ... something's wrong with him ... giving you orders."

"No orders," said Richard. "They weren't orders. He hired me for a job. I'm an independent contractor. He doesn't give me orders. He told me what his needs are. I determine what services are appropriate to meet his needs. That chicken looking guy doesn't give me orders. Nobody gives me orders."

"Yes. Yes. I see that. A request for services."

"It's this woman. I've got to distract her."

"Ah, yes. The woman. I wondered who that woman was."

"What am I going to do with her?"

"I don't usually do it, but I can put a curse on the woman. There are certain things I will need. It will be expensive. Very expensive. I prefer to work with people to remove curses, but you need something else. I would not normally curse somebody. A curse can cause so much pain and anguish. I wouldn't do this for anybody. For you, Richard, I can do it."

"It has to be fast acting."

"You must join with me in this. To make it fast, we must work together. Your belief must be very strong. You need some men. I see one with different color hair."

"Who are those guys with the different hair? What are they doing?"

"They are men known to you. You will talk to them. I can see that. I see you talking to them. I can't understand all. There is wind or something. The sound is garbled. You talk. They talk. I can't make out the words."

~ ~ ~

That night Richard and Catherine sat on the sofa in the living room watching a movie when Kelly arrived home. Richard used a remote to turn off the stereo which he was using for the television sound.

"Babe," he said to Catherine, "you'd better beat your feet back to the bedroom. I've got something to say to Kelly."

"I should be able to hear that," said Catherine. "She's my daughter. I want to hear."

"I told you what to do. Beat your feet back to that bedroom or you're going to have more trouble doing it in a minute."

Catherine left the room.

"Sit," said Richard to Kelly who was standing by the door, her coat still on. Richard pointed to an overstuffed chair, the chair closest to the sofa.

"I'm not a dog," said Kelly.

"All right. Stand in the middle of the floor. I don't give a damn. I've got something to tell you, and I want you to listen good."

"Yeah. What?" Kelly took off her coat and hung it in the hall closet.

"Get your butt back in here. Don't leave the room when I'm talking to you."

Kelly returned to the living room but didn't respond.

"I don't want you to go back to your house for any reason."

"I'll do what I want."

"No. That's where you're wrong. You'll do what I want. I'd hate to see you or your mother get hurt because you went back there."

"Are you threatening me?"

"Yes."

Kelly glared at him.

"I'm telling you that you don't go there no matter what. I don't want you using that house as a bang palace. You'd have every dick in Dorchester County up that twat of yours if you had your way. I wouldn't be surprised if you've had more than half of them already."

"You are disgusting slime."

"Talk sweet to me, baby. I like it when you talk sweet."

"I'm paying rent on that house."

"And you'd better keep it up. I might use that place from time to time, and I don't want your greasy butt out there screwing things up."

"What if I need something?"

"You don't need a damn thing. If you want something, you tell me. I'll get it for you if you really need it and if I feel like it. You go by that place, and I'm telling you, you'll wish you hadn't."

Chapter 28

What Kind of Wife

When Gene woke up the next morning he was aching to see Kelly. Every moment he could spend with her had become precious to him. He had completed his genetic testing, and besides the expected gene for Duchennes Muscular Dystrophy, he had discovered that Kelly was a cystic fibrosis carrier, and that terrified him.

How much longer would he be able to spend time with her? Would she still be alive in a year? Gene didn't know, and he was frightened by the knowledge that if she died soon, which he thought was likely, he would have played an important part in causing that death even if at the time he had been unaware of the significance of the support he provided.

He would stop Dr. Gallagher and Alfred if he could, and then he would leave Davenport Center. The tumultuous, chaotic, unpredictable world outside of Davenport Center would be a challenge for him, but he would meet that challenge. And he would miss the happiness, the contentment, the excitement and the challenge he once felt working for Dr. Gallagher.

The night before, when he got his schedule for the day, he had written a note to Kelly. He would put it in place after breakfast, and he hoped that she would be able to meet him that afternoon in the west wing. His schedule was always demanding, but over the last few days it had been worse than usual. Reviewing and understanding the documents which had been hidden from Marion had taken and would continue to take many hours of his time. At the same time he had a rigorous schedule of medical testing, and he had begun his analysis of the medical literature. Soon he would be going to the medical library at NIH to do research, and it was important to him that he be prepared. The trips to NIH would happen whenever they happened, but the previous evening when Gene picked up his schedule, he had been surprised and a little bit relieved that the first trip hadn't been scheduled yet. He would be ready soon, in a couple of days.

The long hours and the pressure to deal with Kelly and Alfred and Dr. Gallagher and his life at Davenport Center and the baby made it difficult for Gene to think, to understand, to analyze. There was too much similarity between Alfred's story and Kelly's story for Gene's comfort. Maybe all of the pressure was just making him crazy. He would hide the note. He would talk to Kelly.

That morning Kelly knocked at the door of a document storage room identical to the one they had met in previously. Gene jumped up from the chair and opened the door. The stress pulled at the muscles of his face. Kelly seemed wary as he leaned over and kissed her on the cheek.

"It's so good to see you," said Gene.

Kelly smiled.

"I need to ask you some questions. Ok?"

"Sure."

"What's your step-father's last name?" asked Gene.

"Halpin," said Kelly.

"So he adopted you?"

"Yes. I thought I told you that."

"Maybe you did. My mind's not as clear as it has been at times. What was your father's last name?"

"What's the point of this inquisition?"

"I'm just curious. I would like to know what your name used to be." Gene was agitated. Despite his exhaustion, his muscles felt tense, ready to explode. He tried to be as calm as he could be.

"Miller."

Gene was now getting exited. "What was his first name?" he asked as calmly as he could.

"Alfred."

"Alfred?"

"Yes."

Gene was certain that Kelly's father was still alive. Almost certain. But what was the point of telling her yet? The fact was he didn't really know. He wanted to be sure. He had to be positive. If he told her now, that would get her hopes up, and what if he was wrong? Alfred Miller must be a common enough name. Two people could have the name. Even two doctors. Was her father a doctor? That would be a good question.

"Was your father a doctor?"

"Yes."

"Do you have a copy of your father's death certificate?" asked Gene. There was some quality that Kelly and Alfred shared. Gene had noticed it before, but the thought so antagonized him that he had suppressed it.

"Yeah. I do. I took it from Mom's dresser when she married Richard. I didn't want her to have it anymore. She doesn't even know I have it."

"Can you bring it in?"

"Sure." Kelly glanced around the room. "Well actually no. It's at my house. I can't go there. You know. Richard's orders."

"No. I don't know. I know he ordered you to move back home."

"Well he also ordered me not to go by my own house."

"Why?"

"I don't know. Just because he's an evil bastard I guess."

"He's got some reason."

"I figure he got some girlfriend that he either takes there when he needs a release or maybe she's even living there. I can't go by. He threatened to hurt Mom if I did."

"Could I go by?"

"You can't even go to lunch when you want. How would you go by?"

Gene smiled. "I get off this island every once in a while. I'm not in prison you know."

Kelly grunted a grunt of skepticism.

"I've just got work to do. That's all. I'm busy around here. But as it turns out, I'm going by to the medical library at NIH in a couple of days, I think. I'm involved in a literature search. I'll see what turns up on my schedule. I'm going to have to go there."

"Why do you care about his death certificate?"

"I don't mean to be so mysterious." Gene did not want to raise her suspicion more than he already had. "I knew a doctor once, named Alfred Miller. I just wanted to know if it was the same man."

"Wouldn't that be weird, if you knew my father? Al right. Go by if you want. I don't care. Here's the key." She took a ring of keys out of the pocket of her lab coat and started to struggle with it. "I don't need it. Richard won't let me go there anyway. Be careful. The house is way back off the road. Richard drives a black Camaro. If you see it, get out of there. If there's no Camaro, then knock on the door first in case he's got a girlfriend in there. If anybody answers, just say you're selling cookware door to door. If nobody's there it will probably be safe. Just don't stay long. It's in the bottom drawer of the dresser in a wooden box, the death certificate and some other papers. Upstairs. In my bedroom. If you do manage to get by, there are some books on an end table in the living room. I'd appreciate it if you would pick them up for me. I haven't read them yet. And there are a couple of other things, too." She handed Gene the key to the house and put the ring of keys back into her pocket. Then she sat down at the table where Gene worked and made a short list.

"Ok," said Gene when she handed him the list.

~ ~ ~

Catherine was vacuuming the carpet in the living room when Richard showed up before lunch. He left the front door ajar, as he hung his coat in the closet.

"Hello," said Catherine. "I wasn't expecting you for lunch." She laid the hose to the vacuum cleaner along the wall.

"I felt so good today," said Richard, "I wanted to come by. I brought these for you." He leaned over and picked up a cone of white paper with a dozen red roses wrapped inside.

"What's the occasion?" asked Catherine.

"The occasion is I love my wife. I brought you something else." He pushed open the aluminum storm door and lifted a box off the concrete steps. "Here. It's one of those automatic bread makers you've been wanting. I thought it would make your life easier."

"This is ridiculous," she said with excitement and joy in her voice. "Is this my Christmas present?"

"No. No. This is just something I wanted to get for you. Come over on the couch. Let's sit down."

They sat on the sofa, and Catherine balanced the bread maker on her lap.

"Thank you so much. It's just what I wanted."

"I've got to tell you something, Catherine." He lifted the box off her lap and sat it on the floor. He looked into her eyes. "Things are going good for me. I want to share my good fortune with you. We're married. We're supposed to share, you know."

"I know." Catherine smiled and touched his cheek.

"We haven't been on vacation since... well... since we got married."

"We don't have to go on vacations all the time."

"I know, but I know you always wanted to go to the mountains. I made a reservation for us up in the Poconos. We're going after Christmas when everything settles down. I got the bridal suite. It'll be the honeymoon we never had. There's a Jacuzzi in the room and a bathtub shaped like a champagne glass and a fireplace and a heart-shaped bed."

"Oh Richard." Catherine smiled and then started to laugh until tears came to her eyes. "It will be so nice."

"I just want you to know that you're the best thing that ever happened to me. I don't know how I got so lucky. I am tortured sometimes. I know I take it out on you. I can get paranoid and think everybody in the world is trying to hurt me. But I know you love me. I know you're good for me. Don't ever leave me."

"I won't. I never would. I love you, too."

They embraced each other and kissed a long kiss.

"I know I have other friends," said Richard when they leaned back on the couch. "Peter Snyder and Dr. Gallagher."

"Dr. Gallagher?"

"Yes," said Richard. "He doesn't really know me, but I know him. He runs the place where Kelly works, and he has always been good to me... to us. He gives me money... through Peter... when I do things for him. The work is easy and the pay is always high. I just got a good job from him, and I got to work on it this afternoon. Don't cook today. I'll take you to dinner when I get back."

~ ~ ~

It was mid-afternoon when Marion turned from the Rockville Pike onto the outer loop of the Washington Beltway. Traffic was heavy but not congested as she maneuvered across three lanes of traffic from the left lane entrance to the right lane. She passed over a bridge, and an acceleration lane for traffic entering from Old Georgetown Road came up on her right. Seconds later a twenty-year old Chevrolet from the acceleration lane slammed into the right side of her silver-gray Taurus.

The rim of Marion's rear tire caught the bumper of the blue car. The tire exploded as the rim was forced out of shape. Both of Marion's airbags deployed as a result of the sudden jolt. Dark blue paint from the Chevrolet streaked the crushed right rear panel. The cars came to rest on the shoulder to the right of the acceleration lane.

As a dazed Marion emerged from her car, a tow truck pulled off the highway and stopped just in front of the Taurus. The tow truck, painted a powder blue, had a large cab with storage room behind the seats and a dull silver flatbed where a car could be secured.

"My ears are ringing," said Marion.

"I'm so sorry," said a man in overalls who stepped out of the Chevrolet. He spoke with an eastern shore accent. "It's all my fault."

"Ok," said Marion, who looked shaken and disoriented.

Before it was all done, Marion's car was on the bed of the tow truck and Marion was in the passenger seat.

"Where's your garage?" asked Marion, as the light blue truck with black letters painted on the door pulled into the traffic.

"It's in the other direction," said the driver. "I'm going to have to turn around at River Road."

As they started around the curve where the I-270 spur merged with the outer loop of the beltway, Richard, hidden from Marion's view behind the seats, jumped up and pulled a large canvas bag with a rope tie around the open end over Marion's head. The faded green bag was in place before Marion had an opportunity to turn. She struggled and grasped at the bag with her hands.

"What the hell is going on?" screeched Marion.

"Shut up," said Richard. He yanked the rope tight around her neck and pulled her back against the seat.

"Off! Off! Get this off of me!"

"Settle your greasy butt down," said Richard as he yanked hard on the rope, choking Marion and causing a sputtering, gasping sound to emanate from the bag.

She continued to pull at the rope and the open end of the bag which was secured around her neck. Richard yanked harder.

"Stop!" he shouted. With her head back against the headrest, Richard pulled hard on the rope with both hands. "Put your hands down! I don't plan to kill you, but I'd just as soon do it as not."

Marion gasped and sputtered. Her arms flailed. Richard yanked on the rope again.

"Hands down!"

Marion's hands came to rest on her throat. Richard knocked at her fingers with his left hand, pushing her fingers away from her neck. She moved her hands to her lap. Richard loosened his grasp on the rope.

"All right," said Richard. "Good. Listen. This has got to be quick. I don't want these other drivers to begin to wonder what we're doing. You lean forward or I'll break your neck."

Marion leaned forward.

"What do you want?" asked Marion, her voice muffled by the bag.

"Shut up."

"You can have the car."

"Hands behind your back."

Marion complied, and Richard handcuffed her hands together.

"We've got the car already. Didn't want it in the first place. Now you shut up."

With the handcuffs in place, he loosened the rope and pulled the bag further down over Marion. When the closed end of the bag was pulled tight against the top of her head, the open end was about level with her elbows.

"Get down on the floor."

"Eat shit and die," said Marion. Her muffled voice was loud. She didn't move from the seat.

With his fist open, Richard slammed the heel of his hand hard into the back of Marion's head.

"Don't make me tell you stuff twice."

The force of Richard's blow pushed her head up against the dashboard and next to the passenger side window.

"We're coming up to the exit. Get on the floor now."

Marion, who seemed disoriented, fell onto the floor of the cab.

"Don't move," shouted Richard. "Don't talk. Unless you want your face to look like raw hamburger."

With Marion on the floor, Richard pulled himself over the back of the seat. The truck coasted to a stop at the top of the exit ramp onto River Road. The light was red. Richard brought his right foot to rest on Marion's shoulder and his left one on her stomach just below the edge of the canvas bag. He jiggled his left foot to adjust it next to her bent knees. Marion squirmed, but soon his foot was flat against her stomach. He pressed down on it.

"Be still," he said.

Marion stopped moving.

~ ~ ~

That afternoon Kelly left work early.

"Where's Richard?" asked Kelly when she arrived home. She laid her long dark blue coat over the back of a wooden chair.

"He's out," said Catherine. "He's got some work to do this afternoon. Good work. He'll be home in time for dinner."

"That's what I was hoping for," said Kelly. "Let's go. Now is our chance. Get some things together, and let's get out of here."

"That's ridiculous," said Catherine. "Go where?" She sat on the sofa in the living room working on a cross stitch Christmas stocking for Richard. Tugging on the thread she tightened the last stitch in the h in Richard at the top of the stocking. Against the powder blue background with tiny, raised snowflakes the dark blue letters stood out. "Look," she said as she held the fabric up so Kelly could see Santa Claus carrying a tree. "What do you think?"

"It's very nice. You do a remarkable job, but you're making a really nice stocking for a pig."

"Don't say that."

Kelly rolled her eyes and tossed off her mother's comment with a wave of her hand.

"Please, Mom," said Kelly. "Let's go."

"Where do you want to go?" Catherine straightened the thread and turned her attention to the next letter.

"I don't know. Let's just get out of here. I know somebody up in Easton. I haven't talked to her in a year or so, but I'm sure she'll let us stay there for a time."

"Who moved to Easton?"

"Mom, it doesn't matter. We need to get out of here. You need to get out of here. The sicko warden's gone for a few minutes. Let's take advantage of the opportunity."

"Don't talk about him that way, honey." She put the stocking aside. "He gets angry sometimes, but none of us is perfect. He's a loving, thoughtful man and a good provider. I wish you would notice that side of him."

"The man's a pig."

"Richard can be rough around the edges. That doesn't change the fact that he's my husband, and I love him."

"All right, Mom, he's rough around the edges. But please, let's get out of here. I don't know how long we've got."

"We've got plenty of time, honey. Please sit down."

"We don't have time for this. Come on."

"I don't want to go anywhere," said Catherine. "I'm happy here. Richard and I are going out to dinner tonight. He's taking me to dinner."

"Mom, I know he can be nice sometimes. But it's all a trick. You know how you feel when he has one of his tirades. You're not happy here. Nobody could be happy here."

Kelly grasped her mother's arm in an effort to encourage her to get up off the couch. "Come on," said Kelly. "Please. Let's leave now."

"I'm not going anywhere. I want to be with him. I love him."

Kelly tugged at the sleeve of the pink cardigan sweater Catherine was wearing.

"You want me to abandon him just because things aren't perfect?" asked Catherine. "What kind of wife would I be? Please let go of my arm. I don't want to go anywhere."

Kelly let go of the sweater.

Chapter 29

A Physical Response

A couple of hours later Richard was on the phone with Peter.

"That bitch is causing me a lot of trouble," said Richard.

"What do you mean?" asked Peter. "What's she doing?"

"She's screaming and wiggling. She won't shut up. She won't stop moving around."

"What are you talking about?"

"I'm talking about that bitch. Marion. If I didn't have her tied down, she'd be running all over the place."

"Tied down?" Peter's voice had changed. His words were clipped. "What did you do?"

"I kidnapped that bitch, just like you told me to."

"Kidnapped her? I didn't tell you to kidnap her."

"You did."

"I didn't. I told you to distract her."

"Well I'd say she's pretty damn distracted."

"Distract her. Not kidnap her. Distract her. Nothing more."

"Look Peter you are such an ass wipe. You're an ass wipe wimp. You told me to kidnap her. I kidnapped her. That's been done. Now I've got problems. I call your sorry ass up and ask for a little support, and all you can think to do is tell me you didn't tell me to do what you already told me to do. I don't need that. I'm looking for some help here. I've done all the work. I'm asking for a little support. That's all. Is that too much to ask? I don't think so. It's not much. I'm not asking much. So what do you do? I ask for a little help, and what do you do? Instead of helping me, you're wimping out on me and pretending you don't know what I'm talking about."

"I didn't ask you to kidnap her," said Peter in a low voice.

"What?" shouted Richard into the phone. "I can't hear a damn word you're saying."

"I didn't tell you to kidnap her," said Peter in a firm voice.

"You did!"

"I didn't."

"Look asshole, you did. If you say you didn't again, I'm going to come over there and grab you by the throat. Do you want to get your ass kicked?"

There was silence on the phone.

"Peter?"

"Yes."

"I need some support."

"All right," said Peter. "Can anybody hear her scream?" His pace was slower now. Each word was separate, distinct from the others.

"Not where I've got her."

"Alright. Then what do you want?"

"I want something to calm her down. You know all of those damn doctors. That place where you work is crawling with them. Get me something to calm her down."

"What do you want?"

"What do I want?" said Richard. "I told you. I want something to calm her down. Knock her out for a few hours. Whenever the bitch acts up, I'll give her more of it. Get me some pills." Richard paused. "No. No pills. I don't know if I can get her to take pills. I'd have to take the hood off."

"Take the hood off? You've got a hood on her?"

"Yeah. Sure. Then she could see me if I took the hood off. She might not swallow the pills anyway. She might chew them up or spit them out. She's a real bitch. I don't know what she'd do. No pills. Get me something I can shoot into her."

"Have you ever given an injection before?"

"No. But I guess I can figure it out. How hard can it be? I've seen it done lots of times. I bet I could stick a needle through the rubber top of the drug. I bet I'd be able to tap bottles better than just about anybody else in Delmarva."

~ ~ ~

That night, from his home, Peter called Dr. Gallagher.

"You're telling me that you had her kidnapped?" asked Dr. Gallagher.

"Yes," said Peter.

"And that makes sense to you?"

"You said you wanted her out of the way."

"I said I wanted her out of the way. I didn't say I wanted you to end up in jail."

"I'm not going to jail."

"I guess that's yet to be determined," said Dr. Gallagher. "You are one of Davenport Center's most important resources. So you just go along and merrily risk that resource and all the work we've done and all that we hope to accomplish for... for... for I don't even know what."

"You wanted her out of the way. She's out of the way."

"I see. So let me understand this. Kidnapping that woman makes more sense to you than, say, transferring her to another job? Why don't you keep in mind the fact that the benefit to us would be the same."

"Well..."

"Alright. When are you going to let her go?"

"Well... I don't know. What do you think?"

"What do I think?" repeated Dr. Gallagher, his voice dripping sarcasm. "I think you've waited a few minutes too long before you asked that question."

"She is out of the way."

"What is she going to say when you let her go?"

"Say? Well, I don't know what she is going to say."

"Immensely clever," said Dr. Gallagher. "I've got to say that you've handled this in an immensely clever way. First you break the law. And I'm not talking about the violation of some esoteric, technical requirement imposed by some obscure law. I'm talking about the violation of a law that establishes the fundamental order of our society, a law that everyone knows about, understands and supports. So first you violate this law in a clear and obvious way, and then you call me up on a public telephone line and tell me about it. Proud. You should be proud. And I think it is a stroke of genius to do it a couple of days before Christmas. Why should anyone notice her missing at that time?"

"So what do you want me to do now?"

"What you have told me is so idiotic and so fanciful that I can only assume that it is the result of some kind of hallucinogenic response, perhaps to medication. I do not believe that what you described happened. I don't believe that it could have happened. I believe you ought to call your physician or seek help from a psychiatrist."

"You want me to see a psychiatrist?"

"If you want to discuss these hallucinations further, we can meet somewhere other than your office and discuss them. I don't see how it makes any sense to discuss this kind of delusion over the telephone, and I'm not going to do it."

With that, Dr. Gallagher hung up the phone before Peter could respond.

~ ~ ~

The next morning Gene jumped out of bed. Breakfast had been scheduled early. He finished his morning routine as quickly as he could so that he would have a few minutes to write a note to Kelly. After his shower, he went to the small wood desk in the living room and composed a note.

The note read: "Dear Kelly: I know times are hard for us right now. I have so little freedom, and we have so little time together. I have been thinking about our baby. He is due in only five months, and that means there are important decisions we must make soon. I am tortured by the choices we have. I have to go to NIH today. I just want you to know that I love you, and that we will work this out together. I will leave you another note as soon as I can find a place for us to meet. Love, Gene."

Alfred's breakfast, had been scheduled late that morning, and at Dr. Gallagher's request, he was in the main entrance hall inspecting the Christmas decorations and the final preparations for a reception for

VTSs, outside-ins, certain paladins and some invited guests. Breakfast for Alfred had been scheduled to start a few minutes after Gene's was scheduled to end.

After breakfast Gene was scheduled to stop by his lab and pick up a briefcase with papers he would need at NIH. With briefcase in hand, he headed out of the Mission and Conscience Department on the second floor of the east wing. In the public hallway, he set the briefcase next to the wall. At the same time, Alfred entered the public area of the east wing from the south entrance. Alfred entered the hallway where the door to the Mission and Conscience Department was, and he looked to the right. Gene walked away from him, and Alfred paused and waited. Gene leaned over. Alfred watched him insert the note to Kelly behind the door frame. Gene stood. Alfred looked at the door in front of him. Gene turned. Alfred used his ID card to open the door. Gene walked back up the corridor toward Alfred. Alfred looked at him as though he were noticing him for the first time. Gene leaned over and picked up the briefcase.

"Good morning, Gene," said Alfred.

"Morning, Alfred. I'm on my way to NIH."

"Good." Alfred smiled and nodded.

Alfred entered the Mission and Conscience Department and let the door close behind him. Gene went down the hall a little further and marked the doorframe so that Kelly would know to pick up the note.

~ ~ ~

That afternoon Alfred met with Dr. Gallagher in his second floor office.

"I have been keeping my eye on Dr. Nolan, as you suggested," said Alfred.

"Good. Anything interesting?"

"I found this note." Alfred leaned forward from the wing chair, and held the note over the desk.

Dr. Gallagher looked at Alfred's outstretched hand. He cocked his head and then took the cream colored paper.

"What is this?" asked Dr. Gallagher after reading the note. His eyes darted around the room.

"It's a note. Gene hid it behind a doorframe this morning. He was obviously leaving it for a woman named Kelly Halpin. It's addressed to 'Kelly.' I checked the employment records. A Kelly Halpin works here as a lab assistant."

"This is an outrage," shouted Dr. Gallagher. He jumped up out of his chair. The force of his movement slammed the chair into the wall behind his desk.

"Is there anything you want me to do?" asked Alfred.

"Yes. There will be. Where is that bastard? I want him here! Now!"

"He left for NIH early this morning. He's been gone all day. He's not scheduled to be back until early evening."

"This behavior is absolutely intolerable. He'll pay the price for this." Dr. Gallagher paced back and forth in front of the window. "I'm going to grab him by the testicles and yank. Physical response. That's what we'll have first. His body will become compliant. He will follow our direction. He will behave as we direct. We will move his body first. In time his heart, mind and soul will follow. This outrageous behavior must be stopped. It will be stopped."

Chapter 30

She's On Board

Dr. Gallagher walked through the public hallways of Davenport Center, and his presence attracted attention. Everyone knew who he was. His omnipresent image, in photographs hung throughout the building, in a massive oil painting in the central atrium and in various welcome brochures distributed to all who visited the island, insured that everyone recognized him. His animated, entertaining behavior in welcoming and instructional videos contributed to his celebrity. And then there was his behavior in public, always calling attention to himself, always taking charge, always making himself the center of attention. His inexorable drive toward the limelight was occasionally subtle and often entertaining.

After their meeting, Dr. Gallagher, accompanied by Alfred, walked over to the public dining room. A VTS, a round faced woman with waist length jet-black hair, sat near the main entrance. She swooned and, almost fainting, fell back in her chair as Dr. Gallagher passed. Another test subject, a man carrying his lunch on a tray, walked up to Dr. Gallagher.

"Hello, Dr. Gallagher," the man said. "It is an honor to meet you." He rammed his hand straight out, toward Dr. Gallagher's stomach, and waited for the Bloodsworth Island celebrity to grasp it. A distracted Dr. Gallagher didn't notice the hand for a moment, and the tray the man was holding became unstable. A sky blue translucent plastic cup containing dark soda and ice slid to one side of the heavy yellow plastic tray and then spilled, top first, onto the floor. Dr. Gallagher who by this time had noticed the man's extended hand, thrust his toward him out of instinct but recoiled as the tray began to topple. A woman in a uniform consisting of a gray dress and a white apron ran toward the mess. A man in a white coat, white pants and wearing a white paper chef's hat followed her to assist in cleaning up the mess.

"What's with the tard?" asked Dr. Gallagher. He had whispered the question to Alfred, and at the same time tilted his head in the direction of the man who had lost his drink.

Alfred flipped through a list of names secured to a clipboard he carried. "Hallquist," he said. "Yes, here it is," Alfred whispered back. "He's half cow fiber." Cow fiber was a term used by the components of Davenport Center when speaking in public so that if anyone overheard a conversation it would be impossible to make sense of it. Cow fiber meant cystic fibrosis. Half cow fiber meant that the person was a carrier with one gene that coded for cystic fibrosis. A person who was all cow fiber had two genes which coded for the disease, and as a result had cystic fibrosis. "He's scheduled for insight tomorrow." Insight meant infection with the Systus R virus. "He won't be in the here and now for more than a week." A person who was in the here and now was a person who was alive.

"Good," said Dr. Gallagher. "I'm glad I didn't touch him. He lacks the grace and poise we're looking for in future generations." Dr. Gallagher craned his neck to look over the heads of nearby patients and workers and see around the room. "Where's that seductress we're looking for, the one that's poisoned Gene's mind?"

Alfred looked at his watch and then looked at his clipboard once again. "She is scheduled to start lunch right now." Alfred paused and looked around the room himself. "Yes. That's her over there, the one with the long dark hair. I believe she came in right behind us."

Kelly had entered the cafeteria line and was leaning over the cream-colored salad plates with the fine burgundy stripe around the rim. They were laid out on ice, edges touching. Each plate was wrapped in clear plastic which pushed the lettuce, onions, celery and tomatoes flat against the plate. She picked up one, and the heavy weight of the plate caused it to tilt to the side. After looking at it, she set it back into the depression it had made in the ice. Dr. Gallagher walked up from behind. His movement startled her. Recognizing who he was, she smiled a wide grin and did not say anything.

"Ms. Kelly Halpin?" Dr. Gallagher asked.

Kelly nodded.

"My name is Dr. Gallagher. I run this facility."

"I know who you are," said Kelly. "Everyone knows who you are." She smiled.

"Please, go ahead and get your lunch." Dr. Gallagher pointed at the food that lay ahead. "Have whatever you'd like. It's my treat. That is, on the condition that you'll let me dine with you."

"Alright. Thanks. It's very nice of you to offer." She grabbed the same salad plate that she had examined earlier, apparently no longer concerned about the brown lettuce which was pressed hard against the edge of the plate.

A man behind the counter glanced up at Dr. Gallagher. The man with a mustache and and apron had been working while Dr. Gallagher and Kelly talked. Dr. Gallagher followed Kelly in line and the man with the moustache presented him with a bowl of vegetable soup and a triple decker peanut butter and jelly sandwich sliced into quarters.

"Thank you, Carlo. Always looking out for me." The man smiled and waved a small wave with his right hand.

Alfred stood near the entrance in accordance with Dr. Gallagher's directions. He and Dr. Gallagher nodded at each other, as Dr. Gallagher emerged from the cafeteria line.

The room was crowded. Kelly looked for a place to sit. A table next to the large windows that looked north and west toward the center of Bloodsworth Island opened up as Kelly walked by. She claimed the table, and Dr. Gallagher joined her. The view from the window was similar to the view from Dr. Gallagher's second floor office window except facing more to the west and away from Tangier Sound.

When they sat, Dr. Gallagher focused all of his attention, a powerful source of energy, onto Kelly. He ignored the food he had been given and stared at her.

She held her chin close to her chest and giggled a little.

"Why are you laughing?" asked Dr. Gallagher. His voice purred like a fine-tuned car.

"You're staring at me. It's embarrassing."

"I'm just looking. I'm trying to drink you in, to understand you, to know you. Observation is very important. Here at Davenport Center we all know the value of observation."

"That look of yours makes me uncomfortable." Kelly said.

"I'm sorry," said Dr. Gallagher. He raised a spoon to his mouth and sucked in hot vegetable broth. "I was just admiring how beautiful you are. I was thinking how lucky a man would be to have you at his side."

"Thank you for the complement, but I still don't know why you've come to meet with me."

"Your supervisors have commented on your competence and dedication to your work. Admirable qualities. Sometimes at Davenport Center we run specialized studies that are out of the main course of our research. I wanted to know if we could count on you to help us with just such a special project."

"What is it you need?"

"We're doing some testing on a new medication we have developed, and we need somebody who is absolutely reliable to be on call 24 hours a day. You would stay here on the island."

"I always like to help, but…" said Kelly.

"It would take only a week or so. You would work the same number of hours as you work now, but you would stay here at Davenport Center and be on call at other times. There will be many opportunities to socialize. Maybe you can spend time relaxing or getting to know other people who work here, perhaps people you've never met." Dr. Gallagher picked up one of the four sandwich triangles and bit through the three slices of brown bread, two layers of tan colored chunky peanut butter and two layers of purple jelly, cutting the triangle in half.

"Do you always get involved in personnel matters?"

"I like to meet as many people as I can, and I feel that too much time had passed with us both being on the same island having never met. It is important to me to meet the staff members who are performing well."

"I have a number of things going on in my life right now," said Kelly. She put her hands on her lap, grasping at her napkin, and she bit her lip.

"Getting away from all of that may be just the right answer. I find that removing myself from the causes of my stress helps me to think clearly."

"What about my work? Who would take over my duties for Dr. Raines?"

"Don't worry about that, Kelly. We'll take care of everything."

"What about the pay?"

"There will be a bonus. You'll receive your full salary plus differential."

"When would this start?" asked Kelly.

"Right away. This afternoon. You'll need to stay on the island."

"So soon. I don't know."

"It's ok." Dr. Gallagher folded his napkin and placed it back on the table. "We can get someone else. I can see that you have some hesitation about this." He rose from the table.

"Wait!" Kelly said. "I just need a little time to make a decision. There are so many issues."

"How long would you need?" Dr. Gallagher looked down at her.

Kelly looked at the carpet and swayed her right leg around a semi-circle in the pattern. "Can I let you know tomorrow?"

"It would have to be very early." Dr. Gallagher sat back in his seat. "How about this? You can start now doing some of the preparation work. That will help you to understand what the work will be like. Then you can spend the night here as our guest, and then you could tell us your decision first thing in the morning."

"I'll have to call my mother and let her know I won't be home tonight. A phone with an outside line is a hard thing to find on Bloodsworth Island."

"I know," Dr. Gallagher said. "Don't worry. There is a phone in your room. In some ways this will be like a vacation. You'll be able to take advantage of all of the amenities that we extend to our volunteers here."

"Maybe this will give me an opportunity to clear my mind."

"Yes. Good." Dr. Gallagher waved at Alfred who turned and left the room. "This will be a real help. Just wait here. I'll send somebody to take you to your room and help you fill out the necessary paperwork. I'll get somebody over here before you finish your salad."

"But..." said Kelly, "your sandwich and soup. You hardly ate anything."

241

"I'm not really hungry. I had a big breakfast. Thank you for your help."

Dr. Gallagher turned and walked toward the entrance where Alfred had been standing. Alfred returned, as Dr. Gallagher reached the doorway.

"She's on board," said Dr. Gallagher.

"Ms. Vorschrift will take care of her," said Alfred.

"Good. You keep on top of this. I told her she would be helping us to conduct some testing. Keep her busy today doing some kind of setup work. When Gene gets back we'll start to unravel this thing. I want to know what part she played in attempting to destroy our work here. Did Marion set her up? Who else might have sent her? Who do we know who is clever enough and deceptive enough to do this?"

"I don't know, Father."

Dr. Gallagher walked out into the hallway and then turned around. "I think that you had better call Elbridge and Ted. I want this place locked up tighter than Dick's hatband when he gets back. Everyone in their quarters. Components. VTSs. Island Outside-Ins. Everybody."

"Tighter than a tick's hatband?"

"Dick! Dick's hatband. Ticks don't wear hats."

"Shall we do the complete procedure?"

Dr. Gallagher was bothered by Alfred's question, and he appeared to struggle, searching for an answer. His eyes focused on the gray carpet of the circular hallway and then on the dangling Christmas sleigh which hung in the grand entranceway on the other side of the glass. "Alright. I really did not want this for someone who has risen so high in our ranks. Put Dr. Nolan into Harry Sharp's Chair. After we shoot a few electric jolts up his butt we might get the truth out of him. This whole thing makes me so angry I could spit."

"It will be a good instructional example for the others," Alfred said.

"Yes, I suppose there is that. Do you think that we'll be able to rehabilitate him?"

"I'm not sure," Alfred said. "I will need to get at the root of the problem, to see if this can be cured. The Chair is a very effective negotiating tool."

"That it is." There was anger in Dr. Gallagher's face. "Is everything still on schedule for full release of the virus tomorrow?"

"Yes. The replication should be complete by this afternoon. I have notified Ms. Vorshrift of the adjustments to everyone's schedule."

"Good, I would hate to have this disturbance throw off our schedule. The season is perfect for migration of the birds and the resultant dissemination of the virus."

"I'll make sure that everything goes smoothly," said Alfred.

"You'd better," said Dr. Gallagher. "I can't afford any more screw ups."

Chapter 31

Edwin Roybal

Gene left the NIH library early so he would have time to stop by Kelly's house to get the death certificate and some other things Kelly had asked him to bring for her. He got into the fire engine red pickup truck, a new Chevrolet with a black fiberglass cover installed over the bed, which he had been assigned to drive. The truck had the words Davenport Center painted in large white letters on each side of the bed. When Gene got the truck that morning, he had been bothered by the fact that he would be taking such a well-marked vehicle to an unauthorized place. At least Kelly's house was in a remote location, away from prying eyes. The car, which he had driven before, would have been less conspicuous, but the truck was better than the metallic turquoise van which he had never driven and might have been assigned. It had the words Davenport Center painted on the sides in contrasting red, the letters even larger than those used on the bed of the pickup truck.

Gene was anxious as he passed through Church Creek on the way to Kelly's house. He had never been to the house, had never even seen it, but he knew where it was. The sun was fading at a little after 4:00 pm when he turned onto the gravel road that led only to her house. As he approached the weather-beaten, two-story cottage, Gene saw the black Camaro that Kelly had warned him about. He slammed on the brakes and skidded on the gravel. He was worried about the sound. There wasn't room to turn around on the narrow road without driving all the way up to the house. He put the truck in reverse and backed out the driveway, past the mailbox and back onto 335.

It was the right house, cedar shingle siding weathered black by the sun, Richard's Camaro. There was little in the way of a hiding place on the main road, and the bright red pickup truck needed hiding. As it was, the truck would stick out like a man in chains on the Fourth of July. Route 335 ran north and south with narrow shoulders. The gravel road to Kelly's place went off to the east. Some distance south on 335 and taking off to the west, Gene found a similar gravel road that must have led to three houses judging by the number of mail boxes. By backing the truck onto that road, Gene could just see the point where the road to Kelly's house met the main road. He sat and waited and watched. Soon the black Camaro came down the gravel road and turned north, toward Cambridge.

With the black car out of the way, Gene approached Kelly's house for the second time. Worn green shingles with the black asphalt exposed in many places covered most of the roof. Pieces of the shingles were broken and missing and in one place, near the front overhang, the roof plywood was exposed and weathered like the siding. Two stout redbrick chimneys poked out of the roof, one in the front and one in the back. The doors and windows which were once wood had been replaced by aluminum which had become worn, pitted and covered by a greenish-gray discoloration.

The house stood isolated in a place where the trees and low growing vegetation had been cleared. Looking away from the house, the trees, the vegetation, the soft soil, the flat land were more than superficially reminiscent of Bloodsworth Island. An old, leafless oak tree stood above the pines and over the house, guarding it. A wire stretched from a tar soaked electrical pole near the house down to a connector above the side door.

Gene worried about whether he would be missed. Dr. Gallagher must already know that he had left the library an hour earlier than scheduled. He knew so much. Did Dr. Gallagher know that he was at that house at that very moment? Gene decided not to worry about Dr. Gallagher's omnipotence. He needed the death certificate. If the document was genuine, that meant that the Alfred Miller who was Kelly's father was dead.

And who would the Alfred Miller at Bloodsworth Island be? An imposter, of course. Another man with the same name who also happened to be a doctor. And if it wasn't genuine, what would that mean? Did Alfred fake his death to get away from Catherine and Kelly? He was a cold man. He had the capacity to do that. Gene wanted to know.

Gene parked at one corner of the house next to a drain pipe which was loose from the gutter above. Brownish black sludge plugged the hole in the gutter where the pipe had been connected, and water had flowed over the chipped, once white paint of the gutter onto the side of the house causing more damage to the siding in that area.

Gene got out of the truck into the crisp, cold December air and approached the house. Kelly was convinced that the reason Richard wanted Kelly out of the house was so he could keep his mistress there. It seemed like there was some powerful evidence with Richard here in the middle of the day. But there was no other car. Maybe there was one around back. How would the woman get there? She must have been in the car with Richard when he left. The light at dusk had been bad, and Gene had been too far away to see who was in the Camaro.

The small porch at the side door creaked as Gene stepped up onto it. The house was dark, and there were no holiday decorations as there were on some of the houses on the main road. He knocked. No one came to the door. There was no sound inside the house. He knocked again to make sure. He had Kelly's key, but even without it, breaking into this house wouldn't have been difficult.

Comfortable that there was no one in the house, Gene slid the key into the lock and opened the door. The inside of the house was gloomy. All of the shades were drawn, and little of the late afternoon light penetrated into the house. Gene found himself in the dining room as he first entered the house. To the left was a large kitchen, and to the right was a staircase and an entrance to the living room.

Kelly had told him that she kept all of her important papers in her bedroom dresser which was upstairs. The books were in the living room, but Gene had decided that he would get those last. He ascended the staircase, which twisted to the left. The steps were narrow and small. Half the steps creaked as he stepped on them, forewarning anyone that might still be in the house. On the landing at the top of the stairs there was an entranceway with another step up to the right and two doors on the left. Kelly had told him that her room was on the left and the ones on the right were vacant. He could see that the first door on the left led to the bathroom, so he went for the second door which was closed.

Gene opened the door. He saw a figure lying on the bed. The vision jolted him. He fell back into the hallway. There was no movement in the room. That was a surprise. He poked his head through the doorway and looked at the body. It remained still. Maybe the person was dead. It was even darker in the bedroom than the rest of the house, since there were heavy drapes that covered the windows. The body lay on top of the blanket and appeared to be fully clothed.

"Hello," he said. "Hello."

There was no response.

Gene believed that he could make out a skirt, so he assumed that it was a woman he was looking at. As his eyes adjusted to the new level of lighting he noticed something else that was strange. There was something covering her head. Deliberate in his movements, Gene stepped into the room and examined the body. The woman's chest was moving. She was alive. But the breathing was slow, not like normal sleep. He turned on the light.

The bare bulb in the ceiling illuminated the room. There was a tired, worn canvas bag over the woman's head. If this was Richard's girlfriend, Gene concluded, he treated her even worse than he treated Kelly and her mother. The woman was bound at her ankles. Her hands were underneath her, and Gene assumed that they were bound as well.

Gene untied the loop at the base of the bag and removed the canvas from the woman's head. It was Marion. She didn't stir. Gene needed to sit. He joined her on the bed and looked down at the floor. Why would Richard have Marion here?

Examining Marion's body, Gene found that her left arm had small puncture wounds near her inner elbow. He assumed that she had been drugged which accounted for her strange breathing and unconscious state. Turning her slightly to her left he saw that she was handcuffed. He reached into his pocket and pulled out his key chain which held a small pen knife. He nipped at the nylon rope being careful not to cut Marion's legs or ankles. With the bag gone, at least she would be more comfortable.

Not being sure how long she would be unconscious or when Richard might return, Gene felt a new sense of urgency to get what he had come for. He opened the bottom drawer of the dresser and fished below a layer of sweaters to find a lacquered pine box. One foot by one foot, the large square box had a shiny surface which emphasized the wood grain. Gene lifted the lid, set it on the floor and began to look through the papers in the box.

There did not appear to be any organizational strategy for the box. Papers were loose and in no discernable order. Kelly's birth certificate was at the top and then there was a wad of her high school report cards that were paper-clipped together. Her grades looked good from what Gene could see, and it made him wonder why she hadn't gone to college. She had told him once that she had been a bad student and she just didn't want to continue her humiliation at the hands of teachers. Gene realized that her impression that she was not successful at school was not consistent with her performance.

There were a few pictures of Kelly with a woman who Gene assumed to be her mother. They were somewhat similar in hair color and complexion, but Kelly's features were apparently a blend of her mother's and father's. Her mother's face was much rounder than Kelly's, and her eyes were closer together. He put the picture with the other papers that he pulled out on the floor and scolded himself for wasting time.

Near the bottom of the box was a yellowing envelope addressed to Mrs. Catherine Miller. Gene opened the envelope and pulled out the documents inside. A letter described Alfred's death in Germany as Kelly had recited it to him. Attached was the death certificate that Gene had been looking for. Everything about the documents seemed genuine. The envelope was postmarked from Bad Ems, Germany. Gene looked them over for any signs that there was something odd or out of place, and he discovered what he was looking for right away.

Both documents were signed by the same doctor. That, in and of itself, was not so odd. It was the name of the doctor that fascinated Gene. It was Edwin Roybal. Gene knew that Edwin Roybal was the name that Dr. Gallagher used to avoid calls and remove himself from troublesome situations. Gene was certain that Dr. Edwin Roybal never existed on Bloodsworth Island or in Bad Ems, Germany.

Gene pulled a piece of paper from his pocket that contained the list of things that Kelly had requested from her place. The items on the list were various toiletries and clothes and Gene was sure that he would not get everything right. Gene took the death certificate and letter and put them back into the envelope and then placed the entire package in his coat pocket. Taking the rest of the papers off the floor, he put them back in the box and then reburied the box under sweaters in the dresser.

Consulting the list, Gene moved back and forth a few times from the bathroom to the bedroom each time adding a new item or two to the canvas bag that used to be over Marion's head. After he had done his best to get the items that Kelly had requested, he yanked the cord on the bag and threw it down from the top of the staircase. He did not want to waste any more time than he had to walking up and down the stairs. It was going to be enough trouble carrying Marion down the narrow steps.

Gene did a more thorough examination of Marion when he returned to the bedroom this time. He felt her forehead, and her temperature appeared normal. He could not see any bruises or cuts and there did not seem to be swelling anywhere. Her pulse and breathing were both quite slow, but he attributed that to the drug that had made her unconscious. Although he did not look forward to the prospect of moving Marion, he decided that it would be safe to do so. Gene noticed a silver-plated lighter on the bed beside Marion. It had a small gold shovel soldered to the side. He lifted it and looked at the miniature shovel thinking that it was a fascinating thing. He put it in his pocket. He hoped to remember to ask Kelly about it when he saw her.

Richard had kidnapped Marion. That much was clear. Why he had done it was the mystery. He had to get her out of the house and to safety before Richard came back. But Richard had probably just given her another injection, so Gene doubted he would be back soon. At the same time, Gene wanted to protect Kelly. He couldn't just call the police. He knew Kelly had nothing to do with this kidnapping. What would be the point of getting her involved, of bringing the police to her house? And he couldn't go to the police. That would make him even later getting back to Bloodsworth Island, and it would make it clear to Dr. Gallagher that he was incapable of following clear, simple instructions. The best thing to do would be to simply move Marion to a safe place and leave her.

Could Dr. Gallagher have had anything to do with Marion's kidnapping? The thought was shocking to Gene. He couldn't see Dr. Gallagher using such a crude approach with so little likelihood of success. It was obvious that whoever kidnapped Marion would eventually be caught. On the other hand, Gene knew that Dr. Gallagher wanted Marion out of the way. There was no time to figure it all out.

Gene had to get Marion to safety, or at least out of the house. Her body was heavy and difficult to move. Flipping her once more on her side, Gene twisted her body in an attempt to get her in a sitting position. Her body flapped around as he pushed, but he had little luck controlling the movements in the direction that he desired.

After flipping and flopping for several minutes Gene sat on the floor and began to laugh. It was a laugh of exasperation and exhaustion. Then he became terrified that Richard might return. Maybe he forgot something. And Gene knew that Richard had a reputation for irrationality. Unsure of what to try next, Gene remained determined to rescue Marion from this place. Marion was close to the edge of the bed where Gene was sitting. He got up on his knees to face her.

Gene leaned over and tucked his shoulder into Marion's stomach and then lifted her up off the bed. Her topside dangled over his back. He grasped her legs with his interlocked arms. Pivoting in a circle, he turned and headed out of the room toward the stairs. After an initial misstep, Gene concluded that he needed to take one stair at a time. The banister frightened him for it seemed to provide no support. Instead he leaned against the wall on the right side for aid in supporting Marion's weight.

As the stairs turned to open onto the dining room, Gene turned and bumped Marion's head into the wall. Surprised, Gene was knocked off balance, and his weight shifted out of control. His right leg missed the bottom step causing his knee to bend and he lost control of his load. Marion fell off his shoulder and landed in a heap at the bottom of the stairs. The canvas bag that Gene had thrown down earlier cushioned her head. Gene checked her pulse again. Her condition hadn't improved any, but she seemed ok. She had landed on her butt, which appeared to be padded enough to cushion the impact.

Lifting Marion's head, Gene pulled the bag loose and slung it over his shoulder. He then positioned himself at Marion's feet and pulled at her right arm to lift her into a standing position. Once he had accomplished that, he threw her over his shoulder once more and labored his way through the house's side door. This time, Gene was more cautious with her head as he maneuvered through the door, and he gained confidence in his ability to carry her. He was careful to avoid the grass for fear of slipping, so he stayed to the gravel and dirt that made up the driveway.

With great care, he maneuvered the body into position near the rear of the truck. He sat her on the gravel with her head leaning against the bed of the truck. He opened up the tailgate and lifted the black fiberglass bed cover. Gene felt that it would be easier and safer to transport Marion in the bed of the truck, so he laid her down there and once again used the canvas bag as a pillow. He slammed the tailgate shut, secured the bed cover and ran to the cab. There was room to turn around near the house, so Gene did and headed back down the gravel road. It was late now and almost dark. He turned the headlights on.

Gene patted his coat pocket to ensure that the envelope was still there, and he eased back in the seat a little as soon as he turned onto the main road, headed north, toward Cambridge. He had not bothered to close the door to the house, but he didn't think it made that much difference at this point. The road was clear ahead and he looked through the rear-view mirror. There was no one on the road behind him.

Now that he was free from the house, it occurred to Gene that he had no idea what he was going to do with Marion. He wanted to get away from her before she became conscious. He did not know what ramifications it would have for him or for Bloodsworth Island if she thought that he was in someway responsible for the kidnapping. A hospital was not the answer. There would be too many questions, and doctors in all of the area hospitals knew Dr. Gallagher. The presence of a truck with Davenport Center markings would certainly get back to him. Gene couldn't leave her out on the road since she might die from exposure, and Richard might just find her and take her back to that house again. It would be traumatic enough for her, just riding in the freezing bed of the truck.

It had to be someplace public. That meant driving at least as far as Cambridge, since there wasn't much in the way of "public" before that. Gene was worried about getting back to Bloodsworth Island. He had left the library early. But of course he hadn't left early enough to account for shuffling comatose bodies about. This would make him late. Would somebody notice? Gene didn't know. Traffic! Even Ms. Vorschrift couldn't know how bad the traffic might have been. That would provide him with an excuse. "My, the traffic was bad," he could just say. Who could disagree with that? Ms. Vorschrift could shake her head in silent acknowledgment of the traffic problem, but even she couldn't say it didn't happen.

Gene drove to Cambridge. He began scouring the streets for a place that he could put Marion. It had to be warm and close to help, but it couldn't be so public that someone might see him unloading the truck. Semi-public. That's what he needed to find.

Gene drove through the town twice from one end to the other until he found Quick-E Laundromat. The pink building was set back off the road and there were no cars in the parking lot. The lights were on. The neon sign out front advertised twenty-four seven. The building was on the west side of town. There were other buildings within walking distance including a police station.

Gene backed the truck up into the space closest to the door and walked around to ensure that the place was open. He stepped inside. The room was warm. Marion would be comfortable. Gene couldn't find anyone in the building. Returning to the truck, he opened the tailgate and pulled Marion out. After navigating the front door with the limp body on his shoulder, he placed her so that her back was propped up on the change machine. If someone walked into the place, she would be hard to miss.

With some sense of guilt, Gene walked out of the Quick-E Laundromat and left Marion behind. He closed up the back of the truck and drove away. He drove back through town. He was worried about Marion. He stopped at a pay phone next to a diner. The phone was on the edge of the property. He hoped that no one would notice him or the red truck. He could have dialed 911, but he thought he would be better off calling the police department directly. He called information to get the number and then called the police.

"Could I speak to a detective that handles missing persons cases?" Gene asked. He wasn't sure who to talk to.

"I don't know about that," the person answered. It was a woman's voice. "I'll see who I can find."

There was silence. After a couple of minutes another voice came on the line. It was a man's voice this time.

"Hello. Detective Helmbrecht speaking."

"I'm not sure how to say this," Gene started. "Do you know the Quick-E Laundromat on the west side of town?"

"Yeah," said the detective. "Sure. Who is this?"

"Listen. Please."

"All right," said Helmbrecht. "Could you tell me your name?"

"There's a woman in the Quick-E Laundromat. Her name is Marion Latterner. She's unconscious. She's been given some drug, and I believe she needs medical attention. You need to take her to a hospital." Gene hung up the phone.

Chapter 32

Harry Sharp's Chair

Gene disembarked from the Foster Kennedy and headed straight for his lab. The schedule called for him to work in his lab for the next thirty-seven minutes. So many of the principles of Davenport Center had been violated that he didn't bother to review the specifics in his mind, as he often did. He didn't want to attract attention. It would be best, he thought, to avoid all contact with the people of Davenport Center.

Inside the main atrium he saw two VTSs chatting in a lounge area opposite the North Pole display. One of the men was so fat that he didn't quite fit into the beige lounge chair in which he was seated. His shirt was tight. The bottom seam of it rested an inch above the waistband of his sweatpants. The large man's eyes bulged out of his puffy face, and his fingers disappeared into the meaty balls that were his hands.

The other man was thin to the point of emaciation. His head appeared to be shrunken and out of proportion to the rest of his body. Skeleton man had a thin, pointed black beard, which was his most prominent, though not most disturbing, feature. His eyes were sunken. His nose had become narrow and bony. His throat looked as though it had been trimmed away, more on the left than on the right. What remained was streaked with black, perhaps beard growth, and half as wide as Gene expected it to be.

As Gene passed the two men, they stopped talking. The two patients did not look familiar to Gene, but they wore the distinctive sky-blue robes of the Davenport Center VTS. He guessed that they were new to the island.

As Gene moved towards the rear, east staircase, their eyes followed him. They were the only ones in the vast main entranceway, which seemed odd to Gene for early evening. The area was often teeming with people, VTSs having conversations or reading, outside-ins taking a break. Components never socialized with the patients or the outside-ins, but Gene had seen the lobby activities from up above through windows that looked down from the component quarters.

"Do you know who your father is?" asked the fat man. His loud voice echoed throughout the atrium.

Gene had passed the two men, and his back was toward them. It was a strange question spoken too loud for someone sitting nearby. Gene kept walking, but he wondered whether the question could have been directed at him.

"I'm talking to you, Dr. Nolan." The booming voice filled the empty space. "Do you know who your father is?"

The situation was odd. Why would this fat man be waiting for him? Gene became first concerned and then frightened. He turned toward the men who were seated forty feet away.

"Are you talking to me?" asked Gene.

The plump man pointed to the wasted man and said, "Do you think I was talking to him? He's sitting right next to me." The skinny man nodded. "Of course I'm talking to you, Dr. Nolan."

"I don't know you," Gene said. "How do you know my name?"

The large man rose and shook his finger at Gene. "No, I don't think you understand how this works. I ask the questions, and you politely answer them. You never have understood the seventh principle have you? Any information that you need to know will be provided to you. Come over and sit with us."

Gene stood where he was and stared at the men. How would a VTS know about the principles of Davenport Center? Gene felt pressure to get to his lab. But as the fat man approached Gene, he thought it best to acquiesce to the man's request and hear what he had to say. Gene walked toward the men and sat in a chair next to slim, placing the canvas bag he was carrying on his lap so that it could be protected by his arm. Butterball lumbered back over and fell into the chair in which he had been sitting. Gene witnessed tremors in the adipose tissue that covered the man's midsection as he settled back into place.

"Now let's return to an earlier topic of conversation," said the fat man. "Who is your father?"

"I have not seen my father since I was a child," Gene answered. "I don't know where he is."

"This is the worst case I've ever seen, Elbridge," the fat man said. "We have our work cut out for us."

"Yes," thin Elbridge wheezed. The thin man spoke in a throaty whisper. "Dr. Nolan, why are you here?"

"I work here," Gene said. "Why are the two of you here?"

The robust man stared at Gene and rubbed his chin with one of his puffy hands. "You've really learned to think for yourself, haven't you?"

"I don't know what you guys want, or who you are or why you're here, but I really need to be someplace else. This discussion is not on my schedule for today. Perhaps if you submit a request to Sarah Vorschrift time can be set aside for this little talk." Gene had no intention of talking to these strange men again if he could help it.

"Don't worry about your schedule, Gene. You haven't been paying much attention to it anyway. We've already cleared your schedule for the next few days."

"Next few days! I have important work to do."

"It's amazing to me that you have figured out how your own time can be best utilized. It's really amazing." The imposing man looked over at Elbridge with a twisted smile on his face, "Isn't that amazing?"

"It is amazing," said Elbridge without looking at his partner. "Don't you think it's time for us to go?"

"Gene," said the large man, "you'll have to pardon Elbridge. He's a little impatient sometimes. He tries to cut right to the point. He always means well, and this time he's right. It is time for us to go. I'm afraid we'll have to stop all of this chit-chat."

"Good," said Gene as he stood. "Well, it was nice to meet you both," he said, but he didn't believe it. "I have got to be going myself." Gene did not extend his hand.

"No. I don't think you understand, Dr. Nolan. You're coming with us," Elbridge said.

Gene moved away from the two men, back towards the stairwell. As he reached the door to the stairs, he found that he couldn't open it. Gene didn't remember that door being locked in the past. As a matter of fact, he didn't even know that the door had a lock. Gene walked toward the front door, where he had come in from the cold outside.

The entire time, the rotund man and the meager man sat in their seats and watched. The fat man smirked. Elbridge remained serious.

Gene approached the glass doors that opened to the outside, and they too were locked. They had not been when Gene walked in a few minutes before. Pushing on each of the six doors, Gene saw no way out of the room. He tried one more stairwell near the door. When he found that locked, he looked back toward the two men. As Gene stood by the door to the stairwell, the two men got up out of their seats and walked over.

Elbridge pulled a clear plastic strap of his bathrobe pocket. "Please turn around and face the wall," Elbridge said in his sandpaper voice.

Gene stared at them in disbelief. Then, before he could react, the fat man was all over him. Gene could smell the man's putrid body odor as he flipped Gene around and yanked the bag out of his arms.

"Don't break anything, Ted," Elbridge said. "Now please give me your arms."

Gene complied and Elbridge tied the plastic strap around Gene's wrists. Pulling Gene by the elbow, Ted followed Elbridge to the back of the lobby. In shock, Gene no longer knew how to react. Elbridge led them to the back of the room and through a door to some stairs that set them out on the second floor near the public dining room. Gene continued to be surprised by the fact that no one else was around. He couldn't remember ever having seen the public dining room empty before. This time the entire room was empty, and there was no sound coming from the kitchen off to the left, suggesting that there was no one preparing meals either.

This was not an area of the building that Gene frequented, and Gene was surprised when they walked into a hallway at the east of the dining room. Eldridge walked with confidence, like someone who knew where he was going. After several turns, a couple of doors and a trip down a narrow corridor, Gene found himself in a place that he knew well, the Mission and Conscience Department where he worked. Gene had never used the door through which they emerged and was frustrated that it could have been there all this time, and yet he had never been curious about it.

The two men led Gene into the conference room where Gene had met with Dr. Gallagher and other components on many occasions. Gene now knew where they were taking him. Although he had never witnessed it himself, Gene had heard stories about compliance devices that were located adjacent to the conference room. The devices were used to bring components back into line with the philosophies of Davenport Center and were set next to the conference room so that the components could see that justice was dispensed with a firm and even hand. Perhaps if Bruce had committed his indiscretions in Maryland rather than in Ecuador he would have ended up here instead of dead.

There were two sets of collapsing doors on one side of the room. They had always been closed when Gene had been in the conference room. One set of the doors had been opened to reveal a large observation window and a small door. But the room on the other side of the window was dark and the window revealed nothing but blackness.

Gene had heard of one device. It was called compliance by water. A component whose behavior had become inconsistent with the principles of Davenport Center had been placed in a room where the water level was set at about four feet and left for several days. The water level was low enough the man could comfortably stand with his head above water and high enough that he couldn't sit. At first the room wouldn't be all that unpleasant. But there was no way to sleep as the victim's head would fall into the water as sleep came. Over time the sleep depravation and boredom would lead to genuine torment. The last person was placed in the water room shortly before Gene's induction into the body. Gene was told that he screamed for hours from leg cramps that developed one morning during a staff meeting. The story had made Gene anxious, but he had never been certain that the compliance devices existed. Such a device would be inhumane, and Gene didn't see how Dr. Gallagher could ever condone its use. On the other hand, maybe compliance by water was responsible in part for the fact that, as far as Gene knew, all of the components except for himself and Bruce had always complied with all of the principles all of the time.

"Bring him in," Elbridge said as he opened the small door and flipped on the light.

Gene could see through the observation window. Even though he was not sure what he was looking at, Gene became frightened. His legs wobbled and Ted had to lift him into the room since he seemed unable to walk in of his own accord.

A metal chair. That's what Gene saw. This had nothing to do with compliance by water as far as he could tell. It looked like a machine that could be used to electrocute someone. Buried among wires, straps and sharp metal shapes was the unmistakable shape of a chair. This chair was placed on a pedestal in the middle of an otherwise empty room. All of the walls were white. Gene looked back toward the observation window into the conference room. All he could see was his own reflection.

Ted dropped the bag with Kelly's things in it onto the floor by the wall. Elbridge pulled a knife from his pocket and cut the plastic strip that bound Gene's hands.

"Take off your clothes," said Ted in his booming voice.

"What?" asked Gene.

"If you don't take off your clothes, you cannot sit in the chair," rasped Elbridge, as he tossed the plastic strip onto the floor.

"That's OK. I don't want to sit in the chair," said Gene. "We don't need to go through all this. What do you want from me?"

"I want you to take your clothes off," said Elbridge. "If you're going to have trouble with that, Ted can help you."

Gene stood still and defiant.

"Ted, why don't you offer to give this man a little help just to get him started."

Ted lifted his arm and brought the back of his right hand crashing into the side of Gene's face. The force knocked Gene backwards into the wall.

"Take your clothes off," said Elbridge.

Ted moved closer to Gene who had braced himself against the wall with one hand. He used the other to comfort his injured face. Ted raised his arm into the air.

"No," said Gene. "No more help."

Gene took off his coat and the rest of his clothes except his underpants and threw everything into a pile on top of the canvas bag.

"Everything," said Elbridge.

Gene hesitated.

Ted raised his hand again.

Gene pulled off his shorts and tossed them onto the pile. Standing naked in front of the two men, Gene was angered by the way he had been pushed around and forced into this humiliating situation. Gene cupped his genitals with his hands in a last attempt to maintain his dignity and privacy.

"What the hell is this?" asked Ted. He pulled at the aaskuouandy around Gene's neck.

Gene did not respond and he looked at the wall behind Ted.

Ted pulled harder on the cord made from the fiber of tropical vines. It was a sturdy cord, which Gene now appreciated more than ever since he could feel it ripping through the back of his neck. "I asked you a question." But as Gene continued his silence Ted waved his hand at Elbridge who cut the cord that held the aaskouandy around Gene's neck. Ted threw the bird beak onto the pile of Gene's clothes. It landed on top of his briefs where the dark beak stood out against the white fabric.

Gene began to feel guilty about the way that he had behaved over the last days and weeks. He wondered why he had ever defied Dr. Gallagher's rules and decided to question the values that had protected him from the problems of the outside world. He felt uneasy about his relationship with Kelly and the recent visit to her house. How could he have lost control of himself this way and hurt Dr. Gallagher who he cared about so much?

Elbridge pulled at Gene's arm and dragged him up to the chair. "Sit!" he commanded.

Gene sat, unwilling to resist the two any longer. For several moments, the men tied Gene down with leather straps. At his neck, arms, ankles and other places the straps held him tight against the cold metal. Skin sticking to the chair, Gene struggled to find the best position before one part or another got locked into place. The straps pressed small electrodes against Gene's bare skin. Soon the men stood back and admired their work. One last leather strap dangled from a wire in Ted's hand.

"This is the special one," he said and then Gene could feel him placing the object on his scrotum just below the base of his penis.

261

"Alright," rasped Elbridge. "Here are the rules of the game."

Ted walked over to the door and opened it and then threw off the light switch in the room. Then he flipped another switch on the far wall. The reflection of eight colored light bulbs appeared before Gene, reflected off of the back of the observation window. All of the lights were off.

"Can you see the colors on the wall?" Elbridge asked.

"Yeah," Gene replied.

"Look at your fingertips."

Gene couldn't move his head much, but he could see small buttons with colors matching the lights reflected before him. He was able to reach the small buttons with his fingers.

"Go on. Press one."

Gene pressed the red button on the left and felt a sharp electrical jolt to his genitals.

"That's what happens if you hit the wrong button. Want to try again?"

"No."

"Now I'm going to start this thing," said the thin man. "If the yellow light on the right flashes, you're going to want to hit the yellow button on the right within five seconds. If you don't, you're going to get a little electrical reminder that you forgot to press the button. The reminder might come anywhere, to your ankle, to your knee, to your neck, anywhere. You already know what happens if you push a button before the corresponding light flashes. Each time you miss a light or hit the wrong button, the reminders get a little stronger. Let me show you." He leaned over and punched one of the buttons four times. Gene got four jolts to his genitals, each stronger than the last. "Get it right for a time and the reminders go back down."

The yellow light on the left flashed. Gene pushed the yellow button on the left.

"All right," said Elbridge. "I can see you've got the idea. All you have to do is watch for the light and then press the button that matches it. It's easy."

"You shouldn't have any problem with this, Gene," said the big man. "They say that you're a smart one. You've got to pay attention though, and it makes it hard to sleep, impossible really."

"What do you want from me?" Gene asked. He saw the green light on the right flash. He pressed the green button on the right. "I'll do what you want."

"I know you'll do what we want," said Elbridge. "And right now we want you to stay in this chair. That's all. Someone will be by to check in on you in a day or two. I don't know."

The green light on the right flashed again.

Chapter 33

Men Worry Too Much

"We just paid off the mortgage this year," Marion said.

"That's really remarkable. I can't believe that it has been so long since I have been in your house," Peter said. He removed the large yellow and red parka he was wearing and then grabbed Marion's arm as the walked towards the living room.

"Now, Peter," said Marion, "I appreciate you coming out here to visit with me, but I can walk on my own." Even so, Marion wobbled a little when she walked.

"I feel so awful about what happened to you. I just want to do what I can to help," Peter said.

"Now why would you feel awful, Peter? It wasn't your fault." Marion adjusted her skirt as she sat down in her flowered wingback chair.

"You've been living in this house for thirty years have you?" asked Peter. "I remember when you moved in. It can't have been that long ago."

"It wasn't. Doug's had a lot of success in his career, and we thought it would be nice to have one less bill every month."

"Things must be going well for Doug. He was smart not getting a job in the government like us. You must have paid this place off…What? Ten years early?" asked Peter.

"It's only eight years, and you'd be surprised what life is like after you get the kids through college and out of the house." Marion grinned a little, though it turned out more like a grimace.

"So do the police know what happened, I mean, who kidnapped you?"

"Those cops out there in the boonies? Are you kidding?" said Marion. "They're about as befuddled as a heard of cows in a pasture. They don't know why I was kidnapped, who kidnapped me or why I was released. I don't remember much myself. I was unconscious most of the time. They say that I had been injected with sodium-penathol."

"So you don't remember anything?" asked Peter.

"Well, there was the accident, then, I don't know. Noises, shadows, echoes. Nothing substantial. There was this flicking noise I remember." Marion closed her eyes as she sat in the chair. "Flick. Flick. Flick. It was the sound a lighter makes when it's ignited."

"What did the police think of that?"

"I don't know. They didn't seem too interested in anything I had to say. And they didn't tell me too much either. I'm just glad to be here in one piece." Marion looked at Peter and grinned a little. "You sure are curious about all the fine details."

"I just like to stay informed," said Peter. "Do you know who released you?"

"The police said a man called and told them where I could be found. Some laundry place over in Cambridge. But he didn't identify himself. They played a tape of it for me to see if I could identify the voice."

"Was it the kidnapper?"

"I don't know. The tape was bad. There was a lot of noise. I suppose it could have been. It's not much to go on. The voice sounded sort of familiar, but I don't know. I couldn't place it. I know Marcus is mixed up in this somehow. I told the police about him. I hope they go talk to him. Marcus the kidnapper. I know it sounds absurd."

"It does sound absurd. You know he wouldn't be involved in a kidnapping."

"I'll find out."

"So what are your plans now?" asked Peter. "You're going to rest for a while, I hope."

"Oh, maybe for a day or so. I'm going to get back to my audit out on Bloodsworth Island though. They tell me that all work on it stopped after I disappeared." Her voice had changed from pleasant into a grumble. "No doubt, Marcus directed that as well."

"I'm not quite sure what happened," said Peter.

"So, I'll probably rest up through tomorrow and then get back out there the day after."

"So soon!" Peter said. "I really think you should rest for a while, don't you?"

"You sound just like my husband. You men worry too much about us poor, frail women. I can handle myself just fine. And the longer I wait, the more Marcus will do to hide what I'm looking for. I'm so close to getting him now I just can't stop."

"I don't think it's a good idea for you to go back so soon. Those audits can be very strenuous. I'm not sure you're up to it. I really have to say no, Marion."

Marion laughed. "You're saying no to me. Peter, come on. You can't be serious. I know you're my boss and all, but I've never been one for taking orders. I'll be fine. Don't worry about me so much."

"Oh, but I am worried about you, Marion. Quite worried. I think that you are bringing your personal life into your work. I can't say I fully understand what happened between you and Marcus, but your behavior is irrational."

"When I was involved with Marcus, we were both kids. He was completely irresponsible. I found it sort of appealing, since I was always too serious. The man knew, and I suppose still knows, how to be charming when he wants to." Marion paused and looked at the wood shutters that covered the inside of the windows in the living room. "I admit that I was deeply hurt when he broke it off with me, but that has nothing to do with what is happening now."

"Marion, how can I believe that?"

"He is a dangerous man, Peter. I believe I have special insight into this since I was so intimately involved with him. You can't see it on the surface. He looks like everyone else. But the man is the devil. He has masked himself to come here on the Earth with us for awhile, but he means nothing but death and destruction for all of us. He must be stopped before it is too late."

"So you say that your personal convictions will not get in the way of your work?" asked Peter.

Marion did not reply to this remark right away. She sat in silence for a few moments and her typical sour expression turned even darker. She lifted her head up and said, "Well, I'm feeling a little worn out right now. Maybe I should take a nap."

"I think that would be a great idea," said Peter. "Don't rush back to work, Marion. It will still be there when you recover."

"Thanks, Peter." She stood to walk him back to the front door. "I really appreciate your coming to visit me and for being so concerned."

"It's my pleasure, Marion. Good-bye."

Marion stood behind the window in the storm door and watched as Peter got into his Ford Taurus sedan and drove out of the neighborhood. Her husband emerged from the kitchen and stood behind her, hugging her middle. "How did that go?" he asked.

"I don't know," said Marion. "Not very well, I think. Something is wrong. It seems like he's up to something."

"Peter? Is he really capable of being up to anything?"

"Maybe not by himself. I don't know enough yet. I've got to get back to that audit."

Chapter 34

Aaskouandy

Gene was able to keep up with the lights and protect himself from injury for many hours, until he began to lose the ability to focus. Unable to concentrate on the lights and the buttons any longer, he was powerless to prevent the shocks. The electricity came with greater frequency and power. Then at some point, he shocked himself in the genitals three times within an hour. That was it. Despite the exhaustion which had resulted in the mental equivalent of a hangover, he decided that he would do whatever it took to prevent shocks to his genitals. From time to time, the device would provide Gene with an opportunity to rest which might last as long as fifteen minutes. These periods of rest would vary in length but they always ended the same way, with a shock and a mad scramble to clear the mental haze in order to find the right button to press.

His mind had become a jumble of confusion and self-doubt. Deep inside, Gene knew that he must stop Alfred and Dr. Gallagher from killing millions of people, not that he had the power. But the hours of intense mental effort paired with his insecurity and confusion had worn away at his resolve to maintain and fight for his newfound freedom, which in any event he had already lost. Gene wished that he had followed orders. All his aberrant behavior had done was create problems, some insurmountable, for himself and for others. He didn't need to understand everything. He didn't need to know all of the details. If he had just lived by the principles he had taken an oath to support, he would be fine now.

Instead, he was sitting in an uncomfortable, electrified chair, smelling his own excrement. The chair had been designed to collect his liquid and solid waste, but the thing was not as effective as a toilet at washing away the remnants. Now the odor added to the effect of his delirium as he traveled through periods of troubled sleep and confused wakefulness.

He had been hungry for a time, but that was far outweighed by his thirst. Clammy and cool, his skin attempted to hold in what liquid remained in his tissues. His lips had dried and cracked and his throat became sore and irritated. Finding it more difficult to focus on the lights on the wall, he responded to the flashing lights by reflex, and he was surprised at how often he got it right. His eyes fell away from the lights to the reflected image of himself in the chair, and the sight, eyes of death, bleached skin, a look of helplessness, caused him to grimace.

Gene did not want all of the people to die, least of all Kelly. Ted and Elbridge had not told him what they wanted. Gene didn't know who they were. Where was Dr. Gallagher? He had told Gene that he would always protect him. How long were they going to keep him here? Until he died? Gene had wanted to follow the principles, and he knew that he had not followed them. He knew he had been wrong. As he sat in the chair he became committed to the principles. He saw the wisdom that was reflected in their development and promulgation. He would follow them always. He could make that commitment and keep it this time. He was certain of that. Couldn't they just stop this and talk to him?

The lights stopped flashing for the moment.

Gene flexed his hands which had grown weary from the strain. He knew that sleep would soon claim him, but for this moment his mind raced. Looking down to where his clothes lay against the wall, he thought again about the death certificate that he had taken from Kelly's house. Maybe he wouldn't talk to Alfred about it. Talking about the death certificate would violate one principle, but keeping it a secret violated another. Gene doubted his ability to make a decision concerning this or any other matter.

While looking at the pile of clothing on the floor, Gene noticed that a beam of light shone onto the aaskouandy. Gene couldn't find its source. All of his attention focused on the bird beak, and that's when he realized that the beak was the source of the light. A change began to occur and the bird beak grew. The aaskouandy became large, larger than Gene. And it lay on the underwear with the tip of the beak pointing toward the wall. Gene knew he wasn't sleeping. This was no dream. He was sure of that. He thought he was sure of that. He could still smell the excrement from his bowels, and his skin remained clammy. He couldn't dream those things.

Hiaroma's charm began to change shape, but it kept its dark coloring. The aaskouandy shifted and warped until Gene heard a roar emerge from the mass that had developed. He realized that two yellow eyes floated in the blackness, and that's when the dark mass snapped into shape. A melanistic jaguar stood before him, muscles flexed, body tense and ready to pounce. Gene was frightened by the animal's presence and its power.

"Gene," the jaguar said, "you must decide. You alone must control your mind and your fate. This is important, more important than anything else."

Gene recognized the voice of the jaguar. "Decide? Decide what? Hiaroma? Where are you?"

"Yes, Gene Doctor. Among my people the jaguar is a symbol of our ancestors. We fear and respect them. I can transform myself into a jaguar to talk to the ancestors, to seek guidance from them, to talk to you."

"But I can't think. I have no control. I have lost whatever power I might have had."

"Each person must decide. Each person... you... must set your own course. Others can help. I have come to bring you the wisdom of the ancestors. I can help you. They can help you. But you alone must decide."

"Even if I resist, there are too many, and they are too powerful," said Gene. "I can't stop them. It is too late. I am too weak."

The jaguar stood and paced in front of Gene. The black cat with the big chest and well-muscled front legs turned and growled a throaty growl. Then Hiaroma spoke again. "Imposition of one person's will in place of individual choice destroys the human spirit. That force must be resisted no matter what. My people are strong. We fought off domination for millennia. We maintained our independence. Then that freedom was destroyed in an instant. What happened in my village must not happen again. You do have the power. You must ask yourself if you also have the will."

"I don't know what to do. The forces here have overwhelmed me." Gene rattled at the leather straps. "Look! I'm trapped! How can I fight?"

"You know what to do. You have a plan. Do you have the will to follow it, the will to do what is right?" With that, the cat lay back down and the shape changed again. Gene watched as the aaskouandy returned to the shape of an antbird beak and shrunk to its original size.

The light in the ceiling of the room came on. Gene moved his eyes to see the door open. Alfred appeared wearing his violet lab coat with the silver piping and holding a clipboard at his side. He walked around Gene and looked at him.

"Alfred... please... get me out..." Gene said. The blue light on the left flashed.

"I can see that the time in Harry Sharp's chair has not tamed your wild spirit. I guess that application of the therapy over a longer period of time is required in this case." Alfred lifted his clipboard to write some notes and then walked back toward the door.

"No. Please... anything... I'll do anything," Gene said. He thought about Hiaroma.

"Haven't you learned anything? You are to do what you are told. You must learn that. For now you are to stay in this chair."

"What? What do you want... from me?" The red light on the left flashed. The green light on the right flashed a second later.

"That's the problem, Gene. You think too much about your individual needs. You don't acknowledge the importance of the whole organization. Everyone can't think for himself. People can't do whatever they choose, whatever feels right at the moment. It would be total chaos. No organization could operate like that. It takes coordinated effort to broadcast television programs, to produce newspapers, to see that food is delivered to the grocery store, to see that a hospital delivers competent medical service. There must be some central control, some central authority. We all need guidance, Gene. You especially need guidance."

Gene was confused. The yellow light on the right flashed. His mind felt as though it might explode. Mistakes had been made. He would be the first to admit that. He felt powerless and weak, and his life was out of control.

"Mistakes!" said Gene. "I know. Mistakes. I made mistakes."

"Good," said Alfred, surprise in his voice. "It seems like we are making progress. There's a certain hierarchy to things, Gene. There must be order. We must follow the direction of a central authority. Otherwise all of the good that we do, all of our work will be destroyed."

"Yes," said Gene. "Yes..." The yellow light on the right flashed again. "Yes. I... I... was wrong. Mistakes. I made... mistakes."

"Good," said Alfred. "Understanding that will help."

"I... I... tried."

"See. That's what I mean. That's where the problem is." Alfred leaned against the observation window and looked at Gene.

Gene didn't respond. He couldn't. He didn't understand. The blue light on the right flashed.

"That's what I mean," repeated Alfred. "You didn't try hard enough. If you had tried, I mean really tried, you wouldn't be here right now."

"Sorry. I... am... am... sorry."

"Sorry. Sorry's good."

"I see... things. I... I... worry."

"There you go again. Will you ever understand? If you are worrying, you are thinking. To worry, you must imagine that you have some independent control or judgment. If that were true it would simply lead to a world of chaos."

Alfred walked around to the back of the chair and made notes on his clipboard. "There is no need for worry at Davenport Center," he continued. "If you worry, that means you have jumped to some conclusion. If that doesn't amount to independent thought, I don't know what does. You will be told everything you need to know. You have not been provided with sufficient information to understand what we do here. That's why you must learn to acknowledge and accept Dr. Gallagher's guidance. He knows. He understands. He will do what is best for us."

Whatever Alfred wanted, Gene had decided that he would provide, but Alfred's words sounded like gibberish. Gene had tried to be compliant, but in the few words he had spoken Alfred had found defiance instead. Confusion and exhaustion ruled Gene's mind. Desperation would guide whatever words might come next, as Gene felt only tenuous control over himself and limited understanding of the impact of his words.

"Dr. Gallagher lied to you," said Gene. He didn't understand the source of the words or where he found the strength to speak them. "Your daughter is still alive. Your wife is still alive. Dr. Gallagher has hidden those things from you." It was a gamble. For all Gene knew, Alfred had prepared the death certificate.

"Who? What are you talking about?"

"Your daughter." The green light on the left flashed. "She works here at Davenport Center."

"Although components are not to speak of such things, I believe that I told you that my daughter was killed in plane crash many years ago." Alfred spoke in his usual monotone. "Therefore, it would be quite impossible for her to work at Davenport Center."

"She's... alive. She works... here."

"This is highly unusual. An effect that I have never seen produced by The Chair before." Alfred paced around the back side of Harry Sharp's Chair. "So which person who works here at Davenport Center is my long lost daughter, back from the dead."

"Her name is Kelly Halpin. She works for Raines in his lab."

"So your secret lover is really my lost daughter?" asked Alfred.

Gene was not surprised by the question. He knew that he had not been put in Harry Sharp's chair because he had been late returning from the library. In his first few hours in the chair, while he was still lucid, he thought that his relationship with Kelly must have been exposed.

"Yes," said Gene.

"She really must have been put here by someone on the outside." Alfred said. "I'm a little surprised at you, Gene. Will you believe anything? I mean, just because she told you that she was my daughter, you think that it's true?"

"It is... your... daughter," said Gene. "Kelly doesn't even know that she is your daughter. I have your... death certificate. It's in my... jacket." Gene used his tongue to point, and he moved his eyes in the direction of the jacket which hadn't been disturbed since Ted had thrown it onto the floor. Gene didn't know how many hours or days it had been there.

Alfred picked Gene's shirt up off of the jacket, folded it and then laid it in a new pile and then pulled the jacket into the air. The worn envelope fell from its pocket and Alfred picked that up as well. Alfred retrieved the clipboard, unfolded the paper and slid it under the clip. He didn't say anything as he looked at it.

"I suppose you just happened across this paper in her pocketbook while you were having one of your inappropriate and inconsistent meetings with her." said Alfred with some emphasis, a change from his typical monotone.

"No, I got it at her house," Gene realized that with each word he was burying himself deeper. "Look, Kelly's got nothing to do with this. Except... she is your daughter."

"What are you trying to do?" asked Alfred.

"Protect... her," said Gene.

"Protect her?"

"From the... virus. Cystic-fibrosis. She's... a... carrier. Millions will... die. She's is... one."

Alfred didn't argue with Gene. He didn't say anything. He looked at the death certificate. He looked back at Gene.

"Is she... ok?" asked Gene.

"Yeah. I guess so. She has accepted a new work assignment and will be living here at Davenport Center for a time."

"New assignment?" Gene was disturbed by Alfred's apparent disinterest in Kelly. He spoke of Kelly with surprising detachment. Gene did not understand how Alfred could be so cold and analytical. He also knew that living at Davenport Center might make Kelly an ITS with serious consequences whether or not he stopped the release of the virus.

"I am beginning to doubt that you can be reformed using conventional methods," Alfred said. "I need to analyze this further before we can continue." He turned and walked to the door.

"Let me out of the chair," Gene begged.

Alfred switched off the light and left the room.

The blue light on the left side flashed twice, followed by the red light on the right side and the red light of the left side, all within about a second. Gene tried to keep up, but he missed the red light on the left side. He shocked himself twice in the genitals before he found the right button.

All seemed lost to him. He was emotionally and mentally exhausted. The death certificate had had little impact on Alfred, and Alfred didn't seem to care about Kelly. Gene didn't know how much longer he could respond to the lights. The semi-conscious state he had been in before Alfred entered the room would return soon. What would happen if he stopped pushing the buttons altogether? Would the shocks become more and more powerful until he would be electrocuted? He didn't know.

Minutes crawled by. Lights flashed. Gene's desperation became more and more profound. The power and will that Hiaroma spoke about seemed far outside of Gene's reach.

Then the door opened again. Alfred returned. Without speaking, he knelt and began removing the straps around Gene's legs. Deep red marks scored Gene's flesh where the straps had been fastened.

"Alfred ... thank you," said Gene. The green light on the right flashed.

"I'm taking you before Dr. Gallagher."

After the straps had been unbuckled and the electrodes removed from his body, Gene struggled to rise from the chair. He fell backwards causing the urine which had collected on and around the seat to splash. Struggling again, this time with Alfred's silent help, Gene was able to stand on weakened, unsteady legs.

Alfred gathered Gene's clothing and the canvas bag. He motioned for Gene to follow him. Alfred walked and Gene hobbled through the conference room, across the hall and into a bathroom where Gene could wash up before putting his clothes back on.

"Don't take all night," said Alfred, when he deposited Gene in the bathroom.

Gene turned on the water, cupped his hands and leaned over to drink. He sucked down water until he couldn't take anymore. His stomach felt bloated. The thirst was still there, but there was no room for more water. After washing up, he began the painful process of pulling the clothing on over his injured body. The clothes stung in the places where the straps had been, but Gene was grateful to be dressed again.

Alfred poked his head into the bathroom. Gene sat on the floor leaning against the door to one of the stalls. The noise Alfred made startled Gene, and he opened his eyes.

"Where's Kelly?" asked Gene by reflex.

"That is not your concern," said Alfred. "Please keep moving, I do not want to keep Dr. Gallagher waiting any longer." Gene's stomach gurgled and twisted in hunger. Just sitting on the cold tile floor was difficult. Gene was conscious of his surroundings, but everything seemed a little hazy. His eyelids were heavy, and his body ached for sleep.

"The virus," said Gene. "What about the virus?"

The frown on Alfred's face pulled at his eyebrows. Gene thought he might ignore the question, but then he didn't.

"Tomorrow. It's going out tomorrow."

"We must stop it." Gene struggled to stand and fell back onto the floor.

"Don't be ridiculous. It would be wrong to stop it. Dr. Gallagher won't postpone the release."

"But what about Kelly?"

Alfred waved his arm, dismissing Gene's question. "Get yourself ready. I'll be back in a few minutes."

Following another attempt to get up, Gene fell onto the floor once more. After pushing himself onto his side, he slipped into unconsciousness. When he woke with a start, he didn't know whether he had been asleep for seconds, minutes, hours or days. Driven by hunger, he stood and stabilized himself for a moment by holding onto the swinging door of the toilet stall. After establishing some sense of balance he hobbled off in the direction of the public dining room. Alfred was nowhere to be found, not that Gene looked for him. It didn't matter. For the moment, food would take priority.

Out in the circular hallway in the doughnut shaped portion of the building, Gene could see only the darkness of the night sky punctuated by a few glistening stars through the glass pyramids. And no one was about. It must be the middle of the night he realized. He knew he would find food in the pantry off the kitchen.

Chapter 35

To Bloodsworth Island

With his left hand, Richard steered his Camaro through what little traffic there was in downtown Easton at 10:00 pm. Using his right index finger, he probed his ear, brought the finger out and shoved it into his nose. As if rehearsing a ritual, he repeated these motions several times. He seemed to like the way he smelled. Sometimes he would rub his fingers in his crotch and analyze the combinations of urine and sweat that existed there. Each night as he removed his shirt he sniffed at his armpits, lingering there just long enough to ensure that he got a good whiff.

The brick houses of Easton had been built when there was ample wealth in the area, but many of them had suffered with the rest of the economy in that part of the state. Madame Charlotte's place was dark, and there was a parking space under the spruce tree in her front yard. After parking the car with three precise movements, he popped out and ran his hand along the side panel, examining the fresh paint job.

Richard knocked hard when he reached the side door of the house. His breath was visible as clouds of steam puffing out of his lungs and liquefying against the panes of glass in the door. It had grown much colder over the last two days, colder than usual for December. Stars were visible but massive precipitation-bearing clouds blocked sections of most constellations. After several minutes, he knocked again. The door opened and Madame Charlotte poked her head out, looking down the street first in one direction and then the other.

"Get in here." She grabbed Richard's arm and yanked him inside. She examined the street one more time after Richard entered the house and then slammed the door. She wore no shoes and her navy corduroy skirt was lopsided, hanging down more on the left than on the right. Her blossom-covered blouse was no longer tucked. It hung loose over the top of her skirt. Even in this somewhat disheveled state she wore a tremendous number of bracelets, necklaces and rings.

"What do you want?" The pudgy woman stared up at least a foot to look Richard directly in the eyes. "Why are you disturbing me so late at night?"

"I don't know where else to go," Richard said.

"There is a 7-11 at the corner. They're open twenty-four hours a day. I, however, have business hours that are posted on the sign out front. I hear that they make wonderful Slurpees there."

"Madame, I need your help."

"You definitely need help." She looked at his face for a moment, and then the anger in her expression softened. "What is it that you expect from me?"

"I woke up this morning with a dream and haven't been able to shake it off all day. I screwed everything up," Richard whined and held ·his head down. "Everybody's pissed at me: my boss, Catherine, Kelly. Everything I do turns to shit."

"That man who has been haunting you, it's his spirit. Your experiences are so typical of such a haunting. He's taunting you so that you cannot find inner peace and happiness." She looked at his body and then turned toward the center of the house. She turned back to him again. "It's late, but since we are both down here already... I will have to charge you double for the visit."

"Anything." He dug in his pocket and pulled out some bills and handed them to her. "But I need your help."

She took the wad of cash and then led him into the parlor near the foyer where they had been standing. "I'm sorry that the place is so cold. My ex-husband didn't pay his child support check again this month so I had to turn down the heat and give up some other luxuries."

"I'll straighten that bum out for you. Where's he at?"

"That's very sweet Dear, but I don't know where he is. That's my problem. If I could find him I would, as you say, straighten him out myself. Wait here, and don't touch anything." The gypsy shuffled off, bracelets jingling on her arms as she walked, leaving Richard alone in the red room.

There was no incense burning now, but everything in the room reeked from it. The heavy wallpaper was loose in several places, and at the corners it had peeled away from the walls. The muffled, distant sound of unrecognizable voices, television most likely, filtered through the ceiling. Richard sat on a leather couch that faced the door that Madame Charlotte had walked through.

She returned with a beer in one hand and a book in the other. "Come join me at the table." Popping open the beer, she patted on the seat next to her. "There are several levels to the therapy you will need to expel this spirit. Luckily for us, the Earth is as bountiful in health as it is in disease. I believe that wearing a specific crystal might help you combat this spirit, especially while you are sleeping. Would you like me to give you a crystal to help?"

"That would be great, Madame Charlotte." He sat down next to her and took a swig of the beer, and then wiped his sleeve across his face.

She reached behind the table into a drawer in a cabinet that was supported by the wall, since the two back legs were no longer there. After pulling out a dark blue jagged rock, she said, "I would give this one to you at no charge, but it's my last one. I might need one in an emergency, and with my ex-husband's financial curse I can't afford another. I'll give it to you at cost, if that's ok?"

"Sure, Madame."

"It's twenty-five dollars. Here you go." She handed him the crystal that was attached to a small string.

Richard reached into his pocket and pulled out some bills. "Here's fifty. You need to make sure you have enough to eat and take care of the kids."

"You're so sweet. I wish you were available." She folded the bills and hid them in the right pocket of her long skirt. "This is Lapis Lazuli. Wear that around your neck and it will protect you from this evil spirit, and it will reduce your depression. Let us continue discussing your situation. I sense that you were prompted to come here for a special reason. Dreams are powerful messages." The gypsy leaned forward and touched Richard's arm through his black leather jacket. "The dream was about your conflict, wasn't it?"

"You're amazing. I don't know how you do it," Richard said with a smile. "In the dream, I walked into this crowded movie theater. I went there to meet somebody. I only walked down a few rows, and Catherine was sitting there, near the back. But she wasn't alone. Alfred was next to her. I don't even know what he looks like, but I knew it was him. I grabbed Catherine's arm and dragged her out into the lobby."

"So you separated the two of them?"

"Yeah, I guess so."

"That is a good sign. Go on."

"I asked her what she was doing with him. I wanted to know what was going to happen to me."

"So what did she say?"

"All she said was that she didn't know. I can't tell you how that made me feel. I can't live without Catherine. She's more important to me than anything. She's the only good thing in my life. I can't imagine losing her. Especially to some dead guy. I've got to do something to stop this curse."

"This spirit is stronger than any I have dealt with before. That's why I brought this." She pointed to the book that she had brought in earlier and laid on her lap. "This is a spell and knowledge book that has been in my family for generations. I'm told that it goes all the way back to India, where my family has not been for centuries, maybe millennia."

"What does it do?"

"As I started to say, there is something very strange about this spirit. The force is stronger than I usually find coming from beyond the grave. It is like the spirit of a living being. It is no accident that you have ended up where you are. As I have told you in the past, you are destined for a very special purpose in this world and everything that is happening to you is leading you toward this ultimate value which you will provide.

"My elders believe that children are often the cause of disturbances like yours, so Kelly plays a key role here. I believe that Alfred's spirit is less interested in Catherine and desires to protect Kelly in some way."

"What can I do to stop him from bothering me?"

"It's good that you came to me today, because I will need your help in order to find the answer. We must perform a ritual to help us see what path you can take. If you could move over to the couch again for a few moments while I get things set up."

"Can I help?"

"No, Dear. Aren't you the helpful one." Madame Charlotte walked out of the room through a different door this time, this one between the couch and the table. Her voice came from the hallway, but she was not speaking in English. Before long, the television voices were gone, and she scurried back into the room with a small oak case and some cloth under her arms.

After placing the objects on the table, she walked around the room to all three of the entranceways and ensured that they were locked. Digging through the case for a moment, she crossed over to Richard and handed him a craft knife and two candles, one brown and one black. "I need you to carve your full name into both candles. Make sure that the name is in a straight line running from the base of the candle toward the top."

As Richard began carving, she placed the white cloth over a small chest of drawers near the door to the kitchen. At each of the back corners of the dresser, she placed a white candle. In the center, at the back were two empty candleholders. Continuing to place candles on the dresser, she pulled out a purple one, a white and two orange ones. She placed a small incense burner in the front center and lit the incense that was inside. Finally, Madame Charlotte placed the book in the left-hand corner just when Richard was finished with his carving.

"I like the way that incense smells," Richard said. "Cinnamon, right?"

"That's right, Dear." She took the candles and the knife from him and put the candles in the empty holders. "I will need you to remain silent until I call upon you, because I need extreme concentration to find your path."

"Ok, Madame."

"Good. Shall we begin?"

Richard nodded and she sat him back at the table, where there was a mirror lying face up, toward the ceiling.

"Look into the mirror and concentrate on this very troublesome situation."

She returned to the altar and lit both the initial white candles and the candles that Richard had carved. "Here burns the spirit of Richard Halpin, wise in the ways of our mothers and fathers."

Next, she lit the other white candle and said, "Here burn Purity, Truth and Sincerity. They are with him now and always." Then the purple candle was lit. "Here burns Power. Power to overcome the spirit that is haunting him." Finally, lighting the two orange candles, she said, "That which he would scry is attracted to him as is the moth drawn to the candle flame."

Madame Charlotte returned to the table with the book and sat down next to Richard. After pausing for a moment with her eyes closed she said, "Around me are the spirits of my ancestors; through them may it pass the answer for this man. For this I give thanks."

Madame Charlotte gazed into the mirror and Richard sat next to her, looking first at her and then down into the mirror.

"Can you see anything?" asked Richard.

"Not yet. Please remain silent. I need all of my attention to be focused. You must stay focused as well." She reached over and held his hand.

After several moments, she squeezed his hand harder and stared into the mirror for a long while. Then she jerked away her hand and stood up from the table.

"That which was desired has been accomplished. May my ancestors ever be with me and protect me in everything I do." She sat back in the chair and closed her eyes.

Richard looked at her for several minutes, waiting for some sort of motion.

She began to speak, "In my vision I saw a large building, shaped unlike other buildings I know. There was a boat there. Something to do with Kelly."

"She works in a big building," said Richard, "out on an island. You have to take a boat to get there."

"She's in some danger there. Someone is causing her trouble." Madame Charlotte walked back to her altar and blew out the candles that were burning there.

"Probably that boyfriend of hers."

"There's a boyfriend?"

"Yeah. He seems like trouble to me. Always got her crying about one thing or another."

"You must go to her and help her through this problem that she is having. I think that if you protect her, the spirit that is haunting you will leave you alone."

"To Bloodsworth Island?"

"Where?"

"That's where Kelly works."

"Yes. You must go there now and find her. This is the opportunity to place your life back into balance."

"I don't even know if I can get a boat out there at this time of night."

"You must find a way. This opportunity will not come again. There's more. This is important. Of everything I see in the crystal, this is the most important. You must be very careful. Your life and liberty will be threatened. You must be aggressive and quick witted, if you are to have any hope of prevailing. If you hesitate, all will be lost. Remember this above all, act quickly and decisively."

Chapter 36

Voluntary Test Subject

Gene had intended to eat when he got to the pantry, and he did eat some. There were individual serving boxes of puffed rice breakfast cereal. He ate two of those. They weren't as sweet as he liked, so he grabbed a squeeze bottle of chocolate syrup and drank part of that. The last things he ate were some pimento-stuffed olives. He had thought he would eat more, but sleep claimed him.

After several hours Gene awoke. In his sleep, his subconscious had come up with a partial answer to postponing Dr. Gallagher's release of the virus.

Although much recovered from his experience in the chair, he still suffered from pain in his joints and muscles. He made his way back to the Mission and Conscience Department where there was a row of rooms along one wall, all of which were filled with various kinds of birds. There were six of these rooms, and each contained hundreds of birds. The rooms were located directly above the long, narrow bird feeding room which Alfred had shown him. Within the rooms, the birds tended to be broken up by species when it was convenient. Random birds captured in the wild were supposed to go into room number six to await sorting, but sometimes odd birds ended up in the other rooms.

These 3,000 birds were the ones that would be infected with the virus and then released to carry it around the world. Within the rooms, cages could only be found along the west wall, the outside wall of the building. The only thing that separated the birds from the outside was a bank of doors, each of which resembled an automatic garage door.

Alfred was not going to help Gene prevent the release of the virus, and Gene knew that, even if he could find Alfred, it would be useless to ask where the virus was stored. If Gene knew where it was, he could simply destroy it. For the moment, he couldn't stop the spread of the virus, but he could slow it down by eliminating the delivery mechanism.

The first room of birds contained Herons. Gene opened the door and looked inside. Despite Davenport Center's elaborate air filtration system, the stench in the room was overwhelming. The large, blue-gray birds flapped and fussed as he entered. Maybe they hoped he would bring food, not that they could eat more than they already had. Beaks and fluttering wings rattled the cages, and hundreds of pairs of eyes followed his every move. The room was bare with large cages filling all but a narrow aisle. The outer wall of the building provided backs for the huge cages.

Gene returned to the hallway and located a box that protruded from the wall to the left of the door. He ignored the warnings which prohibited tampering with the box. The green button in the back of the box clicked when Gene pressed it. A mechanical sound was followed by the sounds of flapping wings thundering from the room, shaking the hallway door. Gene had released the birds. He opened the door again. Recalcitrant birds were driven into the rising sun and the freezing early morning air when Gene rushed into the room, running as best he could up and down the narrow aisle, flapping his arms like wings and shooing the birds out. When the room was empty, Gene went back into the hallway, pushed the green button again, and the outer garage-like door slammed shut.

He moved down the hallway repeating the same process through gulls, pigeons and swans until he had let go all of the birds that had taken years to collect. Gene felt numb, drained of emotion as he released the birds. It reminded him of pouring bottles of his mother's liquor down the sink when he was a child. He thought freeing the birds would make him feel good, but in the end it made him feel ineffective and small. One delivery mechanism was gone, but Dr. Gallagher had not been stopped.

It was early in the morning, and components of the body would be arriving soon for their triumphant day. Everyone in Davenport Center must have heard the commotion that he was making. To his surprise, no one had appeared to stop him, but he needed to move fast so as not to get caught.

Now it was time to find Kelly and get her off the island. He had no idea what had happened to Alfred, and he was sure Alfred wondered what had happened to him. People, perhaps Elbridge and Ted, might be searching for him. And of course Kelly's room, assuming he could find it in the huge maze that was Davenport Center, might be guarded. There were two ways to find her room. The VTS schedule at Ms. Vorschrift's desk might tell him where Kelly was located, but her desk was located at one end of the component living quarters. That area might not be safe for Gene. It would also be possible to visit each VTS room, an approach which presented its own problems. Of course she might not be in a VTS room.

He took the least direct way to the VTS patient rooms in the hopes of avoiding any trouble, and so far he had been lucky. He hoped that he could smuggle Kelly off the island on the first ferry of the morning. To start, Gene decided to search the group of VTS rooms on the second floor of the east wing. When he arrived on the VTS hallway, no one was in the corridor. He stepped out of the stairwell and began inspecting the rooms.

All of the rooms on the left side were occupied according to the nametags that had been placed outside the rooms. Gene did not want to go into any of the rooms if he didn't have to, so for the moment he decided to assume that the names accurately reflected who was in each room. He felt intense pressure to find her. It might already be too late.

As he reached the end of the hallway, he noticed the door to the room where he had planned to meet Kelly just a few days earlier. He got closer to read the name in the holder. It was Kelly's room. He tried the door, and it opened. Blackness filled the room. The blinds must have been closed. He closed the door behind him, plunging himself into darkness. It would be safer now, outside of the public hallway. After fumbling for a moment, he found the light switch.

"I figured you would show up here sooner or later," said Alfred. He sat in a tan plastic-covered lounge chair in one corner. Kelly wasn't in the room.

Chapter 37

Lucky Charm

Alfred stood near the door in Dr. Gallagher's second floor office. Dr. Gallagher was behind the desk leaning forward, his elbows on the back of his chair, silent anger and frustration dripping from every pore. Gene, exhausted and in pain, sat on the love seat across the room.

"That woman is very disruptive," said Alfred. He was talking about Marion.

"That bitch," said Dr. Gallagher, "can't do half the damage that Dr. Eugene Nolan did. I trusted you," said Dr. Gallagher, looking across the room at Gene. "You fucked me. You'll pay the price."

Gene glared at him without speaking.

"Gene," continued Dr. Gallagher, "I want you to know that I've invited Marion to meet with us this morning, and I asked her to bring an officer from the Maryland State Police. You've got one last chance to beg for forgiveness. If you're not ready to do that, I hope you're ready to take responsibility for your reckless behavior. You caused all of those deaths in Ecuador. If you're not pretty damn contrite pretty damn soon, you're going to jail this afternoon, and I doubt you'll ever see the light of day again." Dr. Gallagher swung the chair around and slammed it into the wall behind the desk.

Anger and resentment boiled within Gene. As he opened his mouth to speak, Dr. Gallagher held up the index finger of his right hand.

"Not yet," said Dr. Gallagher. "Contrition in a minute. I've got to talk to Alfred first."

"I'll talk when I want," said Gene. It was the first time he ever talked back to Dr. Gallagher, but he remained seated on the loveseat, silent, waiting.

"That's where you're wrong," said Dr. Gallagher, the skin on his face drawn taught. "You'll talk when I want. I'll deal with you soon." He looked at Alfred. "Alright. There are a couple of things that we need to do. I want you to inventory all of the Systus-R that we've produced so far. As you do the inventory, move all of the stock into the staging laboratory adjacent to the north dock. There are some seagulls down there, about ten I think. You can infect those birds and then release them. That should do the trick. The Systus-R will spread more slowly thanks to Dr. Nolan, but the result will be the same." Looking back at Gene, he said, "the havoc you wreaked will have no impact in the end. I want you to know that."

Alfred nodded and turned to leave. Dr. Gallagher followed him into the reception area. There, Dr. Gallagher leaned over and whispered so that Gene wouldn't be able to hear. "Would you bring up some Systus Rb virus after the birds are released. Dr. Nolan may need a sedative."

"Yes, Father," said Alfred.

Dr. Gallagher returned to the office, and Kelly, ushered in by Sarah Vorschrift, followed him. "Thank you, Sarah. That will be all for now."

Sarah left, and Kelly said nothing. Gene assumed that she would not know what to do since they were never together except in secret. "Dr. Gallagher knows that we know each other."

"We know each other," repeated Kelly without looking at Gene. "I see that we're in euphemism city. Ok."

"Ms. Halpin, I want you to sit down," said Dr. Gallagher.

Kelly selected a chair near the desk. She was between Dr. Gallagher and Gene with her back toward Gene.

Dr. Gallagher focused his malevolent energy on Kelly. "As the director of this center I'm telling you that I am appalled by your unprofessional and destructive behavior. You are hereby relieved of all your duties and responsibilities. You are persona non grata at Davenport Center and Bloodsworth Island. If you are discovered on the grounds you will be detained and removed."

"No!" shouted Kelly. "You can't fire me. This is a good job. I've always performed my duties. This is outrageous."

"Ms. Halpin, you signed a contract when you came to work for us. In that contract, you were specifically prohibited from engaging in any non-professional relationship with another staff member of Davenport Center. It is clear to me from your confession that a non-professional relationship existed between the two of you here."

"Confession?" said Kelly. "What are you talking about? What confession? You're not the FBI."

"Kelly, there's no point in arguing with him," said Gene.

"I need the money from this job. I can't make this kind of money anywhere else with my education."

"I don't give a damn," said Dr. Gallagher, looking right at Kelly. "Just shut up."

"Don't you dare talk to her like that," said Gene. He rose from his chair. Despite the wobble and the pain, Gene walked toward Dr. Gallagher's desk. Standing up in front of the desk he confronted Dr. Gallagher for the first time in his life. Maybe he was not yet as free as he would one day be, but the subservience was gone, his dependence on Dr. Gallagher was gone.

"I'll talk anyway I like," said Dr. Gallagher.

"No!" shouted Gene as best he could. "You won't."

Gene knew he had crossed the line and that there was no turning back. Still he harbored a genuine fondness for Dr. Gallagher that ran deep, and his mind was still spinning from the time in Harry Sharp's chair.

"You came to me," said Dr. Gallagher, "degraded and despondent, and I gave you life. You killed innocent people, and I supported you and protected you. I provided you with guidance and a set of moral values, and you rebelled. I gave you responsibility, and you betrayed me. Together we here at Davenport Center worked and built, while you engaged in sabotage and destruction."

"I have not attempted to destroy you, Dr. Gallagher." The emotional attachment and fondness and respect Gene felt for Dr. Gallagher left him with some sense of ambivalence.

"And that story you concocted, that Alfred's daughter is still alive and that she works here on Bloodsworth Island, was creative, but it was destructive at the same time. When Alfred first came to me, he was devastated by his daughter's death. What you have done is cruel and heartless."

"You prepared that death certificate. You know you did. And you did it to trick Alfred. Do you live in a world so rich in fantasy that you can't remember what actually happened and what was fabricated? Do fabrications become reality in your world?"

"You messed with that blood sample we took," said Dr. Gallagher, his voice soft. "Alfred said you did. He wanted me to turn against you then, but I wouldn't do it. I loved you. I believed in you. And now I'm paying the price for trusting you. This has been very hard for me. Are you willing to give up a genetically perfect wife and genetically perfect children for I don't know what?"

Gene looked at Dr. Gallagher but didn't answer.

"It is your right," continued Dr. Gallagher, "to build a future for this planet with strong, healthy, genetically perfect children. You are giving that up. Do you realize that?"

Dr. Gallagher looked at Gene with combined anger and sadness. The sadness dissipated, and anger twisted Dr. Gallagher's face. "You are in violation of your oath and of all of the principles," he said.

Gene shook his head. "I won't let you kill Kelly," said Gene. "I'm going to save her."

"Who?" asked Dr. Gallagher. He looked as though he had no idea who Gene was talking about.

"Kelly. Kelly Halpin." He pointed to Kelly sitting in the chair.

"Oh," said Dr. Gallagher. "Right, right, right. Gene, you've always been so naive. People kill each other all the time. It's God's way. It's what God wants. Your mind has been poisoned. It was poisoned before you got here. I've done what I could for you, but you still disappoint. Death is part of life. Killing is part of life. It is a cleansing process. It is the way God has directed us to separate the wheat from the chaff. It's not an exact process."

"Your goal is an honorable one, to free the world of inherited disease, but the price is too high, much too high. Suffering and loss would touch every person on the planet. You can't do it. You shouldn't do it. It's stupid."

"Stupid you say? May I remind you, Dr. Eugene Nolan, that I am Dr. Marcus Gallagher, the director of Davenport Center. What I say governs Bloodsworth Island. What I say is law."

"Maybe at one point but no longer. Today I'm going to change that."

"You won't. There is no one to step in here, and we would be the worse for it if someone prevented us from playing the part we have been selected to play. The killing has never stopped. People kill each other every day. It's an animal instinct inside of us. You say it doesn't happen in families, but it does. Stepfathers kill stepchildren a hundred times more often than natural parents do. It's the drive that brought us all here. God wants men to raise their own children, not the children of some deadbeat who donated sperm and abandoned the child and its mother."

"This is insane," said Gene. "What you're doing can't make sense even to you. I'm going to stop the release of the virus." As Gene started for the door he took Kelly's hand.

"You!" shouted Dr. Gallagher. "Sit down."

"You!" shouted Gene as best he could. "Go to hell."

"No component has ever left Davenport Center alive. No component ever will."

As Dr. Gallagher started toward the door to block Gene's path the phone rang. All ignored it. Dr. Gallagher grabbed Gene's left shoulder and spun him around. With both hands Gene shoved hard against Dr. Gallagher's chest, pushing him back against the desk. Gene put his arm around Kelly and pulled her toward the door.

When Gene and Kelly reached the door they slammed into Marion and a female Maryland State Trooper. Marion and the trooper who had long blond hair and a mannish face and body pushed their way into the room. As Marion closed the door, Dr. Gallagher moved in front of it.

Marion moved to the front of Dr. Gallagher's desk. "I'm here, let's have it." She looked at Dr. Gallagher and seemed to think it was odd that he was standing in front of the office door. The trooper stood midway between Dr. Gallagher and Marion, and Gene and Kelly stood against the wall not far from the door.

"Please have a seat," said Dr. Gallagher. He motioned to the wing chair near where Marion stood.

"No. I'll stand. What are you doing standing in· front of the door?"

"I just don't think anyone should leave the room while we have this discussion."

"I'm sure we'll all stay here," said Marion.

"No we won't," said Gene. "As soon as he gets out of the way, Kelly and I are leaving. This discussion's got nothing to do with me."

"But I'm afraid it does," said Dr. Gallagher.

"Yes," said Marion. "You and I have discussed these matters. Why don't you stay? I'm sure this discussion will be quite short."

"I've really got to get downstairs," said Gene. "Many people will be injured if I don't go."

"Just a few minutes," said Marion. "Please."

"I'll move from the door if the officer here will guard it," said Dr. Gallagher.

Gene could see he had lost this battle. "All right. I'll stay, but it can't be for long."

Dr. Gallagher moved behind his desk. The officer posted herself in front of the door.

"First," Dr. Gallagher said, "I'm glad to see that you've recovered from your attack."

"Alright," said Marion, coldness in her voice. "Can we get on with it?"

"I want to apologize for all of the delays over the last few weeks. I believe that you will understand better after I provide you with a little background information. Right now I want to present you with the detailed report on our work here, the one you requested." He handed her two bright red notebooks, each three inches thick.

"All right," she said again. "I'll take what I can get, but I doubt this represents a fundamental change in your attitude. I know you, Marcus. Don't forget that. And I'm not a child anymore who can be abused and abandoned."

"I know that our behavior over the past couple of months has sent the wrong message. I apologize for that. After you've had an opportunity to review the report you'll see that we've made every effort to cooperate. We want to provide you with everything you've asked for. If the report is deficient in some way, we'll do everything we can to remedy the deficiency. Let me explain some of the things that have been distracting me."

Dr. Gallagher, who had remained standing behind the desk, motioned for Marion to sit as he slid into his chair. Marion sat on the edge of the chair and flipped through one of the binders which she balanced on one knee.

"For years we have been performing charitable services for the indigenous populations of South and Central America. We work under a special grant from the Continental Commission of Indigenous Nations to provide medical services to primitive tribes. A few weeks ago we experienced a terrible tragedy when an entire Orani village in Ecuador was wiped out by disease while one of our medical teams was working at that location."

"I didn't know of your work with the Continental Commission," said Marion.

"Yes," said Dr. Gallagher. "We've never made a big deal about it, but we believe it is a part of our responsibility to the community at large. Anyway, I was shocked when I heard the news about the village. It was a catastrophe which was out of my experience. I couldn't rest until I understood what happened. We began an investigation. Your request for the report coincided with our investigation of this horrible incident. I felt like I had to use all of my resources for the investigation."

"You could have talked to me about this," said Marion. The natural frown on her face was pronounced, as she watched Dr. Gallagher's performance. Skepticism oozed from every part of her body.

"I didn't want to provide you with information that might turn out to be nothing more than baseless conjecture. I had to do the research. I had to understand. The demise of an entire village has a cause, and I wanted to know that cause."

"What did you find?" asked Marion.

"There was negligence at best or intentional wrongdoing at worst. One of the physicians on the expedition to Ecuador apparently had nothing but blatant disregard for the standards required in medical research."

Gene realized that Dr. Gallagher was about to attack him. On the other hand, if he were talking about Alfred, then what he was saying was true.

"Dr. Nolan was experimenting with a novel genetic testing procedure. The concept is exciting, and Dr. Nolan is to be congratulated for the development of that concept. However he took this genetic testing material which he had developed to Ecuador without my knowledge or consent."

"That's not true," said Gene.

"Before it was ready for human testing," continued Dr. Gallagher, "he introduced it into the bodies of all of the villagers. That unauthorized procedure resulted in the deaths of everyone in the village. I don't condone human testing which is not conducted in accordance with FDA regulations, and I don't know what he thought he was doing."

"This is outrageous!" shouted Gene. He looked at Marion. "Dr. Gallagher directed everything that happened in Ecuador. He intentionally killed those people down there. He's getting ready to kill more right now. He wants to blame me, but it won't work."

Dr. Gallagher spoke. "I had assigned Dr. Nolan to act as a liaison between our office and yours when he returned from his trip. I wanted to get him off the island while we performed the investigation. He was supposed to deliver this report to you at that time. It became clear to me later that he has impeded your investigation in an attempt to frame me. I'm very sorry for the fact that I did not see this earlier. I take full responsibility for the report being late."

"No!" shouted Gene, as he moved away from the wall where he had been standing. "This is nothing but a pack of lies."

Dr. Gallagher pushed his chair back away from the desk. "We'll give him a sedative," said Dr. Gallagher. "After that perhaps the officer can take him into custody."

"No!" shouted Gene. The sound was sharp and loud. The shouting made Gene's throat ache. "I'm not taking a sedative. He's trying to kill me. He's going to do it right here before your eyes."

Before anyone could respond to Gene's outburst, the door to Dr. Gallagher's office was forced open. It hit the officer in the back with a crack. Richard stormed into the room.

"Where's Kelly?" said Richard.

Kelly looked at him from her position along the wall, and her eyes met Richard's for an instant. Then Richard's eyes began to dart around the room, from Dr. Gallagher to Marion to the officer.

"Who are you and why have you burst in my office this way?" asked Dr. Gallagher.

"Richard Halpin. I've come for my daughter."

"I'm not your daughter, you lunatic!" Kelly replied.

"Chill out," Richard continued, "I came here to get Kelly and bring her home to her mother where she belongs."

"Don't let me get in your way," said Dr. Gallagher. "Ms. Halpin is through here."

"I'm not going anywhere with him," Kelly said.

"I can't just leave now, Partner." Richard pointed at Marion, "I saw that old bitch on the ferry this morning with her lesbian bodyguard. I knew they were coming to arrest you, Dr. Gallagher. I wasn't going to interfere at first, but I can't let them do it. You've been so good to me. I wanted to help you now that I've got the chance."

"I don't know what you're talking about," said Dr. Gallagher. "Why would they arrest me?"

"They've come to arrest you for kidnapping this ugly bitch," said Richard. "With that ugly mutt, I didn't bang her when I had the chance. I'm surprised they haven't told you yet. I guess they'll tell you when they arrest you."

"What are you talking about?" Dr. Gallagher said. "You must truly be insane."

"No, man. I forgot. You don't know who I am. I'm the guy that Peter hired to kidnap Marion for you. I'm sorry I botched that job up so bad. The way she escaped, I knew they realized I was involved, using Kelly's house and all. But," he said, turning to look at Marion, "how did you know that Dr. Gallagher was involved?"

"You used my house to commit a crime?" shouted Kelly.

Marion turned and looked at Dr. Gallagher.

"I don't know what he's talking about," said Dr. Gallagher. "You can see that he's crazy!"

Marion turned back and looked at Richard. "Crazy he might be." She took one step toward where Richard was standing. "I remember you," she said to Richard. "Peter introduced me to you in that bar on the Rockville Pike."

"That's right," Richard agreed. "And you all had better stop calling me crazy, because it ain't so. Anyway that's where I saw you for the first time. How the hell did you get out of that house? I just don't understand it."

"Peter hired you to kidnap me?" asked Marion.
"That's the part I don't understand. How did you figure out that Peter and Dr. Gallagher were involved?"

"She didn't figure it out," shouted Dr. Gallagher, "because it isn't true."

"That bastard," said Marion, as she walked toward Richard. "Arrest both of them," said Marion addressing the policewoman.

Richard moved, gracefully for a large man, and pulled the gun out of the holster of the cop when she moved towards him. The cop stepped back blocking the other's bodies with her arms.

"Look," said Richard, "I only came here to get Kelly. Her mother is worried about her, and I hate to see my wife unhappy. So, c'mon Kelly, let's get out of here."

"Are you nuts?" asked Kelly. "I'm safer here than with you."

"Kelly, honey, I haven't got a lot of sleep and I'm not in the best mood," Richard said. He waved the gun motioning for Kelly to come over to the door. "Let's just go now, ok."

The ample woman cop dove at Richard's arm to knock the gun from his hand and the movement surprised him. The gun discharged, and the bullet entered the officer's head in the center of the top. Blood and brains splattered onto Marion's face and dress and onto Dr. Gallagher's lab coat. The dead policewoman's body slumped first to its knees and then collapsed face forward onto the floor. Blood pumped out and soaked the thick, soft carpet in the shape of an expanding pear.

Richard stood with the revolver hanging loosely in his hand. "Oh, man. Why did she do that?" Richard dropped the gun at his feet. He looked up at the remaining four who all stared at him in disbelief. "I didn't mean to shoot her. It was an accident."

Kelly screamed and jumped over to where Gene was standing, near the open and unguarded door. Marion stood in front of the chair where she had been sitting.

Gene motioned at Marion to follow him and Kelly through the door.

"Hey," said Richard as he turned to face the door.

Gene didn't speak as he ushered the two women into the waiting room. There he used his magnetic id card to open the door in the wall which led to the Mission and Conscience Department.

"Hey," said Richard again. "Where are you going?" Richard started across the room after them. His left foot got caught under the dead lady officer's arm. Richard went sprawling onto the floor. Gene pulled Kelly through the door to the Mission and Conscience Department. The door swung shut and locked closed before Richard, now splattered with blood, got back to his feet.

"Stop!" shouted Richard. "Kelly, your mother wants you at home!"

Gene wanted to get downstairs to the laboratory where Alfred was gathering the virus and infecting birds. The inventory of the virus which Alfred had been sent to do would, Gene expected, take only a few minutes. Gene knew he had little time to prevent the release of whatever birds remained. He knew that the virus could be destroyed easily with heat. There were gas feeds in all of the labs in the building, and in his pocket he still had the lighter he'd found with Marion.

"Where are we going?" Kelly asked.

"I need to get to Alfred before he releases the birds."

"Alfred?" said Kelly.

Gene didn't respond.

After several turns in the Mission and Conscience Department, Gene found a staircase along the north wall of the building that would take them to the ground floor.

"What birds?" asked Marion. "What's going on here?"

"I can't explain this in detail right now," said Gene as he jumped the last several stairs. His body slammed into the door to the ground floor. He turned and watched the women come down the stairs. "This guy Alfred has got some infected birds. He's about to release them. If he does, many people will die. We've got to stop him."

"What are you going to do to stop him?" asked Marion.

"I don't know."

Gene took them through an outside door on the north side of the building. None of them were prepared for the bitter winter weather two days before Christmas. Marion had left her coat upstairs, and neither Gene nor Kelly had a coat with them. The north dock was off of the east wing. It provided access to the bay through a manmade canal and then a creek. A small aluminum rowboat and two jet-skis, one red and one yellow, were moored there.

Richard and Dr. Gallagher would find them. Time was short. Gene ran toward the dock. Looking through a window, he saw an empty hallway. Moving to the next window, he saw Alfred fiddling with a cart full of test tubes. Dirt and salt residue on the window obscured the view, but he could still make out Alfred standing on one side of the room next to a small group of bird cages. The cages rested on one of the slate counters.

The blustery wind almost whipped the id card from his hand, as Gene went to open a set of double glass doors that led to the laboratory where Alfred worked. Gene opened one of the doors and stepped into the room. Alfred was preparing a syringe with the virus to inject into one of the dozen birds that were in cages along the wall. Marion and Kelly followed Gene into the room.

"Alfred," shouted Gene.

Alfred turned to Gene for a moment and then continued what he was doing, pulling the deadly fluid up into the syringe. He reached for the latch on the cage closest to him, a cage containing a seagull.

"Alfred. Don't do it. Do you want to kill Kelly and all of those other innocent people?"

"Kill me?" Kelly asked.

"Yes," Alfred said. "Because you carry the gene for cystic fibrosis. Everyone carrying the gene will die." He injected the gull in its side, just below the left wing. Then he went back to prepare the syringe again. "I suppose you must have gotten the gene from your mother though."

"My mother, what are you talking about?" Kelly asked.

"Gene, didn't you tell Kelly about me?" asked Alfred.

"No," said Gene. "What with being strapped in an electric chair and witnessing murders, I haven't had an opportunity. Alfred, please put down the syringe and stop this."

"I wouldn't call this murder," said Alfred. "I would call this cleansing. I think that's closer to the mark. Besides you haven't witnessed anything."

"Tell me what?" asked Kelly.

"That I'm your father," Alfred said as he injected the virus into the bird from the second cage. "I'm surprised Gene didn't mention that to you. He was so insistent on telling me. I didn't believe him at first. And Dr. Gallagher said it was a lie. But now when I look at you, I see it's true. You look very much the same as you did when you were a little girl."

"You're my father," said Kelly. "I don't understand."

"I don't understand either," said Marion. "What the hell is going on here?"

"Alfred, do you even know what you're doing?" asked Gene. "Why do you keep injecting those birds? If you know that this is Kelly, why are you trying to kill her?"

"I've dedicated my life to this project. I can't stop it now. I lost Kelly years ago. Nothing can fix that. Get out of here and let me finish what I'm doing. Besides, I'd like to talk to her in a few minutes, when I'm finished with this." He looked at Kelly. "I'd like to talk to you in a few minutes. I would enjoy that. It's been such a long time. There were times when I dreamed you were still alive. I have missed you."

"Alfred, that's it," said Gene. "Don't you see how Dr. Gallagher has used you and destroyed your life? You can reclaim that now."

"You never understood," said Alfred. "I believe in Dr. Gallagher. I believe in what we're doing here. You can't change that. Kelly can't change that."

"You talk about believing in Dr. Gallagher like a child might talk about believing in Santa Claus," observed Marion.

"Not so different, I suppose," said Alfred. He glanced over at Marion.

"No," said Gene. "I won't let you do it." Gene grabbed the arm that Alfred was using to hold the syringe. Gene was not a large man, but Alfred was older and weaker and Gene's surprise attack caused Alfred to drop the syringe on the floor. "Marion, you and Kelly have to go back outside. If Kelly gets exposed to this stuff, she'll die."

Marion pulled on Kelly's arm. Gene could see Kelly mouth the word "Dad" as Marion pulled her away and shut the door to the outside. Alfred leaned over to pick up the syringe, and Gene ran into him, knocking him to the floor.

He could see that there were several tubes of the virus, and Alfred had surely done as Dr. Gallagher had instructed and collected all of the virus into this one room. If Gene could destroy everything in the room, there would be nothing more to release. Dr. Gallagher could manufacture more, but after the events of the day, Gene guessed that it would be a while before that could happen.

As in all of the labs, there were propane fuel outlets along the walls. Here, orange nozzles poked out from two of the walls, and there were many more nozzles than in a typical lab. Perhaps the room had been designed for use as a classroom. Gene could destroy the virus by heat, but the birds were more of a challenge to ensure that they would not infect anyone.

Gene stepped up to one of the orange propane gas spigots and turned the nozzle on. Moving along both walls with the gas nozzles, he opened every gas jet in the room.

"What are you doing?" asked Alfred as he got up from the floor.

"I need to get you out of here," Gene said.

"No."

"Alfred, be reasonable," Gene realized that this was not possible. As Gene attempted to persuade Alfred, the room filled with gas. "Alfred, put the syringe down just for a minute."

Gene moved toward Alfred as though he were going to grab him again. Alfred flung the syringe onto the counter.

"Alright," said Alfred.

"Sit," said Gene.

"Sit? You mean on the floor?"

"Yes. On the floor." Gene sat on the gray speckled tile floor and crossed his legs.

"I've got to turn this gas off."

"No." Gene lunged for Alfred's legs and pulled him to the floor. "Sit. Let's talk for a moment."

"Alright," said Alfred, righting himself on the floor.

The smell of gas was strong and unpleasant.

"Do you realize what you're doing?" asked Gene.

Alfred shook his head as though he were having trouble comprehending the question. "Yes," he said. "Yes, of course. Do you realize what you're doing, trampling on your oath, ignoring the principles?"

"It's your daughter. She's standing out there." Gene glanced up to see Marion and Kelly shivering outside. He felt a gulf between him and Alfred. It was a gulf that he thought he wouldn't be able to bridge.

The other door to the room, the door to the hallway, opened. Gene turned to look. Richard had entered the room. Gene and Alfred got up off the floor and walked over to the counter where the birdcages were.

"Now that you have all wasted my entire morning," Richard said, "it's time to bring an end to this."

"Do you have any idea what you've done?" asked Gene.

Richard grabbed Gene by the arm and pushed him to where his back was against the outside doors. "Where's Kelly? It's time that I took her home to her mother." Richard sniffed. "Whew! Smells like shit in here."

"It's gas," Gene said.

"No duh, genius. Do you think you have to be some big-shot doctor to know what a fart smells like?"

"He doesn't mean intestinal gas," said Alfred. "He's talking about natural gas."

"That's enough out of you, four-eyes." Richard stepped to where Alfred was standing. He turned toward Gene, "Kelly's your girlfriend isn't she? That's what Madame Charlotte said. Well, where is that slut girlfriend of yours?"

"Stop it!" Alfred demanded.

"What's it to you? What business is it of yours how I treat my daughter?"

"She is not your daughter. She's my daughter."

"Her father's been dead for years."

"It's true," said Gene. "He is Kelly's father."

"And I suppose you were there when she was conceived," Richard said to Gene. He looked at Alfred and bellowed. "So what do you have to say for yourself? If you're Kelly's father where the hell have you been all these years?"

As Richard focused his attention on Alfred, Gene pulled the lighter out of his pocket.

Richard continued to accost Alfred. "You're a deadbeat dad. Some money would've helped. You could have sent some money." Richard laughed as he stood in Alfred's face. "You're a worthless piece of crap. Hey! It really stinks in here." He turned his attention back to Gene, "What are you doing?"

Gene did not respond and grabbed for one of the virus racks.

"Hey!" Richard said. "That's my lighter. Where did you get that? Give it to me." Richard pushed Alfred to the floor and then grabbed at Gene's arm. Richard was much stronger than Gene, and Gene did not attempt to struggle.

"My lucky charm," Richard looked at the lighter in fascination. "I wondered what had happened to this.

Gene moved away from Richard and toward the exterior glass doors. He was still worried about how he was going to deal with the virus. Alfred would likely still get up and complete his deadly task. His concentration was broken when he heard the noise of Richard tapping the lighter against the counter.

"The lighter!" Gene shouted. But it was already too late. Gene could see Richard's thumb moving to open the cover of the lighter, initiating a spark.

Gene glanced down at Alfred and saw a look of calmness and satisfaction that he'd never seen before. It looked to him as though Alfred had reached some sort of state of inner peace. Gene could see a flame spread out from the flint below the lighter's cover. As the flame began to engulf Richard's arm, a force hit Gene in the side and lifted him off his feet. He was propelled through the glass door. Spinning and tumbling he flew over the north dock as flames leapt from his clothing.

When he hit the canal he was numbed by the icy coldness of the water. In shock, he flailed his arms to stay afloat. Panic consumed him. He looked, but he couldn't see. The salty water obscured his view of the dock and Davenport Center.

Pulling his face above the surface, he gasped for breath and felt tremendous pain in his chest as he attempted to breathe. He coughed and sputtered water and he struggled to stay afloat. The canal wasn't deep. He could have stood if he had thought to try. An arm reached down behind him and grabbed the back of his shirt collar. He reached back and held onto the arm. The action caused him to spin around, and he could see that Marion and Kelly had untied the small rowboat from the dock and come out to rescue him.

With all of his strength he pulled at the boat to lift himself into it. Just as he managed to get more of his weight into the boat than was outside of it, another explosion boomed back on the first floor of Davenport Center. Gene looked up and saw a plume of flame and smoke billowing out of the ground floor of the building. He pulled his legs into the boat and lay in the bottom. Kelly lifted his head into her lap. Marion rowed the boat further away from Davenport Center. He was frozen from the cold of the water and his face and arms were in pain. Marion produced a rhythmic sound with her paddles hitting the water, interrupted by other small explosions that grew more distant. Kelly rubbed her fingers through his hair, and he fell unconscious.

Epilogue

It was the second week of August when Gene drove down Cedar Lane to enter the north end of the NIH campus. The sun was shining and it was hot enough for Gene to run his air conditioner at full blast. A man jogged by wearing green shorts. Kelly had wanted to come with him on the trip but they agreed in the end that it was better for her to stay behind and finish the packing that they had begun a week earlier.

Gene remembered the last time that he had testified against a professional colleague and what it had done to his career. His stomach felt as if he had eaten razorblades mixed in with the Frosted Flakes that Kelly had poured for him when he got up that morning. The role of wife seemed to agree with her. Gene was amazed at how well she had dealt with the recent trauma. He was not as certain about his own progress though, and he feared that the healing process would take a long time.

Gene was lost in the maze of roads that made up the NIH campus. According to a giant map posted at the side of the road, he was only a few hundred feet from his destination, so he decided to park next to the sign and take the distance on foot. Because of heat outside, he had draped his sports coat over the back of the driver's seat instead of wearing it on the long car ride. He slipped the jacket on, surprised at how difficult it was to get his left arm into the sleeve after so many months of rehabilitation.

Gene thought about Kelly again as he walked the short distance across the well-manicured grass. They both agreed that marriage was the best idea under the circumstances, even though they knew that there were many difficulties that they would have to work through. Gene was proud of himself for taking on the added responsibility of a wife and baby when he wasn't always sure he could take care of himself. They had married on March 16th at the county courthouse in Cambridge. Other than the judge and the court clerk, Kelly's mother Catherine was the only one present. At the time, Catherine was still grief-stricken over the death of Richard and the second death of Alfred. To Gene she had seemed numb to everything that was going on around her.

Since that time, Catherine had improved. The four of them lived together, and Catherine spent much of her time caring for the newborn. The baby often seemed to provide enough work to keep all three of them busy.

When he entered the now familiar hearing room, Marion walked up and greeted him. She wore a bright red dress with a professional cut that set her apart from everyone else in the room.

"Hello, Gene." She smiled, and she gripped both of his hands with hers. It was the warmest greeting that he had ever seen her give anyone. She must have seen concern on his face because she said, "Don't worry. Things are going to work out. It's likely that this whole thing will be over today."

"Thanks," was all he could manage. Although her words were a comfort, he could not help feeling anxious about this proceeding. There were some important people in the room, political appointees, which made Gene all the more nervous. The director of NIH sat in the front row with his entourage of deputies swooning around him, gauging his reactions.

Marion led Gene to the front of the room and sat him at one end of the first row of chairs. "Just wait here and I'll come get you when it's time." She squeezed his shoulder and then walked away, back up the side of the room.

The session was being held to determine if the contract funding which Davenport Center had been receiving should be stopped. Although the answer seemed obvious at this point, the wheels of government bureaucracy kept turning, and one could never determine the outcome of such proceedings. The tribunal had been meeting for three and a half weeks already. Trying to predict the government's actions seemed to Gene like predicting which side of a coin would turn up.

The moderator for the hearing, Peter Snyder's boss, stepped up to the podium to get things underway, and the doors in the back of the room were closed. Everyone sat in folding chairs, and Gene was still uncomfortable sitting in anything made of metal. He occasionally had nightmares about Harry Sharp's Chair. He fidgeted enough for the woman sitting next to him to give him a good stare.

"Marion Latterner has returned to this meeting once more to close testimony in this matter before the funding for Davenport Center is decided upon. I ask that she step forward and present any additional testimony for the record," the moderator said and then sat in his chair next to the podium.

"Thank you, George." She adjusted the microphone down near her mouth. "I know that this information is not welcomed by everyone here today, but I have to tell you that the Federal Government's money has been wasted for the last decade, at least as it has been poured into Davenport Center. Although there have been valuable discoveries made at this island facility, the contractor has done very little over the last eight years to fulfill its obligations under the various contracts.

"You all should have received a copy of my audit report prior to today's meeting. I believe that this spells out how large sums of money from this contract were used to purchase supplies, labor and equipment that were not used to accomplish the government's objectives. I would like to add to this; the testimony of one of the physicians and researchers that worked on Bloodsworth Island during the current contract. Gene, could you come up please?"

When Gene got on the small stage that was only six inches off the floor, he cleared his throat and unfolded a piece of paper that he had shoved in his jacket pocket. "I have prepared a statement that I am going to read." Gene cleared his throat again. He was fascinated how his throat seemed to fill with phlegm just as he needed to talk.

"The work that I performed on Bloodsworth Island, at Davenport Center, was intended for a single purpose. Until six months ago, I assumed that my work was being used to screen and treat patients that were victims of genetic diseases. In December of last year, I discovered by accident that my work was part of a larger project designed to eradicate genetic diseases.

"On the surface this sounds like a noble goal, but I discovered that the mechanism for eradication of the various diseases was the eradication of all of the people who carried the relevant genes. Initially, cystic fibrosis was targeted as a disease that could be eradicated with current technology. I believe that it was intended as the first of many diseases that were going to be attacked in this way.

311

"Over time, as I realized the objectives of Davenport Center I began to take steps to prevent the implementation of the plan. This effort culminated in the partial destruction of Davenport Center and the deaths of a Davenport Center physician and another man. Based on lack of evidence to the contrary, the destruction of the infective agent appears to be complete."

Marion was standing before Gene finished, and she directed him to take her chair next to the podium. "That is the last of the testimony that I have to present." She sat down in the chair next to Gene and the moderator stood again to address the audience.

"Dr. Gallagher is not present today, as he has not been at any of the meetings of this committee. He left Bloodsworth Island on the day of the explosion, and we have not been able to locate him since that time. In addition, there is no representative of Davenport Center present at the hearing today. I believe it is time to turn this matter over to the contract committee for decision. Unless there is any further discussion on this matter, the hearing will close, and the contract committee will deliberate until they come to a conclusion."

A shuffle of feet and chairs erupted in the room, and Gene stayed seated in his chair.

"Don't worry," Marion said. "I think your testimony has sealed the decision. This is all just a formality. Are you all right?"

"I don't know, but I will be in time." Gene continued staring into the room as it began to empty. "What happened with Peter?"

"He was convicted three weeks ago. He kept a complete set of taped telephone conversations in his office. He won't say what they were for, but I guess he thought he was going to write a book one day. The tapes don't implicate Dr. Gallagher. He was obviously careful on the phone. Peter, on the other hand, wasn't so careful. By the way, thanks again for rescuing me."

"I think you've paid me back tenfold," said Gene. "I am so grateful for everything you've done. I know there was a chance I could have ended up in jail for the rest of my life."

"By the way, how are your plans shaping up?" she asked.

"We leave for Ecuador at the end of the week. Kelly and I have decided to take her mother with us, since we're worried about what might happen to her if we leave her here alone. She's been through a lot, discovering that her dead husband was alive and then having both of her husbands killed at the same time. I think we'll all be better off far away from here for a while."

"I wish you the best of luck."

"I feel like I owe something to the Orani that remain down there in the rainforest. I only want to treat people and make their lives better. We'll have a good life there. I think the baby will be accepted and treated well by the Orani."

"Look me up when you get back up this way." Marion got up to leave the room too. Gene rose too, and was surprised when Marion hugged him. "Good-bye and good luck."

"Thanks," Gene said. "Good luck to you in your new job."

"I'll do fine. There are some universities that haven't been complying with the terms of our grants. I'm going to kick them in the butt and get them straightened out."

They walked out of the room together. "I'm sure you will," said Gene.

They parted at the entrance to the building and Gene walked back to his car. As he removed his jacket, he felt the aaskouandy shift around his neck.

"Make your own decisions," he heard Hiaroma's voice say.

"I will," Gene answered. He got in Kelly's car and drove back so they could finish the packing together.